PRAISE FOR THE AESTHETICS OF RESISTANCE, VOLUME 1

"Some of the most gripping—and most beautiful—passages of Weiss's novel appear in detailed examinations of classic paintings by Delacroix, Goya, Brueghel, Géricault, Munch and others, and their bearing on contemporary struggles. . . . Weiss's project has another, deeper aim than advancing the socialist revolution, namely to give voice to fascism's victims, and to preserve the memory of their lives and example—hence the archival nature of his work, with its painstaking attention to the names of fallen comrades."—Noah Isenberg, *The Nation*

"One of the most significant works of postwar German literature. . . . The novel feels like an endless soliloquy on a bare stage, but one that takes the audience on the most amazingly imaginative time-and-space journey, with the narrative perspective cutting like a movie director's camera from one intensely rendered visual detail to the next. . . . [E]xhilaratingly strange, compelling, and original."—Mark M. Anderson, *Bookforum*

"This excellent translation of the first volume of this formidable, convoluted masterpiece makes Weiss's autobiographical novel, one of the major works of literature of the 20th century, available in English for the first time. . . . Essential."—R. C. Conard, *Choice*

"*The Aesthetics of Resistance* writes those who have been culturally and historically excluded back into the story of their time and demands—as modernism does—that we learn to read in a new way. . . . The monuments of modernism today rise like Ozymandias' statue in the sand: *Ulysses*, Proust, Beckett, Pound's *Cantos*, *The Making of Americans*,

The Waste Land. At last, we have an English translation of a work that stands alongside them."—Robert Buckeye, *Review of Contemporary Fiction*

"[*The Aesthetics of Resistance*] gives a rich reward. There are many novels which convey the bitter experience of Europe's twentieth century, but few which range so widely or reflect so deeply on that history."—Brian Hanrahan, *Open Democracy*

"One of the most powerful books of contemporary German literature, this sprawling, spirited work is a novel masquerading as history masquerading as a novel as. . . . The story, magnificently translated by Joachim Neugroschel, is splendid, experimental, and absolutely gripping."—*The Tempest*

"The novel has long enjoyed a prominent place in the German intellectual left. Now that the first volume is finally available from Duke University Press in a superb English translation by Joachim Neugroschel (with a readable and engaging foreword by Fredric Jameson), Weiss's work can finally emerge into the wider public sphere where it deserves to occupy a prominent space."—Inez Hedges, *Socialism and Democracy*

The Aesthetics of Resistance
Volume II

THE
AESTHETICS
OF
RESISTANCE

Volume II

PETER WEISS

Translated by Joel Scott · With an afterword by Jürgen Schutte

DUKE UNIVERSITY PRESS *Durham and London* 2020

Designed by Drew Sisk
Typeset in Trump Mediaeval by Westchester Publishing Services

Library of Congress Cataloging-in-Publication Data for Peter Weiss,
The Aesthetics of Resistance, Volume I, translated by Joachim
Neugroschel, appears below:

Weiss, Peter, 1916–1982
[Aesthetik des Widerstands. Volume I. English]
The aesthetics of resistance : volume I / Peter Weiss ; translated by
Joachim Neugroschel ; with a foreword by Fredric Jameson and a
glossary by Robert Cohen.
p. cm.
ISBN 0-8223-3534-4 (cloth : alk. paper)
ISBN 0-8223-3546-8 (pbk. : alk. paper)
I. Neugroschel, Joachim. II. Title.
PT2685.E5A6513 2005
833'.914–dc22   2004028462

Additional information for Peter Weiss, *The Aesthetics of
Resistance, Volume II*, translated by Joel Scott, appears below:

ISBN 978-1-4780-0614-5 (cloth : alk. paper)
ISBN 978-1-4780-0699-2 (pbk. : alk. paper)
ISBN 978-1-4780-0756-2 (ebook)

The Aesthetics of Resistance, Volume II, was originally published
as *Die Ästhetik des Widerstands, Band II*, © Suhrkamp Verlag,
Frankfurt am Main, 1978. This translation is based on Suhrkamp
Verlag's New Berlin Edition of *Die Ästhetik des Widerstands*
(which includes all three volumes), edited and with an afterword by
Jürgen Schutte (Die Neue Berliner Ausgabe, mit einem editorischen
Nachwort von Jürgen Schutte © Suhrkamp Verlag, Berlin, 2016).

Cover art credit: *Great Altar of Zeus, Pergamon: Hekate with
Her Molossian Dogs and Artemis Battle the Giants Klytios and
Otos(?)*; detail of east frieze. University of Michigan Library Digital
Collections, cco 1.0 Public Domain Dedication, http://quod.lib
.umich.edu/a/aict/x-gas295/gas295.

AN ANONYMOUS DONOR PROVIDED FUNDS TOWARD THE
PUBLICATION OF THIS BOOK. TRANSLATION OF THIS WORK WAS
SUPPORTED BY A GRANT FROM THE GOETHE-INSTITUT, WHICH IS
FUNDED BY THE GERMAN MINISTRY OF FOREIGN AFFAIRS.

Contents

Translator's Acknowledgments

Making this translation truly would not have been possible without the support of a host of individuals and institutions. Some—such as the Goethe Institut, the Robert Bosch Stiftung and the Deutscher Übersetzerfonds, Maison Suger, the Europäisches Übersetzer-Kollegium, and Adam Magyar—provided material support in the way of funding or residencies, in which slices of time could be carved out of my usual schedule of wage labor to focus on this task.

Other individuals have provided support in the process of translation, editing, and reworking. First and foremost among these is Charlotte Thießen, with whom I worked intensively on the entire text. She found countless slips and misreadings, but also pushed me to go back and find something more fitting for sections that I, in my haste and exasperation, wanted to write off as good enough—in other words, to do justice to the strange and unwieldy beauty of this work. She was tolerant when I pestered her mercilessly with questions, often trailing back over old terrain, trying to convince her to see one word and say another when the recalcitrant language of the text rubbed against the grain of my thinking. Tabea Magyar also helped me to resolve many questions about the meaning and tone of the German; and my ability to read and translate this text is in so many ways a result of the love that we've lived. Tom Allen likewise read the entire manuscript in an early version and provided considered suggestions. A number of other people read sections and provided commentary, and I would like to thank Sam Langer, Rory Dufficy, and Marty Hiatt. Daniel Reeve provided invaluable help with the translation of German terminology for medieval Swedish social ranks when I was totally at a loss. I would also like to thank Jesper Festin and Ulrika Wallenström, likewise, for tips on Swedish names and details about Stockholm. Thanks to Bill Bird for trying to help resolve a question about the vocabulary of shoemaking. Thanks also to Jenny Willner, who helped to solve a few last-minute queries and who made me wish we'd crossed paths so much sooner. I also owe thanks to Robert Cohen for his detailed scholarship on the work, and finally to Jürgen Schutte, who sadly passed away while this translation was being completed.

Joel Scott
Berlin, January 2019

THE bearded ebony gnome held the lamp above me in his fists. Settees, enormous upholstered armchairs, tables topped with marble or adorned with intarsia were mirrored in the parquet floor, dark paintings hung on the damask-covered walls, maritime scenes, landscapes, in heavy golden frames. The fireplace mantel rose up like an altar, and from beneath the tripartite Gothic window a spiral staircase led up to the gallery which, with its balustrade full of chinoiserie, ran around the room, dividing the walls in two. Figures lay asleep on the sofas, hunched up on the fauteuils, threadbare items of clothing were tossed over the backs of the chairs, a naked foot jutted out from under a blanket, a flaccid, bloated hand hung down toward the dusty boots. Once again we were camped in one of those spaces that seemed to have no other purpose than to remind us of the dualism that defined our entire project. But this time we had not come to requisition and repurpose the sumptuous property of some temporarily ousted baron of finance but rather to be harbored by the landlord for the span of a few days, before we would move on, each seeking out his own path. Discharged from the collapsing Spanish Republic and having arrived in Paris in the evening, we had taken up quarters in the library of the Cercles des Nations on Rue Casimir-Périer, in this palace which had been erected during the Second Empire for the Marquis d'Estourmelle, and which under its current owner, the Swedish banker Aschberg, had been made available to the movement for world peace and the Committee for the Foundation of a German Popular Front. Utterly exhausted yet unable to sleep, I had walked over to the shelves and stumbled across a book which I pulled down to read. The sentences on the yellowed pages emanated an extraordinarily calming effect, even though the events portrayed moved with certainty toward catastrophe. It was as if, reading of the by-gone events described here, everything that lay torn open within me could be brought to a reconciliation. On the seventeenth of June eighteen sixteen, at seven o'clock in the morning, in good winds, the squadron that had been ordered to Senegal under the command of the frigate captain Mr. de Chaumareys had left the roads of the island of Aix. Four centuries before the departure of the French fleet, Cadamosto, the Venetian, had already sailed up the river in Senegal on behalf of Portugal; the Portuguese had established their trading posts on the coast; they were relieved by the Dutch, who were in turn driven out by the French, who founded the city of Saint-Louis in the delta, making it the center of the slave trade. From this point on, the settlements between Cap Blanc and the Gambia River alternated between French and English rule until the area was left to the French in the Paris treaties of 1815. Having come through the long period of wars, defeated the French, and banished Napoleon to Saint Helena, Great Britain—having received almost all of the colonies they had sought—could afford upon the installation of Louis XVIII to grant France that semi-arid, steppe-covered promontory in the far west of Africa. With access to the natural resources of the south from their base at the Cape of Good Hope and in possession of the fertile banks of the Gambia River and the port of Bathurst, the English furthermore had reserved the right to run the trade in rubber together with the French and to secure it with their own forts and transshipment points. On board the flagship *Medusa* as it steered through the Bay of Biscay were the governor and other func-tionaries who were to administer France's new crown colony, several en-gineers, land surveyors, and settlers, five doctors and two pharmacists for the hospital, a portion of the officers and navy personnel from the three companies that had been assigned to the garrison—each comprising eighty-four men—four storekeepers, six clerks, two notaries, and thirty-one servants, including eight children. In total, three hundred sixty-five people had been sent to Senegal by the Ministry of the Navy—of which approximately two hundred forty went on the frigate, with the others on the corvette *Echo*, the barque *Loire*, and the brig *Argus*—a figure which seemed paltry considering Europe's growing stakes in the African conti-nent and the likelihood of further disputes in the partitioning of the con-quered areas. The undertaking, in its improvised, careless nature, mir-rored the situation in which France found itself: crushed by the burden of war debts which were to be paid to the Bank of England yet at the same time delivered by England and the Allies to apparent stability out of anx-iety over the reemergence of revolutionary impulses. The king, after twenty years of exile, had bestowed the executive positions upon his cronies: aristocrats returned from emigration entirely lacking in experience, animated only by the compulsion to reacquire influence and property. These functionaries were concerned not so much with the task of turning a profit for the court as they were with the possibility of lining their pockets, hoping to find the veins of gold on the upper courses of the Senegal River that had once been reported by the Portuguese. The officers also hoped to gain income from their raids in the bush, from the sale of ivory, skins, and pelts, and the members of the battalions could, at any rate, count on the punitive expeditions against the Berber tribes for some diversion. Other than that, everything seemed to remain within the confines of petty administration, was almost idyllic, having neither the stuff of triumph nor tragedy. But the reader who in November eighteen seventeen delved into the recently published book about the shipwreck of the 5 *Medusa* could see in it how the epoch in which they lived was unfolding out of narrow-mindedness, selfishness, and avarice; he saw an empire with provincial features rising up, he saw the profiteers, and he saw their victims. The suffering of the castaways on the raft of the stranded ship had left him shaken, as it had many others; the account written by the two survivors, Savigny and Corréard, which I read in the contemporaneous German translation on the night of the twentieth of September nineteen thirty-eight and into the twenty-first, introduced him to a wealth of scenes which, after a year of drafting, would result in the constellation that materialized in his great painting. The phases that the painter had gone through in the search for an expression of his indignation became clear to me. Immediately after rounding Cape Finisterre in good weather with a weak northeasterly, an incident occurred that placed the journey under the sign of calamity. Watching the leaping dolphins from the quarterdeck, a scream could be heard; a cabin boy, they said, had fallen overboard and, after having clung to a dangling rope for a few moments, had been carried away in the rapid movement of the ship. With the feel for precision that the authors had already displayed in their listing of the participants of the expedition, and because there was nothing further to report about the victim of the accident, they now described the rescue buoy that had been thrown out. Fastened to a hawser, cobbled together out of pieces of cork, measuring a meter in diameter and bearing a small flagstick, it was able to be sketched by Géricault. Its emptiness, and the emptiness of the water all around, foreshadowed the forsakenness that was soon to come. Madeira, which was reached after ten days, rose up in the reader's vision like a colored engraving, with the city of Funchal, the cottages embedded in flower gardens and forests of date palms, bitter orange, and lemon trees, the slopes of the vineyards lined with laurel and plantain trees. On the following morning the Selvagens Islands were sighted and, at sundown, Tenerife, a spectacle which immediately roused the authors to depict the majestic form of the Pico del Teide, the crown as if wreathed with fire, whereupon they provided the exact height of the mountain and its latitude and longitude. In their mention of the entrance into the bay of Santa Cruz, passing Fort San Cristóbal, they made sure to reminisce on the victory that a handful of French had scored over a fleet of English there, after the drawn-out battle in which Admiral Nelson lost an arm. The squadron moored in the harbor, boats traveled to the city, as wines and fruits were to be bought, and filters in the form of a mortar, as were produced on the island from the volcanic soil. The observations

6   from this visit inspired the painter to create sketches that revealed his tendency to break an event down into various stages. Just as he had been preoccupied with the betrayal and murder of the revolutionary Fualdès while working on the studies for the painting of the shipwreck, depicting the bestial minutiae of the deed in a series of sheets, he also mused over the chroniclers' accounts of the unleashing of passions in Santa Cruz. Fualdès was lured into a brothel, stabbed to death on a table, his blood slurped up by pigs, his body tossed into the river. So in this city, which lay in a swale between slaggy, fissured rocks and jungle-like flora from which cedars and dragon's blood trees shot up, in this city with the squat white houses under the burning sky, a peculiar excitement and lasciviousness began to spread upon the announcement of the arrival of the French. The women stepped out from the doors, hurried toward the strangers appearing in the narrow streets, and invited them to come in for a bite to eat and to make a sacrifice to the goddess of Paphos. Often this occurred in the presence of the men, who had no right to rebel against it, for the Holy Inquisition had once wished it to be so, and the numerous monks on the island took care to maintain the custom. The scintillating heat, the women, untying the strings of their bodices, lifting up their blinding white skirts, hemmed with lace, and flicking them back down, edging forward a pointed, polished black shoe; the naked, intertwined bodies on the beds, the old names of the island, playing on inaccessibility, felicity, the Gardens of the Hesperides, yet also reminding of a fatal danger, the threshold between day and eternal night, the emergence of the basalt columns and phonolite blocks of the foothills, the fragrance of the white-flowering broom at the foot of the crater mountain, the pitchy luster of the obsidian veins in the gray, yellow, and rust-red pumice walls, the clumps of tuff, the smoking fissures and vents of the lateral craters, with congealed lava in iridescent, sulfurous hues, the glassy cone on high, all this conjured up visions in Géricault which caused him to perceive the isolation in which he had placed himself. He tore up what he had drawn, but an agonizing restlessness continued to mark every moment to which he gave pictorial form. Back on the open seas, the fleet passed Cape Bojador on the first of July, and at ten o'clock in the morning reached the Tropic of Cancer, where the passengers found amusement in the baptismal custom, the main purpose of which, according to the authors, was actually the tips that were given to the sailors on this occasion. On the second of July, they set out from Cap Barbas on course for the Gulf of Saint Cyprian. The shore was only half a cannon shot away, the coast clearly visible, with its stretches of desert behind the tall cliffs, onto which the sea broke violently. Following the route set out by the Minister of the Navy, the ships navigated between packs of lurking rocks, dismissing the warnings of some of the sailors; the commander of the frigate believed he had sighted Cap Blanc, but it was soon revealed to be a dense patch of cloud. During the night, the corvette *Echo* burned several charges of gunpowder and hoisted a lantern onto the mizzenmast, but it never once occurred to the officers on watch aboard the *Medusa* to respond to the signals. At daybreak, the plumb line revealed the continuing reduction of the water level; separated from the remaining vessels, the flagship floated toward the long sandbank off the island of Arguin. Even those least practiced in seafaring noticed the yellowish coloring of the waves. All the additional sails on the port side were hoisted in order to gather as much wind as possible for turning, yet the rudder ran aground. For a moment the ship became buoyant again; then, after another jolt, it became lodged at a point measuring only five meters and sixty centimeters deep—and the tide had just reached its highest level. For days on end the painter must have contemplated the events conveyed to him by the following pages of the book. The distress and desperation, the confusion and the torpor were portrayed so palpably that the reader felt as if he were in the midst of the castaways. He heard the screaming, the thundering of the waves breaking on the hull. The sails were lowered, the crow's nest taken down, the booms and bowsprit, powder barrels and woodwork thrown into the ocean; in the bilge, the bottoms were beaten out of the water barrels and they began to pump, but the ship could no longer be saved. The twenty-four cannons, the jettisoning of which would have considerably lightened the load, were left on board in the hope of being able to salvage them later. Since the frigate carried only six smaller boats, which couldn't possibly hold all the passengers and personnel—together more than four hundred people—a raft was hurriedly constructed which, according to the calculations of the governor, was supposed to be able to carry two hundred people. The skies cast over, a storm approached from out at sea, the frigate rolled violently, its bilge burst in the night, the rudder broke off and was left hanging from the stern by nothing but its chain. On the fifth of July, early in the morning, it was decided to immediately clear the wreck, which was threatening to capsize. The soldiers were relegated to the raft, their request to take their muskets and some cartridges denied. They were allowed to retain only their sabers or carbines, while the officers carried shotguns and pistols. The raft—the design sketch of which was reproduced in the book as a copperplate print, and of which the painter would have a model fabricated—was twenty meters long and seven meters wide. Topmasts were fastened to the sides; between them, yards and topgallant masts of the foremast and the main mast were fixed and knotted thick with rigging; on top of these, boards from the decks were nailed at a right angle, broken up by five longer planks which stuck out on the sides by two or three meters; on the bow, two intersecting topgallant yards formed a kind of breastwork; and serving as a handrail— for this is what it was called by those who had the raft built but who had no intention of entrusting their lives to it—was an assortment of all kinds of timber lashed together, barely half a meter tall. At first glance it did seem possible that the two hundred people could fit onto the raft, yet scarcely had some fifty clustered together on it when it began to sink, right up to the railing, and even when the majority of the barrels of food had been jettisoned, after the addition of the remaining castaways they were left standing with water above their waists, pressed so tightly against one another that they couldn't move. There were one hundred forty-nine of them: one hundred twenty soldiers and twenty-nine sailors and passengers, a single woman among them. They had with them six barrels of wine and two barrels of drinking water. A sack of rusk was thrown to them and some sailcloth, even though there was no mast fixed to the raft, and no rudder either. The castaways did not receive the instruments and maps that the captain had promised them. Mr. de Chaumareys hurried away and boarded the officers' boat, which, in addition to twelve oarsmen, held forty-two men. The governor and higher functionaries went in the pinnace along with fourteen oarsmen, making thirty-five people in all, as well as significant baggage. The third boat, rowed by twelve men, was occupied by twenty-eight officers. Thirty people crowded onto the oarless shallop and thirty onto the eight-oared barge which had been intended for the port service in Senegal; and lastly, fifteen ended up on the jolly boat. So at least thirty men must have drowned or stayed behind on board the *Medusa*. The thought of this embarkation, among the roaring and pummeling, while the waves shattered the bulwark and the mast stumps of the overturned frigate, climbing down on rope ladders, on rigging, the cries for help of those who had fallen into the sea, the distorted mouths, the eyes drawn wide with fear, hands straining up and splayed out, the effort of pushing the raft off against the slick side of the ship, the moment when the governor, sitting in an armchair, was winched down into the head boat, such impressions had absorbed the painter before he was overwhelmed by the image of the fully laden raft. It was towed along by the smallest and least seaworthy vessels, and when the oarsmen saw that the boats of the governor and captain were trailing off into the distance, they soon gave up towing and let go of the ropes, themselves battling against the worsening seas. While the flotilla headed for the shore, the raft, unable to be maneuvered, was carried out to sea by the tidal currents. Those gathered together on the raft still did not want to believe they had been abandoned. The coast was visible, as was the island of Arguin with the ruins of the old Portuguese fort; the castaways assumed that the boats would return for them, or that the *Echo*, *Loire*, and *Argus* would spot them. But night fell, and they had still not received help. Powerful swells swept over us. Hurled back and forth, struggling for every breath, hearing the cries of those washed overboard, we longed for the break of day.

There was nobody awake to whom I could have reported my emancipation from the usual daily chores. I stood on the empty Rue Casimir-Périer like a deserter, harried by the thought that I must turn around, return to those still asleep and wait to find out what was to happen next. But then I gave in once more to the pull that had seized me in the hall; I walked via Rue las Cases, past the brick building of Saint Clotilde, toward the small park where two years earlier my father had met with Wehner, where the sparrows were chirping, the pigeons cooing, just as they always had. In the square in the center of the grounds, under the chestnut trees, César Franck, who had been the organist in the church, sat in front of his marble instrument with his arms crossed, his foot resting on the pedal, listening intently to the angel which, resting on its stomach, stretched awkwardly over the back wall and lay his arms around Franck's shoulders while whispering into his side whiskers. Now, in the dim light of dawn, the sea had grown calmer, ten men had been swallowed by the ocean, another twelve, perished, hung pinned between the planks and the boards. I walked down Rue Saint-Dominique, the guards at the entrance to the courtyard of the Ministry of Defense directed their gazes toward me. Suddenly afraid that I could provoke suspicion or be arrested, I slowed my pace. Turning into Rue de Solferino, far off in the distance, above the treetops of the Quai d'Orsay, up at the height of Sacré-Cœur, I saw a newspaper boy riding his bike from door to door; at each building he counted out a bundle and carried it inside: *Chamberlain to Godesberg*, I read on one of the front pages in passing. Rue de Lille marked the end of the gorge of tall, uniform residential buildings; it was followed by the two-story building of the Légion d'Honneur, with its rounded portal, a tricolor on the slanted flagpole above it, and closed shutters on the yellowish-gray, putti-covered façade. Alone or in small groups, pedestri-

ans approached from the boulevard along the riverbank, walking hunched over, hurried; they might have been cleaning ladies, porters, who worked in the ministries where people had worked late into the night, having to empty the stuffed ashtrays and wastepaper baskets, dust off the desks, mop the floors; a restrained silence, a leaden exhaustion lay over the government quarter; these colorless figures, which in the morning mist still had something fluid to them, were familiar to me; they, who were the first inhabitants of the city I encountered, eased my passage into the metropolis, the arrival of these inconspicuous servants provided a familiar background for the impending arrival of the noises; in a moment, their swift and soft steps would be buried under the drumming that the slabs of stone would cause to vibrate on all sides. The actual venture into the unknown began when I had reached the street overlooking the Seine. I followed the railing to the right, suffering an attack of dizziness and delirium. A pole had been torn out of the base of the raft, erected as a mast and fastened with the tow rope, the clapping of the tatters of the sail could be heard and the torque was palpable, the irreparable twisting of the raft due to an overly long, laterally protruding piece of wood. By the second day the refusal to hand over the firearms to the sailors had already proven its purpose. Inebriated, having smashed and drunk a barrel of wine, the crew went after their superiors with axes and knives in a throng around the mast, where the officers held their ground with their pistols. In this burgeoning mutiny, the painter saw the possibility of a great composition arise. But there were still too many people clinging to the planks, their heads hanging down into the water, there was still too much confusion in this mutual onslaught, this struggle for dominance played out on a tiny territory, the antagonism had still not been converted into intimacy, the collective need, the collective horror, had not yet united them. On the ledge of the wall, I opened the street map I had bought the previous evening upon arriving at Gare de Lyon. There would be a lot to do today, decisions would have to be made, important steps for my progression stood before me, yet I had drifted into a haze of multiplicity which made it impossible for me to follow the laws that had previously applied. My every thought was so beleaguered by contradictory impulses, the attempt to gain perspective now seemed so fruitless after this leap from everything solid and binding, that I shelved the question of what was rational and useful and gave myself over to impulses that, without ever revealing their meaning, sought to prevail within me. At this moment, I only knew that I had to continue on through a glut of sediment that had been pressed and woven together so densely that every movement produced as it were a grinding and cracking, and I was not just surrounded by webs of images, tangles of events, it was as if time had also burst, and as if I, by rummaging through its layers, had to crush it between my teeth. But in this condition, which resembled a state of inebriation, of possession, the desire for a form of regulation, of measurement persisted. With satisfaction I realized that behind the boulevard on the opposite bank of the river lay the sculpture-filled Tuileries Gardens, leading up to the elongated façade of the Louvre. It would still be many hours before the museum's gates would open; it was not intended for those who were ready to pay it a visit at the break of dawn, it belonged to the long sleepers, who after a late and generous meal tended to their nightly repose, and were then able to do with their day as they pleased. Yet it didn't matter that I had to wait; I had stolen this day for myself, I could already see myself walking around in the storeroom, in which one after the other of those works of the imagination, of inventiveness, were hanging, where everything was present in the original colors and forms, everything that I had known until now only from second-hand accounts or dubious reproductions. Be not afraid, one of them cried, I am going to get help for you, you'll be seeing me soon, and stepped, amid the general ecstasy, out into the sea. Sixty to sixty-five men perished in the tumult, rusk and drinking water were exhausted, only a barrel of wine was left. What became of the woman, Géricault asked himself. Strangely, the authors had not reported anything further about her, though the fact of a single woman's presence among the men ought to have merited special consideration. He wanted to know whether they had fought over the woman, or whether carnality lost all meaning under the threat of death. He saw himself lying next to her, and he sketched this moment, the two of them surrounded by corpses in the foreground of the raft. The woman was unconscious, he had draped his arm around her, in the other he cradled a naked child, even though there had been no mention of a child on the raft. More and more, the raft became his own world. He clasped the body of the woman, pressed the child against himself, at night, he slept like this, when he awoke, he sensed that his arms were empty, it was a long time before he was able to open his eyes and saw that the ocean had taken from him the woman, the child. As the number of people on the raft became smaller, the painter came closer to the concentration that he needed for the final version of his painting. After the fighting died down, the wish to carry on living for as long as possible underwent a strange transformation. The first people began to cut up the cadavers that were lying around with their knives. Some devoured the raw meat on the spot, others let it dry in the sun, in order to make it more palatable, and those who could not bring themselves to consume this new fare were forced by hunger to do so on the following day. The turbulence was followed by the period of total isolation. In this condition of being torn out of all relations the painter recognized his own situation. He attempted to imagine what it was like, the sinking of teeth into the throat, the leg of a dead human being, and while he drew Ugolino biting into the flesh of his sons, he learned to come to terms with it, as those on the raft had done after letting out a hurried prayer. The naked figures, huddled together on the raft, found themselves in a world deformed by fever and delusion, those still living merged with the dead by consuming them. Drifting about on the plank structure, in cloud-like waters, Géricault felt the penetration of the hand into the slit breast, the grasping of the heart of the person he had hugged goodbye on the previous day. After a week, thirty remained on the raft. The saltwater had driven the skin on their feet and legs to blister and peel, their torsos were covered with contusions and sores. Often they cried and whimpered, at most twenty of them could still hold themselves upright. In the counting and calculating from one day to the next, in the continual withering away of the heap of castaways, in the depictions of the thirst, the running dry of all that was drinkable, the drooling over urine—which bore various aromas, sometimes sweetish, sometimes acrid, of thinner or thicker consistency, cooled in a small tin container— in the description of sucking up the wine ration through a quill, which prolonged the drinking, in the incessant approach of death, the burning of one hour into the next, the painter too heard the seeping of time into infinity, and from this dripping, ticking, and flowing the painting's process of creation was set in motion. Without living through those thirteen days and nights of anguish he wouldn't have been able to find that moment of finality and depict the remaining group in its indivisibility. He was still captivated by individual details, distracted from the conception of completion. There was that little, empty bottle, which had contained rose oil, and which one of them wrested from the other so as to inhale the sweet smell. The painter couldn't shake the thought of the tiny perfume bottle; it roused memories of long-forgotten experiences. For several weeks he took great pains to not portray the objects themselves but rather the emotions, the dream images evoked by the feel of the objects. He knelt on the floor, on top of the drawing paper, the door locked behind him, completely alone with his secrets; for a few days he didn't eat or drink a thing, crawled around on the floorboards, surrounded by hallucinations, his mother, whom he had lost at the age of ten, appeared to him, a violent longing to be close to her overcame him, he reached out to feel her features, drew Phaedra, and himself as Hippolytus, whom the sea monster sought to dash against the rocks, and who was then dragged to his death by horses. For him, existence was drifting around on the raft; he pined for the woman who had replaced his mother, the wife of the brother of his mother, he was torn apart by the guilt of having left her, having disavowed the woman who had borne him a child. I had a desire to learn as much as possible about him, and in the openness that I brought to this day, the expectation that his life would open up before me emerged. Relentless as the permeation of the hazy air by the heightened light were the mounting sounds, every now and then a car drove down the street along the quay, and behind me, the early trains were rolling into Gare d'Orsay. With its coats of arms, helmets, and crowns, its window arches wrapped in patron saints and gods, its clocks set in wreathes, fruit baskets, and cornucopias, its immense golden letters flanked by harps and anchors, the hulking edifice which I turned toward seemed to want to trump the palace above and its halls of artworks. The footsteps of the people exiting the main entrance, most of them dressed in dark hues, briefcases under their arms, were already being drowned out by a metallic buzz, a whirring singing ascending from the city. Compared with the tumors of the industrial age, the titans and muses, the heroes and angels snuggled in together in the niches and tower gables of the side building of the Louvre still had something reserved, chaste about them, and yet these refinements of feudalism were no more laudable than the mountains of pompous sculptures on this side. There was a greater purity of line to be found in the bridge I was walking toward. Its low walls were smoothly cut, the two halves ascended symmetrically to the sharp central seam, four cast-iron lampposts protruding on each side. But Pont Royal also failed to inspire any harmony within me; it was more as if the air, though already flushed with a glow, had become a viscous, dull paste; I had to wring every step out of myself; seized by shivering, I clung to the railing. Only a few days earlier I had still belonged to an irrevocable order, had performed set tasks, had been connected with the actions of others. Now I found myself in a region in which there was a life whose existence we had forgotten just as completely as we had been ignored here. The battlefields lay behind us, the fighting raged on, but the charges, the retreats, the cries of the wounded, the dying voices of the fallen, none of that counted here, everything here was so different that even we lost sight of ourselves, that we could no longer remember what we had actually been fighting for. From our first steps on French soil we were regarded as ejecta; the demobilized soldiers, the masses of refugees were driven into ringed fences of barbed wire, only a small number, with valid passports, were able to evade internment, and this was a hidden path out of a desert, a field of rubble. The expectation of a greeting, a welcome, a sign of solidarity had evaporated, there was no Popular Front here, only the gendarmerie received us, the only place we belonged was in the police archives; henceforth we were to report to the prefecture daily and hold out to be stamped the scrap of paper that signified our existence. I had always seen my path in front of me, made my decisions, even back then, deep in the underground and surrounded by fascism, I had been able to see a way out; only here, in the capital of openness, of enlightenment, were we forced into blindness. On the first evening in Paris we had been suddenly overwhelmed by our sense of estrangement from one another. With the dissolution of our alliance, our natural sense of belonging together had also evaporated; a powerlessness had befallen us with the realization that our ranks had been broken up, that we had been made useless. Only the question of which party we belonged to, or intended to join, contained the suggestion of a continued permanence. Until now I had found my purpose on the side that I was fighting for; now I was confronted with the realization that this spontaneous community was only possible so long as I was among friends and allies, and that this natural cooperation had to be replaced by a binding commitment. At a point in time when the illegal, conspiratorial work in cadres demanded the strictest confinement, it was necessary to join the organized collective; it was only here that it seemed possible to demonstrate our reliability. Yet such a step had been made more difficult by the decentralization of the Party; I didn't even know which group, which country I was responsible for.

The only task now had to be that of rebuilding and strengthening the Party, and I was ready to follow the directives that I would again be receiving. At the same time though, I was drawn to the park gates behind the bridge, watched over by sphinxes, and an immense thirst for knowledge grew within me. I leaned on the stone railing, barges with bunting of colorful pieces of laundry trailed along beneath me; today, when there was a need for the most precise orientation in external reality, today, while the city was holding its breath, awaiting the decisive moves and blows of the protagonists in the diplomatic spectacle, I wanted to head over to the poplars on the upper bank, to that arsenal of images. The thought of being accepted into the Party coalesced with the desire for limitless discoveries; I could already see myself standing before those painted surfaces, see my encounter with Géricault, Delacroix, Courbet, Millet; I wanted to head into the closed organization, into uncompromising struggle, and at the same time, into the absolute freedom of the imagination. Surmounting Pont Royal, I envisioned the path into the Party and the path to art as something singular, something indivisible; political judgment, relentlessness in the face of the enemy, the power of the imagination, all of this came together to form a unity. As I passed the sphinxes, the last line of defense was broken. Here and there in the grounds with the crisscrossing gravel paths someone was walking their dog on a leash. Egyptians and Assyrians, Druids and Gauls, Romans and Goths had been hauled in, beaten into stone, cast in ore, to honor the princes on their warhorses; everywhere guards and rulers loomed, waving their swords and lances, and poets, philosophers, and artists swiveled on their pedestals, passing me along through their arms. No sooner had I leaned back on a bench than silver-gray women appeared before me like ghosts, in long robes, and chased me away with outstretched hands. I had time to ask myself what this actually was, this city, where did it draw its essence, its strength, with which it continuously exerted its influence upon me. It had always been my wish to come to this city, and now that I was here, scarcely tolerated, among the lowest of the low, the task was to not allow it to force me onto my knees. Faced with its buildings and streets, I had to assert myself, in this powerful conglomeration which received its life from all those people who lived within it or had done, I had to look for relationships that could give my consciousness something to hold on to. The architecture and avenues drew the wanderer into their expansiveness, and the light, reflecting off the water and the sandy yellow hues of the walls of the buildings, did its bit to transport them to a realm of levity and devotion. Looking through the central arch of the gate in the forecourt

15

of the Louvre, in honor of the victory at Austerlitz and made of rose marble, the obelisk on Place de la Concorde and the large memorial to the Napoleonic armies at the end of the Champs-Élysées formed a straight line. This perspective, fringed by the gentle green of the rows of trees, drew the gaze into a flight to infinity, running from the symbol of one military triumph to the other, containing all the efforts at attaining absolute power, its format—accommodating the breadth of troops on the march and opening a vista onto unruly masses—was intended to lift our emotions and allow us to perceive imperialism, transformed into grand proportions, as a form of beauty. Considering how tearing down the old districts was supposed to hamper the building of barricades, create a clear field of fire, I saw Paris under the spell of its rulers, saw at all strategic points the mountains of wealth towering over the closed-off quarters of

the tradespeople, the petite bourgeoisie, and the workers. But it wasn't this pattern that gave the city its appearance; the sense of being here, of the presence of all these buildings was instead evoked by the knowledge of the events that, all around, coming from below, had been set in motion again and again, the movements of outrage, of insurgency, which brought their own violence, their own power to fruition. Every building bore a more palpable trace of such actions than of the obligations that had been issued by the dynasties, and if to the nameless masses, who in the alleys had stacked up the stones into barricades, I added those who had entered into the life of the city with their artworks, then I was immediately thrust into a hot and bubbling mêlée that left me gasping for air. Almost all the people who had contributed to shaping my thought had resided here; the fact that their gazes had examined the scenes I was now seeing, that they had crossed this street, placed demands upon me for a moment that were scarcely bearable, but then it encouraged me, for none of these people had managed to transcend their beginnings in an instant either, and it was the ones who were most dear to me who had left behind evidence of their efforts and hardships. Amid the rumble of the traffic, in the chaos of the crowds who were rushing off to tend to their affairs, I approached from Place Vendôme, where I had seen how the column began to list, how it fell and burst. Even if it had also erected itself again like in a film in rewind, encoiled by its copper reliefs packed with nobles, breastplates, army flags, and fasces, which slot together to form a screw thread around the dense masonry of the base, with the spiral staircase inside; the fact that this column bearing Caesar in his laurel crown on the cupola had once been toppled, was still reason enough to leave the lavishly decorated square with confidence. Once, the tall steps to the entrance of the Nationalgalerie in Berlin had sought to hinder our access to art; insignificant and worthless, we had scaled the steps up to the acropolis, which wanted to open itself only to the select few; before the entrance to the Louvre, however, we had only to advance across a threshold, and while the German troops were moving into formation on the Czechoslovakian border, Poland and Hungary were making their own demands for territorial gains, and in Hotel Dreesen on the Rhine preparations were being made for the arrival of the British delegation, the doors were flung open, and I charged in, in the stream of pilgrims, into the enfilade of the halls, bent down inquisitively to the sullen old men sitting on velvet seats with their peaked caps, saw incomparable sights with every step, left and right, gave them just enough time to ring out before continuing straight on, up and down the steps, until I finally ended up in front of the enormous, blackish-brown canvas, which at first conveyed the impression of a sudden extinction and death.

In this first encounter, in those heavily darkened colors—mixed in with asphalt, turned mute and blotchy—I tried to find a trace of those first signs of luminosity that had been present during my conversation with Ayschmann. Gradually, on the seemingly monochrome surface of the image, some yellowish, bluish, greenish tones became discernible. No longer was the feeling of an extremely heightened tension upon discovering the ship on the horizon predominant, but rather an anxiety, a feeling of hopelessness. Only pain and desolation could still be read in the oppressively restrained composition; it was as if, with the sloughing and scabbing of the surface of the paint, everything with a tangible, documentary quality had drained out of the image, and only a mark of the personal catastrophe of the painter had been left behind. But more than disappointment over the dullness of the painting I felt sympathy for Géricault, whose achievements had been surrendered to weathering and decay. The haziness of the picture also led me to planes on which vision had not yet solidified; the appearance of the individual figures spoke of the brooding preparations, and through the shrouding of completion, effervescent, dreamlike elements emerged. The painter had spent a long time in the turmoil of the many, then among the dead and the fading. He saw the solution he was seeking emerge in that second when, with the shrill cry at the appearance of the brig, a complete turnaround occurred, and the bodies, which had been ready to surrender to their demise, sprung back up once more, becoming a wedge against the world of annihilation. He was already close to this conclusion as he read how the castaways, in the midst of the horrors, had been capable of joking, how they forgot their situation for a moment and broke into laughter. If the brig is sent out after us, said one, may God grant it Argus eyes, a play on the name of the ship they were hoping would help them. This showed the painter that even in the most extreme despair, as long as a breath could still be drawn, a will to live persisted. And if he did ultimately end up under the yoke of Hades, and the strain of rebellion passed away, leaving only a necrotic husk, this made his determination, which had cost him all his strength, only greater still. His undertaking had been to paint the final few who had still been able to rise up. And while the raft was being swept around in the frothing, blue-green water, lifted slightly by one wave and drenched by the heavy swell of the next, in the perpetual to and fro, the day of the twenty-first of September intruded upon me from outside. Suddenly, my

18 efforts to understand the image became stuck; it seemed to contain too much of the painter's being, of the uneasiness, the dissatisfaction that ate away at him, it was as if he were somewhere out in the city, as if I had to find him, to interrogate him about the meaning that he had invested in his work, and I left the palace and its imaginary riches. In my attempt to get closer to this tarry scrap of cloth, the inner conflict within me was reactivated. Géricault, son of the fourteenth of July, was familiar with the forces that needed to be directed against ruin, against disintegration; the revolution had been inscribed in him, like a scar; he had striven for the ability to be able to contribute to the establishment of a dominion of the common good, yet he possessed nothing but his artistic language, and even more than this language served him to represent the infirmity of an epoch, it marked the martyrdom that his own exposed nerves were suffering. During the years in which Géricault had developed his craft, the old conditions had been reinstated; in the time of the Restoration, nobody still asked about the First Republic. A passing glance at David's paintings sufficed to confirm how, following the classicist spirit of the revolution, after those soaring idealistic heights, the path to the megalomania of empire had immediately been found. That which was vital in Géricault stood on the side of renewal, which was expressed in his choice of subject matter, in his technique, in the application of paint, the treatment of forms; however, his life was that of someone who was pushed into a corner, isolated; his hatred of haughtiness and the vanity of society drove him to a breakdown. If in the end he spent his time almost exclusively in prisons, madhouses, and morgues, it was because he could only bear to be among the ostracized. They were his kin. Staring into the disillusioned face of the thief, studying the yellowish, pallid skin, the red-rimmed eyes of the madwoman, things fell into place, and his addiction to death found reflection in the sight of the dismembered limbs on the dissecting table, in the bloody heads, severed from their torsos. The rupture within him called up something of the fragmentation to which my generation was also subjected. It was as if we had a gag in our mouths that turned every word we wanted to utter about Spain into a sinister moaning. For more than two years—an eternity for us—people had been fighting there; but here, every thought about the distress in which the Spanish Republic found itself disappeared into padded indifference, dull silence; here, the unspeakable effort of resisting the enemy was covered over by the husk of a false peace. This peace had become a kind of mystical bliss whose preservation lay in the hands of a few people who were equipped with supernatural abilities. The city was indeed pervaded by a tension that encompassed world affairs; people clustered together on all sides discuss- ing the latest news, but the reports they were following with such excitement were nothing more than the story of their own plight distorted into a cheap thriller. Spellbound, the mysterious intrigues kept them on tenterhooks, they were instilled with hope; awaiting a solution, they didn't notice that the threat to Czechoslovakia was a result of the ignorance shown toward Spain; beguiled by the speeches declaiming the honorable character of England and France, they didn't see how interwoven the crimes were. Spain was written off, the threat to Czechoslovakia made into an isolated problem. While in the Spanish vacuum the outcome was still being contested, the mass media of the West served up the maneuvers and countermaneuvers to their audience as a sensational game in which the heroes were the diplomats; they robbed the militant vanguard of the working class of its impact and assigned influence only to the cardboard cutouts of the governing politicians, with no mention of the powerful forces of high finance behind them. The impending advance of a popular movement was drowned out by the flood of rhetoric from the consolidation process of the reactionary forces; the struggle against enslavement was left atrophied beneath distortion and lies. Only recently it had still seemed as if insight and reason could prevail over the forces of destruction; now, dark-clad gentlemen were solemnly and corruptly determining the fate of the nations. They had rejected any and every offer of collaboration from the Soviet Union, had ignored their appeals and warnings, yet they had hurried to the head of the Fascist League, willing to make any concession to avoid getting a raw deal in the redistribution of the markets. Even in the uncertainties and missteps that had been made in Spain, in the doubts and weaknesses that may have overcome us there, for us, that which had been attempted in the Republic took on a luminosity that ought to have singed the rest of Europe; but here, people allowed themselves to be blinded by the salacious reports of shady business dealings, betrayal and plunder were deemed magnanimous efforts to maintain peace. On every street corner we were confronted with the glorification of cynical self-interest; why, we asked ourselves, didn't the workers take to the streets with their flags to express their rage about the betrayal they had been subjected to. Perhaps, we said, they had been exposed to the same shock, the same powerlessness as we had, having been cut off from our tasks, perhaps they too were only now beginning to realize how maliciously their actions had been undermined and weakened over the last few years. Exposed to the forced contingencies of exile, among the escalating instability and panic, we discussed places to which we could

emigrate. If you were presented with the chance of getting to Mexico, North America, Scandinavia, it came with a ban on political activity; you either had to find external support, a guarantee, in order to vegetate abroad with reduced rights, or you had to creep into an unknown country on your own via an illegal border crossing, with counterfeit papers, and then go underground. Beneath the candelabras, the lead-lined windowpanes, at the exquisite tables, the groups sat discussing, gesticulating. The host, with an oddly radiant, satisfied face, paced back and forth among them. For a moment, Hodann could be seen talking to Branting, the Swedish politician; Hodann was viewed with suspicion now, it was known that he was friends with Münzenberg, and though no one knew whether Münzenberg was still a member of the Party or had already been expelled, nor even what he had been accused of, anyone who still had anything to do with him was cut off, neutralized in some vague way. In the upstairs rooms of the house, despite this friction, the Committee for the Foundation of a German Popular Front was meeting, chaired by Heinrich Mann. Since the government would not go along with any Communist initiatives, the gatherings of this small, seclusive circle had something unreal about them, and yet this was the only place where an attempt was being made that could have had any effect on the catastrophe which cast a pall over all of our emotions. Merker, Dahlem, Ackermann, and Abusch were among the spokespeople of the Communist Party; Mewis was in Czechoslovakia at the time; of the Social Democratic functionaries, Braun, Stampfer, Breitscheid, and Hilferding were in attendance, though without authorization to make decisions, unless of course they had been tasked with delaying every possible decision. The structure of the Social Democratic Party, with its executive committee members in Prague and London, had become just as faceless and formless as the French and Spanish socialist parties. It only remained tangible in its craven commitment to the interests of capital. If the Communist Party appeared more amorphous still, it was out of the need for camouflage, the continuation of the struggle in the underground; at the same time, though, for all the emphasis it placed on the efforts to form a united front, it was riven by internal strife. A general mobilization in Czechoslovakia was to be expected; swastika flags, which had been hoisted in Bohemian cities, were taken down; weapons that had been amassed in apartments were seized. I saw before me the kitchen in Warnsdorf, tried to imagine the room empty, in the hope that my parents had gone to Prague. With Katz, Münzenberg's former employee, I discussed whether I should sign up for military service at the Czechoslovakian Embassy, but he advised me to wait. He was living in Paris, and at first I saw him as my father had described him, invoking Wehner's account, but after a short while that description lost all force, the elegance of his clothing inspired no antipathy in me toward him, they seemed to offer him a kind of protection. He was in the city at the behest of the Comintern, among his many tasks was to tend to the members of the International Brigades as they arrived in Paris. In conversation he seemed open, experienced. I had told him about my wish to join the Party, and also mentioned that my awareness of the urgency of the practical issues that needed to be resolved did not preclude my desire to engage in artistic or academic work. Géricault united us. In the afternoon, we walked from Boulevard de Clichy, at the foot of Montmartre, down the narrow yet busy Rue des Martyrs and stepped into the doorway of the building at number twenty-three. The entranceway led us to a paved courtyard. The walls of the formerly elegant building were of a worn gray, the plaster was riddled with cracks; windows, doors, and thresholds were set askew in the masonry. The side wings of the building extended past the garden, which adjoined the courtyard and was populated with a few tall acacias, a copse of maples, and a fence entwined with ivy. Between the iron gates was a fountain with a short trough extending from it for the horses whose stables had been added on the left-hand side at the beginning of the previous century. Katz pointed at the two arched windows and the central, square window in the floor above; there, from November of eighteen seventeen until the autumn of the following year, Géricault had sketched out his picture; to execute the large-scale painting he moved over to a workshop on Rue Louis-le-Grand in Faubourg-du-Roule; then, following the exhibition and his two-year stay in England, he returned to the garden cottage where, on the twenty-sixth of January, eighteen twenty-four, he died as a result of riding accidents. Back then the street had been located in a rural area on the outskirts of the city: passing gardens and scattered country houses, the livestock market and farmsteads, it continued on to the ruins of the Benedictine monastery, to the mills, vineyards, and chalk pits on the Mont des Martyrs. It wasn't until a few decades later that the sprawl of the city reached over the hills, but right up until the early twenties of our century, between the houses in the coiled alleyways and steep steps stood sheds and shacks, shoved on top of one another on the scrubby slopes: this was the Maquis, the sanctuary of the most impoverished. Not far from Place Blanche, Géricault's horse had shied at a fence and thrown him off. The abscess which he developed through the injury burst a few days later when, despite his condition, he took part in the derby at the

Champ de Mars and fell once more. The infection attacked his spine, the vertebrae began to disintegrate, his living body rotted away from within. There he lay, stretched out flat on the bed, partially curtained off in the room with its arched ceiling, surrounded by his paintings and drawings; *The Raft of the Medusa*, taken out of its frame, filled the longer wall; no one had wanted to buy the work, a dealer had suggested cutting up the canvas to sell off the parts as freestanding studies. When Delacroix visited him at the end of December of '23, Géricault weighed no more than a child; the head of the thirty-two-year-old, however, was that of an old man. He had sought out this death as if he had wanted to punish himself, the drive to annihilate himself also made itself evident in his remarks about his work: bah, a vignette, he responded to praise, turning his skeletal face toward the castaways. And yet, right up until his final seconds, he was planning great compositions dealing with the horrors of slavery, the liberation of the victims of the Inquisition. And though the only thing that remained tangible to him was enduring pain and suffering was the only thing that still seemed real to him, he had nevertheless repeatedly overcome death by devising images and had extracted the most acute fervor from his infirmity. Standing under the blackish mass of his work once again on Thursday the twenty-second of September, I noticed how the facial features and gestures of the group, which seemed to meld into a single entity, gradually emerged out of the surrounding darkness. Even though none of the castaways turned their gaze toward the viewer, the painter had intended for the viewer to feel as if they were right next to the raft, it should seem as if they were hanging, with cramped fingers, to one of the boards jutting out from the raft, too exhausted to live to see the rescue. The events taking shape above him no longer concerned him.

You who are standing in front of this picture, said the painter, are the forsaken ones, hope belongs to the ones you've abandoned. The arm of the corpse on the left had originally extended right to the foot of the perished youth on the foremost edge; traces of the painted-over forearm and hand could still be made out. Beneath the ribs, the torso seemed to be torn off: either he had been caught between the planks, folded back into the cavity, or half of him had been devoured. Four corpses lay up front in a row; behind them, three figures were crouched, facing away from the rest; one by the mast, his face buried in his hands, followed by four bodies, half-upright, intersected by one who had fallen back down, then four standing up, huddled close together, and then the last three, two of whom were holding up the one who was highest of all. A greenish-yellow shimmer lay over everyone's skin. As I had examined the reproduction of the painting with Ayschmann in Valencia, much of what was now revealed had already been discernible, but it wasn't until I was confronted with the work, when I became an eye-witness and took in the event in its original character, that I came to comprehend the magnitude of the act of painting it. I began to understand how the arrangement of the forms resulted from creating balances within a process of intensification, how the unity was pieced together out of contrasts. Precisely drawn, dark met with light: the illuminated contour of a profile, a back, a calf muscle, always led to fabric, wood, or flesh lying in shadow, or the black outline of a head, a hand, a hip was set against shimmering cloth, sky, water. That which was contained, controlled in this entanglement conveyed a sense of endurance, this quality being amplified by the fact that the perseverance seemed to be at the same time enveloped by a heavy sorrow. This emotion, the most abiding of all because of its connection with the irretrievable, found expression in the foreground in a full figure, and appeared here and there with its shimmer on a brow, on a temple, a thrown-back cheekbone. And now the expression that had turned toward the possibility of survival with so much energy changed as well; the expectation of rescue was marked by apprehension, waiting held sway, as in the situation in which the anxiety of a dream is to be broken through and waking induced. Those who believed they had seen what was approaching were turned away from the viewer; the few recognizable faces bore the rigidity of inward contemplation. The only one who presented himself entirely to the outside world, who had open space in front of him, was the dark-skinned man, the African; here, the outline also vibrated, the lines of the shoulder, of the cheek seen from behind, of the hair, were in the process of flowing into the cloud, at its outermost, highest point, the dissolution, the dispersion of the group began. As far as I could discern, this light blurring, this shaking of the outline wasn't to be found anywhere else; the blurring must have been applied deliberately as a scarcely appreciable sign of the transgression of the limits of the perceptible. Here, where the transcendence began, the corporeal was also sculpted most starkly, the black colonial soldier Charles was the strongest of the castaways, though according to the reports he was one of the first to die in Saint-Louis after their rescue by the *Argus*, along with the sergeants Lozack and Clairet, the cannoneer Courtade, the artillery sergeant Lavilette, and an unknown sailor from Toulon. Géricault had lived among these people while completing the preliminary studies, during the hot summer. Before he began transferring the composition to the canvas, he often felt as if he were in Saint-Louis, that small city on that island at the mouth of the Senegal River, where the rescued were hauled off the ship, hollow-eyed and bearded, and placed in a corner of the military hospital. Perhaps the painter asked himself if he shouldn't have just started here, with the continuation of the agony on land. The isolated ocean journey was over, and they now found themselves back among sedentary people, in a continuity. The English, who still had control of the garrison, didn't provide them with any help at all. After the weakest had died, the nine survivors—the geographer Corréard and the surgeon Savigny, the captain Dupont and the Lieutenant Heureux, the functionary Bellay and the ensign Coudin, Coste, the sailor, Thomas, the pilot, and the nurse François—prepared themselves for a long period of imprisonment. Géricault lay among them, crawled about on the filthy floor, tried a couple of wobbly steps, then, together with the few who were still able to walk, ventured out onto the street, begging for alms. The flimsiness of the contracts had already been made evident. Since the French occupying troops didn't show up as announced, the English officers and officials saw no reason to leave the village. It wasn't until weeks later that the miserable heap of colonizers arrived after having landed farther north, unarmed and almost without clothes. While Géricault imagined being in Saint-Louis, the great theme of the confusion of an epoch once again began to take form in his vision of the painting. The white race, greedy, beset by violent antagonisms, came crawling onto the shores of Africa; here and there, conquerors had set up shop; following the shipwreck, the dispersed schlepped their emaciated bodies through the sand, dragging their contamination into a black culture already left shaken by centuries of the slave trade. The soldiers, sailors, and passengers, led by the governor and frigate captain, who after the stranding of the *Medusa* had abandoned the raft, had traipsed through the desert into the country of King Zaide. What the painter learned about the arrival of the caravan in the tent city of the regent tore open a new breadth of perspective. After the privations of the march, the French had to rely on the hospitality of the Moorish tribes. They remembered Napoleon. For Géricault as well, the thought that the ousted emperor was still alive on that remote British island was almost a surprise. With the mention of his name, the miserable conquerors sought to lend luster to their origins. Humbly kneeling before the carpet of the king, ringed by spearmen and camel drovers, they traced out the contours of Europe and the north of Africa in the sand, and then their route across the seas. With amazement, the Mohammedan king connected the identity of General Bonaparte, whose army he had seen during a pilgrimage to Mecca, with the world ruler Napoleon. A long thin stroke led from the island of Elba past the columns of Heracles, over the equator, to a point in the South Atlantic, where the great reformer was languishing, unreachable, disempowered, embittered. The strangers received bread and drinks in return for their fabulous account. Thus they reached Saint-Louis, that city that had nothing remarkable to offer. The island was two and a half kilometers long, two hundred meters wide, barely a meter high. The streets strung out in straight lines, the houses uniform, with meager gardens, behind a group of palms the fort with mortars and an arsenal, a few mud huts on the headland at the outlet of the river, named the Point of Barbary. The English politely told the new arrivals that they hadn't yet received an order from their government to decamp from the garrison. Mr. de Chaumareys, dressing himself up with a tricorne and a few salvaged aiguillettes, called in on the infirm and half-starved in the sick bay, promised them better accommodation, care, and food just as soon as the Medusa's cash chest, containing a hundred thousand francs, had been retrieved. He made an agreement with the British representatives to share the goods left behind on board; ships set sail, but scavengers had already found the wreck and taken the safe with them. Whatever had been left behind was sold in the city. For a few days, the dull town became the site of a delirium. Flour barrels were rolled through the swirling dust, bungs were beaten out of the wine barrels, the liquids poured into the gaping mouths of people lying on the ground. Géricault and his companions, haggard, covered in lesions, roaming around barefoot in the chaos, had ocean maps, blankets, hammocks thrown to them. Nautical instruments were taken apart and stuck in the hair of the women as decoration. Children made off with knapsacks and suitcases, dug through papers and books. Ornaments from cabinet fittings were attached to the doors of the huts. Sails, bedsheets were cut up, rigging snaked along the paths. The Africans placed themselves in the role of their masters, kitted themselves out in vests, pantaloons, gilets, rapiers, and large gray overcoats. They brawled over watch chains, jackboots, hung epaulettes and medal ribbons on their glistening skin. In the wild procession, some could be seen firing silver-plated rifles into the air, or keeping watch on the ape-infested thicket through a telescope. Traders didn't want to give the governor the flag, that proud tricolor; blathering, he threw himself onto the sand while the cloth was torn up, and with its blue, its red, it was soon adorning the hips of the dancing villagers. The French were driven off with swinging rapiers, oars, boat hooks. They set off on their ignominious retreat toward Dakar. Until the end of November of that year, the survivors of the raft expedition were left behind in exile, reliant

upon handouts from sympathetic locals, until people remembered them back in France, and the *Loire* was sent after them. It was fitting for this time, overloaded as it was with phantasmagoria, that at the end of August Géricault's son was born, whom he named Hippolyte. The child being registered as descending from unknown parents, the mother being shipped off to the countryside, the child handed over to foster parents, the family's efforts to conceal the scandal from the outside world, all of this contributed to him withdrawing deeper and deeper into his failure, his negation of life. In Roule, where he worked near the Beaujon Hospital, he began to live among the dead. There, in the mortuary, he immersed himself in the study of extinguished flesh. By the time the painting made it into the Louvre for the exhibition, he was living in profound distress. In the Salon Carré, he went unrecognized among the festively dressed ladies and gentlemen, the royal household, the pack of critics; but as he heard the cries of dismay over his coarse and naked attack on all conventions, as he saw their horror in the presence of this naked desperation and heard the disparaging remarks about the colorlessness, the clayey drabness of the painting, he was filled with satisfaction, with pride; it couldn't be more perfect, he thought, the more black contained in it the better. This deep black, this dark gray, as if charged with electricity, these dull umber tones contained the calamity that he sensed with every breath, they predominated even in his juvenilia, the impulses to paint emerged in the strata in which the intolerability of life was rooted. As a twenty-one-year-old he had painted the Flood, which would also ultimately bring down the *Medusa*. In this work, rain sheeted down from low-hanging clouds, the churning water was breaking upon the jagged rocks onto which a few people had clambered; from the sinking raft, a woman was lifting up a child to a man while a youth kneeled on the boards; further away, the hands of a drowning man could still be seen clinging tight to a sinking boat, and a swimming horse, with flared nostrils, carrying a corpse. With this subject matter the young painter had made a variation on a work by Poussin. His predecessor had also foregone all of the typical elements of landscape painting, made the rocks and trees into skeletal forms, and the fall of the water, the stormy skies, into an apocalyptic union; nevertheless, traces of a natural disaster could be made out in the picture. In Géricault, one vision alone was present, a mental apparition; what was lacking was the ark that in Poussin's work promised salvation, floating calmly behind the roofs protruding from the surface of the water; and the moon and lightning of Poussin had given way to a storm, a terror, the likes of which are only to be found in inner turmoil. Poussin had still lent his colors—sparingly applied in a blackish gray—a melodic note, an almost mellow light fell on the figures in their sequence around the boat, the blue and white of the old man by the rudder, the washed-out red of the figure clambering up the side of the boat, the white, yellow, and blue of the woman holding the child swaddled in reddish cloth to the man in the blue shirt on the boulder, and the same red and blue, only more muted, led across to the color sequence of the robes of the figures hanging from the neck of the horse, the drifting plank of wood. Despite all the hopelessness, the damnation in Poussin's painting, the viewer was left with a melancholic prayer; Géricault compelled us to surrender all forms of support, forced us into his fearful dream. Poussin's world was also peculiar, yet in the face of its serenity we kept our composure; Géricault sent us into a panic through which he permitted us to peer into the process of a passionate psychological event. From the same year we have the head of the white horse, resembling the portrait of a person, of a woman; a touch of pink was placed around the vibrating nostrils, the downy skin, the soft swell of the mane, the lock of hair that fell over its brow had been traced with such tenderness, the darkly glimmering eyes bearing the gaze of a lover. And behind this face stood blackest night. On Montmartre, during his final year, he had painted the workshop with the kiln. The dilapidated building, high above the level of Saint-Ouen, had been pushed out to the edge of the world, the clouds mingling with the smoke billowing out of the sheds on the hilltop. With his goat-hair robe and broad slouch hat, the farmhand sleeping between the sacks in the oversized cart, half driven out of the entrance, resembled death, the unharnessed horses stood unguarded in the thunder on the clayey, wheel-shredded path. He had not been able to change his life through painting, even that which could be surveyed from his oeuvre showed no developmental arc, no decisive stylistic transformations, the ten years of his artistic activity were from the outset characterized by the same condition of captivity and by the same intensity with which he sought redemption. There was no help or salvation for him, the tremendous energies which were stored up within him could only find intermittent relief in the pictures he produced; during his brief stay, with madness hanging over him all the while, painting was the instrument with which he confronted the excess pressure building up within him as a revolt against entropy. He who wanted to interrupt the system of oppression and destructiveness saw himself dying a defeated man. And yet it had never before been so clear to me how values could be created in art which could overcome a sense of being penned in, being forsaken, as in his attempts to remedy his melancholy **28** by giving form to his visions. Perhaps he didn't understand what these forces were that were holding him down, perhaps he was so broken that he denied himself the key to interpretation for the signs he had laid bare; in his craft though, he proceeded with enough awareness to realize that with his painterly language he was laying the path for others. As he himself had carried on lines issuing from Michelangelo, Tintoretto, Caravaggio, with the strokes of their brushes Daumier, Courbet, Degas, even van Gogh, in his way, pointed toward Géricault. Suddenly solving the riddle of his life no longer interested me. I knew everything I wanted to know. With his giving and taking, he formed part of the universal relationship and connection which constitute the background of artistic activity.

Oh, I am tired, cried Chamberlain, and threw himself onto the club chair in Downing Street, his rigid hat, his umbrella falling to the floor; he tore open his wing collar, Henderson and Halifax uttered a few encouraging words. Such moments of worry in the face of transactions of tremendous responsibility gave the figures in the second-rate crime novel a human quality; with his exhaustion upon being called to the window to wave to the excited masses, England's prime minister demonstrated just how much he had struggled to avert the threat of war. And it was not just in England and France that the leaders were receiving gratitude and good faith: in Germany as well, there was overwhelming certainty about a favorable outcome to the crisis. Since the suggestions communicated on Thursday, though, the German demands had already been increased, the bomb squadrons were ready for combat, and the armies were awaiting their marching orders. The feudal lords of Poland and Hungary had also underlined their demands, and the Soviet Union warned that in the case of an advance by Polish troops, they would annul the nonaggression treaty between the two countries. That Czechoslovakia had mobilized on Friday the twenty-third did not diminish people's belief in peace; on the warm, late-summer evening, the café terraces and bars on Boulevard de Clichy were jam-packed, and on the promenade, under the still-green foliage of the trees, people were crowding around a street performer who was gulping down live frogs, washing them down with water and throwing the whole lot up with a grimace. A little girl was banging along on the tambourine and dancing, with a monkey on her shoulder. Watching the procedure, as the head, the twitching legs of one frog after the other appeared between the lips of the performer among the spray of the water, Katz said that his artistic talent consisted in feigning the swallowing and the gagging while stowing the creatures in his mouth. When, to the disgusted pleasure of his audience, he declared with a convincing act that a frog had chosen to stay in the warm, dark chamber of his stomach, this ensured him increased earnings when the child went around collecting coins. Later he would surreptitiously transfer the tree frog that he had kept pinned down with his tongue into the glass jug. Van Gogh, said Katz, would have been able to appreciate such a way of earning a living. He walked toward us from a steep alley, in his sheepskin coat, with his rabbit-fur cap, with a bristly red beard, a painting still wet under his arm, one he had painted in the morning at Place Pigalle, and for which he wanted to find a place on the overcrowded walls of the Café du Tambourin. We wandered after this apparition, this shadow, in which a face flared up and died out again. Here, in Montmartre, according to many, it was supposed to be possible to sense the heart of the city. This is where the red light bulbs on the blades of the small windmill were, stuck between roof gables; the glass doors stood open to the jinglejangle all around, figures rushed in and out as swarming daubs of paint, the glasses and bottles were bundles of light, eyes and mouths flitted open, remained effervescent for a few seconds, before being washed away in the breaking waves. If there was a heart beating here, it was the heart of a spinning, whining, artificial market, the heart in a formless heap of shards and junk. People crawled around its outermost stratum, burrowed into it, lodged themselves in it here and there, between tatters of backdrops, themselves hastily decorated and painted. Let's not lose sight of him, said Katz, we'll follow him into that restaurant there, number sixty-six, Boulevard de Clichy, into all this yellow, green, blue, into these reflections, these flashes of zinc, enamel, porcelain, let's barge into the throng and drink a glass of wine at the bar. Van Gogh's ghost had evaporated, there was no

longer a view into the frothing, the sludge of time, we were orbited by
nothing but the present; everything that was perceptible shifted so quickly
and slightly that even we now scarcely seemed to exist and threatened to
disappear in an instant, to drift into oblivion. And then, suddenly, he did
appear, a group of drinkers at the bar had stepped to the side and there he
was, sitting at a small, round table, beneath Japanese woodcuts, still lifes
in luminous yellow, orange-colored strokes, sitting in silence, bent forward with his mouth clamped shut, a furtive, almost malevolent expression, the picture placed in front of him, holding it with his paint-stained
fingers, waiting for people to take note of him and his work. But Lautrec,
Pissarro, Gauguin were carousing, messing around with the hostess, the
dark-featured, plump woman from Rome; then, all of a sudden, a commo-
tion broke out. Bernard, a friend, had approached van Gogh, placed his
hand on his shoulder, sending the painting flying through the air, a brawl
broke out, the waiter, his white apron flapping, wrapped his arm around
the neck of the man in fur, a frenetic twisting in the direction of the door,
Gauguin, encased in his cape, in the shadows cast by his broad-brimmed
hat, didn't look up. We walked out, a police whistle could be heard, we
couldn't allow ourselves to be grabbed and led off to be interrogated, arrested, kicked out of the country because of a punch-up caused by a
painter drunk on absinthe. Though he had only one thing in mind, said
Katz, to ensure that he and his comrades could subsist, to struggle so that
he and they could possess means of production: a bit of paint, a piece of
canvas, a few paintbrushes. He wanted no more than his right to work,
ownership of his own work, he wanted the free association of artistic
workers, rebelled against the ignominy of having to cart his productions
to the junk dealer time and again. If this was the heart of the city, then it
lay buried under dust and rubbish, a mountain had grown over it, layer
upon layer, a fetid draft blew toward us from the heights, through the
troughs and hollows. Van Gogh had been tossed into the stream of pedestrians, stood stunned at first, wanted to go back into the bar, but then
changed his mind, staggered on, into the arms of Corot, Monet, Seurat,
whom he didn't recognize, walked across Place Blanche, up Rue Lepic.
This Place Blanche, this meeting place of nocturnal flâneurs, this circus,
which had seen Sue, Bretonne, and Nerval, Hugo, Balzac, and Vigny,
Baudelaire, Verlaine, and Rimbaud flitting past, this square, where hurried business was carried out and furtive liaisons emerged that found
sanctuary in the alleys branching off it, this Place Blanche, white from
the footprints of the workers from the chalk pits, white from the sluggish
processions coming down the hillside, climbing up from the chalk facto-

ries on Rue Blanche, intersected by a hefty stampede of horse hooves, this white square, over which the horse swept with its rider, disappearing behind bobbing green omnibuses, this square was now a raucous, filthy cauldron from which we fled, in pursuit of a fugitive. At the spot where Rue Lepic described an arc before heading up to the summit, in the third story of the building at number fifty-four, van Gogh lived with his brother. From his window with the low, iron railing, he could look out onto the Moulin de la Galette, behind the picket fences, among the shrubbery, the skewed huts on the embankment. Fifty years later, only one of the mills was left, as an ornament on the tower above the wooden walls of a cabaret, in whose courtyard people danced under paper lanterns. If he wasn't cowering up there in his dark room, between the large closet and the base burner stove, then he had gone running up to Place du Tertre, having elbowed his way through the crowd, through the dense flocks of families, groups of friends, old and young, sitting at the wooden tables under the trees, celebrating in their own way with food and drink this evening of peace, and the thought of the unshakability of this peace, was holed up over in the building site around the basilica of Sacré-Cœur; we thought we could hear his whining coming from over near Saint-Pierre. The door to the oldest church in the city stood open, a few people knelt in prayer on the pews, more than a millennium lay stacked up in their stone. The construction of the cloister had been ordered in commemoration of the martyrs who had hidden from the Romans in the mountain caves by Louis the Fat and Queen Adelaide, whose straw-covered country estate was located in the neighboring woodlands. Built on the foundations of a Roman temple, held up by Roman arches and Gothic pillars, interspersed with masonry which still bore traces of being burned down during the great revolution, pieced back together and given a roof by the stooges of the counterrevolution, there stood the abbey, which in the spring of seventy-one had served as a munitions depot and field hospital. Though the figure with a pig's head riding a billy goat and the sanctimonious patron saint of the city, Genevieve, mocked all the efforts which had been expended on the heights of the mountain, and most things up here had been turned to ashes and rubble, it was still the place where the Commune had entrenched itself. Perhaps because of this, the thought had emerged that the heart of the city beat in this pile of debris, because this is where the fleeing had found their hideouts, the insurrectionists their defensive positions. Not just the saints Denis, Rustique, and Éleuthère but Marat and the insurgents of eighteen thirty-four and forty-eight had also escaped their pursuers in the chasms and shafts of Mons Martyrum.

The cathedral made of frosting had been nothing in the face of the cannons of the national guard that had once been assembled here. The mountain had always been a site of refuge, of perseverance, of dogged resistance, the picturesque cladding had only been applied by later generations; the bohemian milieu, the bandits and cocottes, formed part of its temporary seizure by the bourgeoisie; the mountain itself, with its secret heartbeat, was the property of those who went about their work in silence. Van Gogh had disappeared, but in the houses someone may still have been living here or there who had seen him skulking through the alleys at night. The smell of mildew and decay predominated, and yet suddenly it no longer seemed as if we had climbed a burial mound, we didn't turn back when we thought of those who had lived here, they had left behind traces, signs of resistance, objects of extreme mental concentration. The

political vanguard and the artistic avant-garde had been based on this mountain. The connection with the people who had been at work before us always bore the same significance as an opening up of the path into the future. In that sense we are traditionalists, said Katz. We can't believe in anything that is to come if we don't know how to appreciate that which has gone before. Thus, the people who were eating and drinking on Place du Tertre in that moment, as the world was threatening to fall apart, held tight to the continuity of life. Generals and foreign ministers were flying back and forth between London and Paris, in their briefcases the documents for their bargaining and conning, the big players were at their rotten business, the small fries were sitting at narrow tables rammed into the earth, and by gathering together here they announced their contempt for everything that was objectionable, which didn't belong to them. For a few hours, threatened with death, they praised tranquility. We had arrived at Rue Ravignan via a narrow alley that opened out onto the sloped plaza of the same name. Here, scrawny trees stood around one of those fountains, of which there were so many in this city, made of cast iron, painted green, sheltered by a dome which held up nymphs in a round dance. The streetlamps illuminated the low wall of the building on the edge of the square, it was all scratched up, patches of plaster had fallen off it; the entrance, with its gates sagging in their hinges, led past a set of wooden steps and a rusty drain into an angular courtyard covered in scraggy scrub. Beside Rue Garreau was a sprawling, roughly patched together building, with ladders leading up aslant to the upper levels and matte windows, some with cardboard nailed over them. On the roofs, which ascended like steps, between tall, tin chimneys, there were fixtures for skylight panes. Nothing could be more crumbling, rotten, expired than this shed-like housing, which had been nicknamed Bateau-Lavoir after the floating laundries on the Seine, and which resembled a river steamer stranded between the cliffs of the firewall. Once upon a time, washing had been done here in a particular way; behind this splitting wooden cladding, cleaned of slag, our century of painting and poetry had unfolded. A stay in the sheds couldn't have been idyllic back then either, in summer it was hot as an oven in there, icy cold, drafty in winter. The outsiders of culture had scampered into these nooks and crannies because they offered cheap shelter. Utrillo, Picasso, Gris, Braque, Herbin, Apollinaire, Laurencin, Brancusi, Severini, Modigliani, Derain, Reverdy, Salmon, Gertrude Stein, and Max Jacob had been housed in the stalls or visited them; there, beneath the cracked glass, on the top level of the tattered roof, the *Demoiselles d'Avignon* had glimpsed the hazy shimmer of the world, and below, on the ground floor, the size of a barn, held up by rough wooden posts, the fabulous feast had been held in honor of the customs officer, Rousseau. He was enthroned on a chair placed on a crate, surrounded by foliage and bunting, playing a child's violin. It was as if the celebrations on Place du Tertre were for him as well, and as if they were commemorating the Communards up above, and under the echo of the laughing voices I felt at home in this city. It was only back in the library in Rue Casimir-Périer that I found myself back on unstable terrain. The Soviet Union had asserted that, in the event of a German invasion, they would fulfill their duties to defend Czechoslovakia. The French reservists had been called up, on Saturday, at three o'clock in the afternoon, the enlistment orders were stuck to the walls of the municipal buildings, tens of thousands of working men headed to the railway stations to wait for the military trains. Daladier, accompanied by General Gamelin, reported to the press and pointed out the extreme gravity of the situation. The stocky petit bourgeois with the bull's neck struck patriotic tones, attempting to tauten his bloated face and present himself as a respectable man burdened by the obligations of France's alliances. He needed the tension surrounding the question of whether France would stand by Czechoslovakia, whether it would come to all-out war, in order for his later breach of faith to transform into a relief. His composure, his dignity, his readiness to take historic actions were to be remembered when the hour of retreat arrived, dressed up as a clever act of statesmanship. He presented himself as the courageous man who had already raised his old service rifle, had the enemy in his sights; and this is how he would be remembered, when he had been reduced to a mere puppet show of cowardice. This shrewd game would lead the people from hope to sudden fear

33

and back to hope again; the same occurred in England, the haggard old man with the thickly trimmed moustache above his crooked, grinning mouth, with the golden watch chain dangling from his vest, and the lord with the greyhound face beside him, announced the preparations for mobilization; in Hyde Park, in Saint James's Park, in Green Park, trenches and dugouts were excavated. Thus, in order to confront growing unrest in France, the rulers had placed the male population under the spell of military service; the reminder of national pride trumpeted by the press impeded any possible attempts at disruption. The halls of the Cercle des Nations were abuzz with arguments; Scandinavian union representatives, representatives of the Spanish relief efforts, politicians, and Party functionaries debated with one another in the rooms decked with expensive tapestries; the word was that Pieck had come from Moscow, the Central Committee had issued a call for a collective struggle against fascism, the metaphysically overblown defensive will of the Western powers coincided with the outbreaks of hysterical defamation with which the Greater German Reich sought to demoralize Czechoslovakia into surrendering the Sudetenland. In addition, rumors were spread that England and France, now united with the Soviet Union, would stand up to the aggressor. On the morning of the twenty-fifth, I sat once again in the park on our street, on a bank among the well-trimmed shrubbery, accompanied by the tolling of the bells of Saint Clotilde. The families were heading to Mass in their Sunday bests, the children scrubbed clean and groomed; soon, prayers would be echoing out from the pulpits for the protection of the system for whose downfall the rebellious had gathered together so often and in vain. The city towered monstrously, what dwarves we were within it, what audacity it had been to erect barricades here in the streets, to hold off the owners of the arsenal behind them for a day, a couple of days. I was some kind of straggler, who, like countless others now and before, was crouched in a corner, cursing their inferiority, plotting their revenge for the annihilation of their kin. But they wanted to see us this powerless, shoved into the bushes like this, those bloodsuckers, their well-salaried blowhards had managed to get the masses of millions to keep quiet, fall into line, while up above them, out of reach, the speculation and extortion continued apace. Once more I hurried along the quay and over the bridge, perhaps I would only be granted one more day to see what I longed to see. And again, upon visiting the hideout, I asked myself whether this was a form of evasion, of delaying other, important decisions, whether all of my earlier hesitation about joining the Party couldn't be traced back to my tendency toward doubt, my rejection of completion, of finality, which was immediately followed by the justification that I first of all had to be sure of myself before I could venture to take on other responsibilities. The rows of images were endless. In a small painting by Meissonier, I saw the power relation between the inhabitants of the streets and the masters of the arsenal depicted even more convincingly than in Delacroix's work with the figure of Liberty at the barricade. No wider than the span of a hand, without decorative embellishments or noticeable composition, as soberly as a piece of reportage it conveyed what the painter had seen in June of forty-eight: an alley, its windows and doors barricaded and shutters down, where, between the cobblestones that had been tossed together into piles, the blood-covered corpses of the insurrectionaries lay. The image bore the stillness that followed the catastrophe. The murderers were nowhere to be seen, they kept their distance in this hour of ignominious victory, only their sorry victims lay there, their clothes shredded, in the foreground, a man on his back in red trousers, one foot missing its shoe, another with his hand pressed on the wound in his chest, on the curb, a boy lying on his stomach, next to him a lost cap, an old man, his pointed red beard sticking up in the air, up front, a little light on the shattered stones, in the background of the empty street, deepening darkness. And yet it wasn't this unassuming image that I took with me as my final impression as I was driven out of the temple but rather the thought of a panel, also almost miniature, in which Saint Rainerius flew through the air, in front of the smooth wall of the prison in which he had blown a hole, with a wave of his hand, in order to free the paupers who had been thrown into the cellar. The saint wasn't floating: he was roaring around like a bullet, his legs disappearing in a flaming cloud. The wall that he was set against was of a cool gray, a few of the prisoners had already escaped from the hole at its juncture with the smooth earth, fleeing toward the left on the square and into an alleyway off in the distance, while another, in gown and belt, was in the process of heaving himself out of the dungeon. There was a tiny, dark door in the foreground, above some steps on the short side of the building, with the opening revealing the thickness of the stone walls. The bleak, cube-like building took up two-thirds of the space of the image, the gray scale was divided into three, from the light gray of the shadowless, regular surface of the ground to the muted gray of the front with the protruding staircase. The building in the background on the corner of the alleyway, half castle, half market hall, exhibited arrow slits at the top, and beneath, a row of arched, shuttered windows bore slanted awnings which sheltered the stalls, the doors of which were pulled shut. The patch of sky in the upper left and the halo of Rainerius were rendered in gold leaf. Off in the distance I had heard the ringing of the handbells; now their tinkling was approaching, mixed in with yells, a babble of voices, and the scuffing of steps. The guards appeared, swinging their bells, pushing a swarm of visitors in front of them. They laid their hands on the lingerers, shaking a shoulder here, tugging at an arm there; after years of drawn-out, bitter waiting, they had remembered their authority. They had an important task to carry out today, emptying the Louvre for the evacuation of the images. Through the Trecento, the Quattrocento the little bells clanged, the increasingly hostile commands, the whistles, the clicks of the tongue, the clapping of hands, past Martini, Fra Angelico, one of the guards, with an olive-colored face, had stopped beside me in admonishment, another had made it to Martorell, to the triptych of Saint George, who, naked but for a loincloth, was kneeling at the post, his hands bound in front of him, and, his mouth half agape, was staring into the distance with a somewhat foolish expression while four dignified, bearded men with devout expressions on their faces took to him with knotted cords and rods, and the panels left and right showed how he was dragged to the execution site and his head lopped off. This small picture, which the guards pushed me away from, suddenly took up more space in me than Géricault's painting; it contained little in the way of deliberate confrontations with an entire epoch, didn't seek to unfurl everything that was questionable and the complexes associated with the creative process, it was just there, existing completely for itself, as a symbol, formed once by Sassetta, who lived from thirteen ninety-two until fourteen fifty in Siena. I couldn't yet define what the image had stirred within me, but it had to do with the simplicity of expression, the freshness and directness of the vision, the combination of objectivity and abstraction with the sharpness and clarity of the colors and forms. Walking backward, my gaze directed toward the horizontal, flying figure, I drew away, feeling relaxation, levity; ladders were already being carried over; the demounting began, and we were tossed out into the mobilization, into the expectation of war. Hang him, hang him, came the familiar roar from the loudspeakers on Monday, as the ringleader baited the people against Beneš. Our patience has run out, he bellowed, the Sudetenland has to be given back to the Reich now, and then, with booming conviction, he had been a frontline soldier himself, knew how dreadful war was, hoped he could spare the German people the same. Then on to the king of England, keep your spirits up, have faith in your government, who with God's help will find a just and peaceful solution. The great bluff was taken to extremes. The

Western powers declared themselves willing to come to the aid of Czechoslovakia, the British fleet mobilized, Berlin also announced their plans to mobilize on Wednesday, and under the cover of this deceptive maneuver, England's and France's large corporations sold their Czech shares, at a profit, to the firms in Germany that were ready and waiting to take over the industries. On Wednesday, there was no longer any mention of a coalition between England and France with the Soviet Union nor of carrying out a general mobilization; instead, the so-called four-power conference was announced, that intimate gentlemen's gathering that was to take place in Munich on the twenty-ninth of September. Amid all the menacing clamor, the patriotic pledges, the business had been settled, Czechoslovakia had been left with no other option than to cede the regions being demanded. It became evident that a political strategy that had been carried out for two decades was now nearing its fulfillment. For England and France, and all the countries allied with them under the pretense of neutrality, the desire to isolate and cut off the Soviet Union possessed greater weight than the fear of fascism. When the governing politicians of Western Europe spoke of peace, washing their hands as they did so, for them this peace meant the crippling of socialism, and when, before flying out, Chamberlain and Daladier let it be known that no price was too great when it came to salvaging peace, they were counting on the possibility of being able to confine the conflict to a clash between Germany and its only foe, which for them, lying in wait, could work out to their advantage, to their eventual triumph. The Soviet state alone would not be able to come to the aid of Czechoslovakia; it had to prepare itself for its own defense. All pacts of mutual defense fell apart. The English and French hypocrites met with the chief thief and his Italian sidekick in order to organize the skyrocketing of the stock prices, and during the night, at twelve thirty, they arranged themselves behind the table with the unfurled map of Czechoslovakia, strewn with circles drawn with brightly colored pencils, for their historic snapshot, all lined up, staring out at us the next morning from the front pages of every newspaper with their sinister, pinched faces. It wasn't just Czechoslovakia that they had sold off, they had thrown all of Europe into the bargain bin. Yet this elicited jubilation, rapture, people embraced each other in tears, in speechless delirium. *Heil Chamberlain*, they cried out over in Germany, and, everything is all right, said the old man with the top hat upon his arrival in Croydon, peace for our time, he pledged, pulling into London, and now the crowds streamed onto the streets of Paris as well, onto Le Bourget Airport, onto Rue La Fayette, onto Boulevard Haussmann, to greet their miracle worker and shower him with flowers, to celebrate the victory of the ruling classes. Once more, capital had transformed its eternally brewing bankruptcy into an aggressive display of power, enveloped by the flashes of the reflection of the sun, the trustees of the businesses waved graciously from their black limousines to the seduced and the duped, who tried to break through the police lines at the intersections. They all wanted peace, they wanted to live in tranquility, and they didn't dare ask about the kind of peace, they merely marveled at what they had been given, something they hadn't brought about themselves. It was small-business owners, employees, petit bourgeois who were gathering there in throngs, they had rushed out of their shops, offices, government departments, even from the odd workshop; a couple of bricklayers lingered on the scaffolding as spectators, otherwise workers were few and

far between, they were out in the factories; we traveled with the metro to the north, into the outskirts; there, a despondent silence prevailed, the intoxication of relief hadn't made it out that far. A dull, restrained rage could be felt, but also exhaustion, consternation, resignation. Those who lived here knew that this was not the peace they had sought, and which corresponded to their being. They knew that this peace was merely staving off the war, buying time to build up arms, for even more looting and pillaging. Without them, no war could be waged, but they hadn't yet reached the point of shaking off the inhuman coercion which lay upon them. They who hated war were forced to work for the war. To stay alive they had to produce the material which could only bring them mutilation and death. The call to come together, to hold firm, had petered out, the fetid stench of the addiction to wealth was brewing, the flowers which had been tossed to the oppressors were laid on the grave of the unknown soldier, forming a mountain, honoring the millions of coming sacrifices. This system, which was maintained by the profiteers and which brought abasement and subjugation to its populations, to smash this system once and for all, that was the task that still awaited us, that demanded all our strength and that drove us in this hour of defeat and exhaustion to continue looking for the only weapon with which the enemy could be defeated, the weapon of unity.

Then the streets broke into a flutter of red. We filed into the rows of the marchers. We were a thousand, five thousand, eight thousand. There was no fire that descended upon the city, it was the source of a blaze that had begun to form. This march was a beginning. We were survivors from the previous demonstrations. We pushed forward through narrow channels.

To our sides stood the heavily armed security forces. Our footsteps
evoked the memory of the processions which had been streaming through
the cities for two decades. Once, these footsteps had borne the power of
a class, everything else had been drowned out by the chanting. Now the
voices rung hollow in the fortified city; each one could be singled out and
counted. From the side streets came the piercing cries of the members of
the Croix-de-Feu. The police gave the nationalists free reign. Though we
might have been few, we knew we formed part of great armies. The many
were isolated from us, tied up, numbed, regaining their energy. Many were
also waging struggles far away, in China, in Southeast Asia, just a few
hundred of us would have sufficed to show that we wouldn't give up. The
cohort of those who had returned from Spain walked in a dense pack.
Here and there, their tattered flags were met with cries of belonging. We
could sense the discrepancy in the fact that we were commemorating the   **39**
Spanish advance while we ourselves were in retreat. Every beginning,
every conclusion of these mass protests was present in the movement in
the rows, from childhood we knew these slogans to come together, passed
from street to street, this resolve that emerged through walking together,
this violence, which was imbued in our demands, and the dissolution as
well, which we couldn't evade, the separation that forced everyone to
maintain their endurance. For a few hours, we disregarded the ban on the
expression of opinions, on agitation. Under the cover of internationalism, individually, anonymously, we belonged to those who were making
calls to resist the swindlers and profiteers. Peace could not yet be forced
to conform to the conditions of the workers. We had been set back a long
way. During the last great war, the idea of this peace had penetrated the
atmosphere of enmity. Our fathers had fought for it. In one country,
though, the idea had prevailed. For us, this one country was the guarantee that it would not be possible to smother the idea here either. We
parted ways in Clignancourt. Armored cars were sitting in the courtyard
of the barracks on the boulevard. Only at us, always at us, would the barrels of the cannons be aimed. The faces of our fellow travelers were gray
and exhausted. They had begun to resemble the miserable, filthy façades
of the district. Just a moment ago, as we were streaming through the
streets, a brightness had shone upon them. This brightness belonged to
the city as well, and could be won back. A sense of confidence prevailed
over the trepidation that had emerged as the small groups had dissipated in
the streets. Impressions of the city that I had taken in over the past few days
were unfurling their force. I thought I could find somewhere to stay here.
Forget about Paris, said Katz. You've reached that point where the city

teases us with the possibility of an unscathed life. It flatters us with its famous light, it entices us with its airy expanses, only to repudiate us once more; it is so close, and yet always out of reach. But I had been offered a job in La Brévière, the home for orphaned Spanish children set up by Aschberg in the Forest of Compiègne. For us, said Katz, at the Porte des Poissonniers, among the racket making its way over from the freight yard, other homes are being planned. If there is a war, and perhaps even under this rotten peace, they will take us in, unless they decide to deliver us into German care instead. But where should I go, I asked, should I attempt to make it to Oslo, like Hodann, or head back to Prague. The trip into Czechoslovakia, which was also the country for which he was responsible, could be fatal, said Katz. Germany would not be satisfied with devouring the Sudetenland, but rather, with the consent of the West, would

quickly swallow the entire state. He advised me to summon all my cunning and guile to get to Sweden. The entry of a group of Czechoslovakian metalworkers was planned, set up by the Swedish union; he wanted to speak with Aschberg and Branting and ask them to help me to join them. But the invitation had stirred up the discord within the workers' movement again; it was only open to Social Democrats, and the fact that I had been in Spain would make it even more difficult for me to get in. It's good that you don't belong to a party, he said. Your father is a Social Democrat. For your parents, who are in immediate danger, emigration to Sweden should be facilitated. You are an antifascist without party affiliations; everything else about your life, he said, as we walked down Rue des Poissonniers, you should now keep quiet. Your task is to reach terra firma, so that you can continue your education and prepare yourself for the work that you are destined for. Today, surrounded by snitches, cheats, and agitators, we need to be able to dissimulate, to conceal our true intentions. Keep yourself in check. Travel to Sweden via legal channels. Find yourself some kind of livelihood. Be careful when making contacts. Get to know the situation in the country. Make up your mind later. The street that ran beside the railway line grew narrower, the paving came to an end, to the left were a few sheds and abandoned workshops which backed onto the wall of a cemetery. The ancient Rue des Poissonniers, who used to transport their catch here from the northern bends of the river to the markets, had become a bumpy trail, lined by heaps of trash. Behind the short, crumbling wall, the gravestones could be seen, grown over with scrub; to the right, freight trains rattled past the wooden fence. We got to talking about the divisions in the Party, which affected all the work we did, and then I mentioned Münzenberg, with whom Katz had been close for years. Changing the topic, he initially replied that nowadays, in anticipation of major confrontations, all political organizations were investigating and measuring the scope of their potency, that the focus of the parties at the moment was to strengthen the positions from which developments could then be steered, and that the reshuffling and purges would produce the concentration necessary for drawing out the battle lines. Asked about the events of the autumn of thirty-six, he hinted at a number of things relating to the differences of opinion and misunderstandings that had led to the break with Münzenberg. In nineteen thirty-five, he said, as the Comintern decided on the policy of the Popular Front, Münzenberg was still among the advocates of the united proletarian front. It was to be built from the ground up, against the Social Democratic leadership. In the eyes of the Comintern as well, the proletarian front represented the foundations for a broad antifascist alliance. Without the unity of the working class, alliances with other groupings were impossible. Proletarian unity was supposed to prevent the front from becoming an instrument of reactionary forces. But proletarian leadership could also be identical with the leadership of the Communist Party. This allowed the oppositional relationship to Social Democracy to be maintained. With their unity of action, the French parties had gotten further than anyone else. After the victory of the Popular Front in France, in May of thirty-six, the attempts to overcome the contradictions between the two German parties were desperately needed. But there was no mass organization standing behind the German party leaders. Their internal conflicts could not take place in public, carried out by the working class. They had to be carried out in the secrecy of exile. Initially, efforts toward a common front could only be tactical, maintaining clear and constant divisions between the parties. With his emphasis on the priority of the proletariat, said Katz, Münzenberg gave sustenance to the argument that the Communist Party just wanted to place the Front in the service of their hegemonic designs. Even though the only goal was to establish contacts between isolated cadres, splintered groups, people of indeterminate number from all social classes, so long as it could be assumed that they were opponents of the war, of National Socialism, the antagonisms surrounding perspectives on the future formation of a state began to grow apparent. There was also disagreement on the question of illegal collaboration. In his memorandum from September concerning the situation in Germany, although Münzenberg did emphasize that the key struggles had to occur in the country itself, he argued that, given the paralysis of the opposition, the ideological and propagandistic activity could only be led from abroad. At this time, the Central Committee too had decided to expand the underground cells, despite also claiming that the progressive groups were growing. Thus, Münzenberg suddenly ended up in the vicinity of the Social Democratic position, according to which (admittedly for reasons of self-preservation) the parties ought to limit themselves to activities outside of the country. The Communist Party had also regularly altered its evaluations and assessments of the news issuing from Germany: at times, a prevailing passivity and lethargy could be observed, and then, as in the fall of thirty-six, there was a belief that unrest was brewing among the populace. In principle, then, Münzenberg's shifting views were not inconsistent with the behavior of the Central Committee; it was just that their resolutions were made in consultation with the Comintern, while Münzenberg's decisions were made according to his own judgment. Now that the need to strictly follow Party lines was greater than ever, this unpredictability posed a threat to the Party, and would also end up having fateful effects for him personally. In September, said Katz, Münzenberg's suggestion to intensify activities abroad had not signified a turn toward the Social Democratic position; it had only been after his return from Moscow that he came into close contact with Social Democrats and liberals. Back then, he said, in response to my question, Wehner was likely in touch with leading Social Democrats such as Breitscheid, Herz, Grzesinsky, Braun, and Kuttner, but that was largely carried out in accordance with the Party's intention of driving a wedge between the executive committee and a number of individuals who seemed willing to cooperate. Up until this trip, Münzenberg too had acted in accordance with the plan of winning over a group of oppositional Social Democrats for the Communist front policy. But why, I asked, was Wehner hostile toward him, when he too had fallen under suspicion from the Comintern. If he was now, as we knew, being subjected to the same kind of interrogations as the Control Commission now had in store for Münzenberg, then the reason must have been that he was accused of maintaining relations with the Social Democratic camp that were of an all-too-intimate nature. It was only in July of this year that the investigations had come to a conclusion, recommending Wehner's rehabilitation. He had been required to answer forty-two questions in writing, elaborating verbally, questions about his social background, about people he knew, about conversations he had had with Social Democratic functionaries, trips he had made, and party and union activities in which he had previously engaged. Katz remained silent for a while. With the extreme tension of these times, this kind of evidence, based on secondhand accounts, formed part of a reality that we couldn't evade. Since it was connected with our own existence, we took note of it and would sometimes bring it up among our closest friends. The disagreements within the Party leadership, said Katz, may have appeared minimal; however, they contained profound differences, which in the context of the re-forming of the Central Committee and the Politburo were now becoming more pointed. Unlike with Münzenberg, Wehner did not want demonstrative declarations but rather patient, silent action in order to establish some initial form of mutual trust. I recalled a remark of Hodann's concerning the rivalry between Ackermann and Merker, Münzenberg and Wehner, and between them and the group around Ulbricht. Officially, Thälmann, who was in a German prison, was still the leader of the Party. Once Schehr, who was acting as his proxy, had been murdered, Pieck took over the leadership. The young Politburo candidate Wehner was not just interested in enjoying their support but also in proving his independence from the Soviet Party, to whom Pieck was beholden. It might have been the case that the conflicts now taking place, which had ensnarled the remaining members of the Central Committee—Dahlem, Florin, Dengel, Abusch, and Eisler—and aspirants to leadership posts, such as Mewis, Kowalski, and Knöchel, were brought about by the continually intensifying fear of being found wanting in the eyes of the supreme arbiters of the Party and being liquidated, just as their comrades Remmele, Flieg, Neumann, Kippenberger, and Eberlein had been. Or was it rather that, I asked, in the never-ending wrestle for primacy between the Communist and Social Democratic parties, the character of those who brought about this policy was also necessarily marked by the urge to exercise power. I don't want to speak about power, said Katz, but rather of toughness, of a toughness toward each other and toward oneself, without which there is no survival. Wehner had to prove his party loyalty. Münzenberg also continued to stress his loyalty to the Party in thirty-seven. It was he, said Katz, who provided the Comintern with the lion's share of the incriminating material against Wehner. Yet while he still purported to be in agreement with the Soviet Party, the contradictions in his work were growing. Münzenberg had always been headstrong, he said, inclined to make decisions under his own steam, but now he was acting out of an isolation which seemed to be deeply rooted in his nature. As long as the Party possessed a solid form, he could fulfill his duties; his inventiveness served him well in all posts. As the organization collapsed and we had to contract, said Katz, that which we had come to know in him as generous, expansive, became unclear, utopian. During this conversation, I didn't manage to get a sense of the antagonisms within the Party. And again, the solution of viewing the Party as something absolute pressed upon me, that we had to look past all of its controversies: a solution that could never fit with my endeavors. The arduous work that was now being carried out in order to make the Party functional again demanded a particularly clear and unambiguous course. I touched upon another problem, one that I had wondered about for a long time, by asking Katz how he had been able to break off contact with Münzenberg, with whom he had been close for a decade. His reply was brief and referred only to the meaninglessness of personal friendships if they could no longer be reconciled with the interests of the Party. Besides, he said, his interaction with Münzenberg is no breach of discipline. He and Šmeral, the founder of the Czechoslovakian Party, had indeed taken over Münzenberg's duties, but Šmeral had not yet been hit by the thunderbolt, as they used to say. With the rapid changes now facing us, the dissatisfaction with him might be quickly set aside. At the end of the cemetery wall, the path—a vestige of a medieval trading route—opened out into a garbage dump, whose swollen lumps and clumpy excrescences let off isolated threads of smoke. People lived in the burrows, in the shacks made of planks of wood, cardboard, corrugated iron, washing hung on strings, women approached from the river with buckets, a group of workers, thermos flasks and lunchboxes under their arms, trudged over between the hills, children played in the rubble and rubbish on the railway embankment. The tracks and rows of line poles became lost in the haze at the height of Saint-Denis. Katz continued on, as if he were headed somewhere in particular. Attack, attack, he said, that was always Münzenberg's motto. But this posture of the eternal warrior was the result not of an excess of strength but rather of a weakness, a fear. Father is coming: that was the first danger he had known. His father's room was a sacred site; the children were never permitted to enter it. Often drunk, his father, who was an innkeeper, would tear his shotgun from the wall and threaten to shoot his family dead, the whole lot of them. I'll shoot you up, this cry followed him into the night, he didn't dare fall asleep, for fear of being set upon by his father. Often he was ordered into the tavern to clean glasses and bottles. Münzenberg often described to me, said Katz, how, while being bullied and manhandled, he would be forced to wash a glass four or five times, with his father still finding a smudge on it. Go and hang yourself, you bum, his father would cry, throwing him a rope. I see him in that primeval world, said Katz. Standing there, rope in hand, in the smoke-filled bar in a village by the name of Friemar, on the banks of the Nesse, a kerosene lamp swinging above the bar, the deer antlers on the wall casting large shadows. Farmers sitting around the tables, wrapped up in winter clothing, with froth in their moustaches. A wan, gaunt woman plods up the steps, turns around once more to check on the boy. Upstairs in her room, she gets into bed, to die. Then the five-year-old climbs up the steps with the rope. He crawls into the attic. Nobody comes after him. This life is worth nothing, that is his first lesson; for a man who later dedicated his whole life to making the lives of others worth living. To understand Münzenberg, he said, you have to understand this mix of regions that he comes from, between the Harz and the Thuringian Forest, between the Saale and the Werra, this area which produced rulers with names like Ludwig the Bearded and Ludwig the Iron, Heinrich the Illustrious and Albrecht the Degenerate, Friedrich the Brave and Friedrich the Serious, Friedrich the Simple and Friedrich the Strict, these godforsaken estates, where Waltershausen also lies, where poor Hölderlin found work as a tutor, but which is also not far from Weimar and Jena, and where Gotha and Erfurt emerged as emblems of social democracy. In a few early sketches, said Katz, Münzenberg described the tavern in which he grew up. Back then he stayed close to the truth, though over the course of the years he sought to reconcile himself with this milieu, even showed a certain affection and esteem for his father. Münzenberg was slight as a child, like his mother. His sister and two brothers resembled their robust father. His father had once shot at his eldest brother, who fled through the window, never came back. From that point on, the youngest child too was gripped by the desire to get away. As an eleven-year-old, with a sack full of hunks of bread over his shoulder, he stole out of the house one morning. He want to go to Africa, to enlist with the Boers in the war against the English. The gendarmes picked him up outside Eisenach and brought him back to his father. Two more years of abuse came to a sudden end when his father fired a load of lead shot into his head. Münzenberg had always refused to see it as a suicide, said Katz. The old man had only wanted to clean his shotgun and, as usual, had been drunk. But the torment did not end with the conclusion of his childhood suffering. He received his first apprenticeship in Gotha, and now the master possessed the paternal right to corporal punishment. He was to be trained as a barber. In the opinion of his siblings, this occupation was suited to his feeble frame. The workday lasted from five thirty in the morning until nine at night, Sundays from seven till one. There were no days off or breaks during the day. That was nineteen hundred four. In the village schools in Friemar and Eberstadt he had learned to read and write a little. He was still unaware of the association of apprentices and young workers that had just been founded in Berlin, neither had he heard of Bernstein's appeal to the youth to defend themselves against the assaults of the masters. The fact that it took a few more years before he dared to join meetings might have been related to the fact that he'd had a heavy stutter hammered into him. He bore this muteness, this reticence within himself. He was also confused by the city, after his time in the drab countryside, in the watering hole for poachers and petty thieves. Back then, Gotha had thirty thousand inhabitants. It was a workers' city, with an iron foundry and machine works, a steam-powered dairy, porcelain production, and a meat industry. His Gotha program, Münzenberg always used to say, consisted of scoldings and slaps, of frothing shaving cream and sweeping floors. Every Saturday there was barber practice on live models. The apprentices had to shave the inmates of the home for the elderly, about a hundred men. For a few hours, they, the downtrod-

46   den, were for once allowed to be the strong. The old men would run away from them, be overpowered, held to the floor. The stubble was hard as the ends of wires, the blades dull, tearing off shreds of skin as they scraped across it. Five pennies is what the city of Gotha paid the master for every pensioner treated in this manner. Münzenberg's Erfurt program began in a shoe factory, in nineteen hundred six, when he arrived in the city on the banks of the Gera. During the twelve-hour working day sorting lasts in the stretching section, amid the screeching of the machines, the hammering, he schooled himself in speaking; no one could hear him there, and he wanted to prepare himself for participating in discussions. Something had occurred: he had joined an association, the workers' education association named Propaganda; he didn't yet know what that was, propaganda, he just sensed that in this gathering of young workers his life was going to change. Not only did the big city—home to some seventy-five thousand people—reveal itself to him, he also began to count himself among the masses of the working people, he was no longer an isolated individual, he belonged to the people who worked in the shoe factories, the breweries and railway workshops, in clothes manufacturing, the yarn bleaching plants, the wool dying works, in the production of locomotives, turbines, and agricultural machines; soon enough he was able to utter the word propaganda, he took part—every now and then interrupted by the choking and sputtering of his speech impediment—in political education, in the dissemination of social demands. Anybody who knows him, said Katz, can still recognize that tendency toward stammering today, above all when it came to his interaction with the authorities in the Party. He overcame his inhibition with his cry: attack, attack. Soon enough he was a well-known speaker and agitator, head of the Free Youth, leader of discussions, campaigns, demonstrations, and yet he retained his independence, hated the lords and masters, took no part in the factional conflict in the Party, struggled against everything that sought to box him in, set off on his journeyman years in the summer, came back to Zurich in nineteen ten, where he immediately joined the youth organization. When I was working for Piscator, said Katz, we looked at the play that Münzenberg had written as a twenty-five-year-old, by which time he had long been a member of the central committee of the Socialist Youth. The preparations for the Zimmerwald Conference, the efforts to create a new International was one thing, but the turmoil that continued within him, this nightmare of violence and foul screaming, was another thing entirely. Katz had stopped on a patch of compacted earth on which a few tents were pitched. A dancing bear was chained to a post, with a nose ring, flies swarming around it; gypsies were sat by the bonfire. Katz demonstrated the roles of the play, in which Münzenberg expressed the things that had burdened him at the time of his activity with Lenin. The roar of his father was still blaring in his ears. I'll gun down the lot of them, yelled Katz, not concerning himself with the fact that the gypsies were looking over at him. He played the father, waved his fist. Silence, you dog, he yelled toward the son, who wanted to protest. Good luck with that big mouth of yours. The gypsies stepped closer to listen to the stranger. Come, father, said the mother, supper is ready. Scoff your slop yourself, answered the father. I'm gonna bring some order into this rabble. You should be ashamed of yourself, said the son softly, for threatening Mother and your children. Then the father started up again. I wish I were strong and brutish enough to fight you with your own means, said the son. I'd strangle you. From the cowed stance of the son, Katz sprung up into the enormousness of the father. The gypsies looked on in amazement. Rascal, miserable, screamed the father, I'll beat you until you can't even crawl anymore. No beating, no beating, begged the son. Katz intimated how the son attempted to defend himself. No, I can't, you planted cowardice in my blood. At this, the father: I'll beat in your skull, beat you to death. Katz pantomimed reaching for the shotgun. One shot. God Almighty, cried the mother. Right in the head. *Schund* [Trash] is what Münzenberg titled this piece, which Piscator had given him to revise. He wanted nothing more to do with it. Said he'd purged it from his body when he wrote it, that ought to be enough. Immediately went back to defending his father—who had been similar to him, in his restlessness, his ferocity. And yet his entire childhood could be found in this drama, and an indication of the unspeakable effort that he must have had to make to work his way out of the dullness of the backwoods to a conception of the world. But Katz had not led me to this barren neighborhood on the edge of Saint-Ouen in order to perform Münzenberg's juvenilia for me against a fitting backdrop. His intention was, as now became clear, to visit the gypsies. He told me to wait. A young woman in a long, thick, puffy skirt walked toward him, took him by the hand, and walked with him through the swirling swarm of blowflies. The family members retreated to the fire. The bear grunted by the post. Katz disappeared inside the tent with the woman.

Either we start very early, said Münzenberg, or we'll never make it. In our club, we apprentices studied history, politics, art, and literature, and that was all done in a very orderly fashion, one of us would sit up front at the lectern, ring the bell, one of the young workers would stand up, give his presentation, which was followed by discussion, with each person raising their hand. Until then, I had been reading Jules Verne, Cooper, Karl May, played cards; now I was acquainting myself with Lassalle, Engels, Bebel, Mehring, Haeckel, and Forel. The strict discipline was one of the foundations of the gatherings. We sixteen-year-olds would wear our Sunday best with stand-up collars. In casting off our sweaty work shirts, in getting changed after the day in the factory, we were in a sense preparing ourselves for an existence on a higher plane. But that year, nineteen hundred six, bore down on me like a waterfall. The solemn beginning quickly turned into a stormy confrontation with our circumstances at work, in the union, the Party. From the older heads we received only condescension, rejection. In the meeting room they only wanted to allow presentations which, as they put it, were tailored to the cognitive abilities of the youth. We ended up being part of a process of transformation without knowing anything about the conflicting opinions among the Party leadership. Reformism, revisionism, for us, that was nothing but reactionary thought. We railed against the debasement within the Party, its abandonment of the revolution, its nationalism, its policy of forming an alliance with capital, with the military. Though we retained the ordered structure of our studies, we also possessed a readiness for revolt, for we viewed a logical, systematic attitude as a prerequisite for participation in the building of a party such as had been organized in Russia following the events of nineteen hundred five. Within a few years we developed a new concept of the proletarian youth, and we drew this from our experience of the abuse that had been meted out to us. When I arrived in Zurich, much of it still bore the influence of our readings of Herzen, Kropotkin,

Bakunin; anarchism belonged to the first stage of revolutionary struggle, which was a generational struggle, and before we found our way to Plekhanov, Lenin, to *Iskra*—which also coincided with our shift toward the Bolsheviks—we read Dostoyevsky, Ibsen, and Strindberg. There were always, he said, two apparently contradictory forces working within us: one demanding patience, discipline, the other spurring on our radicalism; one constructive, the other raging against rigid relations; and then it turned out that these were just two sides of the same coin, and that both had to be accommodated if we wanted to realize our full potential. Ibsen, Strindberg, they would almost have elicited our expulsion from the workers' union, for, in the eyes of some functionaries, such literature promoted moral decay. They considered the reading of realist, socially critical novels and plays more dangerous than the scientific instructions for social transformation found in our nascent studies of Marx. The name of the progenitor was not yet frowned upon within the Party, but in the depictions of the downfall of bourgeois institutions, particularly the family, the old-guard Social Democrats sensed a danger that also seemed to threaten their own organizational apparatus. The fear of a ruthless analysis of human coexistence, which inevitably led to animosity toward art and literature, this impulse that was always confined to the unconscious, immediately denied when put up for debate, continued to cling to the workers' movement as a petit-bourgeois, reactionary hangover that was responsible for its tendency to make compromises, its narrow-mindedness and dogmatism. In our struggle to break the old educational ideals, in our effort to find a new form of life, we came across those who demanded that the coming revolution be total, that the entire human being be seized by it, from the impulses of dreams through to practical actions. In nineteen twelve we had caught wind of these signs of cultural upheaval and we immediately incorporated them into our political onslaught. That which, four years later, was so emphatically expressed at Cabaret Voltaire by those who had fled the orgy of mass murder, we soaked up in its first inklings. Living surrounded by international newspapers and periodicals, by flyers and manifestos, emissaries traveling to and fro, we had absorbed the creations of the likes of Cravan, Picabia, Duchamp, Arp, and Apollinaire, nobody knew where we had developed the openness for such experimentation, the explanation was perhaps simply once more that our senses had been sharpened by all the humiliations and castigations. I hate assaults, wanton violence, punch-ups, he cried, and yet we belong to the generation that arrived at scientific thinking through misery and poverty, through a constant attempt to escape from figures of authority, through homelessness and vagrancy. I don't want to glorify that in any way. There are better ways to gain a sense for recognizing connections. But we were taught this insight through violence and terror. The new came, as always, from Paris. In an age when capital was preparing the most enormous episode of plunder and barbarism ever seen, we dogged, haggard former messenger boys, who were supposed to be made into wolves, found our way to the idea of fraternity, to a celebration, the kind that had often rung out here in this city, in the midst of the most brutal brawl. With these words he came to a standstill, swung his arms out wide, standing in the Parc des Expositions, behind the Porte de Versailles, where the suburb of Vanves began. The gray of his eyes was of an almost blinding brightness. With his stocky figure, his high brow and dark hair, he resembled Hodann; in their mannerisms of speech and gesture their affinity was even more prominent. Münzenberg had founded another periodical; he was always longing for such a mouthpiece. Cut off from the Party, he had found a funder in Aschberg—that peculiar patron of the left—and the first issue was just about to appear, in October. Thomas, Heinrich, and Klaus Mann, Arnold and Stefan Zweig, Feuchtwanger, Kerr, Döblin, Olden, Schifrin, Roth, Schickele, Werfel, Ernst Weiss, and Graf were all involved; Hodann was also providing him with contributions—I had accompanied him to Münzenberg's apartment on the corner of Rue Voisembert and Rue du Quatre-Septembre, in a new building which clashed with the soot-blackened tenement houses of the neighborhood. Having ended up in a conversation, Münzenberg dragged us out, first of all to a bistro on Avenue Renan, then past the warehouses, under the railway bridge, into the exhibition park, all spaces were too cramped for him, he needed plazas, fields, panoramas around him, and with his knickerbockers and laced boots, he looked to be dressed to go mountain climbing. His thoughts always seemed to be in a dialogue with the outside world, it was as if he grasped every word, every image out of a boundlessness, and yet his most incidental remark was marked by a strong inner resonance. With spluttering laughter, Hodann mentioned that there should no longer be any room in the Party for a man like Münzenberg. If for no other reason, he said, than that you write that the most precious thing in the Party is the militant, the member, the person. That is an insult to the all-powerful leadership. And how can you advocate freedom of opinion today, he cried. How can you write that the paper will maintain its independence. Independence, that is a lack of partisanship, that is subterfuge, so as to be able to criticize the Third International, the Soviet Union. Independence, even from the Second International, is worthless today, because everything is either/or, for or against. I asked myself whether these motives could indeed suffice for Münzenberg's expulsion. The explanation seemed to me to lie in the concentration of power, in the clash of rivalries. As far as I was able to judge, Münzenberg and the other leaders of the Party wanted the same thing. It was just that the call to come together was not to be issued by him, but rather by the group that was now taking over the Politburo. What other option was he left with besides editing a paper himself in which he could advocate the idea of unity. Working toward this unity, even from divergent starting points, was better than remaining silent. And yet for him, a man who had contributed to the establishment of the Communist International, this forced independence must have meant a loss of belonging, an agonizing sense of being severed from all attachments. In nineteen fourteen, he said, when we made a stand against the Social Democrats' support for the war, we were thrown out of the Party, all of the youth associations were dissolved by the geriatric leadership due to their antimilitary stance. There was one revolutionary stream approaching us from the Russian underground, with its political charge; and from Paris, the current of the artistic revolution. The two collided above us in Zurich, but not in order to numb us, but rather to exculpate us, to deliver us unto clarity. In September of nineteen fourteen, said Münzenberg, I stood next to Lenin for the first time. Radek and Bukharin had already arrived in Switzerland a few weeks earlier, while the Austrians still had Lenin interned in Kraków. At the end of the month, Trotsky arrived in Zurich. When I think about that time, he said—about the monstrous supremacy of the warmongers, and about those few who in Bern, later in Zurich, often starving, always pressed for money, living in meager quarters, planned to smash the rule of greed— their feat in October still seems virtually unimaginable. That Lenin immediately put me to work, he said, spurred me on, but it also brought a certain sense of unease; his personality was so dominating, his strength as a leader so indisputable, that something inside of me still wanted to rebel against him. I never even came close to forming a connection with Trotsky. We Young Socialists were involved in printing and distributing his pamphlets about the war and the International, smuggling them across the border into Germany in the winter. In Trotsky's presence something adventurous, anarchistic always arose; he was at once fanatic and bohemian, just as interested in discussing Jarry, Kandinsky, Marinetti, Picasso, or de Chirico as insurrectional strategy. With their conflicts, fought out primarily in the press, Lenin and Trotsky complemented one another. Trotsky was the only one who dared to express his own opinion in front of Lenin. It was precisely because of this independence that Lenin appreciated him. Their hefty clashes were not testament to irreconcilable differences but rather to an inextinguishable, dialectical vitality. Just as the revolutionary moment could only develop out of antagonisms, out of paradoxical preconditions, artistic development was also unthinkable without tensions, conflicts, extreme strain. It's not something I've often spoken about, said Münzenberg, and perhaps I am only now seeing it clearly, now that I've been maneuvered into this isolated position, but my political ideas were strongly linked to the image of a cultural revolution. In the summer before the Zimmerwald Conference, in the clandestine meetings, the heated conversations among small groups of professional revolutionaries, we were steered in the direction that from then on was supposed to apply to all of our activities. The splinter groups from the old Erfurt Party found their way to a common line, declared their revolutionary program on the fifth of September. Our paper as well, *Freie Jugend* [Free Youth], was renamed *Jugend Internationale* [Youth International], relationships were being forged between countries, we could not imagine anything but the struggle against the war turning into a proletarian world revolution. Zimmerwald was a beginning, he said, full of halfmeasures. And while we were organizing the next meeting, in Kienthal, in order to advance Lenin's International, the artistic revolts—seeming much more intransigent, more cunning than our activities—overtook us. The tumult that arose when the word *Dada* was snatched blindly from a French dictionary on the eighth of February nineteen sixteen made us temporarily forget our conviction that the material revolution was inseparable from the intellectual. The artists in Spiegelgasse were as unaware of their actual task—namely of complementing the political revolution—as the politicians who refused to assign any revolutionary capacities to art. Huelsenbeck, Ball, Tzara, Arp, and the other drumming, freely associating poets on the stage declared all political and social ambitions rotten and corrupt, they despised sober-mindedness and planning as prerequisites for the success of the revolution, saw only chaos as being fruitful, but were unaware of how they were running the risk of once again replacing that which had been toppled with something mystical, irrational. They called what they produced anti-art. We, on the other hand, had no interest in breaking with the works of the past, we saw a historical continuity between them and the evidentiary signs of new social relations. Cutting ourselves off from earlier achievements would have meant placing ourselves in a vacuum. Because of this, our agreement with many manifestations was accompanied by a resistance; we often gave the productions a different meaning than what was intended by the creators. Since early nineteen sixteen, Spiegelgasse had housed the entire revolution, for that was when Lenin moved in there as well. The old man, as we called him—for that is what the forty-five-year-old already resembled, with his almost bare skull—condemned the spleen of the artists, their veneration of uselessness, as was being expressed in the performances in the grotto. The planning took place at the top of the hunchbacked alley; deep down below, fantastical unreason was unleashed. Spiegelgasse became the symbol of the violent coupling of the waking and the dreaming revolution. I asked Münzenberg about where the alley was situated. From the Limmatquai, said Münzenberg, you walk along Marktgasse, turn into Münstergasse, and it's the first one on your left, going straight up the hill. The first door on the left, with few stairs in front of it, leads to the cabaret. At night, a racket pervades from the low, arched windows that makes the walls shudder. I can still see Radek, he says, the way he stretches his arms out to the side to prop up the walls of the narrow alley. From there it was straight up the Zürichberg, over bumpy cobblestones, to the square that joins up with Napfgasse and where the building in which Lavater had lived was located. He had received Goethe there, in seventeen sixty five, I think it was, before the supporter of the French Revolution became a counterrevolutionary, he also received a visit, on a hike, from the young Hölderlin. Büchner had often walked across this square, while he was a lecturer in anatomy at Zurich University; he lived until his death a dozen paces farther up, in the building on the corner of Spiegelgasse, the Brunnenturm. Next door, number fourteen it was, where the alley fell away again, Lenin and Krupskaya had rented a room, on the second floor, at the shoemaker Kammerer's place. He had his workshop on the corner, number twelve. I often stopped in at his place, reminiscing about old times. Münzenberg had stopped at some scaffolding, wanted to scuttle up the ladder, I held him back. Yeah, he yelled, the room was about four meters long, three meters wide, the ceiling not much more than two meters high. Dark-stained wooden molding crisscrossing the walls. Two windows, the curtains usually drawn shut. Beside the door an iron stove, with the chimney bent off at a right angle. Shoved between the oven and the corner of the room, a table, where they ate, and a narrow sofa. In the corner by the window, a washstand with a small bowl. Which was also used for writing. Above it, a mirror hung from the molding. The double bed in the center. Dominating the room. Fluffed up pillows, huge duvets. Then a few chairs, a chest of drawers. Otherwise no space. You had to shuffle sideways. They had negotiated the right to use the kitchen. Rent was twenty-eight francs a month. Apart from the innkeepers, there were also other occupants. Emigrants. An Italian, a few Austrian actors, a German woman with her children. In the morning, Lenin would wait at the front door so that the postman didn't have to climb the steps with all the letters and newspapers. He stored his correspondence in cardboard boxes that Kammerer had given him. Below the label *Bottine* were the names of Gorky, Bukharin, Zinoviev, Luxemburg, Chicherin, Shlyapnikov, Trotsky. Yes, said Münzenberg, the drumming from the depths could be heard from up here, at night, when the windows could be opened. They opened onto the courtyard. Had to be kept closed during the day, and even still a relentless, cloying stench of blood and entrails pervaded the rooms through all the cracks. There was a sausage factory below. Lenin alternated between complaining about the

rattling of the meat grinder and the drumbeats. Now we had climbed up the wooden stairs, were standing at the railing, overlooking the trees, the pavilions. Münzenberg could still see Spiegelgasse before him, which descended from the Brunnenturm to the narrow street that was named after the fences that bordered a series of gardens. Kammerer stepped out in front of the entrance to his shop, arched back at an angle, inspecting the rows of shoes in the window. Out the front of Restaurant zum Jakobsbrunnen, on the ground floor of the building of number fourteen, draymen were setting down cases full of clinking bottles. It was bright here: the alley opposite opened out into a forecourt. Above numbers sixteen and eighteen ran Ruff's butcher's shop, with a proud announcement between gold garlands that their sausages had received the highest of accolades. It was Lenin's most trying year, said Münzenberg. Behind him, three years of ostracism, more than one and a half decades of exile. Being cut off from the events in Russia had become almost unbearable. His colleagues scattered across the world. Contact with them made difficult. His health poor. Sleeplessness. Splitting headaches. We were often frightened by his gaunt face. Moments when he felt stranded. The continual fear of missing the revolutionary situation, arriving too late. Sometimes, at meetings, in the Schwarzer Adler at Stüssihof, he managed to perk up. But his vitality seemed artificial, hectic. Then he'd go back to sitting for hours on end, brooding. A monstrous energy stored within him. Every day, from nine till six, he was in the libraries. Writing, writing. The book on imperialism, countless articles, flyers, pamphlets. Who visited him in his apartment, I asked. Only a few people, said Münzenberg. Krupskaya was ill as well. They lived largely in isolation. Zinoviev came occasionally, Balabanoff, Radek too. Or people he had invited after meeting them at gatherings, hoping to influence them. If there were more than three guests there, they sat on the bed. Agitation, furor, as Radek expressed his disbelief that the war would bring about the proletarian revolution. Did he ever meet Armand, I asked Münzenberg. Just the one time, he said, evasively. The mention of this name touched upon something that went too far, was too violent to be absorbed. What was she like, I asked again. There was something intoxicating about her, he said. Big hat, veil, plumes. Then: we younger ones wanted to introduce Lenin to writers, artists, wanted to drag him out of his isolation. But he would just sit there with his watch in his hand, staring at the second hand. From time to time I lost track of him, said Münzenberg. He homed in on a single point. For us there was so much to do. We drifted about the city. Münzenberg pressed his nose flat with his index finger. How can I convey, he said, what happened in those foundational months. If we spoke of the two poles of the revolution, he said, then we were invoking knowledge that we had attained primarily via philosophical channels. Even if it seemed that the artistic revolution was being waged on a different front than the political one, and was not fighting for social changes, in positioning itself against the tired conventions and seeking to smash norms that had long ago revealed their coercive character, it was indeed related to our revolution. With its struggle for the liberation of forms, of movements, for the renewal of language, of the gaze, it had to exert an influence on our senses, our search for a transformed existence. Art has no power over reality, said the politicians. And with reality they meant solely the reality of the external world. They didn't see how threadbare this reality had become. In Switzerland, all events that were important to us took place in a strange shelteredness. Zimmerwald was a rural idyll, close to Bern, suited to forest getaways, relaxing holidays. Kienthal was a village at the foot of the Blüemlisalp. It wasn't until we arrived at the train station that we found out where the conspiratorial journey was headed. Along the Lötschberg railway line to Reichenbach, in the Bernese Oberland, then, like a group of tourists, in hay carts to Hotel Bären. Spiegelgasse consisted of traditional, noble-looking houses, with gables and turrets, as if made of gingerbread. But behind the windows, explosive material was gathering. With our dreams, ideas, and plans, we were reshaping reality. At the end of April of sixteen, we dislodged our meeting place from its idyllic frame and transported it into a world-historical context. But what, the artists down in the alley might have asked themselves—presuming they were even taking notice of our activities at all—could the Kienthal Resolution achieve. Weren't the differences of opinion between the socialist factions still present, weren't the German and Russian groups still split into two hostile camps, hadn't the social chauvinists once again managed to prevent the foundation of a Third International, were the proletarians not still shooting at each other from the trenches, wasn't the only place to find meaningful activity among those who rejected all order. The aim, said Münzenberg, was to mount the hypothesis of a comprehensive social and artistic revolution, and then to produce the evidence of the interrelation of the components, which until that moment had always been treated separately. To do so we didn't need to demand that art, which had assigned itself the task of toppling the intellectual reality, also bear a political mission. It did what its means were best suited to do. Nor was it incumbent upon politics to drag art along with it. The new, he said, still insufficiently outlined even today, consists in recognizing the two forces

in their unique characteristics and equivalence, not to pit them against one another but rather to bring their parallel courses, their simultaneous creations together to form a common denominator. What did match up was the intensity of revolutionary artistic and political actions, as well as their internationalist objectives. What seemed irreconcilable was the derision, the irony of the one, with the seriousness, the sense of responsibility of the other. Citizens, students, workers, vagabonds, drifters of the world, unite, sang the Dadaists, in a mockery of the call from Kienthal to the working-class soldiers of the world. And if in April of sixteen it seemed as if the arm of the arts was reaching past us with exaggerated drama, said Münzenberg, a year later, the masses of working people in Russia did rise up, and Lenin's theses drowned out the bubbling broth of words at the soirées in Cabaret Voltaire. We had imagined something, he said, which couldn't yet be defined, which for now consisted only of premonitions, intimations. In nineteen seventeen we had little time left to continue pursuing the trains of thought which underpinned the idea of the cultural revolution; surprisingly, they were later taken up by Lenin, who despite refusing to see even the beginning of a politicization of the arts in the uproar in Spiegelgasse, declared that the revolutionary must possess the capacity to dream. Because practical daily tasks always took precedence, it seemed as if this term, *cultural revolution*, which Lenin used frequently during his final months, had receded into the background; yet according to its meaning, conceived by Lenin primarily as an opposing force to the bureaucratized, doctrinaire party apparatus, it continued to have an effect on us. Now that the time seems ripe for bringing together the lines that formed back then, I see that with *cultural revolution* we were referring to the break that formed the prerequisite for the fulfillment of the political struggle. Lenin spoke of a laborious process, and even I, during the years in which I lost sight of my earlier ideas, had attempted to put art in the service of the Party, to force it to promote the cause of ideological education. But art is the means, he said, of loosening the rigidity of political institutions, and of reminding us of the diversity of our perceptions. Propaganda, said Münzenberg with a laugh, and we watched the traffic streaming back and forth along Avenue Renan, between Issy and Porte de Versailles, circulating around the roundabout, flowing into Boulevard Victor, Boulevard Lefebvre, into the never-ending Rue Vaugirard, behind the gray sea of roofs we saw the green of the park of the Michelet school and the military training fields which stretched on until the Seine, propaganda, he said, I was tasked with creating this apparatus, it had to be conjured up out of nothing and made into a weapon to confront the powerful press of the bourgeoisie; with our writings we 57 had to gain influence over the millions of people who for half a century had been numbed, inundated with lies and trash, we had to publish the truth about their situation. From that point on—it began in the summer of twenty-one, he said pensively—I scarcely concerned myself with art itself, I might have dealt with cultural questions in my journalism, but our focus from the Zurich years was never mentioned. Artistic, literary elements had to be absorbed into the needs of the political propaganda. We measured quality according to the extent to which a work served to strengthen the Party, to ameliorate the hardship afflicting the Soviet state. The catastrophic famine and the aftereffects of the civil war had to be overcome. The foundation of the Workers International Relief coincided with the release of the first illustrated workers' newspaper. Lenin had summoned me. During the war, he had contributed to the formation of our Young Communist International; now, with the revolution having remained isolated, he called on me to initiate the international aid efforts. My first visit to the Kremlin. As Münzenberg paused, as if he had only now become aware of the chasm that had opened up between July of twenty-one and October of thirty-eight, I asked about the setting in which he met Lenin, what the rooms were like. Once again I wanted to picture every single detail that formed part of the environment of an event; if a mental image did not materialize before me, I pressed for further details. His apartment was in the long building with its deeply recessed windows, the former arsenal, right on the northeastern corner of the wall between Manege Square and Red Square, on the top floor, at the end of the vaulted corridor in which the footsteps rolled like muffled thunder. Located next to the parlor was Lenin's personal library, Münzenberg recalled having seen some books by Nexø, in English, Heine's collected works, a few volumes by Bebel, Mehring, Lenau's poems, Hugo's novels, Hauptmann's *The Weavers*, *Man of Straw* by Heinrich Mann; apart from that, primarily pamphlets against Social Democracy, disputes between Mensheviks and Bolsheviks. He was shown through the conference room—the room of the Council of Ministers, in which wicker chairs with flared backs sat around the large, green-topped table and old maps of Russia and Western Europe hung on the walls—into Lenin's small office. There was a leather sofa and four leather club chairs for guests, Lenin himself used a simple wicker chair, behind him he had two short, rotating book stands with reference books, literature he had just used, stuffed with slips of paper. Two telephones sat on the desk, along with a bronze sculpture. It wasn't until Münzenberg had told me about the palm in the wooden bucket in front of the window, about the portrait of Marx against a red background painted by a worker, about the white-tiled stove and the adjoining room of the telephone operators and had mentioned the faded maps, which here too hung from the wood-paneled walls, that it occurred to him what the sculpture depicted—namely, an ape, sitting in contemplation, one hand on its chin, the other hand holding a human skull. And his apartment, I asked. It was along the same corridor. In his bedroom there was a narrow brass bed with pillows piled up high, next to it a nightstand, on top a small arc lamp with a silk shade, the same set-up could be found in Krupskaya's room, as well as a desk with a blue-green tablecloth and a wardrobe with mirrored panels. One could look from the windows onto the courtyard in front of the gate of Troitskaya Tower. The kitchen, that's where you sat for a cup of tea, a piece of bread; hectored by my persistent questions, Münzenberg described the wooden seats at the table with its oilcloth, the iron stove, the coal bucket, the basket with kindling and pieces of firewood, the sink, the vitrine, a few cups inside it, no two of the same kind, a couple of plates, small pots, bowls, an iron heating up on the stove. But then, after having been cajoled into talking about it, all of this must have seemed to him a distraction from things that were more important at this point in time; and yet his storytelling had conveyed the impression that the things he was evoking were more present to him than all the efforts at a reorientation that his newspaper—optimistically named *Die Zukunft* [The Future]—was supposed to work toward. It was as if he were embarrassed to have divulged so much about himself. He jumped down the rungs of the metal frame, Hodann held him back by the arm to keep him from running away from us, no, cried Münzenberg, I won't do them the favor of throwing myself down on my knees and apologizing, that is the difference between me and my accused comrades, I still stand behind everything I've done, I'm still the same person I've become, I dare to criticize what needs to be criticized. For this criticism does not serve the purpose of damaging the Soviet state but of promoting it. What I wrote more than a decade and a half ago, that the first workers' state has to be protected, I write now as well, and I am finally addressing what Lenin, already gravely ill, saw before him, the cultural revolution, to usher in an epoch of democratization. And for that they slander me, he cried, them, the grovelers, the opportunists, Katz, who was my apprentice, Šmeral, who was a member of the Imperial Council of the Habsburgs when we founded the Young Communist International, they try to gag me, because I refuse to agree with their hypocrisies, they try to get rid of me, because I am inconvenient for them. As Katz stepped out of the tent he was staring at his open hands, as if to read what had been pre- **59** saged in their lines. He stayed silent for a long time on the way back through the tunnel, and then his voice, with its sparse words, was different, barely recognizable. Beware the ropes, he said, assuming her Bohemian-tinged German, she saw only rope, only rope, from which we hang.

The melodrama of the violent crimes that were playing out before us today would have found a form a hundred years ago in the works of Sue, which mirrored contemporary events through their serial structure, their shady, questionable characters, their details painted in often lurid colors. Now and then I would pick up one of his novels, which formed part of the inventory of Aschberg's library; reading them provoked contradictory reactions: the style of the revelations from a world of taverns and hideouts, of ballrooms and bordellos, of card sharps and secret agents, of thieves and stockjobbers originally turned me off somewhat, until in the accumulation of the loucheness, eccentricity, and vulgarity I recognized the means for representing a particular social situation. Marx and Engels had handed down a one-sided judgment on the author of the *Mystères de Paris*, the *Fleur de Marie*, and the *Juif errant*, charging him with a tendency toward mysteriousness, to cruelty, to a belief in miracles, redemption, and grace, which he expressed in his characters. For them, Sue was a blinded, an isolated figure, for whom the city, filled with life, became a mere idea; one who reduced everything that revealed itself to him to his own hallucinations. Though they were willing to see a critical approach in his depictions of a civilization gone feral, of lawlessness and inequality in the state, they still maintained that, in the countless scenes full of fury and the thirst for revenge, he was only satiating his hunger for the self-abasement of humanity, that he used the contrition and penance that followed deeds of extreme brutality only in order to transform reality into smoke and mirrors. For all their appreciation of the political implications that Sue, influenced by the theories of Fourier and Proudhon, drew from his knowledge of economic misery, for them he remained a confused, sentimental petit bourgeois who, having failed in his personal life, found success and a comfortable livelihood in depicting moral degradation. His work, however, as dubious and speculative as it might have often appeared, could only be understood if it was related to Sade and Bretonne; then, in the depiction of modes of torture and oppression, the humanistic and moral intentions emerged, the mystifications were nothing but the rug the rulers pulled over their scheming; the accentuation of the brutal

punishments, of iniquity, served to denounce an entire system. Moreover, the fantastical encounters with pimps and prostitutes, with butlers, porters, and poor man's lawyers, the surprising glimpses into hidden doorways and spaces; the bridges, colonnades, and embankments appearing in half-light, the descriptions of cryptic figures floating by, all reflected an outlook that was emerging in the first half of the nineteenth century, not just in a number of literary works but also in the visual arts, above all in the graphic arts, and which reached their high point in the etchings of Meryon, which I discovered in the Bibliothèque Nationale, and in Baudelaire's *Les Fleurs du mal*. My study of Géricault and of that forgotten illustrator and printmaker who perished in poverty and mental derangement had taught me something about life in this city, something that expressed less the susceptibility to morbidity and decadence that had repulsed Marx and Engels than a deepening of the real, in which precisely and objectively reproduced details were assigned the character of dream. Such an extremely personal vision, without which the art of Lautréamont and Rimbaud would not have been possible, formed part of this city, it could only, as Münzenberg said in his considerations on the cultural revolution, come from Paris. His conception of the interrelation of the social and political with the poetic, the visionary, pointed toward the intellectual world of those who refused to accept the existing paradigms and rules, who were able to make the imposing buildings transparent and to recognize the events within them, who could make a fleetingly glanced face into a reflection of the doom, the calamity of an era. Münzenberg had referred to an artistic way of life that encompassed everything that we understood under openness, unreservedness, the will for renewal; for him, the visual revolution meant a path to more richly composed concepts that corresponded more closely to reality. In their aversion toward Sue and the admiration that they showed toward Balzac, Marx and Engels joined in on the mockery which the great historian of *La Comédie humaine* showered on the literarily inferior depicter of morals. Sue, the son of an anatomist who had provided Géricault with corpses to use as models while he was creating his preparatory studies for *The Raft of the Medusa*, had originally been a ship's doctor, and only came to writing after long voyages on the seas. In the eyes of Balzac, and of the two masters of social analysis, he would always remain a dilettante, completely unable to detach impressions from emotion, which is why he wrote such turgid tales. Balzac's condemnation of Sue was not related solely to the fact that Sue strayed into hunting grounds that Balzac claimed for himself alone but also to the fact that Sue, as a representative of the left, was an advocate of a socialist revolution. Balzac, with his affinity for the nobility, was a reactionary, and yet he was viewed as progressive by Marx and Engels because he was able to depict the class to which he himself belonged with all of its contradictions and symptoms of decay. For Marx and Engels, Balzac's artistic superiority was obvious; they had no feeling for the criteria of gaucheness, of ambiguity, which comprised Sue's originality. In the figure of the prostitute Marie, he conveyed his attitude toward the terror of the bourgeoisie most clearly; she retained her dignity in her downfall, she put up a fight, until she was made to disavow and destroy herself by society's most underhanded instrument of oppression, the church. Setting out from a sympathy with her fate, he forged on into regions for which there were still no benchmarks of investigation; here too he followed in the footsteps of Restif de la Bretonne, who, while addressing the bizarre and the obscene, sought to lay the foundations for a new, materialist outlook, anticipating communist doctrine in the middle of the eighteenth century. Like Bretonne, Sue stood on the side of the poorest, despised art that allowed itself to be exploited by the ruling classes, and believed that poems ought to be scratched into walls and bridge vaults, able to be read by vagabonds, surrendered to the elements. During my time in Paris, the mere mention of a name, the broaching of a topic, would cause disparate connections to resonate; all the motifs of my being were present, like an organ register that would someday come to resound fully. Which is why I also accepted the encounters in their haphazardness, their brevity, the conversations in their abruptness. What remained fragmentary in one articulation would find its continuation in another encounter. I moved through this time as if by circular paths which screwed deeper and deeper, unnoticeably, turning my stay in Paris into a *saison en enfer*; there was a reason why Münzenberg had said to me, read Rimbaud, there you have everything that makes poetry complex, as well as everything that brings about its demise. With its riotous attitude, its provocation of heated contradictions, he said, this art form was also associated with a form of society, and yet it gives the impression that it was hurrying ahead of its time, that it was conceived from a future position. There, as in Hölderlin as well, a consciousness extended far beyond its own contemporary moment; this phenomenon, he said, endows us with a particularly keen sense of hearing, enables us to assess our personal project with more focused attention. Much of what I experienced in Paris was more of a guessing, I lacked the prior knowledge required to understand most of the things that confronted me, and the strain of arriving at some kind of understanding would often leave me confused. From our fleeting encounters I wasn't able to interpret Münzenberg's essential nature. In the way he would digress or break off as soon as he got close to important material, it seemed to me as if he were himself marked by the strife that was afflicting the Party. He liked to point out that he was free, that nothing could get to him; but it was inevitable that the things that were savaging the Party he had helped to build would also eat away at him, it would have been unimaginable for somebody who had intervened so deeply in all the entanglements and flash points not to have been seized by the political phantasms of his time. I took in what he and Katz described from their opposing standpoints; the flitting from one topic to another produced a polarization, a principle that also shaped the appearance of the Party. We sensed the burden under which the Party labored, it often brought us to the brink of despair, yet there was no alternative; that which was infected would fall off; people, many of the best, perhaps, would go down in the process, it was shameful that such sacrifices were being demanded, we jolted up from our sleep in terror, wandered restlessly to and fro, had no solution, but stopping was unthinkable, as long as there was life, there could be no standstill. We cursed ourselves for being so helpless, for being unable to bring a stop to the distortions, we beat our brows on the walls in rage that our knowledge was so limited, that we weren't able to explain, in a manner enlightening for everybody, what was going on and what had to be done; we sensed our blindness, we threw ourselves on the floor when it was no longer possible to stand upright in the midst of the onslaught of slander; over and over we were forced to crawl like this, this terrible dragging ourselves about as if stricken by a plague, and everything happened in this city, in which, alongside the paralyzing internal conflicts in the Party and the bourgeois intrigues, suddenly, one of the slain pulled himself up and began to dance. It was at Carré de l'Odéon, at the spot where, before the old quarter was torn down and opened up by Boulevard Saint-Germain, Rue de l'École de Médicine had intersected Rue Carret on its way toward Rue de l'Ancienne-Comédie. There might have also been roasted chestnuts being sold from carts back then, like they were today beside the steps of the metro; the pungent aroma, the yell of the vendor unchanged. In his rambles through the alleyways, Sue had also seen the ragged figure, initially crouching vacantly on the edge of the street, who jumped up suddenly as if he'd been wound up, and he would have surely, like Meryon after him, spent plenty of time observing the house with the corner tower beginning on the first floor, for Marat had lived overlooking the inner courtyard and met his demise there. Meryon had depicted a peculiar throng around the house. Like now, the people were hurrying across the square, or lingering in pairs and small groups, a conspiratorial air colored their demeanor, a tall covered wagon drove toward us from the side street, the two women sitting up front, one of them holding the reins, seemed not to notice the horse shying, they were turned toward each other, deep in conversation, as if in a basket of calm in the middle of the hustle and bustle. The artist had adorned the stone under the ledge of the tower with the initial of his own and Marat's name, above the street sign another name was visible that was still obscure to me, *Cabat*. The shop window on the left was filled with spices, in front of the bakery, on the opposite side of the road, a few people bore tall, formless bundles on their backs, and high above, on a rooftop pedestal, two naked figures could be glimpsed, in combat, the one forced onto his knees, the other raising his hand to deliver the mortal blow. Every groove, every patch of plaster that had fallen off, every store sign on the walls of the buildings had been depicted with precision, but from the heavens, goddesses flew down, a Fury, her grimace surrounded by billowing waves of hair and veils, a sword tethered to a scale pan, hurtling into the tower building, and a Grace, an Aurora, holding an open book with the inscription *Fiat Lux*, while a small genius, losing his wings, throws himself into the air. In eighteen seventy-one, when Sue died in exile, banished from France following Louis Napoleon's coup d'état, at the time of the military dictatorship and the colonial wars of conquest in Indochina, Meryon, fearing his own persecution, had shrouded the house of the friend of the people and revolutionary with deeply cryptic symbols. The cryptogram bore the traces of his anxiety: the lurking and creeping, the waiting for plots could be felt all around the buildings. Now it was where the length of the building of the medical faculty ran. At the grandfather clock, the prearranged meeting point, a man and a woman embraced, the clochard danced, swaying and singing, hinted with contemplative gestures that he wasn't bothered in the slightest by the lack of success of his begging, and as a group up ahead at the steps leading down to the metro went to part ways, he jumped toward them, shoved his hand between their leave-taking hands, shook them, bowed chivalrously, and his participation in the parting was remunerated with laughter. It wasn't just the sudden proximity of people that touched us; buildings also took on life. The sight of them was like the manifestation of a painting, a statue, only the buildings were more alive, resembled organisms. Through the eyes that had observed them for centuries, the hands that had touched them, their exteriors had become sensitive like a skin, and their interiors swelled with the breath of generations. For this reason, often when I was confronted by such an entity, one that had been erected by human hands, I would find myself caught in a dialogue. At that time, Meryon was still able to walk from the intersection into the narrow courtyard, fenced off on the sides by tall firewalls, and look up to the windows behind which Marat had lived. I only found photographs, in the Musée Carnavalet, that showed the corner building, in a state of demolition, in eighteen sixty-four. A staircase with the wall torn away, a richly ornamented balustrade on the curvature of the steps, a living room above, floral wallpaper, an open fireplace, then a sketch, a floor plan of the apartment, an indication of Corday's path through the building to the little room in the corner, an A designating Marat's bathtub, a B the location of the murderess, everything rendered in fine, shaky watercolors, faded memory on crinkled paper. And the imaginary encounters were always entwined with what was occurring in that moment, they were flushed with reality, the historical relationships were absorbed alongside the measures and assessments arising from the political situation, from our work assignments. On the twenty-third of October, the day before his departure, Hodann collapsed. The overpowering mental pressure had triggered an asthma attack. Branting and Münzenberg were present; I had come from the Spanish Aid office, had registered the newly arrived children, whom I was to send in the next convoy to Compiègne, to the home La Brévière; I rushed from the rooms in the wings of the building where the medical staff were now housed, across the courtyard, past the Roman fountain, up into the conference room in which, illuminated by the chandeliers that were duplicated in the mirrors on the walls, Hodann lay on his side on the sofa, his knees pulled up toward his torso. His friends were tending to him, but he was already in the process of overcoming the attack; his face waxen, wet with sweat, he pronounced his own diagnosis: obstruction of expectoration through bronchitic symptoms resulting from emphysemic mutations to the inferior lobe, had me inject him with a codeine solution, demanded that we pay no attention to his ailment, sat upright and continued the conversation without interruption. The topic had been dogmatism, which the French Party was intensifying in an attempt to combat its disintegration, and a number of Hodann's remarks led me to suspect that he had moved closer to Münzenberg's position. At a time when they ought to be pursuing an independent, broad, democratic politics, one tailored to their own country, their adherence to the directives coming from the Comintern could only have disastrous effects. The German Communists as well, he said, were now using the Committee for the Foundation of a Popular Front for the exclusive interests of their own party. It was less his statements than the tone in which they were delivered that left me unsettled; Hodann's intolerance in the face of errors that had been committed, of poor decisions, was all too familiar to me for me to be able to view it as an ideological deviation, but it now seemed to me that he was no longer willing to defend the Party as he had been earlier, despite all the difficulties that had arisen. His critique was characterized by a sense of disappointment and demoralization, betraying an anxious, conflictual relationship. The discussion subjected me once again to the conflict of double loyalty, yet on that evening I ascribed his agitation primarily to nerves in anticipation of his departure for Norway. I refrained from referring to the opinions that he had once divulged to me on the trip between Albacete and Denia, according to which every hint of a feeling of dislocation robbed us of some of our strength to act. In switching countries, he had said, we must always preserve the continuity of our political stance. It wasn't until a few days later, in the Château de La Brévière, on the edge of a medieval village in the forest of Compiègne, in the attic, upon whose ceiling a lantern was casting shadows of bare branches, that this moment returned to me once more, as a penitence, in which I had to tussle with my mistrust. My silence could be traced back to his impending departure, to my long-standing affection and deference toward him, but also to feelings of hurt and, as I now recognized, of fear and cowardice, for Branting had guaranteed my entry into Sweden. Together with a financial guarantee from the banker Aschberg, Branting, the Social Democrat lawyer and politician, chair of the Swedish Committee on Spain and supporter of the antifascist Popular Front, provided me with my only chance of getting anywhere. Katz had repeatedly urged me to accept the offer, but also to be careful, the German Communist Party was planning on relocating a base to Sweden, Mewis had been tasked with directing the section, it would be possible to put me in touch with him. The combination of the necessity of cooperating with radical Social Democrats—which I had always considered a prerequisite to maintaining a socialist front—with the admonition to maintain a distinction between the parties left me uncertain; despite his sympathies for the Soviet Union, I didn't know how far Branting could be trusted; and Aschberg too, a backer of the Soviet state since the October Revolution, always presenting himself as a humanist and a democrat, had something unsettling about him, with the thought of his princely estates and finances, which were indeed partially used for the benefit of the persecuted, but in disproportionately larger amounts were invested in banks and industries. Acknowledging my half-

heartedness, my tactical reticence, I had to make my peace with dissimulations and secret paths. During the night in La Brévière, that castle with its sixty rooms, erected in the pompous style of Napoleon III, once a hunting lodge with a stud, now a place where children stayed, their wailing and periodic yelps ringing through the halls, I was overcome by fever. I had not been ill a single time in Spain; now, far away from battle, my blood was racing and sizzling, my throat and lungs on fire. The shadows of the branches seesawed up and down to the noise of the rain, a child seemed to be whimpering right beside my bed, the castle was a showcase, a menagerie, where the Spanish orphans were placed on display for the arriving delegations, where the headmistress ran a strict, unjust regime, where, upon a suggestion for the improvement of some arrangements, I had been told that I, as a refugee, had no right to say anything. I jumped up, looked down through the window at a deer standing on a hill, motionless, glistening, haloed by the spray of the rain. On the twenty-fourth of October, Hodann had flown out from Le Bourget in the evening; after seeing Bremen and Hamburg as glimmering mounds in the twilight, he landed in Kastrup and continued on to Oslo the following morning. He hadn't concealed his fear on the way to the airport, and I could still feel his hand shaking in mine; now, at least for the time being, he was safe. I thought back on the conversation upstairs in the hall of the Cercle des Nations; the deer stared up at me, the leaves swirling through the park behind it. Some of Münzenberg's statements must have referred to things that had been mentioned earlier; I thought I could trace them back to his decision to announce his split with the Party, in order to preempt his excommunication by the Central Committee. Hodann's answer hinted that the Party had not yet made a decision; it was still of the opinion that all points of contention had to be discussed and reconciled. Neither you nor the Party, he said to Münzenberg, can afford for you to leave. In the eyes of the Party, countered Münzenberg, I have long been leading a pleasant life in the bourgeois camp. Branting attempted to appease him. Now, with the most extreme concentration of energy being required, he said, all personal disagreements had to recede. Shivering, I crawled into bed, but saw the opulent stucco work above me which filled the ceiling of the hall in Rue Casimir-Périer, the putti on their pedestals, the bacchanalian, allegorical figures of the ceiling painting, time and again, something painted or sculpted by another hand interfered with the monumental image that Münzenberg sketched out for us, pacing silently to and fro on the thick rugs, and which he wrapped around the hostile forces he had fought against his entire life. He went back to what he might have been talking about before I arrived. France would not fight against fascism, he said; the haute bourgeoisie would even form alliances with the fascists if it meant preventing a reemergence of the workers' front. The strike movement and the mass actions that were emerging would be smashed with the most brutal means, ushering in a mood of passivity. The mechanism depicted by Münzenberg, which allowed the ruling classes to reconsolidate their position after every crisis, took on the proportions of a nightmare. One of the difficulties of following the vision was that his words became increasingly interrupted by the stammering which lay beneath all of his efforts at expression. And so at times while he was holding forth I would see him among the highwaymen in the seedy drinking dens of the Thuringian Forest, the heads of roe bucks and wild boars appeared behind him, his face illuminated by the flickering of the rocking kerosene lamp. The will to liberation was buried under mountains of money, the voice of revolt made mute by the droning of the rotary presses, the walls of living bodies that raised themselves up out of the depths were nothing against the flurry of bullets that instantly ploughed through them. Their riches enabled the despots to keep henchmen everywhere, but how could these hordes, these armies, who themselves came from poverty, be willing to offer themselves up to the powerful: why did they not turn their weapons against them instead of against those who were as lowly as they were. Because money numbed them, because the lies engendered by money left their brains matted, because the pay, their tiny portion of the enormous profit, gave them a sense of supremacy, made them adventurous, fed a greed to reap profit in them. They were unable to see past their own hand, raised, ready to strike, they were steered from control panels high above them, at the press of a button, through the resonance of a membrane. The most terrifying aspect of Münzenberg's hallucination was the unshakeable, sovereign reign of the owners. They claimed as their own everything that we too were striving for—perspective, the ability to organize, consistency—and while our armies allowed themselves to be fractured, their shock troops were everywhere diligently at work. We had to hide ourselves away, we burrowed below the ground, they ruled the states, we had to arduously recruit allies, they drew on hoarded reserves, we printed flyers in secret, distributed them at the factory gates, ready to flee, calling for global solidarity, they speculated brazenly, openly, internationally, sucked the continents dry. He brushed away the fact that people were fighting in Spain, in China, in Indochina, that in France too, the workers hoped to win back their strength. I no longer knew, that night in La Brévière, what was fact and what imagination, a cancerous sore was spreading in every living thing, consciousness was devouring itself, everything orderly became contagion, the earthly mêleé served to elicit nothing but agony, we chose our own floggers, our torturers, it was we who provoked the insane actions, we who enforced the madness; I cried that it wasn't so, that it couldn't be so, that we possessed reason. Reason would prevail, I heard myself say, to Münzenberg's laughter, and, but you were in Lenin's room, I said to him, and soothed myself with this thought, you have seen him with your own eyes, but he just shrugged his shoulders, asked what has that got to do with anything. I saw the brownish-yellow map of Belarus that he had described in Lenin's office in the Kremlin, and it was already being permeated by a lighter gray, I was confusing it with the map in another interior, it hung wide, crumbling, unfurled on the wall behind the easel, next to the model with the wreath of leaves, it echoed in the studio of the painter Vermeer, clad in black, there, with cogs and rows of islands, the North Sea coast stretched out, *De Noord See* it read, clearly legible, Hodann had flown toward the North Sea, he had seen the sudden glitter of the course of the Weser, he was overcome by the fear that the engine would suddenly give out, that the propellers would stand still, that the craft would descend for an emergency landing, into the arms of the hangmen. Then I was no longer sure whose journey this was, mine, Hodann's, or Münzenberg's. Münzenberg had gotten to talking about his visit to Stockholm, in May of nineteen seventeen, as a delegate of the Young Communist International. On the way from Zurich, and again on the return leg, he had traveled through Germany, constantly expecting to be arrested on the train, his vision of this monstrous Germania fused with Hodann's panic about the Reich, which was making its preparations for war, and with my own image of the country in which I had grown up and which I had abandoned. Far away from this dangerous world was Sweden, with the provincial feel of its capital; Münzenberg had recalled that the congress participants had been welcomed at the train station by a wind orchestra, with each appearance on the podium being accompanied by fanfare. Stockholm, in the lead-up to the summer of seventeen, after Lenin's *April Theses* but half a year before October, was still the ideal home of capitalism. In their arrogance, the rulers didn't pay much mind to who all these new arrivals were, Balabanoff, Lunacharsky, Chicherin, Manuilsky, Sokolnikov, Shlyapnikov; Lenin had also stepped out of the train station here a month earlier, unrecognized, on his way to Petrograd, together with Zinoviev, Krupskaya, Armand, Radek. And yet, said Münzenberg, in that idyllic city, perched on bodies of water and surrounded by forests, in those days, there were work stoppages, mass demonstra- tions, hunger marches, and a new party, the Social Democratic Left Party, had just been founded. But it was just that in this city, said Münzenberg, the people who hit the streets were beaten up as quick as a flash by the mounted police, the military, and driven out; in next to no time, the blood stains were washed from the cobblestones, and even the revisionists held their positions as if the radicals had never existed. And today, the country could still be held up as an example of the gentle progress of reforms, of the harmony between the buyers and sellers of labor power. There was one more thing I wanted to ask Münzenberg about, whether he had met my father back then, when he passed through Bremen, but he had become just as hazy as Hodann, and the cities began to melt into one another as well; I asked myself what I had to do with Bremen, with Hamburg, with Stockholm. The only thing I was certain of was that I was lying in a bed. Stretched out on a bed I lay and knew that I was in a hotel room. A clunky, angular protrusion ran from the floor up to the ceiling, the wallpaper was of a shabby, greenish gray, the lace curtains in the window were drawn open, bunched together by thick cords, outside there was a muted, misty light, and beside me, on her side, her face resting on her hand, lay my mother, looking at me. Now it occurred to me that we had set off from Bremen, on the trip to Berlin we had stopped off in Hamburg for a day, my father had traveled ahead in order to rent an apartment, in a moment, we would walk down to the harbor and through the Elbe Tunnel, I had desperately wanted to set foot inside this tunnel, deep beneath the masses of water, the large ships. Soon enough we were walking through the hall with the glass cupola, we walked down the spiral staircase and along the narrow footpath, on the road automobiles and carriages rattled, horses' hooves stomped. I drew a longitudinal section of the tunnel in the hotel room, or later on the train, with my pencil I drew the steps, the elevator, which hung from enormous cogs, drew the cars inside it, the coach with its driver, the little men walking back and forth in the tube, the frigates and ocean liners above and, like a fata morgana, the silhouette of the shoreline with towers and warehouse gables. I was absorbed in the act of drawing, attempting to solve a technical miracle, but something wasn't right, I didn't know where my mother was, just a moment ago, she had been holding my hand, below, in the dead-straight passage, a terrible uncertainty emerged as to where I could have lost her, perhaps she had been kidnapped, I heard only a screaming and moaning, people hurried past, there was a crashing sound, as if panes of glass had been shattered, the crowd was pushing a woman ahead of them, a sign

hung around her neck with the inscription *Jidd*, in Jewish lettering, perhaps it was my mother, I made my way through the throng, but the woman was no longer to be seen; what was now being asked of me outstripped my reserves, something that lay beyond my grasp was supposed to be molded into a concept, are you still clinging to the conviction that nothing is inexplicable, asked Münzenberg, do you consider all puzzles solvable, yes, I wanted to cry, but I didn't produce a sound, all searching would be in vain, but still I walked as if I could see tracks, clues in front of me, even if it was too late, all was lost, I would continue walking, to the train station, from platform to platform, chase after a train, pull myself up on the railing, jump back down, until I found a carriage with a sign announcing my destination, there had to be some meaning, an objective, I had to fight off fatigue, not slacken in my endeavor, my destination had already been decided, it was just that I had forgotten the name of the city, hands pointed in the direction I had to pursue, something was called out to me through the smoke of the locomotive, but shrill voices drowned out the cries, children's voices, they were crying for help, in Basque, I hurried out into the adjoining room, the dormitory, where children, shivering, drenched in sweat, threw themselves at me.

The train traveled slowly along the narrow bridge into the station, with a high-pitched tooting of its signal horn it had emerged from the tunnel under the southern hills of the city, rolled across the sluice's retaining wall, past the fishery harbor, the floating fish market, the crowded, gabled façades of the houses of the old town, along the canal and the steeply ascending walls of Riddarholmen, at Klara quay the red and white striped boom gates had been lowered, between city hall and Tegelbacken the automobiles and trams were backed up, the sleepers creaked under the wheels of the train, the iron side panels of the bridge rattled, pedestrians on the narrow sidewalk next to the tracks leaned back against the railing, looked up toward the windows of the carriage gliding by above them, behind which the passengers stood, arriving from Berlin, Hamburg, Paris, a wet snow was falling, the ice lay gray on the fjord, the flounder drifted about in the chopped up channel and around the white steamers of Lake Mälaren sitting by the wharf, the water looked black, a filthy sludge covered the cobblestones on the street leading down to the square with the building housing Tysta Mari. The two women at the boom gate could also see the signs on the train, hear the whistling from the platform, the rattling of the luggage carts, the drawn-out sound of the train braking. Bischoff herself was supposed to travel through here soon as well, in the opposite direction, accompanied by plain-clothed police officers; she asked herself whether her chaperone could really be so oblivious to what it meant for her; the police matron had spoken about her upcoming trip with such nonchalance, as if she were discussing the homeward journey of a tourist. As the gates rose with a ring, the cars began to move and the trams—current collectors hitting the sparking cables—to advance, she could have thrown herself to the side, make off, maybe find a spot to hide between the market stands at the back of the Klara shorefront or in one of the boats that were moored there; but she knew she wouldn't do it, she had given the matron her word of honor as a condition for the stroll. Before she was to be extradited, the privilege had been bestowed upon her of getting to know the city, of which she had only seen a little, since shortly after her arrival she had been transferred to the prison for those on remand. But, since she was in Stockholm, the matron had said, she could hardly be denied the beauty of the city. They had headed down the street from the prison on Bergsgatan. It was dreary, clammy, but that didn't matter, said Bischoff, she found the city beautiful nevertheless, by which she meant the freedom which she had been loaned for this day. It was pleasant to walk through the streets, to look into the shop windows, to brush past other people, and she agreed with the matron that the view of the buildings with their battlements and cupolas over on the cliff tops of the southern part of the city and of the round medieval towers and the palaces of Riddarholmen was without compare, and part of that beauty was also the anticipation of being able to glean something about the political situation from newspapers. The oblivious friendliness of the police matron, who wanted to give the prisoner a souvenir picture of the city before her deportation, had initially dismayed her, but then she accepted her mix of courtesy and barbarism as a quality that the present moment produced among those who believed they had nothing to do with the upheavals surrounding them. It had in fact seemed to her at times during the three weeks she had spent in custody as if her minder were not capable of imagining what awaited her, a fugitive Communist, in Germany. Then she would be made uneasy again by the discrepancy in the character of this woman, who approached her with an almost helpful demeanor, and at the same time was cooperating with the Gestapo. Perhaps she did have the right to break her word to the police matron—who, though she had taken on the responsibility for returning her to prison, was also willing to hand her over to the enemy—and to use the next available opportunity to escape this mortal danger. She had arrived in Stockholm in late December, had immediately reported to the Red Aid office on Mälartor-

get, and was put up by a Swedish comrade. She had reached Sweden illegally via a circuitous path from the Soviet Union and hoped to then return to Germany to resume her work in the underground. She knew that, by legalizing her presence in the country as a political refugee, her personal information would end up with the German authorities. On the fourth of January, she had given in to the urging of her comrades, who were inexperienced in the conspiratorial struggle, to register herself with the police. Five days later police officers picked her up from her apartment. There are two gentlemen here, they want to speak with you; this sentence, with which her comrade's mother approached her, did not surprise her. She was used to these kinds of encounters. The interrogation began immediately, even before she was taken to the police headquarters. To the question of how she had entered the country, she responded that she had taken the ferry from Copenhagen to Malmö, where she'd chosen the exit for Scandinavians. She didn't mention the fact that during the last three years she had lived in the Soviet Union. Questioned about her entry to Denmark, she responded that she had crossed the border from Schleswig-Holstein. The authorities worked quickly and effectively. After a few days, the police commissioner Söderström had found out that she had worked since nineteen thirty as a stenographer for the Central Committee of the Communist Party, then in the agitprop division, and, from thirty-three, in the secretariat of the illegal Party. This information had been passed on to the German investigators by Lass, a former member of the Communist Youth Association. The interrogations in the remand prison then concentrated on her work during the past five years, but she refused to provide information other than that she had stayed in hiding as an opponent of fascism. She spent the waiting period—already certain that the German agencies had demanded her extradition—in the fortress-like building behind the police station, with its windows barred from the inside, in a spacious, clean cell, which had a fold-up bed, a leather sofa, table and chair, but no washing facilities. Her meals were brought over from a restaurant. She even received malt beer. She was the only political prisoner in the women's section; in the washroom and the common room she only ever came across women who had been arrested for vagrancy, as it was called, for prostitution or for having had abortions. These women were not alien to her, she was happy to have this chance to get an insight into the society which projected such a harmonious appearance to the outside world, she was among fellow travelers, whose hardships within the Swedish welfare state was no less dire than the misery she knew from Berlin. She was thirty-seven years old, politically active since her earliest youth. In nineteen fifteen she had become a member of the Association of the Socialist Working Youth, and then a Communist. Her father, a Social Democrat, had also originally stuck with Luxemburg and Liebknecht but had later rejoined the Social Democratic Party. You lot with your dictatorship of the proletariat, he once said, to which she countered that there were only two dictatorships, that of capital and that of the proletariat, and that she chose the latter. But she owed her political education to him. She remembered how on the fourth of August of nineteen fourteen, as the war bonds were approved, he had wept and said over and over that the workers would resist. He remained active, in the left wing of the Party. While she was still a child, she had learned what house searches and detentions were, had walked through police barriers with a briefcase full of compromising material. When she looked back on her life up to that point, she saw it as being entirely in the service of the Party. This day in Stockholm too entered into an unbreakable chain of commitments. There was no sacrifice for her. The illegal work was a natural consequence of all her earlier activity. She had jobs to carry out, and this took place anonymously, inconspicuously, silently. She had not seen her husband for almost five years. Head of the Junge Volksbühne and the Syndicate for Working Culture, he had been sent to the Wehlheiden penitentiary in Kassel after his arrest in thirty-four. If she considered personal impulses, it might have been the thought of being nearer to him that had contributed to the wish to once again be put to work in Germany. She didn't even carry a photo of her daughter, whom she had left behind in the Soviet Union. She could picture the fourteen-year-old clearly, and she did this with complete calm, knowing that she was safe, in the children's home in Ivanovo. It surprised the matron that her charge looked so normal, not at all how she imagined a revolutionary. Back in the prison she had noticed how the detainee tended to her clothing, her personal hygiene; she had expressed her surprise about the fact that a person who behaved so properly could be a Communist. Communists, so she had heard, were filthy, treacherous, and thieving, a danger to the country. Bischoff had always made an effort to look after her clothes: her blue suit, which she had owned for years and wore often, looked new. But it wasn't just that she knew that unkemptness makes you suspicious; it was also a result of her belief that as a Communist she always had to present herself as exemplary, and that part of that was cleanliness. She was level-headed and attentive because she was aware that, at all times, her fate depended upon how she reacted to any incident. She always had to be training her eyes, had to be able capture what

was happening around her with a single glance. Nothing was without a cause, and she could be afraid of nothing. Suddenly it became impossible to flee again. It was as if she had been tasked with carrying out an educational mission, however small, during her time with the matron. She mustn't let the matron down and confirm her belief that Communists are traitors and liars. They had left behind the city hall, the tower of which sought to conjure up a Venice of the North; they had arrived at Tegelbacken, observed the front pages of the newspaper stands next to Tysta Mari; Bischoff wanted to know what the headlines said, but listened patiently as the matron explained to her how Mari's surname had been Lindström, and how she'd owned an inn at the beginning of the previous century on that street, the one leading to Saint James's Church. She had curly blond hair and was soft, peaceful, and quiet. Then Bischoff asked what was written there about Barcelona; that the assault on Barcelona has begun, said the matron, that the outer suburbs have been seized by Moroccan troops. Bischoff wanted to know more, but to avoid making the matron suspicious she agreed that they should carry out their tour of the city first. The matron bought a newspaper and took it with her, in order to read from it later, when they stopped at a café. Though Bischoff demanded no understanding from the matron for her situation, she well understood her companion. She respected the matron's determination to allow her, the prisoner, to share in something that for the matron was valuable and fascinating. While Bischoff walked along beside her through the streets of the newspaper quarter, past the big windows behind which bands of paper raced through the rollers, she could imagine what this city was for someone who lived and worked here. The matron had a connection with these buildings, these alleys and squares, with all their signs, symbols, and monuments, the city was a component of her life, it contained her own past, and for her it was brimming with history. But if the matron was unable to convey more of this wealth to her than mere general facts, it might have had to do with the sudden feeling that her charge would never be able to make a home here, and that she was actually giving her a farewell tour through the city. In order to relieve herself of the unease, the feeling of shame, she said she was sure it would all turn out for the best, she had also read the letter from the German authorities, in which they gave their assurance that the extradited refugees would receive just treatment. Bischoff had stopped. She sensed only that she couldn't allow herself to be surprised, that she couldn't lose control. She glimpsed past the matron into one of those bare, uninviting, brownish ale houses, numerous in that quarter, in which printers with blackened hands, a few old people, men in shabby clothing, sat at the wooden tables, detached, with vacant expressions, as if in the waiting room of a train station. She would gladly have entered, but her guide would have none of that. On the way to Brunkeberg she spoke of a battle that had been fought there between the Swedish farmers and the Danish occupying troops. There must still be a lot of skeletons and helmets and weapons lying in the earth beneath the buildings, thought Bischoff. The name of the military leader, Sten Sture, didn't ring any bells. The sight of the telephone tower, on the other hand, which rose high above the roofs, and of the vegetable market on the square, brought her closer to the city and made her forget the fleetingness of her visit. The hulking iron construction, with masts encaged in filigree metalwork on the four corners, and below, by the fountain with the wide handles, in the trampled snow, the women at the stands with their faces all wrapped up; to her, this contained something of the matter that made up the character of a city, and she tried to explain it to the matron. The women were stomping in their clunky bast shoes, their faces were ruddy, their breath rose in a fog, they weighed their wares on their handheld scales with small copper weights, placed winter apples, turnips, potatoes, and fresh lettuce from the greenhouse in paper, and above them this metal framework loomed, this emblem of technology which was able to bring together the voices from across the whole world through buzzing wires. She wasn't sure if the matron could follow what she was saying. As they continued walking, she gave her another example to illustrate what she understood as the social fabric of a city. In the prison cell there was no pencil, no writing paper, a form of punishment that breached the rules applying to political prisoners. One day, a couple of builders had been working in front of her window repairing the façade. They had waved at her a few times, had found out why she had been locked up, and when she asked, they had passed her a few sheets of paper and a carpenter's pencil through the ventilation flap. That's how I got this worn out, flat stub of a blue pencil, she said, which the workers let me have, it went without saying, they didn't ask about bureaucratic provisions, I needed the pencil and they gave it to me, out of natural solidarity. The snow was now falling thick and soft, the façade of the castle appeared as a broad and dark reclining mass, with diagonal bastions leading up to it; on the right, the parliament building loomed imperiously; the National Bank was tacked on to the back; that the two colossuses were so deeply enmeshed, embraced each other so intimately, was a perfect reflection of the nature of these institutions. The columned portal to the building had an Egyptian air to it, from which the building that

formed the seat of government broadened into the distance. The chambers of the Council of State were also located in these rows of buildings, which left between them a narrow gorge that extended into the old town. Down below, in the café, under the rows of windows already lit up in the morning, devouring the crumbly, sweet pastries, she was again beset by the thought of how little time she had left. The matron had opened the newspaper. To begin with, there had been an orderly retreat on the Catalonian front. While Tarragona was being evacuated, the Republic had launched a counteroffensive in Brunete. The Italian troops had retreated, and just as gains seemed to be within reach for the Republicans, German reinforcements arrived, tanks, air squadrons. Yes, said the matron, in Paris there were demonstrations demanding the opening of the Pyrenean border, with a cry of *weapons for Spain*. The Socialist International in Brussels had also demanded that the embargo be lifted. But the workers' movement was powerless in the wake of the dispersal of the most recent strikes in Paris, in November. Daladier was able to hold to his blockade policy unchallenged. Chamberlain, having returned from negotiations in Rome and an audience with the Pope, supported him, and also, he has been put forward as a candidate for the Peace Prize. Peace, that meant the pact between fascism, the Falange, the Holy See, and English and French high finance. Bischoff wanted to know more about Barcelona. The matron read aloud that, following heavy bombing raids, the populace was preparing to defend the city, in rain and thick fog. Barricades in the streets, siege conditions in the entire Republican sector. Then came a detailed report on the gala of the Swedish-German Society in the winter garden of the Hotel Royal. Among the more than a thousand attendees, many diplomats and high-ranking officers had been present. They had finished their coffees, they should continue their stroll. They walked along the narrow street through the floating flakes. Now and then cries rang out from the rooftops, a guard stopped the pedestrians, and shovelfuls of snow fell onto the piles at the edges of the alleys. They walked between walls of snow toward the harbor; cranes and the hulls of a few larger ships could be made out in the milky drift. The view won't reach far today, said the matron, but they traveled up in the lift anyway, the roundabout at the sluice sank back down, the crossbeams of the iron tower glided past, at first trams, automobiles, omnibuses were still visible below, a horseman on a raised pedestal with outstretched hand, then, in the flickering, there was nothing but formless shadows moving about. In the narrow cabin, Bischoff was standing right in front of the woman operating the lift; her face was furrowed with deep creases, a woolen scarf wrapped around her head; with clammy fingers polished a leaden gray by the coins, she stuffed the money into her conductor's purse. You have to imagine how the waters and islands open out when the view is clear, said the matron as they reached the drafty gangway. Bischoff listened silently to the matron's attempts to conjure the panorama out of the snow, and the more they were enveloped by blindness the more magnificently the matron wanted the picture of her city to appear before the prisoner. Bischoff thanked her, it was almost as if she were the one who now had to do the consoling, yes, she said, she could picture everything clearly, on the left the arches of the Västerbron, on the right the forested hills of Hammarby, behind the islet with the castle, Djurgården, Ladugårdslandet, the industrial areas around the Värtan strait, Lidingö. When the matron asked about her family, probably only in order to express compassion, in her way, Bischoff grew cautious. It could be, she thought, that this rambling promenade was all in the service of one thing, getting her to open up, getting her talking, for her to reveal something about the things that she had kept from the interrogators. For a second she felt nothing but rage toward her minder. Up here in the snow, there was nobody else around. She could have thrown the police matron over the edge, walked away. She wondered if the bait of freedom had been held out in front of her to beguile her into revealing herself. Had she once again made the mistake of being gullible, just as she had a month ago, when she listened to advice that flew in the face of her better judgment. She still hadn't learned her lesson. Hadn't resisted contact with emigrants during the days before her arrest. She had come to the attention of the police through their chatter, she was certain about that. She had walked into their trap because she had been willing to have a false sense of freedom dangled in front of her for a few hours. A risible idea anyway, that one person could give freedom to another. Freedom was something she had to grab with her own hands. She stood across from the police matron. She was around Bischoff's age, was somewhat taller, more powerful, had light brown, marcelled hair, an oval face, with fine features, a soft gaze, was dressed tastefully, clothes made to measure, came from a good bourgeois family according to all appearances. And yet if her posture betrayed a slight rigidity it was because she was pressing her hand on her shoulder bag, almost as if she were ready to grab for a firearm. But Bischoff had never noticed this capacity for dissimulation during their encounters in the prison. The matron had apologized to her for the light that was left on in her cell at night, and for having to glance through the peephole every now and then because some detainees have, as she explained, attempted or committed suicide. She had also expressed her embarrassment about the prison library, which only contained religious and patriotic writings, had given her, because she was not permitted other reading material, a dictionary, so that she could at least study languages, as if these might be of use to her in anticipation of her deportation. There would be no reunion with loved ones for her in Germany, she said. And at that moment the matron wrapped her arm around Bischoff's; it was impossible to ascertain whether this was a gesture of intimacy or of caution, lest the prisoner make an attempt to throw herself over the railing into the blurring depths. The fact that she was telling herself that such an escape route wasn't an option made Bischoff realize that this possibility must indeed have occurred to her. Then they walked down a steep alley, and on the way back to the prison she confronted the question of what advice the Party might have been able to give her to help her cope with her situation. Would it be viewed as right or wrong that she, only to avoid breaking her word, remained with someone who, despite a few redeeming qualities, was in the service of the enemy. But she had to make the decision herself. She didn't know whether she was once again committing an error, in this country in which hypocrisy could scarcely be distinguished from indifference, in which ignorance formed part of all the inept attempts at washing over and smoothing out, in which political contours melted away. When they reached the prison she was almost relieved, she allowed herself to be led through the halls by the matron, and it was only as the bolt fell shut with a bang behind the cell door that she was seized by despondency at having to assent to this divide, in which one side, struggling until the very last, had to place themselves in chains, while the other, continually capitulating, resided in a sense of security and smug satisfaction. Stretched out on the leather sofa, she heard the footsteps of the matron trailing off. Heard the police officers who, in dealing with her case, compliantly carried out their duties in the section that investigated offences that were directed against the security of the state; and so the matron must have also viewed it as her mission to neutralize anybody who was said to have been a danger to society.

Though it might well have seemed as if all of these maneuvers were being carried out in an undecided, obscure realm, they were actually underpinned by precise plans and agreements, and though things were ambiguous, this ambiguity was a tool that was consciously deployed to keep the regulations as malleable as possible, so they could then be fitted to each arising situation. That the apparatus had to remain unrecognizable **79** was an international rule, this was the precondition of its effectiveness. The person who was identified in police queries and reports on the other side of the border mustn't know anything about the magnitude and progress of the procedure, so that, when the mechanism of the secret service then rained down upon them, they were immediately rendered powerless. The detained refugee had no access to legal representation, they were beyond the law, or rather, they were implicated in a higher, interstate legality which presupposed their total isolation and personal neutralization, and which positioned the interest of the nation alone as decisive. The disenfranchisement of the foreigner was a necessary component of the praxis, for this circumvented the possible question of whether this was someone who had been displaced for political reasons, who could make a claim for asylum that the constitution would have to grant. Around the beginning of thirty-nine it had become evident that the immigration law passed by parliament two years earlier, which did not define the concept of political asylum, instead leaving the decision on whether a new arrival should be accepted or expelled to the individual agencies, fit perfectly with the policy of keeping the country free from undesired immigration and, in the face of the growing numbers of exiles from Germany, Austria, now Czechoslovakia as well, of thwarting any notion that Sweden might be a state of refuge. Those who wanted to stand by the disenfranchised—in addition to representatives of the Communist Party and Red Aid, a number of Social Democrats, as well as liberal-minded members of the bourgeoisie, writers, journalists—had to overcome the entire court system, which presented itself as suprapartisan but which was heavily hamstrung by the edicts that served to maintain the purity of the race and to prevent Bolshevization. It took exceptional courage, great endurance, and impeccable contacts to reach one of those who were in danger and to find out what their situation was. Those who were being detained in prison—meaning that they had already arrived in the country, legally or illegally—represented only a tiny portion of all those who were turned away at the border because they didn't possess an entry visa or because the three-centimeter-high *J* could be seen in red in the left-hand corner of the first page of their passport, a mark whose introduction the Swedish authorities had themselves helped to institute. The press scarcely took notice of this incessant crush, this pleading to be let in, this confrontation between those with homes and those without, between the guardians and protectors of a state and those who had been wrenched from all forms of belonging. The failure to mention the daily tragedy at the border crossings was a reflection of the tactic of not allowing anything of the essential material of our time to penetrate into the fabric of the *folkhemmet*, the people's home. The order of Swedish society remained undisturbed. In this country in which capital governed unhindered, and Social Democracy tended to the equilibrium between the classes, the will to resist had long ago been hollowed out. And where the workers' energy to act had been paralyzed, it was to be expected that the petite bourgeoisie gained influence and were cultivating classes which not only saw themselves as responsible for maintaining the prevailing peace but were also willing to take measures that broke through their usual contentment and contourlessness. It was still almost impossible to detect and identify the urge to exercise violence in the long Swedish night. None of the activities of the authorities could be described as a breach of a liberal, democratic outlook. The arrests and extraditions took place in an orderly manner, there was nothing dubious about the connections with the security police of other states; it was not just Berlin and Vienna that were included in the communications: an exchange of criminological information was also maintained with Paris, London, and New York. Since the conference in Évian in July of thirty-eight, the committee of the Western powers, having been called together to tackle the problem of emigration, had primarily been interested in keeping immigration to their own regions as low as possible or to prevent it altogether. Anybody who entered the country illegally had already committed a crime in doing so, and if the information revealed that they were a Communist, they ended up at the mercy of the collective defense front, which ran right across Europe. Through the tightening of checkpoints and the right to deport afforded by new laws, border guards received powers that allowed them to make discretionary decisions. If there was a suspicion that one of the arrivals did not, as the formulation went, intend to return to their rightful country, the directive was issued not to let them in. The mortal danger that was associated with their return was not taken into consideration. In fulfilling their duties, the officers were given plenty of opportunities to train their eye. Even before they demanded to see a person's papers, they were able to differentiate between the moneyed, acceptable ones with entry visas in hand, and the helpless and impoverished, the expatriated, the hounded Jews, the politically active. Even though there was no sign of a threat of Communist infiltration, and the country's small Party could be kept under strict surveillance, camouflaged beneath this hazy, almost distracted-seeming nonchalance, the protective regulations had the precise ideological objective of expressing respect and deference toward the German Reich **81** without revealing a direct relation of dependence. It was impossible to determine whether the turning away of a refugee or the particularly severe treatment of a detainee was to be traced back to the individual zeal of this or that section chief, or to the directives of the Social Security offices, the Ministry of Justice, or the Foreign Ministry, and who could be declared responsible for the individual cases. If an arrest and its consequences didn't remain entirely under wraps, it was a result of the intervention of that small, always constant circle of people who were in conflict with these cold-blooded decrees, who monitored the events, and who would—often with just hours, minutes to act—make a rescue attempt. Bischoff, called up once again for interrogation, where she was posed questions that she had already answered numerous times, had to set out on one of those feverish campaigns that, with petitions, parliamentary inquiries, letters of guarantee, telephone calls to members of the government, led to either the postponement or prevention of an extradition, or to a sheepish silence after its failure. A tug of war began to emerge between the proponents of jurisprudence, of humanitarian thought, and the representatives of destructiveness; and every time the former were able to record a victory, the opposing side pushed for harsher measures. At times it seemed as if this latter camp, which included many of the top military officials, the majority of the business sector, and numerous figures from academia and public life, was destined to get the upper hand. Month by month it became ever clearer how this coarsening was expanding its sphere of influence. We who had experienced the rise of fascism saw ourselves returned to that creeping, indefinable primary state of being. The terminology transformed, the pronouncements upon persecuted groups grew more ruthless. The rulers hardly needed to concern themselves with recruiting for their *Schutzstaffel* any more; the driving mechanisms of brutalization delivered them their lackeys, and they were mostly drawn from the ranks of those who had previously experienced discrimination and contempt. As the influence and power of chauvinism and reactionary thought grew, so did our desire to encounter signs of an organized defense and to find access to groups that were on the same splintered front as us. What was happening in this country served, it was explained, to maintain calm, order, and national independence. The intolerance shown to the refugees formed part of the diplomacy which hoped to buy them neutrality from the powerful state in the center of Europe. To the outside world, this neutrality presented itself as incorruptible. References were made to the dozens and hundreds of people who had

been let in over the course of the last five years. The argument that the most important task was to maintain this neutrality—an argument that radical politicians also supported—served as cover for all those who had smelled blood and advocated for the propagation of the war against the foreign and anything suspected of being revolutionary. While tens of thousands fled over the French border from the Spanish Republic, and in Barcelona the salvos of the execution squads could be heard, Swedish entrepreneurs were sounding out the conditions for a trade deal with nationalist Spain; leading industrialists had landed in Madrid, evaluating the prospects of imminent business transactions as positive. English and French manufacturers were also looking forward to normalized economic relations. After President Azaña had fled, the Western powers wanted to drive Negrín, who intended to defend the remnants of the Republic, to capitulation, and on the island of Minorca British troops intervened to expedite the Republican defeat. The last troop of returning Swedish volunteers had been welcomed at the Stockholm railway station by members of the Committee for Spain. The address was strained, the song trailed off feebly. The small regiment, accompanied by police officers, moved through the hall that evening, through the throngs of people rushing to the commuter trains, past the fountain with its lions' mouths spouting water and the stone globe of the earth resting on top. The men, their faces haggard, wearing berets, aroused little attention. And had everyone around them discovered that they had fought in the International Brigades, it would have been swallowed up by indifference. And yet a year ago there had been a broad popular movement to support Spain; right into the winter isolated appeals were still being made; but now, with the downfall of the Republic, a paralysis of the will to intervene had taken hold, the oppressive realization that the resistance no longer had any use. Another procession could be seen on the streets of the city a week later, on the sixth of February. Those walking there did not part ways in anonymity. The police were not there to carry out surveillance but were marching at the front. More than five hundred students came, trainee pharmacists, dentists, and doctors in the preppy white caps of their clan, with national flags, with music, placards, banners, and torches. They had set off from the Östermalm square, their destination the public event at the Victoria Hall in Norra Bantorget. They were demanding the immediate cessation of the immigration of foreign doctors, of the importation of intellectual emigrants and Jews. From this day forth, the medical occupations were to be reserved for Swedish graduates. Sweden for the Swedes, they cried in chorus. Crowds of onlookers lined their path. In this country, we had to keep our heads down and look for another underground hideout. We had departed Paris on the day that had come to be known as Kristallnacht. Upon our arrival in Malmö we had to declare on the registration form whether we were of Jewish heritage, on our mother's side or on our father's. We stole into the country under the cover of the Swedish metalworkers' union. Even with our Czechoslovakian passports we resembled stowaways. In Paris I had invoked my father, denied all connections to the Communist Party, kept quiet about my year in Spain. I had been issued a provisional residence and work permit thanks to a recommendation sent by Aschberg to the management of the Alfa Laval works in Stockholm, with the note that, through experience acquired previously in the Berlin branch, I was suited to work in the separator plant. This was the narrowest of all imaginable paths, a shabby path founded on half-truths and hypocrisies, and yet it was the only path available to me. It didn't make me seem trustworthy, and it couldn't guarantee my safety. During my first three months in the country I scarcely left the street where the factory was located, where I had been given a trial as a cleaner and stoker in the tinning workshop and where I had also rented a furnished room, in the building at number thirty-seven. The wide, drafty Fleminggatan sufficed me: it extended straight as an arrow from the bridge leading over the railway grounds on Kungsgatan to the steep slope of Stadshagen. Because my shift began at four in the morning and by the time I headed home after a meal in the canteen, the wintry darkness was already setting in, I saw it mostly by night. It took almost three months for me to overcome the gloom that had descended upon me after leaving Paris. It wasn't just that everything here, unlike in Paris, was dull and muted; I had seen things as we crossed the border into

Sweden that had left a mark on me, and their effects only intensified during the ensuing period. We had arrived in Helsingborg as two Jewish families were being deported, after having made their way to Denmark via arduous paths and then catching the Swedish railway ferry. The derogatory remarks we heard from our travel companions were compounded by later remarks which revealed their contempt for Jews and their scorn for the Communist Party and the Soviet Union. The schism within the workers' movement seemed to run even deeper here than in Germany or France, where, despite tactical divisions, the rudiments of a unity had always been visible. In Sweden, it was as if the leadership of the Social Democratic Party and the Trade Union Federation had eliminated any of the collaboration among workers that we had come to know growing up, or had relegated it to the realm of the unspoken. Their ruthless attitude

had already been demonstrated during the selection of the group that was to travel to Sweden, when a few supposed members of the Communist Party were immediately excluded. Though I had been aware that aid was supposed to be provided only to Social Democratic workers, that I had only been accepted because I didn't belong to a party and because the planning office had learned of my father's position, I was still dismayed by the fact that those who were most at risk were being delivered to their doom by the trade union. This compulsion to one-sided solidarity plagued us upon our arrival on the peninsula, and it was doubly oppressive, as we took our first steps on Swedish soil, that we, just to save our own skins, had to suppress our reactions. First screaming, then moaning desperately, finally falling silent, broken, the two families, the one with a small baby, the other with grandparents and a couple of children, from Bohemia, were forcibly carried back to the ferry, and this at a time when, in Germany, the synagogues were being set alight, the Jewish shops smashed up, the racially condemned hunted through the streets. It was this imposed silence that tormented me in those first months, and it was a silence born not of urgent political duty but rather of petty fear, that the tiniest suspicious utterance could lead to instant dismissal, to being thrown out of the country. I knew I wouldn't have received my papers had I not still been in possession of a valid passport. With the renunciation of all political activity, to which I had had to pledge on my forms, and my admission into the union section demanded by my hosts, I had been neutralized. These limitations, combined with my linguistic difficulties, contributed to the fact that a distance initially separated me and my coworkers in the factory. And yet, as I came to discover, almost half of the six hundred fifty workers were sympathetic to the Communist Party or belonged to it—

and the Communists often reached a majority in the union elections. Always taking care to remain reserved, I made an effort to get to know the workers in my immediate environment and to find out who among them I could trust. Their beliefs could be divined from the tone with which they commented upon political events, above all when it came to questions regarding refugees. If the topic of a successful or an impeded deportation was raised, the entire structure of a struggle otherwise hidden in anonymity became visible, in which the smallest result in favor of those whose freedom could be revoked at any moment, or those who found themselves in the uncertainty of imprisonment, sparked new hope in us. Fleminggatan, by night, in the twilight of the afternoon and on the desolation of Sundays, Fleminggatan, with its funeral parlors, furniture warehouses, pawnbrokers, and meager shopfronts, Fleminggatan, with its blue trams rattling past, brakes screeching, Fleminggatan, with its view onto the King's Bridge square, the market hall, the bare-branched trees on the canal and the distant hills behind the cleft in the houses, Fleminggatan on the way to work and on the way back home, Fleminggatan, seen from the window in my room, up in the fourth floor, opposite Saint Erik Hospital, in the grounds of which, up by the fence, the green barracks for women in labor stood next to the chapel in which the dead were laid out, Fleminggatan, that old, gray industrial street, came to be the epitome of the uniform and the foreign. Only once did I step through the portal with the fanned semicircle of the stained-glass upper window into the plant's administration building, and I was sent back from the grand reception hall to the street and to the entrance to the courtyard, only once did I see the mirrored finish of the mahogany on the walls and the columns from which the ceiling arches sprouted with their coiling plaster ornaments, did I stand at the counter in front of the majestic desks and hand one of the clerks my letter, while virgins looked down upon me, the tips of their nipples protruding from beneath sheer garments, leaning out of their niches onto centrifuges, palm fronds and laurel wreaths in their hands, and then I had no further business in that tower-crowned corner building. It was not the gentlemen at the desks under the scalloped light fixtures who were responsible for me, with their French cuffs, stiff collars, and black suits; it was the workshop engineer who was in charge of hiring workers, in the office off the second courtyard from the gate. This enormous, antiquated factory was like a fortress. The buildings within the square were arranged in a labyrinthine fashion, the narrow courtyards between them, accessed through gateways, were divided up by sheds and connecting wings. I walked along the forking paths between the guard houses with my papers. My letter from the banker, my certificate of employment from Berlin, my stamped passport, my membership card for the metalworkers' trade union, these were all documents that should have filled me with confidence, and yet it was as if I were not presenting myself as labor power but were begging the engineer, whom I ran into in a dark room above the loading ramp, for alms. People were needed on the lathes, in the assembly halls, in the packing section, but I would be considered for a menial job at best. Actually, I was told, the company wasn't hiring any foreigners except in the offices, where relations were maintained with the branches of the corporation in almost every country in the world. Were it to occur as an exception in my case, he said, inspecting my documents with a weary benevolence, it would just be as a trial for the time being. With this, I understood, the wage had been pushed down as low as possible; the engineer knew I could not pass up any offer. I was supposed to receive eighty öre an hour. This was the minimum wage set out in the collective bargaining agreement. That I was classified as an unskilled worker and was once again made into an errand boy, a runner, was to be expected; my father had gone through something similar. The engineer's evasiveness, his provisional acceptance accompanied by the remark that I had first of all to prove my suitability, his imprecise instructions, which left me confused about what I was actually going to be doing, this was all part of a beginning that I knew well enough. I could make myself useful in the tinning workshop, pushing the trolleys full of bars, heating up the smelter; they got me to shovel coal, to fill up and empty the acid vats, jobs for which it was difficult to find local workers. I had always been a foreigner at my workplace, the last to be taken, the first, when necessary, to be let go, but here I was also lacking everything that had formerly balanced out the precarity: researching, studying, and planning with like-minded people had given the day some value, and I couldn't even ask about these things, for it would have betrayed intentions that had no place here. A pressing suffocation could be felt in the courtyards. I was always deep below, surrounded by the blackish-red brick walls, the grimy, brown, plastered façades, in the coal pit near the bulky block of the boiler house, beneath the monstrous smoke stack, on the tracks with the trolleys, in the tangle of gangways, in the low-ceilinged rooms with the acid vats and smelting furnaces. All of the work spaces that we were able to reach faced toward the interior of the compound; barely a ray of light fell through the windows. And yet everything was just as it was supposed to be. The thudding of the steam hammer was there to toughen us. We had to show that we were up to the enduring thunder. The forge in the coal yard was a black grotto, the system of rods and levers, flywheels, pipes, and pylons were patchily lit by light bulbs. The drive belts thrummed, the lathe chisels screeched in the machine halls, the end of which was impossible to make out in the smoke and metal dust. We had to defy the deafening drumming, everything that sought to break us down, in order to find our way to ourselves. To be a worker meant going through the unspeakable wear and tear every day, while somehow maintaining our strength, so as to, someday, when the time came, seize hold of everything. After heating up the crucible at four o'clock in the morning, it took three hours for the tin to melt. During that time, the manufactured centrifuges were carted in and had to be submerged in the tubs of hydrochloric acid to be cleaned. We usually had no time to put on our protective masks. Hampered by the stiff oilskin coats and wearing large gauntlets, we lowered the pieces on chains, the vapors penetrated our lungs like knives. Coughing, our eyes watering, we heaved the smoldering, dripping masses out of the vats and transported them to the tin crucibles, where they had to arrive still damp, plunging into the boiling metal with a hiss. With the constant to and fro, the eternally recurring bending, stretching, the reaching out of hands, many a day passed in a void of thought that was only interrupted by the moments when we stood between the curved tin walls of the toilet, on the threshold to the courtyard above the coal shaft, and, staring into the smoky skies, relieved ourselves. And though there was no communication between me and my comrades beyond a wave, a reference to actions to be performed, a mute compliance, and though it might also have seemed as if nobody had yet discovered anything about my background, an agreement had soon arisen among us that asked after no language or heritage, a bond to one another through the collective dragging, the drudgery we carried out together. I recalled my father's rules, to recognize the necessity in every detail of work, to view no activity as lowly, and, in carrying them out, to never abandon concentration, engagement; and there, even before I was able to progress from my existence as a refugee into the realm of political action, this feeling of solidarity kicked in, drawing its being from the sight of a gesture, a face. Though I might not have received a better wage than the underpaid women in the quality-control section for finished materials, even long-established workers only rarely—by increasing their production rates—reached an hourly wage in excess of one krona thirty-five or fifty, and many were forced to work additional hours as tram conductors, as ushers in cinemas; one even worked Sundays as an attendant at the Skansen nature reserve. As I was waiting for the opportune moment to alter my situation, Selin, the foreman in the tinning workshop, shop steward of the workshop club, approached me. When he asked me to come with him, one Saturday in early February after quitting time, I didn't yet know that he had divined the motivations behind my seeming contentment. He joined me, as if by chance, in front of the factory gate, we walked across the street, up Scheelegatan, he didn't say anything that could have made me suspicious, seemed only to want to speak about typical work issues. Over behind the town hall, between the black trees in the snow, the police headquarters was visible, with its white moldings, balustrades, and balconies, its light-green, ornamental cupolas as if erected from a construction set, and across from the imposing, square town hall tower, topped with a helmet-shaped cupola, lay the fenced-in front garden of a squat, elongated building with its pilastered façade. Narrow paths led along the sides of the towering wall that sealed off the property; on the left, at the steps of the Amaranten, was an inconspicuous café that Selin told me to enter, mentioning casually that a common acquaintance, Rogeby, was awaiting us.

His parents separated in the year of hunger, nineteen seventeen. The seven-year-old ended up with his father, a carpenter in the prison workshop in Karlstad, by Lake Vänern; his two siblings were assigned to their ailing mother. The father resided in a room with a stove in one of the wooden houses on the edge of the city. Because his father's working hours stretched from seven in the morning to seven in the evening, the boy was left to his own devices, except for the hours he spent at elementary school. His father had left a few slices of dry bread for him to gnaw on. The pantry was empty but for a jar of pickled beets. Father won't notice, thought the boy, if I grab a beet. He pushed the table over to the open cupboard, lifted the chair onto it, reached the top shelf, then put everything back in its place. His father discovered the theft that same evening. A few drops of the red vinegary brine had trickled out. The father laid into the boy's head, his behind. His screaming could be heard throughout the neighborhood. Back then, committees were being sent out to investigate the nutritional condition of the children. When they asked him where the bruised spots on his body came from, he said he had fallen from the table. But the real reason came out, the child was taken away from the father and given into the care of a pastor. But here, with his well-off host, he was subjected to attacks that hit him harder than his father's blows. He was used to beatings; they were part of everyday life. It was only with the punishments of the priest that this took on the dimensions of injustice and violence. Once, after a scuffle on the street, the boy had picked up a scarf that had been lying on the ground and shoved it into his schoolbag, to give it back to its owner the following day. The clergyman, who had caught sight of the piece of cloth, didn't believe the boy's explanation. He took him between his knees, clenched him tight. The father was of low status, he was no match for the government agencies. The cleric was authority incarnate. If he said he had stolen the scarf, then the boy had to agree with him. To begin with he wanted to resist, wanted to refuse to make a confession, but the fat knees that enveloped him disgusted him; to get out of this humiliating situation he admitted to the theft that he hadn't committed. Even lower than his father, a foster child who lived from the mercy of others, he atoned once more for the crime of his mere existence. Thrown out of the church home as a liar and a thief, he was handed over to another family to be disciplined. He was beyond help, downtrodden. He was sent up toward Charlottenberg, to Sunne, to peasants who needed cheap help. The river valleys of Värmland, the forests of Finnmark on the Norwegian border, these might have been landscapes full of wide-open spaces, but for him they were realms of bondage. During his years with the cottagers, the question of what it might be like to have his own life grew inside of him. His final foster father, in Karlstorp, on a farm with four cows, a horse, and some poultry, suffered from shingles, yet didn't want to be taken to the hospital, because in the hospital they stab you to death with knives, he said; so he only called quacks, at whose hands he wasted away, stinking, his body disfigured by blisters and boils. He didn't grieve for the farmer, had never been fond of him, but he kept the foster mother in his thoughts. She came from the family of a provost, was an Anabaptist, and at times had shown him kindness. He was also allowed to read the books that she kept in a basket in the attic. *The Count of Monte Cristo*, *Tristan and Isolde*, titles behind which an alien world opened up, but when he thought about what had driven him out into the workplace as a fourteen-year-old, it had not been dreaming but raw necessity. He went from being a serf to a day-laborer with the raftsmen on the river. He had to measure out the lumber, two tape lads worked each shift, one would hold the measuring tape against the lower end of the stump, the other had to walk up to where it had been cut and yell out the measurement, which was added to the list by the scribe, then the piece was rolled into the water to be chained on. He could still hear the cries: *Thirteen foot, thirteen foot heave-ho*. Two kronor twenty-five is what he earned a day; that was a lot for someone who had always been penniless. He grew broad, strong, bought himself tobacco, Tiger brand;

lodging with the trader cost seventy-five öre. This job lasted an entire summer, then he had to look around for work again. I need work, work, that was the pulse that pursued him incessantly. In the forest, felling trees, he hewed into his leg, and thanks to the insurance he received more on sick leave than he had while working. He received three kronor fifty a day and was able to set aside sixty kronor, with which he bought a suit and a pair of shoes, to look for a job in the city. But there was no work for him there, and he didn't want to go back to the country, to the forest. He was too young to get hired on a freighter, but he heard it was possible to apply to the cabin boy corps as a sixteen-year-old—and because for that he needed the permission of his guardian, he had to track down his father once again. His father refused to place his name at the bottom of the letter; the lad threatened to forge his signature; he, the foreman of the car-

penter's workshop, would then be responsible for the shame of his son being sent to prison. Actually he had wanted to talk to the old man, tell him about his experiences, after their separation of almost a decade he had wanted to meet him as a free and independent being. There was nothing left of their family ties; if they had ever existed, they were long forgotten now. And yet his father clung to the role that he had once played, barking and hurling his fists about; but he found himself driven back by his son, had the paper shoved in front of him, the pen pressed into his hand; it wasn't rage that the lad felt, it was more like pity. The prison carpenter had not lost only him: both of the other children had been taken from him; he hadn't found a second wife; and the mother of his children had been living in an asylum for years, delirious. The boy stood waiting; his desire to make it out of this narrow, dull world was so strong that his father was forced to give in. As he left, the boy was unable to turn and face him. That's how the sixteen-year-old made it to Marstrand, on the training ship named after the harbor. In summer, the three-master cruised around in the Kattegat and Skagerrak; in the winter they maintained the battery. Trained as an artillery mechanic and armorer, after two years he ended up at the Stockholm naval base. Alongside his regimented life-style, for ten kronor a month he tried to prepare himself for his high school diploma via correspondence, but at nineteen, having been pro-moted to corporal, he was discharged because Communist flyers had been found in his locker. This was at a time when unemployment was rising in the country, when Sweden was joining the economic crisis, and the deep rift in society that the Social Democratic Party and the bour-geoisie had previously attempted to conceal was becoming evident, a rift that both parties soon sought to paint back over. He didn't have to ask himself in nineteen thirty how he had become a Communist; a singular logic had led him to the Party, a continual experience of the contradiction between the strong and the weak, the powerful and the exploited, an unarticulated drive at first, then a conscious will to resist injustice. The restructurings of finance capital caused that condition referred to as a *depression* to manifest on the global markets, and it was primarily those who were already disempowered who felt its crushing weight. The creation of armies of idle workers was carried out in order to spread demoralization and despondency among the proletariat. With the losses in production, anybody who still dared to strike now and invoke their rights had to expect instant, violent retaliatory action. The clashes of the workers with the strikebreakers, the police, and the military culminated in Ådalen, and there was a direct line connecting the shots fired at the protestors to the intensified persecution of Communists and the closer alignment of the union leadership with the business community that was set down in writing in Saltsjöbaden in December of thirty-eight. Expelled from the Royal Navy with unemployment at thirty percent, he could no longer find work on land. Until the outbreak of the civil war in Spain, he worked at sea as an ordinary seaman and machinist, hired illegally, saw harbors that were identical to one another, read books, from which he always learned something new, began himself to write stories, letters, addressed to people whose names he didn't know, and who lived all over the place, and the writing was just as natural as the manual labor on board, not corresponding to some desire, but to a necessity. When I asked this calm, contemplative fellow traveler, in one of our conversations in Cueva la Potita, what had made him, a country boy from drab villages out in Värmland, set out to sea and become an internationalist, he answered, with a shrug of the shoulders and a smile, that it had probably been the force of historical materialism. When he, having picked up a little German and English on his long sea voyages, told me—back then, in the autumn before the Battle of Teruel—about his childhood, he brought to life not just to me, but also to himself, something of a world which seemed to be marked by shades of medieval damnation. The twenty years that have passed since then, he said, may seem long to me because I have transformed myself fundamentally, but living conditions are still in many respects almost identical, you can still find people there who live as if in primeval times, ruled by ignorance and superstition. I remembered now, sitting across from Rogeby in the café next to the Piper summerhouse, how he had witnessed the death of the farmer who was too scared to go to the doctor, preferring instead to be treated with salves concocted by a witch. I saw the small room before me in which the mother lay in bed with the three children, and the father on the floor beside it, in his work clothes with a jacket rolled up under his head, and then the room he lived in with his father, the one with the open fireplace, the stout, brick chimney, the pile of brushwood, here too they slept in their clothes, which had a sourish smell, the father lay on the kitchen bank, the boy in the compartment underneath, in the narrow coffin. Just as he described to me the table, stained a yellowish brown, the roughly hewn floorboards, the yard outside with the outhouse with the pump that often froze in winter, he was also able to depict the little room in which his foster father would lay into him. The pastor would sit in a tall, carved chair, the pendulum of the grandfather clock moving back and forth, a white, embroidered cloth on the table, the sunlight filtering through the slit in the billowing tulle curtains, and on the wall, Jesus suffering the little children to come unto him. His sympathy and compassion for his father, who had been embittered by constriction and hardship, and for his mother, who had been broken by poverty, were just as strong as the outrage he showed toward the powerful.

At a meeting in the Party office up on Kungsgatan, Selin had got to talking about his team in the workshop and had mentioned the unskilled laborer who was part of the Czechoslovakian group that had been evacuated from Paris. In the autumn of thirty-eight, before the occupation of Bohemia and Moravia, this man had spent time among the International Brigades. He had surreptitiously pointed me out to Rogeby as I exited the factory. Thus, long before he organized our encounter, he had been aware of my origins, and had waited to feel me out, to find out whether I had since made other commitments. During his last few months in Spain, Rogeby had been a reporter for the Party newspaper and was still working in the editorial office now. Yet he and Selin advised me not to make any contact with the Party for the time being. I was not to expose myself to any risks, they said; I had to continue to abstain from any political expression. Right now it was a matter of just keeping my job in the separator plant. Even if, later, when the time was right, tasks were to be assigned to me, my not belonging to the Party would be an advantage anyway. We had left the café, the snow lay atop the roofs, and on the trees in front of the Piperska Muren, icicles hung from the gutters. Through gray, trampled snow we walked beside the bars to the path on the other side. Here, where the steps led up to the new buildings and scaffolding on the blasted Kungsklippan, Rogeby lived at the foot of the steps in an apartment building. From the window of his furnished room you could see the garden building, which, formerly the seat of the Order of Amarante and the Order of Coldin, now housed a restaurant and a venue for private gatherings. In one hall formally dressed gentlemen were dining by candlelight, waiters in livery served the dishes, speeches were given. Those gathered presented themselves publicly, proudly, with brilliant white shirtfronts, while we, like conspirators, were hiding out in this room with its bourgeois furnishings. That evening we turned our minds to the topic that had preoccupied us in Berlin, in Spain, in Paris, and whose relevance had been revitalized by the recent conference of the German Party at an undisclosed location that was referred to as Bern. Bern, the name a nod to Zimmerwald, was this time a house in the middle of nowhere in the South of Paris. As usual, we had to content ourselves with the meeting minutes that had been condensed down to a few directives. The question had been posed of the extent to which an antifascist front was still possible, and of how it might be possible to activate the internal opposition in Germany and to circumvent the system of surveillance and denunciation. After the failure of the Popular Front in France and in Spain, and after the years of rejections on the part of the German Social Democratic leadership, there no longer seemed to be any of the preconditions necessary for joint action by the workers' parties. And yet the resolution spoke of the willingness of the masses to come together and transcend party divisions. The number of people in Germany who were resisting the warmongering, it said, was growing. There was even an estimation that the dissatisfaction among the populace could induce a crisis. But with the call for a coalition among all progressively minded forces, the goal of creating a democratic republic liberated from monopoly capital, and an emphasis on the continuation of the struggle for socialism, the reservations of the Social Democrats were bound to surface. The hope for a return to the traditions of the Weimar Republic did not allow the establishment of a unity party as had been suggested by the Communists. For the Social Democratic Party leadership, it was clear that this unity was intended only to secure hegemony for the Communist Party. The political interests of the Party were more important to the Social Democratic leadership than a last-ditch attempt to form a united front. Only a war, they claimed, could remove the National Socialist dictatorship. They chose catastrophe over the risk of entering into an alliance with the Communist Party in which Social Democracy might come off second-best. The Social Democratic fatalism was matched on the other side by the delusion propounded by the Communists that the German working class would now place their trust in the Soviet Union's commitment to peace. We could only imagine the differences of opinion that must have preceded the resolutions that had been conveyed to us from the outer Parisian suburb of Draveil, and yet we didn't want to view them as the product of wishful thinking but rather as an appeal to the cells in the underground, to buoy their spirits, to show them that the Party was still intact and capable of action. Even in our hideout on Coldinutrappan we were exposed to the threatening clouds that imperialism had cast over all continents. Everywhere, conversations like ours now had to take place, in which the question was addressed of how we, with our limited strength, our decimated groups, could withstand the plans for annihilation. The social antagonism which had always been clearly visible in Germany, said Rogeby, had largely been muted in Sweden over the past few decades by the hope of the realization of the welfare state. Though the older workers still bore within them the experiences of the great strike movements from the turn of the century, and though there had also been violent confrontations around nineteen thirty, the development was always flattened out by the reforms to the working day. Despite an early, prerevolutionary situation in June of nineteen seventeen, the newly founded Left Party, which later became the Communist Party, was never able to gain ground in this country. The workers stuck to the old party that the unions were attached to, and which, since the fight for the right to vote and the eight-hour day, offered them the guarantee of implementing social and economic improvements. Continually riven by splits and fractures, torn between loyalty to the Comintern and the desire to achieve independence, the Communist Party could at most make suggestions, which, though they indirectly promoted a progressive evolution, didn't lead to a continual program through which they could gain access to the populace. Even at the elections of nineteen thirty-eight, when it had become clear what kinds of depredations the ruling class were planning, they weren't able to scrape together a mere four percent of the vote. Over the past three years, many workers had mentioned the events in the Soviet Union as the reason for their mistrust. The economic boom had given them a false sense of security. Criticizing the lack of democracy in the workers' state, they didn't see that they were being robbed of their own force of initiative. Weakened by the times of hardship, once the market became stable they allowed themselves to be brought to heel by the industrialists. They had to be focused on retaining the governing position of the Social Democratic Party, and through this, the expansion of what had been achieved to date. But with the accord between the union leadership and the employers' association a few months earlier, a peace had been produced in which the organizations of the workers and the procurers of labor were described as equal parties, but in which the decision-making power over production remained the preserve of the owners of capital. Under the guise of shared responsibility, economic stability had been won, with the workers abstaining from making use of the means of class struggle. The remains of radical ideology were debased and traded off for a depoliticized popular education. At the round table covered by a lace tablecloth, in the weak glow of the lamp with its parchment shade, we spoke about the continual attempts to portray the intellectuals as a parasitic group and to sever them from the working classes and throw them in with the bourgeoisie. The effect of this manipulation, apparently guided by the intention of foregrounding our autonomy, hampered our ongoing development toward scientific thought. We had been familiar with it since our youth. Particularly the people who grew up in the countryside, said Rogeby, must have seen in educated people a species of human being who wanted to discipline us. The provost, the school teacher, the town doctor, the mayor and the other civil servants, they all belonged to a hierarchy whose upper echelons were out of our reach. In our cramped quarters, our sweaty lodgings, we were left with no alternative but to see the world of art, of literature, as something entirely foreign, hostile. The mere contrast between the modest rooms in which parents and children resided together, and the rectory, the manor, determined the dimensions of our cultural perspective. The longer we remained in our isolation, the more irrefutable the opinion seemed that education only benefited an elite. Only those who made it into the city at a young age, gained access to libraries, and progressed from simple writings to the works of the classics noticed that there was an intellectual form of labor that was related to the manual, that both activities interacted with one another, supported and advanced one another. And if the influence of anti-intellectualism was growing not only among the Social Democrats but also within our own Party, it was because of attempts to censor things, to keep things from us. None of us deny, said Rogeby, that of those who have acquired a formal education and are able to choose an academic career there are many who are only concerned with their own advancement, who don't consider us, who never contemplate our disadvantage; but how could we forget that the majority of people whose ideas have been decisive for our struggle came from their ranks. I don't know what they call themselves, he said, whether they have ever seen themselves as intellectuals. Some came from working families, most from bourgeois households. The only thing that matters is what they made out of their background, the extent to which they have committed their energy to the overthrow of social relations. In examining their works, it becomes apparent which side they are on. The guardians of working culture often say that the intellectuals sit on their high horses, know it all, want to indoctrinate and lead us, while we alone are capable of changing our own circumstances. Such an opinion excludes the idea of an evolution, a maturation, and obstructs the prospect of education one day being made available to all of us. Without this process, it is not possible for the working class to gain an understanding of the tasks that have been bestowed upon them. These do not consist only in contributing to the social and economic transformation of society, but also in participating in a reconception of the means of expression. A reactionary, anti-intellectual streak has crept into our movement. Anybody who disdains erudition and an appreciation of art is opposed to thought. Communist functionaries put up barriers because they are afraid that bourgeois ideology might corrode the revolutionary ethos. Even more damaging is what the leading Social Democrats are doing, for they, entrusted with government posts, have reached a position from which they could promote the expansion of consciousness; they have the workers behind them, could spur them on, provide them with unlimited access to the products of culture. But they are full of fear that intellectual activity, progressive study, awareness of international conflicts, participation in the actual liberation struggle, might break through the barriers they have built up. They may well be for education, but only for education that does not critique the hybrid situation they have manufactured in alliance with the bourgeoisie, this political system and its mixed economy combining remnants of socialism with the capitalist profit motive. Seemingly objective, they stress that, although they have seized the power of the government, the bourgeoisie continues to play the decisive role and that they can therefore only maintain their ongoing efforts at striking a balance. What they fail to mention—but is borne out daily in their actions—is that they have long ago given up their notions of industrial democracy in favor of the capitalist system of production. But for each day that they preserve the country's neutrality, they can point to the rectitude of their actions, and the workers are forced to agree with them. The years of deprivation are still too close for them to want to risk anything they have won. They know what it means to brace themselves for their dismissal every single day. For them, whose lives hang on the calculation of a few öre of their wages, a new conflict situation would be akin to a defeat. We are also concerned, he said, with keeping our country out of the war that everyone is expecting. But while we're at it, we are looking into ways that the war itself might still be avoided. The politicians, instead of doing everything to counter the warmongers, now see the war as unavoidable. They have not made a single effort to motivate the Social Democratic International to form a defensive front. They are waiting, like their friends among the German émigrés, like their friends in France and England. They long ago issued their answer to the appeal from Paris. They underline their position with a demonstration. They have invited Scheidemann to Stockholm, said Rogeby, the liquidator of the November Revolution. Tonight, the seventh of February, he's supposed to hold a talk in the meeting house of the workers' association, with the revealing title "Between Two World Wars." The fact that, right now, at a time when two more German Communists, Drogemuller and Bischoff, had been picked up and were going to be deported, the community of workers upon whom it was incumbent to prevent the militant past of Social Democracy from falling into oblivion is opening its doors to the mummy of the former prime minister—the man who had declared the republic of the counterrevolution—was an open declaration of enmity. And yet, said Selin, we must continue our efforts to establish a dialogue. We are reliant upon the support of Social Democrats like Branting, Ström, Wigforss, Undén. Compact defense, he said, from Police Commissioner Söderström to Foreign Minister Sandler. But the concept of the Popular Front cannot be brushed aside so long as there are a few democrats and humanists left, even if we have to force them to give us a hand every single time. This is a reflection of the situation in which we find ourselves. Thus, at this hour, as it was growing dark and the wet trees in the garden glittered under the light falling from the window, the urging and pleading started up again; perhaps it was already too late, perhaps the prisoners had already been handed over to the officers tasked with their expulsion, and they were already on a train somewhere, or a ship, and while we stared out, and as a toast was made over in the ballroom, it was as if the straining of our senses might allow us to make out the cries for help off on the horizon.

The garden of the comital Piper family had been renowned for its follies and artificial grottoes, its floral landscaping, orangeries, and labyrinths. For the pedestrians on Trädgårdsgatan, which was now called Scheelegatan, the view into the complex was blocked by tall walls. Inside, on the grass surrounding the fountains and sculptures, celebrations were held, the music could be heard, and in the evening, the people could delight in the fireworks. Until the beginning of the previous century an island of flower gardens, country houses, and hunting grounds, a destination for day trips for the residents of the city, Kungsholmen gradually became the domain of tradespeople and manufacturers. Following the belated fall of feudalism, tanners and sail makers, potters and brick burners settled on the banks, and some of their small wooden houses stood for a long time between the growing, mechanized workshops, foundries, armories, and breweries. The chestnut woodlands and rows of lindens lining the boulevards were felled; on the corner of the shore of Lake Mälaren, where the stone bridge leads to Tegelbacken, loomed the steam-powered fire mill—that flagship building of modern industry—and on the leftover parcels of land, barracks and field hospitals had been constructed. As the century drew to a close, tree-lined hills could be seen only here and there, along with the odd grave, some shrubbery in unfenced squares between the

sprawling buildings with billowing chimneys, the long rows of tenements for the workers of the neighborhood. The reserve of the nobility had become a proletarian district; in times of scarcity, the erstwhile island of luxury was called the hillock of hunger. A few garden allotments and plots of land on the edge of the Pipers' property held out the longest, until, in the years leading up to the World War, the town hall and the police station with the remand center were built here, and only one last mill remained standing on the hill behind the Grundberg metalworking plant when it was incorporated into the separator plant around the turn of the century. At that time Fleminggatan was not yet sealed, and the old country road, which bore the name Reparebansgatan, after the rope makers who plied their trade on a long, covered pathway, was furrowed by the wheels of the trucks, churned up by the hooves of the horses; early in the morning and in the evening, the processions of workers would traipse along through the dirt, the mud. Where the street began, beside the Kungsbron, behind the wooden fence, there was still an area where planks were stored, and where the sheds of carpenters, firewood vendors, and junk dealers were located. Below, on the swampy banks of the canal connecting Riddarfjärden with Lake Karlberg and Lake Ulvsunda, barges were moored. Leaning on the windowsill in my room, just before those of us who lived here were overcome by sleep, I was able to gain an insight into something that had been buried during the day; in this moment something like an ability to think emerged, senses began to stir that were capable of taking in the details of the otherwise unremarkable occurrences surrounding me. Fleminggatan was empty, trams traveled past only now and then, no one was on the streets who didn't have some reason to be here, and the people who lived here retired at an early hour. On the right-hand side, the mass of the factory could be made out behind a block of houses with no lights in the windows; the living quarters inside were swollen with a heavy breathing, an ongoing sucking in and expelling of air; in the wheezing constriction, bodies lay shoved together, flaccid, unconscious. And though it might have seemed to me that now, shrugging off my fatigue, I could become clear-sighted, I didn't yet know what to investigate. It had something to do with being transplanted from free movement to a tightly fenced-in area. The European continent, with its wealth of relationships and tasks, had sunk away, and an onerous search for new connections had begun. The path out of direct participation in political events and tussles into the realm of a grinding monotony introduced me to that form of passivity that had always posed the greatest threat to our confidence. The workplace was dominated by the old and expended. Sometimes it seemed as if I had drifted into a kind of illiteracy, in which there was nothing but a dreary immutability, an ongoing standstill, and in which every impulse was seized by an indifference, every approach to contemplation pulverized. Nevertheless, even if it exhausted me more than the physical exertion, this too was instructive for me. I had almost forgotten this condition of self-limitation, against which my father had always struggled and which I had tackled with my comrades in Berlin. My conversation with Rogeby and Selin had reintroduced me to the problem. Earlier, the political tension, the subsumption of our actions into larger contexts had protected us from a downward slide into numbness. Even when we were in the subterranean world of the disempowered, everything that formed a part of our work had been connected to Party-related planning. Now that I was beginning to understand the language of the land, and could take part—albeit deficiently—in discussions, I initially could not understand the separation between practical matters and political consequences. Even the Communists in our workshop dealt only with questions that were of direct interest to the entire workforce. No ideological points of view were brought up, no radical critique of society was made. Later I came to understand that their influence was restricted at that time to negotiations over wages, piece rates, reforms to workplace hygiene, and the like. Working with long-term goals in mind, they were able to gain influence in union affairs. With the small minority that they represented within the workers' movement, it was tactically significant that they had managed to gain strong representation in important industries, in leadership positions in the unions. The demands being made by the Communist Party had to be tactically adapted to the interests of the left wing of the Social Democrats, for it was only with the support of the governing party that they could even partially be realized. When dealing with everyday details left me unsatisfied and the apathy toward international perspectives weighed upon me, I thought about the situation of the workers in Germany. I wondered if, despite being largely the result of decades of making compromises and abandoning revolutionary traditions, this atmosphere of restraint, which often felt like indifference, might actually be an expression of increased durability. The faces of the workers certainly spoke of being involved in a struggle for their rights, but the calm that they brought to this struggle seemed to stem from the conviction that they had strong organizations behind them. The power of their class expressed itself in the power of the unions, and this was a power that limited itself voluntarily. In contrast to the heated thinking that I had come to know in Germany and that had hurled the

workers' movement there into catastrophe, the fundamental attitude of the workers here was a democratic one, they were convinced that conditions could be changed in their favor, gradually, through parliamentary ballots. They would not allow themselves to be dragged into a dictatorship. They preferred negotiation to violent clashes. The sense of justice that prevailed among them caused them to appreciate the achievements of the Communist functionaries. But the sober-mindedness of the workers didn't necessarily justify the stance of the Social Democrats. Much of the conduct of the workers was directed against the upper echelons of their party, and was also at odds with the decrees of the union leadership. They were simply more patient than the workers I had grown up with. Yet on this evening, by the windowsill overlooking Fleminggatan, I was of the opinion that the struggle I had been a part of in Spain, and before that in the clandestine cells in Berlin, must still live on within these workers as well, and must still be able to be retrieved from old experiences. I saw them in front of me, in their apparently reduced capacity for action, not protesting, adapting themselves to uniformity, and I recognized that, under the current conditions, only minor tasks, only miniscule shifts here and there were possible. But it wasn't just this that I was contemplating, with my brow against the windowpane. The plant over there, with the chimney still smoking at night, was a walled colossus; I could see its labyrinths before me, so different from the playful paths in Pipers Park, could imagine how the industries had grown around the wooded hills and patches of meadow and how the business owners were praised for having given the populace work, and the pride of those who viewed themselves as the founders of the wealth of the nation could be read in the gables and towers of the administrative buildings. The poorhouse, the home for the elderly, now an entrance building for the hospital across from it, was covered in ledges and turrets as if embellishing a palace. The growth of the city, the tearing down of the old, the continual process of paving the way for the new, the lingering of a world that now existed only in dreamlike images, and the unquestioned domination of the now, all of this could be reflected upon; but then came the other thing, that which was difficult to fathom, which could only find a place in one's own contemplation. Sitting on the edge of the bed by the window, in the narrow room between the kitchen and the room in which the other tenants were sleeping, next to me a table, a chair, behind me a cockle stove in which a few pieces of wood that I had gathered on the banks of the canal were burning, I saw something develop for which I had no words, and which I wanted to explain to myself. Perhaps it was the sight of the trees that conjured up this emotion. Their bare boughs, the thin tips of the branches stood out clearly against the overcast sky, which was reflecting the reddish light of the city. From root systems reaching out into the earth, these peculiar trunks grew upward and then stretched arms out in all directions. The earth was a sphere rolling through space. I could see a small section of that sphere, with a hospital park, a fence, an empty street. The trees were imbued with growth. Sap seeped upward through the ramifications to the knots in which the germs of the leaves lay hidden. The branches shivered, stirred in the gentle wind. The city was inhabited. From the area in front of the railway station came the muted sounds of the freight trains. Tomorrow, the branches would stretch out toward the light. In a matter of weeks, their buds would open. The trees were palpating the air, the expanse, they were receptive, like the bird that rose up from the shadows, floating upward and disappearing behind the rooftops. Perhaps, I thought, everything on earth, as it rotates in space, is one big hearkening and sensing of countless nerve fibers and tentacles, of the finest materials and organs of all imaginable forms, that all life is merely there to feel and, in continual excitation, to emerge from blindness to understanding. In the end it was nothing more than the silent presence of the trees in the yard—where less than two decades ago the discarded old men, shattered from work, would stagger around among hosts of foundlings and the sudden screams of a woman in labor in the squat barracks beside the house of the dead—which allowed me to perceive the sensitivity of our planet. I wouldn't have been able to say anything more about it; it went no further than a fleeting intimation, this expansive view led only to a thought that, although it then fell once more into oblivion, still offered relief, because it brought an end to a long period of estrangement. I knew that I no longer had to stay alone in the enclosure of the island, that I could venture into the city, and the path that I was now taking into the night was a final tour around a self-imposed isolation. A starting point had been given. When I tried to imagine this period of three months, I perceived it as a sound, as a dull, metallic whirring. Surrounded by this echo I walked down the four flights of stairs; from the two top stories the helmet-like cupola of the town hall was visible through the courtyard windows, sinking step by step; below, along the foot of the wall, mounds of snow lay on the concrete; between the trash cans, the laundry, were sprawling puddles. I walked past the factory. With its corners encased in light-colored bricks and window arches, its ornamental gables, the unlit management building protruded from the long façade of the workshop building that led down to the canal. In the machine rooms, the lights

were burning for the night shift. The humming of the rotary pistons and drive belts could be heard from the steeply sloping path. On the right, behind the fence, was the tangle of shacks and sheds, smelling of damp wood, roofing paper, mold. The water was still frozen, stilts protruded from the surface of the ice, half-collapsed boat houses, warehouses, lop-sided jetties were lined up on the embankments; I climbed over piles of stones and walked along the escarpment beneath the hospital park. At the pier on the other side a mastless brig was moored, a houseboat, but long dead, only the skewed flagpole on the stern still seemed to have tales to tell of voyages on the seas. In the railway yards out the back, accompanied by whistling and spinning signal lights, train carriages were being switched. From a thicket of rangy, knobbly willows, the towering pedestals of the Saint Erik Bridge emerged; up above, a bus zoomed off over the blackness and silence. At the entrance to Kungsholmen, the bridge was flanked by two massive constructions rising out of the cliff-like defense towers; I descended through gorges and arrived at the Kronoberg parklands, which were nestled between tall, perforated crater walls. Surrounded by a cast-iron fence, the old Jewish cemetery—once situated off on its own, near a saltpeter mine down where the forests of Stadshagen began—now formed part of the park, hiding its weathered gravestones behind thick tree trunks. Here and there, a lamp shimmered from one of the holes in the uniform stone façades, scarcely visible paths snaked around the hills and spat me out on the street leading to the prison at the police headquarters. It was mid-February. The attempts to prevent Drögemüller's deportation had failed. He was taken to Mälmo by train and packed onto a ferry to Copenhagen, with the Danish authorities signing for the delivery. The Communist politician Senander had appeared in parliament to speak out against these recent human shipments. The speaker's hammer had struck down the reading of his expulsion papers, in which, according to royal decree, a one-year prison term was threatened upon reentry. Nobody could be found who would have been able to assist Drögemüller. But on this night, in one of the cells, its hatch illuminated, Bischoff was getting ready to move out. In the evening, the head interrogator had asked her what she would say if they let her go. At first she didn't answer, as she thought that the remark, which came out of the blue, was some kind of ruse. But then the decision was repeated: she would be allowed to leave the prison the following morning. Both her reprieve and the sentence that had been handed down to the other prisoner each bore the same lack of feeling that arises where people have total power to decide over life and death. Three weeks earlier, she had been guided through Stockholm by the police matron. She had been left with no doubt that she would **103** never see this city again. Suddenly she had been granted permission to stay. The arbitrariness of the process prevented her from feeling any gratitude. She just asked herself why she had been pardoned while others were being cast out. In her conversation with the officer, the game of hide-and-seek carried on a little longer. She was asked what she intended to do now, as a stateless person. Claim her right to political asylum, as stipulated in international conventions, she said. And to what ends, she was asked, did she want to use said asylum. To work, it didn't matter as what. Political work, asked the superintendent. She was aware, she said, that political activity is forbidden to foreigners. The papers to apply for a residence permit were already lying on the table in front of her. Next to them, a letter with the stamp of the German Federal Police was visible. The letter contained notification of her denaturalization. The officer shoved the forms toward her. She signed everything that had to be signed. She confirmed that she would register her address. As she signed the declaration to abstain from political activities, she thought that her energy for political action had only grown stronger through her experiences over the last few weeks. She didn't ask who had arranged her release. Such questions were not posed in her line of work. The superintendent let on that he was amazed by her lack of expressions of joy. His reaction was marked by the same apparent childishness she had noticed in the matron. She could read no cruelty in his face. It had become her custom to produce a kind of profile of her counterparts at every encounter, and she stored the characteristics she had gathered in this way in an internal register. She memorized the fat lips of the police officer, sagging slightly at the corners, his round, well-nourished cheeks, watery, light-blue eyes and brownish, brushed-back hair, thinned out above the temples. It was a smooth, friendly face, as belonged to those who knew how to protect themselves from the worries and suffering of others, how to carry out anonymously assigned tasks that did not affect their personalities, a face that could serve as a symbol for the neutrality and respectability of the country. So where did she wish to go tomorrow, she was asked, and immediately she answered, to the Red Aid on Mälartorget. She knew there was a candor in which everything could be concealed. A person who lived for illegal, revolutionary work could never appear to be hiding anything.

The collapse began on the fifteenth of March. In the preceding month, which I attempted to view under the banner of mobility and planning, an anxious expectation had set in once more. As it had a year ago in Spain, the calamity that had followed elicited forms of strength in us that we had scarcely imagined existed and that enabled us to face defeat with composure. Breaking out of my isolation, forging relationships with a number of comrades helped to make endurance possible. In the weeks preceding the takeover of Czechoslovakia, I had already approached the metalworkers' union to investigate how I could ascertain my parents' whereabouts, and how their passage to Sweden could be arranged. But neither the unions nor the Refugee Aid nor the Czechoslovakian Family Reunification Service in Stockholm could manage to find out where my parents were; after the German troops marched into Prague, the only remaining hope was that they had been able to escape across the Polish border. At that point a desperate arm wrestle began, between the people making efforts to help those in danger and the ones passing the resolutions who were committed to quashing every intervention. At a time when the need was at its greatest, the unwillingness to offer support also reached its apogee. The more restrictive instructions to the embassies and passport offices had proven successful. With the political refugees having been criminalized and the racially persecuted dismissed as undesirable, there was no reason to expect a rush at the border any more. This applied not only to Sweden but to all as yet unscathed countries in Europe. Just as the German government gave assurances that they would not make any further significant territorial claims, the West could announce that there was no longer a significant refugee problem. Only those who managed to smuggle out capital, who had rich patrons or connections to the upper echelons of industry, or were able to establish themselves as entrepreneurs could expect an exception. The minimal support previously provided by the confederation of trade unions ran dry, not, as officially stated, due to a lack of economic resources but because of a breakdown in communication with the Party leadership in Prague, which meant that reliable information could no longer be gathered about applicants. As the definitive confrontation drew nearer, the universal exclusion of those suspected of being Communists grew more explicit. The half-heartedly commenced negotiations with the League of Nations and in England, along with the initiative of the Nansen Committee in Prague, ultimately meant that a few hundred of the hundreds of thousands of fleeing people would end up in international allocation. In order to keep their own countries unaffected, there was a concerted effort to transport the refugees to Madagascar, British Guiana, Rhodesia, and other far-flung regions, but the only places still available were a few small settlements in Mexico and the Dominican Republic. Since the majority of refugees were of Jewish descent, the Swedish Foreign Minister Sandler gave the conciliatory explanation that their admittance could negatively influence public opinion in the country, and with this he found support from the Jewish community in Stockholm, who wanted nothing to do with their fellow believers from the East, whom they viewed as inferior. Yet something of a desire for justice began to take shape in the populace. It wasn't yet a defined stance, merely the first signs of a general sense of compassion. Individual trade unions—those of the metalworkers, agricultural workers, forestry workers, municipal workers, and typographers—advocated for effective efforts at assistance, while among the representatives of the parliament and the business community, and within the nationalist groups, talk could be heard about the danger of Judaization. With this, the persecution that immediately took on a systematic form in occupied Czechoslovakia extended into the Nordic kingdom, which had made a name for itself for its liberal and progressive attitudes. No broad public debate took place. The measures to shield against the catastrophe on the part of the government and dominating parties had already grown too strong. Only the Communist press and a few liberal newspapers addressed this immense problem, to no avail. On the fifteenth of March, the Western world had revealed its utter bankruptcy. It was not a bankruptcy of falling share prices, however—the activity on the stock markets, especially on the metal markets, was lively—but the dissolution of the last semblance of moral values. They no longer even attempted to cover up their duplicity. According to the official statements from the world of diplomacy, getting involved in the fate of the displaced would only have fostered panic. The only aim was self-preservation. The cry of outrage that hung over Europe was smothered. With the melting snow, the burgeoning spring, we were all enveloped by the reign of death. Just as the Western powers sat by as Czechoslovakia was destroyed, a few days later they looked on as the Spanish Republic fell. They hadn't just contributed to the crushing of both democracies; it was their own handiwork. They kept quiet about the fact that they had given fascism a helping hand, assisted by the neutral governments. Likewise, as reports filtered in about the horrors, the terror in the conquered countries, the statesmen clung to an appearance of normalcy. There was no reason, so they said, to interfere in the affairs of other nations. Reports of torture and deportations were played down as fairy tales. We were forbidden to speak about the events; from Switzerland all the way to Scandinavia, any foreigner who dared to attract the attention of their reluctant hosts by expressing their own opinions was placed in custody or thrown out. Every utterance that could be considered political

was akin to self-incrimination. We were reminded how incredibly lucky we were. We were to replace every stirring of criticism with gratitude. Having slipped through a loophole in the laws of the Swedish state ourselves, we had no right to make accusations about these restrictive measures. We still wanted to view our presence here as a transitional situation. We learned the language, assimilated into working life, shunning the thought that we could ever make a life here. And how, I said to Bischoff, are we then supposed to feel a sense of belonging in this country that lets us know how unwelcome we are at every opportunity. She looked at me with astonishment, said that was irrelevant, since we were only waiting to be put to work elsewhere. She could find no complaint against Sweden, she said, for this country was acting in accordance with a system we had been familiar with for a long time, whose foundations are threatened by the tiniest hint at concessions. Sweden, she said, is for her a small piece of a world that draws its power precisely from the elimination of proletarian internationalism. At the moment, the only thing we can do here is barricade ourselves in our cells, she said, but, in the long run, we will inherit the greater power, for while we are connected to all continents, the West is fractured, their selfishness is testament to nothing but their fear of collapse. What is this ostentatious Europe, she said, compared with the enormous, as yet untapped sections of the earth from which one day a force will grow, in the face of which our miserable present will recede into oblivion. And if this state of perseverance makes us anxious, we should think of what awaits the Soviet state. Everything is now aimed at its annihilation. Even the unspeakable things happening to the people in the countries occupied by fascism failed to unsettle her; for a long time now she had been tied up in this process, which had not even come close to reaching its climax. Sweden seems out of the way, but it is cemented in with the rest of the West, she said, and just as the events in one land bleed into the events and decisions in the other countries, the fate of the peoples of the world is a singular one, indivisible, the torture and murders form part of a universal order, it is not possible for us to single out the lot of any individual. I wouldn't even know whether I could feel sympathy for this or that person were I to hear of their agony, so all-encompassing is the collective pain. Only as a totality, she said, can the misdeeds be tackled, only as a totality can they be remedied. And then, with the seemingly unbearable things we have to bear, there are still those small, inconspicuous actions that also lend something purposeful to our presence in this land that does everything it can to degrade us. With which she meant the hours that she spent going around to the construction sites with the collection box for the Red Aid. She couldn't be accused of politi- cal activity for this, the workers' parties themselves ran this organization, and if she agitated, then she did so inconspicuously, by reminding people about Spain, about those who had been executed in Germany. The workers who gave her donations from their measly wages knew her, with friendly derision they called her the schoolteacher, because during their short breaks she gave them lessons about the history of fascism, and in a form that could not be construed as propaganda by an informant; factual, mixed in with anecdotes that conveyed easily recognizable, everyday situations to her audience. Otherwise, she found work as a cleaning lady, for eighty öre an hour, even mopped floors in the Ministry of Foreign Affairs, dusted off desks there on which important papers were left lying around, until the employment agency's error was discovered and she was immediately dismissed and transferred to private houses to sweep and scrub. As she recounted this event to me, she emphasized that quality which she had already identified in the appearance of the police matron and which, amid all the disrespect that had been meted out to her, presented itself as a kind of innocence of being. This elicited a conflict in her, she said, resulting from the fact that although she sees her adversaries as shaped by their upbringing, she also detests them as stooges of the rulers. With the domestic servants and menials, she explained, she was always searching for signs that would indicate something of the consciousness of their oppression, and often, standing in front of a person who had just hurled the most vulgar abuse at her, she would catch herself wondering how they could be won over. In which other European country, Bischoff said, laughing, would it be possible to put a political refugee, released from prison, to work cleaning rooms in the Ministry of Foreign

Affairs, and what's more, rooms in which the shelves were filled with books in Russian, including Lenin's *Collected Works*—and she didn't even believe it was some kind of trick in order to catch her spying. Rather, she said, it spoke to a fundamental naiveté, to a lack of talent for intrigue, which, supplemented by the manifold support of comrades, might one day lead to the production of an image of this country that would counter the oppressive one handed down from the era of its genesis. From my very first encounter with her in the immigration office of the social welfare agency on Riddarholmen, where the emigrants would arrive with fearful looks and cowed shoulders, she had exuded an immediate straightforwardness that seemed to imply that the hassle of filling out forms and getting documents stamped couldn't get to her at all. It was almost with curiosity, with a certain pleasure, that she had stepped into the long, wooden shed, which was located below a palace from Sweden's epoch as a great power, with which it was connected by a gangway. This shack, with its cramped, musty waiting room and the counters where we were processed, resembled the quickly cobbled-together buildings that were familiar to us from border-crossing stations and detention camps and that—from its smeared blotting paper to the potbelly stove—conformed with the meagerness and makeshift nature of our living situation. The imposing buildings from the sixteenth and seventeenth centuries—which, with their noble façades, their courtyards, and round towers, lined the island and encircled the church of Gustav Vasa—accentuated the architectural style of the buildings intended for the homeless. This was the age of the wooden sheds in which people were herded together in order to be added to lists and sent on to be fed, to the refuge, to be interned or liquidated. And high above us, the windows were left open to let in the light which, reflecting off the waters of the Mälaren, fell into the exquisitely decorated rooms in which the Sparres, Bondes, and Wrangels, the Rosenhanes, Hessensteins, Stenbecks, and Oxenstiernas had once had their seat. We could take solace, said Bischoff, in the fact that, earlier, there had been only goats grazing around an abbey of the Gray Friars here; and she made this remark with a glance at the trail of miserable figures edging over from Munkbron. In addition to Bischoff, I had recognized Lindner, who had worked as a nurse at La Brévière, that haunted home in the forest of Compiègne. We had both lost our citizenship by this point, and she too was here to pick up her alien's passport. Bischoff was living at her place on Hägerstenvägen, in Aspudden, a suburb in the south of the city where scores of foreigners had found cheap accommodation; her room with kitchenette cost fifty-six kronor a month. Lindner too, a former member of the Young Communist League and the Red Students' League whose father had disappeared in thirty-three while imprisoned, and whose husband had fallen in April of thirty-eight on the Ebro, cleaned apartments for an hourly wage. It was not until we had left the office that we began to speak to each other. That we only exchanged a brief greeting upon recognizing each other among strangers and then arranged to wait for each other outside with a wave had become a rule for each of us. Lindner and Bischoff had gone ahead, I could see them at the end of the path to the quay, clerks from the government offices that were accommodated in the island's stately houses were sitting on the benches and the stone steps by the water, the midday sun was giving off warmth, people were consuming their packed snacks, dockworkers were also taking their breaks here beside the cargo which was to be loaded onto the steamers of the Mälaren. From the square where we sat down next to one another as if by chance, on the opposite side of the fjord we could see the long, southern quay, which ran from the sluice to the Västerbron. The yellow and ochre-colored buildings of the old town jostled up the slope, nested into one another, the trenches of the stairways, alleys, and forecourts lay deep in shadow, a forest of chimneys grew out of the glistening roofs, towered over by a castle-like building with a tall turret. Further to the right, workshops, squat red wooden houses, warehouses, and production plants ran alongside craggy cliff faces. A few freight cars stood on the path by the banks; slowly, a small locomotive rolled past, expelling bulbous clouds of steam; the cranes were lifting sand, gravel, slabs of stone from Gotland off the barges and loading them into piles. The aliens' passports we had received afforded the women an income as domestic servants, me work as a metalworker; every three months, after renewed evaluation of our behavior, we could apply for an extension. Czechoslovakia, Spain had fallen, the Germans now had their sights on the Memel Territory, Danzig, Poland, and we were sitting in the March sun, our fatigue after the work-day, begun at four in the morning, was evaporating, the ringing in our ears also dissipating, the bright, expansive view onto the water calmed us, our kin were dead or disappeared, yet we were enveloped by something like a feeling of security. At this first meeting, Bischoff had said it had to be a mark of our weakness if we thought we could find nothing here but a hand-ful of like-minded comrades; we should be making an effort to extract more from the situation. To begin with, she too could see nothing but ambiguous events; it seemed to her as if something were always being covered up here. I never knew, she said, whether some kind of scam was being cooked up behind the curtains or if a harmless rearranging was taking place; but then I thought that this haziness had to be related to my ignorance of the country and its customs and mores. Perhaps the only people we could trust now were those with whom we stood in a collective struggle, but the noises from the harbor and the shipyard all the way over on Pålsundet and the peaceful activities surrounding us made it impossible for us to believe that someone could harbor malicious intentions toward us; the government agencies and offices were the same all over; sure, they wanted to make us their slaves, but the world of work was infinitely more expansive, and one we were familiar with. Yet it was precisely the peacefulness, the tranquility of the image with which we were faced here, that made us think of the severity and peril that accompanied our existence. How, we asked ourselves, could the day proceed so uninterrupted, with all the treachery that had descended upon Europe; and we

110   could only explain this naiveté to ourselves by postulating that the dimensions of the horror were too great to be grasped. And it was precisely in people's inability to imagine their own obliteration that fascism found its precondition. Within an immediate context every individual can imagine defending themselves, but what lay beyond the discontent about the deformity that pressed upon us was no longer conceivable; the moment we made an approach toward everyday rebellion, we ran up against the first impenetrable bastions, and from there, increasingly sealed off, the branches of iniquity extended outward. How was an individual at their workbench, at their stall, supposed to sense something of the murderous lust of those who had emerged from the typical regimes, how should they, held hostage by their worries, grasp something of the phantasms dreamt up by the despots. Thus, inexorably, the poison from the realm of depravity and the greed for profit seeped into every group, syndicate, and organization, dissolved their ties, their mutual relationships, undermined the integrity of their representatives, and this development was able to proceed so successfully because the soil in which it now grew had been fertilized for years. A beautiful, clear day at the end of May, with gulls over the water, twenty years after the end of the war of our fathers, twenty years of misfired efforts at transforming society, and we were sitting on the harbor wall, no different from the gullible, the betrayed people around us, like countless others we had attempted to improve the situation with subtle interventions, and like everyone else we had failed. Even the final line of defense upon which we had still pinned hope, the workers in France, had been defeated. Lindner told us about the days in Paris, in late November, early December, as the general strike that had erupted was crushed. She shielded her eyes from the glaring light as she conjured up what she had seen, the scattered crowds fleeing through the salvos, the truncheons raining down, the wounded and dead on the pavement, those who had been seized being tossed into police wagons, the tattered red flags, the gloating headlines of the newspapers. The notion of the Popular Front no longer existed, the right to strike no longer existed, the right to assembly had been dissolved, wrath could no longer rise up, only a shivering, a powerless groaning remained. Bischoff had put her arm around Lindner's shoulder. Those animals, she said, will not prevail.

The two hacked-off heads lay on the crumpled, gray-white, blood-stained cloth. Cushions, shoved under the sheet, were propping them up. Were the rough-cut cross sections of their throats and the watery trickles of blood not visible, they could have conveyed the impression of a couple who had been surprised by death while lying beside one another in their bed. The picture was painted with black and white and a minimal addition of brownish and reddish hues. The woman's visage was tilted toward the man. Her mouth was slightly open; between the eyelids, ringed in shadow, a point of the white of her eye glistened. Oddly bare, her ear protruded from her hair, cropped short for the guillotine. The face of the man, with the hint of a beard across his collapsed cheeks, was still marked by terror. His eyes were open, clouded and skewed, sunken deep in their sockets; his mouth was also ajar: the gaping lips, the teeth, the tongue still seemed to carry their final cry. They must have dragged him to the guillotine; the woman had given up sooner. It would have been disrespectful to compare the extinguished quality on her face with a sort of peacefulness; for how, even after the arrival of her eternal rest, could the thought of peace be connected with her existence. And yet her features—a faint glow on the temple, cheekbone, nose, and chin—contained a softness, her head lay there like an overly ripe, fallen piece of fruit. The man had been ripped from his existence. The chin muscles, the sharply bulging nose, and the crudely dimpled contour of the bare skull still expressed an energetic tension. If the woman had been completely divested of power, he had violently resisted for as long as there had been a breath left in him. The painting was hung on the wall of a small side room in the National Museum. Through a window, my gaze fell over the stream and onto the castle and the wide street leading up to the obelisk. Traffic flowed back and forth on the Skeppsbron. As I turned back to the small canvas, the agony captured there grew more piercing. Once more I was face-to-face with Géricault. On this Sunday, in the first days of May, half a year after my arrival in Stockholm, Paris rose up within me, overwhelming.

Once again I was following Géricault, into Beaujon Hospital in the suburb of Roule, into the Salpêtrière, into the morgue, where his study of the definitive had taken him. The fascination that death had exerted upon him mirrored his desire to confront the moment in which everything is over. I began to understand why he craved such a counterbalance to his activity. In doing so, he put his desire for truth to the test. His work had to withstand the final moment, the irrevocable. At the sight of these corpses, every remnant of vanity and self-deception in him withered away. I had walked along the narrow path at the foot of the retaining wall between Pont Saint-Michel and the Petit Pont. There, where the blocky building of the morgue had been located, overlooking the quay, next to a steep set of stairs leading up from the embankment, the great palace of the police prefecture now loomed, on the Quai du Marché-Neuf. In Géri-

cault's time, the Petit Pont was still nestled between two tall defensive walls, and from the bridge, which rested on arches of great ashlar blocks, a gate led into the throng of tall and slender buildings over which the cathedral towered. In one of his most remarkable prints, Meryon had captured the old mortuary, the former abattoir on the market. He too had been drawn to this building, because its cold interior contained the ter- rifying antithesis to the vision of civilization of which the city boasted. He had lifted the quarter on the front edge of which the mortuary house stood out of its surroundings and depicted it as a sealed world. Black smoke billowed from the two smokestacks of the mortuary house, as if, inside, in the ovens, rags, damp clothing, perhaps also decomposed body parts, bodies were being incinerated. A strip of the Seine was visible on the bottom edge of the sheet. One of the long, flat laundry boats was sit- ting moored at the embankment. Women were leaning over the railing, rinsing and wringing out towels; shirts and sheets were hung up to dry under the slanted wooden roof. The barge, with a ladder running along the side of the vessel, and with poles and ropes on the deck, filled the entire width of the water's edge; on board, people were working, unperturbed by the events unfolding directly above them. On the left, behind the boat, on the corner of the embankment, steps rose up out of the water. From this point, the scene of the salvaging of the dead body began to take form, with its intermeshing movements and gestures signaling their continued upward procession. The drowned man had been hauled out of the river in which the women were washing their laundry, was now lying face-up in the arms of the two people carrying him. Standing in front of the group was a thin woman in a long gown, her hair out, arched so far back in de- spair that her spine almost formed a right angle, her hands thrust over her face, a child behind her like a small tree swept bare of leaves. The constable, with rapier and tricorne, was showing the way from the stony bank, above the drainpipe of a sewer, to the steps in the middle of the wall. A couple of other women, rushing down the steps, were being held back by a guard. On the left, the brightly lit surface of the wall past which the dead man was being carried, his hands scraping along the ground; on the right, on the squat substructure, the morgue with its deep-set windows half-covered by thick, protruding shutters. A kinked drainpipe led down from the roof to the cobblestones of the path along the embankment, with tufts of grass growing in the cracks. Below the mass of the houses stacked up in the background, which dominated the upper section of the image, and the broad, vertically divided mid-section of the wall, the small figures were almost lost in the left-hand corner, having just emerged from the hard shadow. Onlookers were sitting, crouching and standing on the ledge of the wall, some of them leaning on the edge, they were gathered together casually, as on the balcony of a theater, while curious gawkers were propped on the railings of distant windows. Distributed across various levels, water, barge, embankment, wall, building façades, plumes of smoke, attics, an event unfurled that at first glance seemed to fit into a typical cityscape, and only gradually revealed its complicated drama. The workers, sealed off in the elongated cavity of the ship's hull, were facing forward, the path along the embankment was the stage for the actors in a pantomime. Passers-by and street vendors had come down to the wall of the quay from the market stands with the curiosity that accidents arouse. Yet only a few of them expressed surprise, sympathy; the others were indifferently taking in the free show, which was probably an everyday occurrence. The marketplace was hidden behind the height of the wall. The cloud of smoke from one of the chimneys, blown sideways, hung above it; the houses must have been continuously blanketed by the acrid stench. From the thick chimney on the right, the smoke ascended to the jumble of rooftops, which, on the upper edge of the sheet, revealed a stippled section of sky fluttering with crows. Among all this, the main subject, the morgue, stood there abandoned, as if it had nothing to do with the motivation for creating the image. It could just as well have been some sprawling warehouse; barge poles were leaning against the basement wall, arranged around an anchor; a rope was fastened to the wall with pieces of sailcloth hanging from it. Both Meryon and Géricault knew what it looked like inside. In a moment, the dead man would be lying on one of the stone tables in the hall among other perished souls, among nameless suicides, people who had starved to death, fallen victim to drugs, been executed; and then the people would step back from the wall, commerce would continue. Heavy, oblique shadows, bright sections of façades with square window openings, horizontal and vertical lines, between them tiny figures, a dead man, a broken woman, a helpless child, a precisely framed cityscape, a view into a limbo that had to be entered by those who sought to walk the path of knowledge. I had spent a long time thinking about Meryon's engraving; unable to get my hands on a reproduction, I had even sketched it. On Sunday afternoon, in my room on Fleminggatan, I sat over this paper that I had produced in Paris, tried to call to mind a conversation about the second and third cantos of the *Inferno*, from long ago. The absence of my close friends Coppi and Heilmann had formed part of the desolation of the past months. I could also now find the time that I needed to come to myself, I could always skim off a few hours from the wear and tear of the day. It was just that earlier we had been so in tune with each other in our group that everything we uttered was immediately expanded upon by one of the others, every question had led to answers and follow-up questions on which we honed our thinking. Alone with my thoughts, I was often overcome by despondency. I tried to imagine Heilmann's voice declaiming the verses of terza rima. I could see his face, the movement of his lips. Yet what I heard remained fuzzy, could not be brought into alignment with my thoughts. I experienced something of that which we had anticipated in our discussions back at the cemetery of the Saint Hedwig parish, namely, the instant in which, despite having already made resolutions and begun activities, we had to hesitate and start over. That had been on that dark slope, at the spot where the steep, rough path drops away. I had paused there with Heilmann and Coppi, had also encountered Ayschmann, Géricault, and Meryon there. This was the state of realizing that we had strayed from the straight path, whatever the straight path was, as if something like that ever even existed for us. We only knew that there was no possibility of return and that we had to liberate ourselves from our fear of continuing on. I called out to Heilmann and Coppi through the open window overlooking the hospital grounds, which were beginning to grow verdant. Among the blossoming bushes, a pregnant woman was pacing to and fro. The driver of a tram that was rolling past stepped on his pedal-operated bell at a person hurrying across the tracks. How did it go again, I yelled, how did it go, when the speaker had entered the city from which the path spiraled down into the underworld. And then I heard something of the torrent of noises which, captured in just a few verses, contained all forsakenness, all exile. Back in Paris this tintinnabulation had pursued me, though I had been unable to determine its origin; now, above the budding trees, I was able to distinguish the individual elements in the eddy of sounds drifting through the air. From the jangling of the iron wheels, the fading of the bell, the rattling of the car engines, the hard thudding of the steps, a sigh, a single cry of lament was released, and was joined by many identical voices; a scraping and grazing emerged, as in a crowd of people scuffing about endlessly, I could hear the lips opening, tongues stirring, teeth grinding and chattering, words in all languages sought to emerge from the murmur of voices, a whistle, a clapping of hands, a cry of pain, of rage, cut through the stammering, whispering, and singing. In this way, those who had been cast out moved forward like shadows, toward the border river, the Acheron, which a ferryman would take us across, a man so awful in appearance that we'd have swooned on the spot. Yet I didn't sink to the ground, as if overcome by sleep, but rather hurtled down the steps, inside the screw thread of the stairwell, whose mother-of-pearl coloring was shot through with a network of thin cracks containing scattered holes and deeply scratched streaks. Descending from landing to landing, I saw the roofs of the courtyard buildings growing upward, covering the tower of the town hall, I walked along Fleminggatan, past the bicycle workshop, the coal vendor, the shop windows full of urns and coffins, the gray-green beer hall with people sitting motionlessly at stained tables, past the factory, the wooden fence, and onto the Kungsbron above the broad expanse of the railway tracks and the forest of railway cable poles. At this late afternoon hour, the sun shone directly into Kungsgatan; behind me, from the dark blocks at the end of the street, the tower of the town hall rose up once more, backlit, as if made of translucent fabric. On the sides of the main street, the pedestrians trailed back and forth, with their long shadows, washing past one another in streams; here and there waves and eddies formed, stagnated, twisted and turned, and in the middle, in opposing directions, the glistening automobiles glided along, between them the trams whose front carriages shot blinding reflections, one of them bearing a number two, the other an eleven, in their round, cyclopean eyes. Through the flowing, swirling Sunday throngs, I walked down the Kungsgatan beneath protruding signs, leaning to the side, tracing arches through the sunlit bodies that collected in front of the shop windows. In the vitrines, the inimitably sophisticated gentlemen were displaying casual trousers, sports jackets, fleecy tops, brightly colored neckties, lightweight shoes and sandals, raincoats, felt hats and peaked caps that they were planning to wear in summer, while ladies, also made of plastic, writhing ecstatically, smiling seductively, touted their suits and silk blouses, their light underwear, floral bathing attire, and their headdresses made of petals and foam; and I walked across Sveavägen to the office building on the corner, where Hodann had been quartered in the cellar since his arrival from Norway.

Three floors below street level in a cramped, stiflingly warm room, he was lying on an oilcloth sofa, his hands clasped beneath his head. Shelves full of files and medical preparations extended up to the pipes running along the ceiling, one wall was filled with cages in which rabbits were sniffing and scratching. At the basin, a woman was preparing coffee with laboratory equipment on an electric hot plate. He had not received a license to practice medicine in Sweden. He had been taken on by his colleague Ottesen-Jensen, whom he had known since his time in Berlin and whose sexology institute was located upstairs in the same building, to help her with patient consultations. As the woman, a refugee from Prague who had accompanied him from Oslo, poured the boiling water through the packed filter in the glass funnel, for a few moments, the aroma of the coffee shrouded the acrid odor of the rabbits, which were undergoing pregnancy tests and other examinations. This thing I'm lying on, said Hodann, reaching his hand out toward me, is our marital bed. The woman lifted his head a little, poured the drink into his mouth from a retort. He feigned contentment with a throaty hiss. The plan is, he said with a laugh, that I use my not inconsiderable experience to secretly build up a correspondence service, in violation of the decree from the Swedish medical association. The woman had walked over to a tall, metallic stool, where she sat motionless, alert. The whisper of the rabbits was emanating from the cages; they were pressing their rosy nostrils against the bars, their ears twitching, incisors glinting, holding little parcels of dried grass in their paws. The thing with Münzenberg, he said, propping himself up with his arms, was that his relationship with the Party had become untenable due to his ongoing clashes with Abusch, Eisler, and Dahlem. Pieck, Dimitrov, and Manuilsky had initially been favorably disposed toward him, while Ulbricht's group in Moscow was working against him. Dogmatism, jealousy on the part of the exiled leaders. Eisler published the newspaper of the Central Committee, *Die Internationale* [The International]. Abusch was editor-in-chief of the *Rote Fahne* [Red Flag]. The newspapers were smuggled into Germany in order to convey the positions of the Party to the underground cells. For them, Münzenberg was the great rival. He had reproached them for overestimating the strength of the German working class. He didn't believe that the masses would topple the fascist dictatorship of their own accord. You still haven't learned anything from the errors of judgment from before thirty-three, Münzenberg would tell them. For this he was accused of Trotskyism, because, back then, Trotsky had been the only one to recognize the magnitude of the danger. They set about falsifying Münzenberg's past. Having procured money for the Party like no other, he was declared an ally of capitalism. While the tactic of the Popular Front was being pursued, they tried to blame him for their setbacks, because he, with his adherence to the united proletarian front, was driving away the Social Democrats. And yet there was no one in the Party who would have been better positioned to attract and unite representatives from all strata. Münzenberg had urged them to establish a propaganda apparatus that could compete with that of Goebbels. He was overestimating fascism, he was told. By losing faith in the proletariat, he was assuming a petit-bourgeois standpoint. The arguments that were hurled at him were contradictory, confused, irrational. Time and again he warned against placing faith in the German workers' capacities for struggle. It was clear that the actions of the workers were not founded upon class consciousness but were rather the result of propagandistic influences. Means had to be found to break the dullness and stubbornness, the reactionary poisoning that had been promoted in the people to prepare them for participation in the war. He believed he was capable of opening their eyes. He was accused of arrogance, of having designs on a leadership role. That was what mattered, the maintenance of the coterie favored by the Soviets. In their quest for survival, this group destroyed all who proposed a divergent opinion. You know, Hodann said to me, how we clung to the protection of the Soviet Union, knowing that without them we'd never be able to defeat fascism. To this day, Münzenberg has never allowed himself to stoop to anti-Soviet rhetoric, even though he has been subjected to the same condemnation that has been handed down to his comrades. His staunchest opponent in Paris was Dahlem, who gave him the ultimatum, late in the summer of thirty-eight, of either apologizing or being expelled. Münzenberg did not return compliantly to Moscow, like Bukharin, handing himself over to the Control Commission. He'd been under continual surveillance ever since. His post was intercepted. His previous colleagues were poisoned against him. Wehner was cold toward him, wary. He was ambitious, thirty-two years old. Ascending through the ranks was only possible through constant vigilance. He was the most silent of all. Katz too refused to fall in line. They tried to convince him that he was the one who had actually given these ideas to Münzenberg. Katz was too smart to believe that; he was all too familiar with Münzenberg's achievements over the last two decades. But how strong does one have to be, said Hodann, sitting up, to withstand the systematic manipulation of the Party. And I saw that, in Hodann too, that which had begun to take form in Paris had now reached its fruition. I understood Katz, he said. In the end, he could either make a declaration of loyalty or get a bullet in the back of the skull. Münzenberg's life, said Hodann, is in danger. Renegades had been murdered abroad. No reason to expect him to be spared. And now, he said, on the tenth of March, he had published an open letter in his newspaper announcing that he was leaving the Party. And as Hodann quoted Münzenberg, I could see him standing in front of me, stooped forward, his left hand laid flat on the tabletop, right hand raised, writing in the air with his finger, broad and powerful, his Thuringian dialect mixing with Hodann's Berliner intonations. Hodann

adopted Münzenberg's explanation. My experiences over the past two years, he said, have convinced me that it is impossible to clarify and settle political differences of opinion within the Party in its current form. My conflict with the leadership can be traced back to issues relating to the Party program, the propaganda methods, the internal democracy of the Party, and of the conception of the relation of the Party to the individual members. We were all in agreement about the principle of democratic centralism, about the defense of the rights of all minorities and all loyal critique, about the autonomy of the different Party organizations, about the recognition of the right to elect and dismiss all representatives, to hold them accountable for their actions. Not until we find our way back to these principles can the correct relationship between the Party and its members be reconstructed. The Party is made up of the sum of all its individual members. The impending revolutionary war can only be won by individuals whose discipline is voluntary, not drummed in through regimentation and commands. Not the apparatus but the members—the individual man, the individual woman, the politically thinking human being, the growing, creative individual—they are the Party. If the many cannot be convinced that the strategy and tactics employed by the leadership are correct, then every attempt to instill discipline is doomed to remain a grotesque tale, a fiction. It is we who invented the Party, and who continue to do so; we are the Party, not the idol up there, the wrathful God, who presumes the right to determine our fate. I have separated myself from the leadership, from their apparatus, said Münzenberg, but not from the thousands who have been unjustly pushed out by anonymous forces, without due process, with no chance to defend themselves. Hodann bent forward, brushed his hand across his face. The woman jumped up from her seat, stood ready to hold Hodann, attempted to prevent him from continuing his discourse. Münzenberg, he said, had no intentions of renouncing the Soviet Union, nor of founding his own faction within the Party or confining his activity to a particular group; he will carry on working to create a large, all-encompassing unity party. But what was this voice now worth, I asked myself, as Hodann lay down, this isolated voice in Paris, with no organization behind it, which would never manage to divert the Party from its course, a voice that, regardless of how stubbornly it might express a conviction, could ultimately only speak of its isolation. Nevertheless I agreed with him. I could only judge him as I had gotten to know him. I had heard dubious things about him, but I imagined that his perspective had been too broad to be reconciled with his comrades' narrower thinking, which was founded upon an absolute adherence to centralist decrees. The position he expounded was mean- ingless in the face of the opinion of those with more power. This group had to maintain the Party in the face of existential threats. Whether he was selfish, or smug, as he was accused of being, I couldn't judge; I also didn't know if his nearest colleagues were simply careerists, as he would often claim. There had to be explanations for the situation somewhere. It's just that they would remain locked up, forever inaccessible. For me, all of this had to recede into the background. I could not yet say anything about my own possibilities, could not yet prove that I possessed the aptitude for illegal political work; the only thing that I knew for sure was that, without my participation in the political struggle, there would be no future for me either. A few weeks ago, Rogeby had arranged for me to meet with Mewis. He had left his lodgings in Malmö for a few days to come to Stockholm. In the afternoon, we walked across the fields of Ladugård, on the edge of the functionalist neighborhood of Gärdet, which was still under construction. Actually, the only thing that came out of the meeting was the suggestion that later, perhaps in late summer, I might be put to use procuring materials for a newspaper that was being planned. The rest of the casual remarks resulted only in impulses, which didn't began to sink in until a few days later, reigniting a sense of the enormous insulation and confinement of working in the political underground. As in our encounter at Villa Candida, I was set upon by a greenish, blueish gaze and a handful of questions; once again Mewis seemed like a stranger to me, utterly different from people like Hodann, Münzenberg, who revealed their personal character. Sitting behind Hodann, who was breathing heavily to combat an oncoming cramp, I thought about the hidden, conspiratorial world in which, every six weeks, carefully planned trips from Trelleborg to Sassnitz took place, with counterfeit Swedish passports, trips on which instructors visited their contacts in Berlin, Hamburg, Bremen, cities in which the cells inside the industries, the mass organizations, the urban districts were being built up, in which, in Berlin alone, there were still three thousand Communists carrying out their daily, painstaking work, in which messages were exchanged between groups that never numbered more than three to four members, reports were obtained, pamphlets produced and distributed. The world in which Coppi and Heilmann lived moved closer to me, a world in which, through furtive actions, the membrane in an instrument or the thread in a motor would be positioned incorrectly, in which the wrong parts would be installed in locomotives and planes, grenades and artillery. Back from their trip to Germany, the representatives of the Party disappeared again into

their Swedish hideouts, nobody asked after their names, they were put up by workers, sailors, down below, solidarity remained intact, down below, in primitive workshops, changes were made to identity papers, photos swapped, stamps transferred using peeled boiled eggs, cooked not too hard, down below, no single word was uttered in vain in the industrious battle against the monstrous structures of the enemy. Hodann too continued with what he had begun, even if he, like Münzenberg, had ended up in an inopportune position. As an opponent of fascism he still found himself on the same front that had been occupied by the Communist Party, and for this front, despite all the antagonism, unity remained a necessity. At the conference in Paris at the end of January there had been talk of a form of unity from above. Perhaps this was linked to the realization that the fissures were too deep for them to close organically, that this unity could be produced only through an exercise of power by the person who had won the upper hand. For me, not yet having solid forms in front of me, not even able to see a section of my own path before me, orienting myself toward some kind of commonality was the only thing I could hold onto. As in Cueva la Potita and in the field hospital near Denia, in his Stockholm catacomb Hodann sought to overcome worries and depression through activity. Of all the forms of pity that he disdained as hangovers from Christendom, the one he most loathed was self-pity. No one could be helped by any kind of empathy for their own suffering, and, what's more, it merely became a means of excusing one's failure to intervene. An emotional response was worth nothing unless it led to direct practical assistance, and once this had been set in motion, all emotions ought to fall away. The strength and endurance that he demanded from himself had to exceed all normal dimensions because a significant

portion of his strength was expended in combating his illness. While fear
plagued him in the form of asthma attacks, outwardly he radiated nothing but confidence. He had always refused to speak about the cause of his
distress. His insightfulness about the psychological backgrounds of the
illnesses of others was matched only by his coolness and stoicism in the
face of the pressure that burdened him. Whenever he tried to hide something from himself, when a conflict—usually of a political nature—
remained unresolved, he would be overcome by respiratory distress.
Often, while we were together in Spain, I had wished he would surrender
some of his self-control and ask for help, but he continued to show nothing but equanimity. His throat was full of rattling. He spat into a paper
bag that the woman had handed him. And though just a moment ago his
features had borne the stamp of terror, his eyes staring blackly, he was
now smiling once more, looking at me, filled with self-deprecation, as   **121**
the woman washed and dried off his face. I sensed her jealousy toward
me; a possessiveness emanated from her, just as it had from Lindbaek, his
previous partner, but with Lindbaek it had been demanding, almost violent, while with her it was protective, full of self-sacrifice. With the sniffing and chewing from the cages around me in my ears like a ceaseless
rustling, I asked myself what could have led Hodann, who always spoke
so disparagingly about the couple form of marriage, to this woman. Perhaps his isolation had become so overwhelming that he craved the sense
of security that this woman conjured up. Soon, she said, they would move,
they had been offered a small apartment out in Kristineberg, she had already been to look at furniture, at the emigrants' welfare center, she spoke
of tables, chairs, crockery, curtains, calculated how much of Hodann's
wage would be left over once the rent was taken out, and Hodann, forging
ahead from his meager new beginnings in exile to the hope of expanded
professional opportunities, said that progressive Swedish doctors would
surely be willing to work with him, the renowned specialist; swatting
away the weakness that sought to take root once more, making a show of
his energy, he pulled himself up, pointed upward, where the city we had
almost forgotten now placed itself on top of us like a cauldron; then, out
of nowhere, he brought up Kautsky, the son of the patriarch, he was a
friend from his school days, also mentioned Brecht, both lived in the suburb of Viggbyholm as guests at the boarding school; Kautsky was a doctor
as well, also affected by the Swedish ban on employing foreigners; Brecht
had come from Denmark with his family while they waited for a visa to
enter the United States, he was to be provided with a house soon. Hodann
suggested that we visit them that same day, the woman wanted to object,

but he was already walking past her through the scraping and snapping, and, by managing to set his own vitality in motion, he also transformed the room in which I had found him: it no longer resembled a dungeon as much as a random, makeshift hideout, one in which it was possible to take shelter and make plans.

Near the farm stables on the way to the school, in the spruce woodlands, Ossietzky's daughter was sitting by the edge of the path on a tall wooden table used for loading and unloading milk buckets. On the left, behind a ditch and a fence, pastures sprawled, with the freshly plowed furrows of the field running off to the right. She had come to Viggbyholm in nineteen thirty-six, through the foresight of the Swedish committee founded to support her father. Prior to that, as the first political refugee child from Germany, she had spent three years at the Dartington Hall boarding school in the south of England. Even before I found out who she was, I had been struck by her air of total isolation. I didn't follow Hodann and his wife—who had been picked up from the train by Kautsky and his family—to the school building, but lingered on the unplowed strip beside the field. After a long silence, she asked whether I wanted to join the institution as a student, but then she quickly surmised that I too had probably also already left school. She told me that she was still living here but worked during the week as a housemaid in the city, in Enebyberg. Do you ever get the urge to just smash some glass, she asked abruptly. When she's holding one of those glasses that she has taken out of the vitrine, she continued, she can't resist the urge to drop it, despite knowing that the woman of the house, the wife of a bookkeeper, would deduct the value from her wage. And on top of that the ranting and raving about it being a particularly rare piece, even though it's only part of a cheap set. The laugh around her broad, slender mouth was childish, but also bore a hint of rebellion. Her black hair hung long and smooth over her shoulders. The shape of her brownish hands, which she held in front of her on her knees, betrayed a particular strength. On her mother's side she descended from an Indian princess, she explained; on her father's side from a Polish knight, who during Metternich's time had fought for the freedom of his country. As I leaned onto the edge of the wooden frame next to her, as if getting into position to listen to a fairy tale, her voice took on a bitter, jagged tone, and her greenish-gray eyes inspected me with mistrust; I sensed that the tiniest sign of disbelief would have scared her off. In England, she said, she first lived at Russell's house, and was then sent to Devon to join his and Huxley's children at the experimental school near Exeter. Gusts of wind blew her hair into her face. Her mix of Swedish and English filtering through the strands. She said she'd been brought up among the elite who were supposed to tend to the survival of the British Empire, that she had grown up under the impression that she was destined for great things. Toller, an outsider, had been among her protectors in this endeavor, had fostered her interest in dance and theater, and, before she even graduated from high school, arranged for her to sit the test for the acting school at the Old Vic, which she passed at the age of sixteen and after which she was summoned to Sweden. It was at this point that she mentioned her father's name for the first time. When, in November of thirty-six, he had been awarded the Peace Prize by the Nobel Committee, and she had been taken in as the daughter of one of the most prominent prisoners in Germany and invited by Sundberg, the rector, to visit the boarding school, she was still expecting, in accordance with her father's wishes, to receive a portion of the prize money of one hundred thousand marks to put toward her theatrical education. She said she didn't want to go into the details of the embezzlement that was committed by the Gestapo. Eighty marks a month were apportioned to her father's care, and, while her mother had received one mark a day during the final months of his life, the rest ended up in the hands of the fraudsters. Gravely ill after years of torture, her father was transferred—as a result of the pressure of international opinion—from the camp in the swamp near Esterwegen to Berlin and was put up in a small clinic run by a doctor by the name of Dosquet, who had a close relationship with the Reichsmarschall. One year ago, she said, propping herself up with her hands on the edge of the plank of wood, sitting up and talking with her face looking skyward, shortly after Easter of thirty-eight, I found out how he had died through a letter that had been smuggled out. They'd said he had suffered from tuberculosis, heart failure. But he never had respiratory problems; he had a strong physical constitution, she said. With appropriate care he could have been saved; but the bloated con man in the white general's uniform, the number-two man in the state, had ordered his murder. His stay at the Nordend sanitorium in Niederschönhausen was covered by sixty francs a month that were sent from Paris by the League of Human Rights. The patient lay in a shed-like building in the garden, in a small room divided by a chest-high wooden partition. A suitcase, a few cardboard boxes, a plank of wood with a few books arranged on it, that was all that he owned. His pulmonary condition, she said, had been injected into him in small doses during his years in the camp. The gradual destruction of his body was intended to drive him, officially in protective custody, to put an end to his life himself. Yet because he continued to hold firm, and because a dead prisoner, as experience had shown, swayed international opinion less than one that was still breathing, his elimination was ordered. Her informant, she said, had told her how the condition of the prisoner had visibly deteriorated shortly after a visit from the marshal; he was certain that the patient had received an overdose of tuberculosis bacteria, which, given his general physical infirmity, was certain to bring about his death. The word *dispatched* had been uttered. During the final days, the nurse refused him the blanket he had asked for in the damp and drafty room. And once he could no longer be helped, she said, and the protests of the global community had petered out, the attention she had received had also diminished; though she remained a guest of the school foundation, she was told with increasing frequency, especially by Kronheimer, the headmistress, that she should get the idea of being destined to be an actor or dancer out of her head, and that she needed first of all to learn to work. Back when her father had received the Nobel Prize, she had been paraded around as a celebrity, swarmed by photographers and journalists; she had even secured permission to join Håkonsson's theatrical school in Stockholm, with the committee putting up the costs. However, in the fall of thirty-eight, when Toller—in Stockholm for a few days—recommended her to Brunius, the director of the theater, she was gruffly turned away with the explanation that firstly, as a foreigner, she could not be admitted to a state school; and secondly, that with her accent, she would never be able to learn stage elocution. She jumped down from her seat. For a second I thought she would rush off, but then she walked with me to the school grounds. I had to consider, she said, that staying in boarding schools had been the normal state of affairs for her since her early adolescence, the fascists had not been the first to stick her father in prison, the government of the Weimar Republic had put him behind bars for his struggle against the Junkers and militarists; while he was in Tegel, she had attended the gymnasium at the Gray Abbey, Bismarck's old school in Breite Strasse, where as the daughter of someone found guilty of high treason she was bullied and, because she refused to perform the national salute, expelled. It wasn't until October of thirty-eight, when I was eighteen, she said, that Toller outlined to me the consequences of the events of the ensuing years. Just as, a year earlier, even though I had known how my father was being treated in the prisons and camps, his loving letters, which he was able to get to me through my mother, and all the articles, campaigns, and activities to support him had nourished the belief within me that he would one day be released; after

124

his death, I likewise thought there had to be some form of expiation, re-demption. I had left Germany as a thirteen-year-old, had lived a sheltered life despite the drifting about, had never belonged to a nation, was a citizen of the world, and only now, as Toller showed me the defamation that was being marshaled against him, did I understand the reach of the lust for destruction. Toller, the pacifist, had replaced a part of my father for me; shortly before he continued on to Oslo, this gentle, warm human being was called a mass murderer by the Norwegian newspaper *Fritt Folk* [Free People]; he, the wandering Jew, they wrote, flutters about from land to land, a hater of Germanic culture, in the pay of Communism, to sow the seeds of depredation and war. If you would speak German, I said, I'd un-derstand you better. She stopped still, stared at me with a look of horror under which her facial features threatened to collapse. So who are you then, she said, suddenly lisping, I thought you were Swedish. She stood before me in her thin, ratty dress, which must have been a hand-me-down and which she had long since grown out of, her hands now hanging lifelessly. I can't speak that language any more, she said. My parents, I said, are workers, they were driven from their home by the occupation of the Sudetenland, where they were now I didn't know, I myself work in the separator plant as a tinner, for an hourly wage of one krona, the rent for my room on Fleminggatan is forty kronor a month. I didn't know why I was explaining all of this to her; perhaps it was nervousness. She grabbed my hand, pulled me backward, away from the school buildings in front of us. We could go to Hodann's place, she said, I've visited him once before, he is a mentor, a helper, but let's not go to the others. His wife, she just wants to fuss over me, and the Kautskys, those dignified, cultivated people, and Sundberg, my host, regardless of how proper, how compas-sionate and open-minded he can be within the confines of his religious humanism, I can't look any of them in the eyes, I'm all betrayal in the face of their benevolence, I can't handle that they view me as their charge. Here at the school they want to teach me to experience nature, she said, that'll put my mind at ease, they say, and I have tried to feel something looking out at the fields with their cowpats, at the wires charged with low voltage current between the posts, at the swampy creek, at the piles of stones that the farmer has picked from his field. I stared at the sky, the clouds, and the only thing I felt was that I don't belong here. I reminded her about Brecht, but she didn't want to hear anything about Brecht either; he was only interested in meeting influential people, she said. We had arrived back at the road; she was walking at a rapid pace toward the hill with the villas. It is now seven years, she said, since I last saw my father, before his, what's it called, *transfer* to the Tegel penitentiary; then he was still well-fed, wearing a coat and hat, collar and tie, and since then, it was like in a film, I could only see images cross-fading into one another, they became more and more uncanny, mask-like, from the camp in Sonnenburg, where he wore that big patch sewn over his heart with the number five hundred sixty-two, then, lined up in rank and file, his clothes hanging off him, eyes sunken, nose enormous, mouth clenched together, barely able to keep himself up with his spade, in the east wing, station five, then in Papenburg Esterwegen, near the Dutch border on the Ems, hunched over, peeling potatoes, then, in late thirty-four, now emaciated to a skeleton, lying on a cot, then hanging between two figures in black uniforms, pale as a sheet, one swollen eye, teeth beaten in, a broken leg, poorly healed and dragging behind him at an angle, then that double photo, his skull across from the pompous face of Hamsun, who taunted, berated the inmate, who was one of the leaders in the months-long battle against him being awarded the prize; I vomited, threw up, she said, his books, which I once loved, *Hunger, Pan, Victoria,* I tore up, then, in February thirty-eight, the cadaver dressed up as a civilian one last time before a jury in Berlin Mitte, in profile, straining to hold his head upright, then nothing but the vision of him lying in the filthy corner of the shed, the nurse keeping guard behind the wooden partition, in the hospital garden the blackthorn blossoming, on the fourth of May, thirty-eight, at three o'clock in the afternoon, as the Catholic sister was reciting *pray for us pray for us* over him, through to the final plaster husk that an unknown sculptor, sneaking into the death room by night, took of his face and managed to smuggle out of the country; an utterly alien mask, cold, resembling those of Schiller and Blake. We walked up the street, and now, she said, because nobody knew what to do with her anymore, the Jewish headmistress of our school pours out on me everything that in my childhood in Germany was most insidious, the authoritarianism, the terrorizing shackles of discipline; she, herself a refugee from that disgraceful country, scowls that if I don't work then I don't eat either, and these respectable people stand around agreeing, confirm that I, as a nothing, a beggar, should be content with the alms that I receive. We had reached the railway station. She wanted to travel with me into the city, she said. When I pointed out that Hodann was expecting us, she simply responded that we could let him know by telephone. It was the first time someone had walked through the doorway of my apartment with me and accompanied me into my room. My fellow lodgers were sitting in the kitchen having dinner, it was getting raucous, they had produced brandy with their own distilling device, the drinking songs were reverberating through the wall. I saw my accommodation through the eyes of a guest. It resembled a cell. Slender bed, table, chair, chest of drawers, tiled stove. Not one book, just a few papers on the tabletop. I had nothing to offer her, I didn't want to go into the kitchen. I should put out the lamp, she said. Just the wan pre-summer sky, the lights from the street were illuminating walls and ceiling, reflections from the headlights of passing cars sliding across the room every now and then. At least you have a view of the park, she said. And it was also the first time that I spoke about my time in Spain in this country. It grew darker. My visitor had stretched herself out on the bed; I sat by the window. Gradually things grew silent in the kitchen and the adjacent room; a workday was to come, with an early morning. For a fraction of a second I saw myself sticking my card into the slot of the time clock at four o'clock in the morning and pulling down the lever. **127** How had I managed to adapt here, she asked. She has been in this country for almost three years, and until now had acquainted herself only with the effort it takes to survive. After her aborted attempt to make it in the theater, she had given up hopes of further education, was just vegetating. It's not the emigration, she said, that gave her the feeling of not belonging, she had always emigrated, immigrated, moved on, impermanence was in her family's blood. My father's grandparents, she said, still spoke Polish, my mother was born in India, brought up in England, my father's parents moved from Upper Silesia to Hamburg, where, before the war, my father met my mother, who was an adherent of Pankhurst, a suffragette. They married in a village in Essex in nineteen thirteen, then traveled back to Germany, lived in Hamburg, Berlin, were often on the road for their magazine, for the antiwar movement. The problem was that there was always a pettiness and narrow-mindedness that cropped up to counter the internationalism in which she had grown up. In Berlin she had been called a foreigner, a Jew, because of her dark skin, her dark hair; in the Viggbyholm school the kids called her Indian, American Indian. In England, for a while, she had entertained the dream of having an origin. I wanted something to imagine, surrounded by all these scions of the upper class. I dug up my great-grandfather, Palmer, the general in the Queen's Guard, who married the daughter of a maharaja in Hyderabad after entering the fray during some massacre to protect the Indian dynasty. I surrounded myself with the images of his possessions, his estates, the bank he founded; behind him stood the East India Company, the might of colonialism. And my mother, I didn't see her as a suffragette who held agitating speeches in Hyde Park, who went on a hunger strike in prison, but

in a past replete with marble palaces flanked by palm trees, with mauso-
leums, with servants, slaves, fakirs, one of whom—and this seemed particularly romantic to me—stood for years leaning on a wall, his arm
crippled, having become like the branch of a tree. I could connect this
legendary world with the nobles, lords, and soldiers from my father's lineage; this is how I pretended to have a family history beneath which I
could conceal my insecurity. Perhaps it would have been better, she said,
if instead of being taken in abroad for the sake of my father, I'd been
forced to start out in the poverty that was actually my reality. I could see
her mouth moving, hear her words, but was unable to respond to her with
my experiences of exclusion; it would only have sounded hollow to her, or
moralizing, had I brought up my own privations. I also knew that this was
her day, that she was in no way ready to listen to me, to provide me with

understanding; I just said that I had managed to find my way here because
I had been presented with a job opportunity; everything else, I said, I had
put on hold. But then she did respond, saying, the fact that you have forged
a political path has helped you; nobody invited me into any youth group,
I was always a kind of exception, I was always brought here or taken
there to one shelter after another. I could have learned from my mother,
she said, but my mother was never there, for her I was a Sunday guest;
and I idealized my father in every way, I made a hero out of him, a man it
was impossible to talk to, impossible to embrace, one who could only be
deified. All of this has only now become apparent to me, since fall, since
Toller's departure to America. At heart, I think I'm a practical person, a
materialist. I wanted to see myself as European, cosmopolitan. But I didn't
know how to make use of my circumstances for my development, I allowed the role of the emigrant to be foisted upon me, and on top of that the
other role as well, the role of woman. She sat up straight. Being an emigrant and being a woman, she said, that is a double reduction. An emigrant
is not a human being, just a shadow trying to resemble one. A woman is
a thing that has no right to make demands. To put up with both at the
same time, that was too much to bear. I know that when I hurl glasses on
the floor I end up in pieces myself. In Viggbyholm nobody has any sympathy for that: the slightest attempt to hint at my difficulties just leads
to stares, first of bewilderment and then of annoyance. How can I forget,
they say, that people have helped me, that they stood up for my father.
And that criticism is fair enough, but, at the same time, the things that
drove us to flee, that annihilated my father and countless others, do not
exist here. This Europe that we come from is formless. I'm still the odd
one out. If I ever try to show something of my independence, people close

up, as if they were facing a terrible, unbearable conflict. Get a job as a maid, say my benefactors, learn stenography, then you can find employment in an office. She lay down. I have tried to fit in, she said, you have to belong somewhere, I tell myself. And then this Sweden engulfs me. Sweden is an island, with enormous forests, with fields and lakes, hills and mountains, here and there, huts painted red. Europe is miles away and exotic. Can you still picture what it looks like there, she asked, when you want to think your way out, do those long, long stretches of coast not close in around you. She fell silent; I thought she had fallen asleep. Then I heard her laugh all of a sudden. You know, she said, now I have truly sunk from the highest caste to the untouchables.

Bleary-eyed in the steam of the boilers, I said her name over and over again. Just as she had adorned her life for years with fantastical ornaments to overcome her lack of belonging, she was now weighed down by a dream which her parents had bestowed upon her, the dream of a name which quixotically encompassed everything that had been denied her father and mother during the volatile time after the end of the war, this name that like a blossom expressed the joy of her parents over their child, the hopes they had for her, their visions of relaxation and peace. The fact that they, in their harried, militant existence, named their daughter Rosalinde added a particular agony to the things that her father had to suffer through, and that her mother had to bear daily under the surveillance of the Gestapo; the agony of thwarted ambition, of utterly miscarried desire. And though she never said anything about it, I could imagine how being ruthlessly severed from a once-dreamt miracle could impact upon her and burden her with a sense of guilt; for she did get away, was spirited away, while her father and mother had been left behind in the torture chambers. My parents had also stayed behind, without leaving a trace. For Ossietzky's daughter, as for me, it was now a matter of finding a way to outlast, to surmount the obstacles obstructing our intentions and desires. It was harder for her to free herself from her confinement. She, the nineteen-year-old, found herself in a conflicting position that could make her helpless, apathetic; for me, my year in the International Brigades had given me something to hold onto that continued to exist, even as Spain was now being subjected to such horrific mutilation. Time and again over the following weeks, questions arose about the events there, and about the factors that had led to the collapse. The way that political decay could affect individuals was reflected in Rosalinde's being. On the twenty-third of May she found out about Toller's death, through a news item that I had missed as I browsed the dominant news of the day. As she told me how he had hung from the belt of a bathrobe in the shower next to his room in the Mayflower Hotel the previous day, her voice failing, I initially thought she was speaking of something she'd dreamt, but for her this image was more real than the continuity that I, together with Rogeby, Bischoff, and Lindner, had been attempting to construct from fragmentary reports. The front pages of the newspapers had announced that England and France had accepted the Soviet Union's suggestion of an alliance, and that they were now prepared to offer mutual military support in the event of any future assaults. It was expected that Poland and Romania would join the coalition. Yet, by the next day, reservations were tacked on to these headlines; we asked ourselves what the small suggested changes being considered by the British could mean. On the thirtieth of

May, the signing of the agreement seemed imminent, an assertion that was then revoked on the first of June, with the explanation that insufficient assurances had been made by the Soviets regarding the Baltic states and Finland. We saw the state of affairs before us like an enormous, increasingly blurred network, in which here and there the course of individual threads could be made out. On the seventeenth of March, two days after the occupation of Prague, the Soviet government had called England, France, Poland, and Romania to an urgent conference to discuss issues related to a common plan of action. With the pressure of the territorial claims that Germany was asserting in Poland, after all their previous evasion, England and France's obligations toward Poland forced them to begin to discuss protective measures. There was still no talk of an alliance, despite the fact that Germany was demanding the seizure of Danzig and the surrender of the Polish Corridor. The British scheming to delay the accord could be traced back to the fact that the Western powers, supported by the United States, continued to cling to the tactic of driving Germany into a one-sided war with the Soviet Union. With British approval, the German government, as we later learned, had suggested Poland receive compensation at the expense of the Soviets. During our discussions in Rogeby's room, we lay a map beneath the tapestry of events, almost like a grid, to lend more solidity to the fluctuations and disruptions of the diplomatic games. In the wake of the annexation of the Memel Territory on the twenty-third of March and the escalating diatribes against Poland, the British refusal to provide aid in the event of an attack on the Baltic states was tantamount to a rejection of the alliance. Germany and the Soviet Union had no common border. A German assault would have to take place via Poland, Lithuania, or Latvia. From Finland,

Leningrad was within range of artillery shelling. The Baltic border states, Poland, and Romania had reactionary, semifascist governments, which, though certainly concerned with retaining their national independence from Germany, were also reluctant to enter into a defensive alliance with the Soviet Union. Playing to these regimes, the Western powers rejected the Soviet request for right of passage through Polish and Baltic regions in the event of an eastward German advance. They wanted to avoid strengthening the Soviet state by acknowledging that Poland and the Baltic region belonged to its sphere of influence. From the political formulae and arabesques, it was possible to surmise that England and France were willing to enter into a military alliance in the event of a direct attack. Yet a direct attack was impossible. And in the event of an indirect attack, they completely ruled out providing support. The Soviet Union understood an indirect attack as the kind of infiltration that was currently being carried out in Danzig through the injection of German citizens. The only thing the British riddles implied was that the Soviet Union would have to defend their western and northwestern borders alone. Never completely rejecting the notion of an alliance, while simultaneously negotiating with the German government, England was trying to save its own skin. The British position was formulated unequivocally on the fifteenth of April in a demand to the Soviet Union to guarantee support to their neighboring countries in the event of war. With this cynical declaration, the prerequisites for further negotiations seemed to have been nullified. Two days later, though, England had received a renewed Soviet appeal to seal a military pact. The British response made it clear that the Western powers saw a direct attack on the Soviet Union's neighboring states as merely an indirect threat, and could not consider themselves obliged to allow the pact to enter into force in such a situation. It was only when public opinion began to waver in England, when an opposition led by Churchill emerged, that the British government was forced in early May to give in to the pressure for an effective Eastern Front, or at least to elicit the appearance of giving in, in order to convey the impression they were acting on their own initiative. Political changes had also taken place in the Soviet Union, though their consequences would only become visible as June progressed. According to a tiny report on the back page of *Pravda*, Litvinov, the advocate of a democratic united front, was relieved of his office as people's commissar for foreign affairs on the second of May and had been replaced by Molotov. The British maneuver in mid-May to resume the discussions was portrayed by the bourgeois press as a great feat in the effort to keep the peace, while the Soviet Union was described as dragging their feet. Henceforth England could bask in praise for its efforts at establishing an alliance, while the Soviet Union, through its intransigence, bore the blame for the delays. Just how uninterested the British government was in an alliance was revealed by the fact that they never engaged in the negotiations at the highest level. It was not, as the Soviets had demanded, the foreign secretary who traveled to Moscow on the eighth of June, but Strang, a subordinate civil servant, who stayed for several weeks without, as the press noted, arousing Molotov's interest. Meanwhile, the German troops were carrying out exercises on the Siegfried Line, and Danzig, adorned with waving swastika flags, was in a festive fervor. On Sunday the eighteenth of July, the voice of Goebbels rang out in Danzig, announcing that the Führer would soon visit this German city, which belonged in the Reich. On top of the familiar barking

issuing from the radios was the undeniable fact that Germany had become a coveted object at the center of this tug-of-war. Halifax had expressed his desire to reach an understanding between the people of Britain and Germany, English finance emissaries had traveled to Germany to draw up contracts, and as bait for an agreement, the government of the Reich had been offered access to colonies. And now, suddenly—or so it seemed to us, since we were only ever confronted with final outcomes—a shift became perceptible in the tone of the Soviet Union toward Germany. On the twenty-third of June, coinciding with Molotov's rejection of the British offer, negotiations were initiated in Moscow with Schulenburg, the German ambassador. Initially, in the ongoing back and forth over the alliance, we thought that the Soviet rapprochement with Germany was a means to pressure the Western powers into a binding outcome. Then, as the summer progressed, and with an alliance not yet having been secured, a peculiar calm descended over Europe in early July, and we discovered that a ten-year Soviet-German trade agreement had been signed, amounting to sums in the billions. With a single blow, the power relations had shifted. England and France stood isolated. There was talk of a détente between the Soviet Union and Germany. For a long time we were left puzzled by this event, which was at odds with the previously unrelenting struggle against fascism. Still reeling from the mass murders of Republican prisoners in Spain, we asked ourselves what other price would have to be paid to maintain the peace. There was no reason, said Rogeby, for this commercial partnership between the Soviet state and Germany to cause us to curtail our political goals. The West's animosity had forced the Soviet Union to take new measures for its protection. We were standing in front of an enormous picture. From afar, it resembled a world landscape, a battle painting by Patinir or Altdorfer, and yet it was composed of ciphers, of forms and figures that were foreign to us and which we were attempting to decipher, piecemeal, through perpetual study and comparison. After the rainy mid-summer, the streets of the city had emptied out, most people had headed to the countryside on vacation. With the ominous silence, we who had stayed behind fell into a kind of lethargy. Once again we could sense our isolation and lack of motivation, the terrible uniformity of our days. We often spoke about visiting Brecht, in the hope of finding explanations there about the origins of this spectral uneventfulness, but we always put it off. In the end it wasn't through Hodann—who often visited Brecht at his home—that the encounter eventuated, but through a messenger, a vagabond, an enigmatic and questionable apparition, a true product of the age. Hodann had always evaded my pleading to allow me to accompany him to see Brecht, either because he had changed his mind about our earlier agreement or because Brecht had demanded total isolation. The messenger on horseback who turned up unexpectedly and delivered the invitation to us was Tombrock, the painter. Though I was always looking to avoid this scrawny man with the filthy, tousled hair and piercing gaze, he had grabbed hold of me, seized me. Like a demon who curses everyone who doesn't want to listen to him, he had gotten close to Rosalinde as well, had dealings with Lindner, and even had the sober-minded Bischoff under his spell. For him, Sweden was not a foreign land but a hunting ground through which he stalked. The forty-five-year-old, who came from a working-class family from Westphalia, called Herring as a child due to his meager frame, had ended up in the pits at the age of sixteen, where small, slender people were needed. He led the draft horses below the ground, pushed carts of coal, lugged wooden sleepers about, then went to sea as a cabin boy. There, as he once told me and Rosalinde, who was carrying a bundle of his drawings for him, it was like in Benninghofen, near Hörde: you were jostled, shoved, kicked, you had to peel potatoes, wash the dishes, and scrub the decks. All things great and beautiful in this world, he said, belong to the rich. That this was nothing new to me provoked his wrath. He disdained the way that I hung about in the factory to create surplus value for the owners at a starvation wage, told me to throw in my job, become a vagabond, to beg, and to realize my desire to paint and write. Only then, he said, ranting and raving, do you have the right to call yourself a prole. He had done away with all self-deception once and for all before the World War, when he was hired to work on Braker's fishing boat *Gut Heil* and used to take his intestines to market. Joined the revolution in the

Ruhr, ended up in prison, in the correctional facility, then on the street. There, he said, among the poorest, is where you'll find your school, never in the academies, that you can only get into if you bend over backward and sideward sucking up. He was self-taught, and his clumsy drawings with their dense lines, their distorted forms, and awkward perspective seemed convincing enough, though there was also junk among them, kitsch produced for quick sale. The women he reeled in took care of the sale of his wares. He was married, had a couple of kids, lived somewhere in Råsunda, but had a few other places where he could stop in for the night. He sent his wife, a seamstress, to the people's houses, the workers' clubs, and if she didn't offload enough sheets, he'd tear and cut her sewing to pieces, lay into her, he would admit, not without a certain pride. What drove the daughter of Ossietzky, I asked myself, to use her name to help him out. Even more difficult for me to understand was that Bischoff, with bruised patches on her arms and face from his blows, continued looking for buyers for a collection of his pictures. This scrounger and bum was now rambling about his friendship with Brecht and invited us to participate in a get-together at Brecht's house. We were to travel separately, at different times, from Humlegården along the Lidingö line, on foot or by bicycle, to Vasavägen station, and from there via Riddarvägen to number one Lövstigen. We were to enter the garden of a wooden house, painted dark red, from the forest side, and only if we didn't see anyone on the way. His instructions sounded over the top, but the precautions were necessary, for not only was Brecht under surveillance and all of us forbidden to engage in meetings of a conspiratorial nature, but a number of Party functionaries, who were living in Sweden illegally, were also expected.

The brown suburban train traveled past the clinker-brick stadium, crowned by its towers, and the expansive, fenced-in complex of the free port. The large ships from the Baltic Sea sat in the basins; trolleys full of coal were transported over the street with winches and up to the industries surrounding the gasworks; heavy, acrid smoke ascended from the smokestacks of the factories and drifted over to the forested banks of the island we were approaching via the narrow bridge with its iron arches. Lidingö, out past Värtan, had a rural look about it. Nestled at the foot of the slopes and on the edge of the forests were conglomerations of opulent villas; passing through gorges and fields, we finally arrived at the village station. From Riddarvägen, the house that had been provided to Brecht by the sculptor Santesson could already be glimpsed behind the rocky ridges, between pine trees and a few birches; it was taller than it was wide, though the clunky, oddly proportioned form was partially concealed by the shrubbery. Jasmine bushes stood by the white posts of the gate, their fragrance mingling with the aroma of elderflower. I walked toward the house through a flittering of foliage, grasses, and daubs of sun; curved gray boulders protruded from the mossy ground like half-buried elephants. Leaves brushed across my face as I looked for the entrance to the studio, which was built onto the rear of the house. Behind a trellis there were two steps leading to the open door of the work space. As I entered, I heard Tombrock announcing my arrival with my first name. Despite the white-washed walls and tall windows, the workshop was shrouded in a dusky darkness, the light stolen by the surrounding trees. It was difficult to make out the size of the room because of the numerous tables dotted around it. In the corner near the door to the hall was a balustrade on wooden posts, with a narrow stairway leading up to it, a sofa bed at the top and a bookshelf affixed above it. Those present sat in a semicircle on stools and boxes; somewhat off to the side, beneath the little mezzanine, with his back to the window, a narrow-shouldered figure was huddled in a deep leather armchair. I sat down on a chest, next to Bischoff. We were still waiting for a number of visitors to arrive. Once my eyes had adapted to the subdued light, I estimated the size of the studio at about seven meters by five meters. There was a workbench, on trestles, running be-neath the windows on the longer wall, packed with bundles of paper and newspaper clippings; at a right angle, a long table on tall legs jutted into the room, laden with manuscripts, books, and an old-fashioned type-writer with a worn ribbon. Farther along stood tripods—the kind used for modeling clay—platforms, and frames, one of them holding a model of a stage pieced together from little sticks, sheets of cardboard, small boxes, and scraps of cloth. Beside the armchair, a woman with short, light hair sat straight-backed, wearing a loose-hanging burlap robe, and made steno-graphic notes upon the sudden commencement of the discussion, usually at a wave, a nod from the person sitting next to her. Brecht was smaller, wirier than I had imagined. His face was pale and pasty. He was wearing a collarless brown jacket made of slick leather. Behind the thick lenses of his horn-rimmed glasses, his red-ringed, close-set eyes had a frozen, slightly teary gaze, which was interrupted every so often by a heavy blink. He tapped the ash from the cigar that he was sucking and chewing on into a large copper bowl. Bowls of the same kind were distributed among the tables in the room. One of the guests was reporting on the conditions in the camps near Perpignan. At first I hadn't recognized Branting. He had just returned from southern France, where he had been looking into possibilities for evacuating children. His speech was fatigued, stuttering. It was as if he were straining to express something unimaginable. The listeners didn't move a muscle. His words permeated into the sensory realm of every one of them. Many of us possessed memories of that ocher-yellow, sun-bathed town in the lowlands on the edge of the Pyrenees. The shores of the Mediterranean lay an hour and a half away by foot. After a day's walk, the border crossings in the hills and foothills could be reached. Thousands had set off from there to sneak past the border guards and join the Republican army. We looked at the city and its fortifications from various perspectives, from the Roman ruins through to the forts and citadels of later centuries. Almost one hundred fifty thousand people had now been penned up behind barbed wire, some under open skies, some in makeshift barracks. The collection points were located a few kilometers outside the city, on the edge of some dried-out fields. As winter drew to a close, in the cold, the downpours, the people had traipsed northward, demoralized by the aerial assaults on Barcelona. Corpses lay on the edges of the paths; some of the women were carrying their dead children in their arms. There was hardly any food left in the villages, and their first, meager meal didn't come until they arrived at the emergency quarters in Figueras. Starving, exhausted, some still shaking at the thought of the massacre that the Falangist colonial troops had carried out on the streets, the expelled had wandered across the mountains and were met at the border by the Senegalese soldiers of the Garde Mobile and shoved into livestock wagons with rifle butts. The Africans from the old slave colony, forced into the army, gave back what had previously been doled out to them. Under the pretense that they had not paid any customs duties, what was left of the refugees' belongings was taken from them: watches, jewelry, fountain pens, even reading glasses, headscarves, combs. Having arrived in Perpignan, the men were separated from the women, the women had their children torn away from them. Day and night, the crying, pleading, and whimpering could be heard issuing from the train station. On the siding at the station stood the rows of freight cars that hadn't been let into Spain by the French government, fully loaded with machine guns, cannons, anti-aircraft artillery, and munitions stamped with Soviet postage markings. From the city, over which the Cathedral of Saint Jean and the Moorish castle loomed, the masses of people had been forced into the different enclosures. The most terrible place of all, said Branting, was in the special camp for children; not even our appeal to the local populace led to an alleviation of the misery, and the few who responded weren't able to prevent the deaths from exhaustion and emaciation. Children lay on the earth in tangled groups. With the arrival of the Republican army, which had provided cover for the retreat of the civilians, hope raised its head again for a few days before giving way to even greater demoralization. The soldiers had crossed the border in ordered columns: they didn't view themselves as defeated, and their posture still bore the stamp of their just struggle. Women had broken through the gates of the camp, walked out to look for their sons, to find their husbands. They were chased back into the pens with gunfire. Even those who had managed to reach Perpignan in automobiles and find accommodation in hotels or private homes were arrested, robbed of their money, and put in the camps. The Republican troops had to accept the jeers and mockery of the French units to whom they had handed over their weapons, and by whom they had expected to be taken in and shown support. For the first time, Brecht's voice could be heard. Turning to Trepte, the director who had staged a new production of the piece about Señora Carrar in Sweden and who had requested from Brecht a prologue and epilogue adapted to the altered circumstances, he said sharply, croakily, that the broader context surrounding the plot was no longer tenable, had to be rewritten. So he had relocated Señora Carrar, her son, and her brothers to the French camp. In order to pass the time, a few guards asked them questions about the lost war, which were then answered with the plot of the play. The conclusion was supposed to teach the audience that the struggle, despite the current defeat, had to be continued. He had believed he could convey the resilience of the figures in this way. The impression was created that French soldiers and Spanish workers, the one lot as guards, the others as prisoners, could talk to each other. Perhaps it was also important to maintain this class-centric hypothesis. If it were still possible to bring about changes at all, they would have to be built on the foundations of this solidarity. However, according to Branting's report, such a solution no longer reflected reality. What was now revealing itself was the turning point in the phase of the preliminary battles leading up to the great war of annihilation that would engulf the entire continent, the entire planet. The degradation of individual reactions had been initiated, and had already left behind profound traces. The simple dramatic fable of the kind that had only recently still been possible to write suddenly belonged to a world buried under rubble. The French workers had allowed Blum to smash the Popular Front and Daladier to institute a regime of terror. Those fleeing Spanish fascism were greeted by the fascism taking hold in France. Brecht saw that what was now taking shape no longer fit in the space of a chamber play, but rather in the landscape of *Dulle Griet*, or of the *Triumph of*

Death, as Brueghel had painted them. He had the open, wide-format book brought over from a table. For a while it seemed as if the only thing that interested him anymore was this skeletal woman, this rural Fury who, with a frozen gaze and gaping mouth, a breastplate over her apron and a sack full of loot slung over her shoulder, swinging her sword amid flames and fumes, hurried through exploded cities populated by lascivious, slobbering, trunk-bearing, fish-like, reptilian beings; or that red, sandy shoreline brimming with hosts of skeletons, who, to the clang of bells, fanfares, and kettledrums, descended upon the people in amphibious wagons and other armored vehicles, in rectangular shock-troop formations behind tall shields, oozing out of bunkers, laying into them with scythes, hoes, fire tongs, pitch torches, grindstones, nets, throwing them headlong into ponds, forcing them into cages, caves, and onto the barren hills, breaking them on the wheel, beheading them, and stringing them up on rows of gallows. But then he suddenly wanted to know how the Popular Front had held up in the Spanish combat zones. As the ensuing reports were delivered, it became clear that he had called together adherents of various political groups in order to draw conclusions about the causes of the Republican collapse from their conflicting viewpoints. It was as if his isolated position in the room also mirrored a reservation toward the attendees. His gaze at the guests was cool yet exhibited extreme concentration. Often he impatiently steered digressive remarks back to the topic with a nervous shrug of the shoulders. And you really managed to pull together, he asked upon mention of a troop made up of socialists, anarchists, Social Democrats, and Communists. His concerted attention became the focal point for the divergent analyses being offered up. Were his curiosity to wane even slightly, the circle would have fallen apart. Discord had already begun to emerge between the proponents of the view that it was the failure to wage guerilla war, a revolutionary civil war, that had led to the defeat, and others who defended conventional static warfare as the only possibility, even if, given the material superiority of the enemy, it had no chance of producing victory. Most agreed that the lack of involvement by the Social Democratic leadership, as well as the stance of the French and British governments—with their policies of noninterference—was tantamount to a sabotage of the Republican cause and bore the lion's share of the blame for the capitulation. The leadership of the German Party was represented by Warnke, Verner, and Mewis. Verner said that, even in the wake of the decision to dissolve the International Brigades, the will to fight had by no means been broken. Even in February, before Casado's coup, there was still so much confidence that

Modesto, who had pulled out of Barcelona after its fall, initially withdrawing with his troops to France, would return to the country to establish a new defensive front. It was only because France refused to allow the weapons in—despite the fact that Germany and Italy were not honoring their agreement to withdraw their troops—that it was no longer possible to carry out campaigns on a larger scale. The Soviet Union, said another, should never have allowed the Western powers to pressure it into ceasing its military aid. An altercation broke out between one speaker, who blamed the collapse in Spain on the discord in the Soviet Party, and Warnke, who saw the Soviet Union as the prerequisite for maintaining peace. I had been drawn from my spot to the table near the window by the flickering of the images in the book that had been returned to the woman with the ash-blond hair and which she had since set back down. I pushed a kitchen chair toward the table, turned the book toward me, and inspected the reproductions. Almost two years earlier, in the bookstore in Warnsdorf, I had had these pictures in front of me; now, after my experiences in Spain, they emitted a new force. Often I had asked myself how it could ever be possible to convey impressions of war, since even in precise descriptions they always lost something of their essence. There was something alien that clung to the experiences being conveyed, realistic depictions were only able to cover a tiny detail, under which lay the nightmarish terror, the panicked confusion, unresolved. Here, everything was erupting from beneath the earth, enticed by the figure of Megaera. There was the swirling ash, the brittle earth, there were the tree branches withered by the heat, the demolished walls, there were the helmeted heads of the scouts behind shutters, there was the carnage in gateways and caves, the search for shelter beneath boulders, there was the familiar—excessively clear in every detail—and there was the brooding, the plotting; there was the phantasmagoria of deceitfulness, of betrayal, of shamelessness and disgraceful deeds; everything was equally palpable in the tumult. The combination of the spawns of madness with the gestures and movements of startled, agonized individuals created a situation that approximated that derangement and clairvoyance we had sometimes felt, if only for a few seconds. In those moments, staring at sand dunes and piles of stones, faces would emerge from furrows and holes, roots, charred beams would transform into bodies lying in wait, dust-gray shrubs on the edge of paths turned into the raised barrels of guns, and from this threshold between flash-like impressions and delusions other apparitions proliferated, characterized by the disgust that was never far from fear. Forced into the position of murdering out of self-defense, we had struggled not to lose our minds, not to allow them to be deformed, in the face of this image that bore down on us irresistibly, licked us, fondled us, stroked our skin gruesomely, strained its bristles, trunks, suckers, fangs, and claws toward us. Here, drastic and brazen, everything was gathered which pursued the business of forging rumors, stacking decks, sowing intrigue; apish, feathered vermin crouched in dangling baubles, under bell jars, in hollow, giant eggs, their snouts and beaks wide open, ready to spit bile, tar, to rain down lead shot; on one roof a demon sat with legs splayed, his clothes bunched up, baring his ass, a spoon stuck in the budding excrement. These scrambling slurry buckets, these insects with hats and fishing rods, these spiders, weaving harp strings to catch their prey, these hybrids of maggot and fish, insect and rodent: this was the brood that otherwise kept itself hidden from us,

which was constantly at work, these were the parasites, the plague bringers; they almost seemed comfortable, displaying bloated, priestly mugs; though they seemed to lie there sedately they could disappear in an instant, and whoever dared to try to squash them and managed to actually do it would soon have to watch as they multiplied into swarms of bugs as they burst. People suffering from the fever brought on by infected wounds were most capable of recognizing the intrusion of this hellish reign; we had often heard people whose eyes had been shot out, whose arms, legs had been ripped off, pleading for us to get that animal there, that goat, that owl, that snapping carp or whatever it was away from their bed, to swat away those blowflies. Once the threshold to the unreal had been crossed, the apparitions, as Brueghel had depicted them, assumed an immediate tangibility. The materialization of the huge, scaled faced, with one empty eye, the other glittering darkly, the eyelids propped open like shutters, the hideous rat's tail coiling out of one of the nostrils, a watchtower sprouting out of its stony brow, the gaping gob, from which a teeming cloaca was gushing forth, it was the tyrant who had installed his reign in all countries in which the struggle was being carried out, smothered, rekindled again; ringed by shot-up walls, the bastion of power rose up, clashes ensued all over the place, blazes broke out, captives lay bundled together; off in the distance, behind gorges, unreachable, in the mountains against the red sky stood a giant jug, promising coolness, relief. Dulle Griet trounced through the field like a sutler, holding her bag of stolen wares in her iron-clad hand; she lived from war, extracted profit from it, the seam of her skirt brushed over a horde of women who hewed into advancing mongrels with flails and pans, slitting open their bellies, ripping out their innards, plundering a shop as they fled, making off with sacks of flour, loaves of bread, ham, only to be overwhelmed at the next corner by other beasts. These faces were still etched into my retina when Mewis asked me to recount my activities on the front. Only three months after the end of the war, many of our memories already seemed to have become unreliable, the things we wanted to hold on to had already become enveloped in a dense web of mendacious chronicling, the events were disappearing into a world of myth, and this was true for both sides, ours and the enemy's. Any object we wanted to pick up and study had been deformed; it was not just the fear of violating a truth that had been determined from above that impeded us in retrieving its tangibility but also the desire to allow our own failure to fade into oblivion. Thinking about the infinite patience, the courage, the exertion of every individual, the defeat of the Republic seemed inexplicable. The possibility of defeat had been unimaginable, there had been nothing but perseverance, enthu- siasm; the imputation that the sacrifices had been made in vain was unbearable. But if we now had to identify reasons for the collapse, then we had to attempt to trace it back to the insufficiency of our imagination. We hadn't been sufficiently initiated into the all-consuming conspiracies, we had held out in our hideouts, had relied upon our good will, our ideal of justice; our understanding of the manipulations that were being carried out all around us was not sharp enough; no, that's not how it was, it was precisely the quarrels, the deceptions, the outbreaks of enmity between the parties, the smoke and mirrors of propaganda, the forked tongues of diplomacy, the evidence of our own weakness and disorganization that had besieged us, and we had denied these unsettling realities in order to carry on. The feigned confidence, the belief in the resilience of our actions, so highly praised, held up so high as an example, became our demise. Yet how could we have been capable of anything else, I asked myself; after all, there was only ever the one day standing before us, there was no room for anything but trust in the military and political leadership, who were engaged in the same efforts at perseverance as we were. And while I was straining to express something of these thoughts, through the window I saw a gaunt, dark-haired woman behind the bushes, a cigarette in a long holder between her lips, washing laundry in a zinc tub. In the summery warmth, she was wearing only a pink petticoat, she meticulously rinsed every item, rung it out, hung it on a line strung between a birch and an apple tree, and then climbed into the foaming soapy water, sat still, leaning back, pulling her knees toward her, smoking a newly lit cigarette, staring up into the glittering foliage. Later, while other people were talking and my gaze was gliding back and forth between the woman in the garden and the secretary with the demure, girlish face; and then from her to a third, athletic woman who had sat herself by Brecht's feet, I felt as if I was getting a sense of what Tombrock, the buccaneer, referred to as his bond with Brecht. The assistant with the light blond hair, whose features called to mind a drawing by Kollwitz, waited patiently for Brecht's instructions; resigned, the woman outside remained in her isolation; and the one who had laid her arm on his knee, as if she wanted to make a special claim to him, also signaled with her alertness, her continual observation, that she was willing to subjugate herself to him. If the painter's relations with women mirrored his often amateurish, brutal, slapdash products, then Brecht's patriarchal air was unaffected, could scarcely be distinguished from absolute self-confidence. Without knowing more about his personality than the posture he assumed in that armchair and his cold, demanding voice, I thought that Brecht, with the right that was founded in the compensation of his achievements, presumed that everyone he waved at should come to him, that everyone should help and support him, everyone let him pick their brains and bring him what he needed. I struggled against the thought that it should be enough of an honor to be allowed to enter into his house, and thought that he might at least have offered us a glass of water. In the smoke-filled, oppressive humidity, and under the aftereffects of the tension of offering an opinion on contentious, dangerous questions before all these authorities, I was dripping in sweat. The green outside was calling to me like freedom.

That green. That green that Lorca sang of, said Gallego, his gaze directed at the Swedish coast as it streamed past. Green wind, green branches. The ship out on the sea. Stahlmann stood beside him, leaning on the railing of the ship that they would take from Le Havre to Leningrad. That dense, succulent green we'd dreamt of in the rocky soil, in the russet dust of Andalusia, and then in the desert, in the blinding sand around Bogari. He was trying to convey to his German comrade, who during the war had led a partisan column, something of the days, the weeks, the almost five months that had elapsed since the collapse. Actually, since he was thinking of the palace of El Pardo, in which he had been barricaded with his unit until the twenty-fourth of March, he had to reach even further back, to his childhood in the village of Siles, near Jaén, where he had been born to peasants and had worked as a herder in the scraggy highlands. I first received shoes, he said, when my mother sent me into the city at sixteen years of age to learn to read and write and get a trade, after the death of my father. To begin with he couldn't wear the shoes, as the soles of his feet were tough from traipsing around in the mountains, the arid slopes. Apart from attending school, he initially had few options other than going back to herd livestock. While he and his thirty men, members of the Party and the youth organization, were holding the Pardo, behind the windows on the first floor, bolstered with sandbags, he often thought about his origins, his trajectory up until the outbreak of the war. That they held out for three weeks was nothing extraordinary; it was the natural consequence of a path that he had been on since joining the youth association as a seventeen-year-old. Looking at the chandeliers beneath the ceiling, with its hosts of painted angels, at the gilded chairs along the walls of the hall in which he was holed up, the last few years had pieced themselves together inside of him to form an indissoluble whole. It felt as if he had come directly from his village to defend the city and the country here, at this advanced position. Broad, darker sections in the fabric covering of the walls showed where Goya's tapestries had been. The floral patterns of the mosaics on the floor were strewn with bullet casings. Sleeping figures lay beneath brocade curtains, while the others kept watch at the loopholes. In July of thirty-six, he said, all poverty, all misery came to an end for us, we were now embarking upon the struggle for our liberation. I had grown up among children who died young, the infirm, unemployed, and beggars. Even in the city only a minimum of food could be rustled up. And yet here, without money, with no occupation, he had met young people who were preparing themselves for a revolution in the country. After evening classes and late-night study, after a few years of school and political education, he had become the youth leader of the province, and in October of thirty-four, as a participant in the general strike and insurrection, he had ended up in prison together with tens of thousands. By the beginning of the war, at twenty-one years of age, a country lad, a herder who didn't even know how many men made up a battalion, he was named a major in the People's Army. But everyone, he said, received unimaginable strength from the certainty that the struggle would lead to the extinction of injustice, of need. From one day to the next, their faces transformed. The harried, careworn look in their features gave way to the expression of joyful confidence. We didn't perform miracles, he said, but rather carried out actions for which we had been preparing for a long time. The difficult times lay behind us. Reaching for our weapons triggered the onset of our relief. Which is why, right up to the very last moment, capitulation remained unthinkable. Though we knew we were cut off in the Pardo, we were still waiting, hour by hour, to be rescued. Behind the fence, just a few meters away from us, were the Falangist marksmen. Tanks had advanced. They yelled out that we should surrender, that Madrid was occupied by Casado's troops. And yet, he said, since everything I had learned had been acquired in the battle against a superior power, in the third week of March I still believed that the struggle would continue, that victory was possible. How could we have imagined that we were alone. Such a thought would necessarily fly in the face of all our previous knowledge. We'd have been cursing ourselves if, in our palace, which had been spared the heavy artillery so that it could remain intact for el Caudillo as a residence, we had entertained the notion that all support was exhausted. Cowering at the machine gun, he had remembered how awestruck he had been by the arrival of the International Brigades. That was the first time he had seen people from another country. The foreigners wore the same uniform as he did; he stood alongside them in the same army. The sense of belonging had been intensified further by the fact that they could not speak with one another. He became acquainted with the solidarity that required no common language. And now, he said pensively, we had the fascists directly in front of us. Our rations were running out. We prepared ourselves to stay to the final cartridge. Our medic assured us he could still operate on each of us at least seven times. We wouldn't have left the Pardo if somebody hadn't managed to sneak through to us to deliver the order to withdraw. We still refused to believe that Madrid had fallen. Plenty of cities had fallen and the war had continued to be waged. The north was lost, but Modesto was gathering units for a counterattack. To outsiders this might have seemed absurd. For us it was the right decision. Even at the Battle of the Ebro we'd only have needed a few more hours and the enemy would have been forced to retreat. But the reinforcements never came. Why, we asked ourselves, would the reinforcements not make it to us this time. For an eternity, the enemy's front line had been frail, demoralized. After the unspeakable efforts of the people, it was unthinkable that the reactionaries could win out. The building we were in, he said, was not just any palace, it had been one of the main seats of feudalism, a royal estate since the Middle Ages, expanded by Carlos the Third, filled by the fourth Carlos with the masterpieces of Velázquez, Murillo, Goya. You know the picture, he said to Stahlmann, in which Goya captured the royal family, fourteen figures, puffed up, witch-like, puppet-like, looking addled and adipose, in shimmering robes, pompous uniforms. We had promised ourselves that the palace would stay in our possession, that the cretins, whose power was now only recognizable in their rustling, shimmering clothing, would never again return to these chambers. But we were urged to hurry. In Madrid, having been recognized by England and France, the armies were preparing their victory parades. I was caught in the contradiction between my mission of bringing my group to safety and my desire to continue the revolutionary struggle. My indecision was resolved by my duty to save the lives of my comrades. We had to accept a partial defeat. We had to make it through in order to continue the struggle elsewhere. Everything that followed, in its seeming arbitrariness, its improvised nature, taught me one thing, that there is rarely a situation with no way out, and that failure merely meant failing to find that way out. As the green Swedish coast receded, and the waves, sliced through by the bow, rolled frothing along the side of the ship, he asked himself how their withdrawal from the Pardo, with its flash-like impressions, could be translated into words. Before daybreak they had heard a bellowing voice issuing from the entrance, the iron gates had been opened, an ambulance drove up to the main entrance. The driver of the wagon, carrying identification issued by the anarchists, who were among Casado's guards, had convinced the soldiers out front with the volume of his voice that he had orders to remove the Republicans from the palace. Gallego could still see himself in the mirror above the open fireplace, flanked by candlestick holders, while he fixed up his filth-encrusted hair with his fingers. Then they jumped down the marble steps, in a moment the doors of the automobile were slamming shut behind them, they raced down the road, through the plains, away from the bluish, snow-topped mountains of the Guadarrama to the barracks, where the driver, yelling once more and waving his papers, demanded gas, and, because his audacity aroused the impression that he was one of them, the Falangists gave it to him as well. Thus they broke through the blockades surrounding Madrid, and they went on like that, traversing the country, until they reached Mazarrón, just outside Cartagena. Traveling across the Baltic Sea, with everything lying behind him, he was able to depict it in this way, and yet it had not been picaresque, as it now sounded, accompanied by laughter. We were surrounded by terror, he said, by panic. Through the window of the ambulance they saw the city shot to bits, the streams of refugees, the Italian tanks, the plundering fascist troops. At one point, they drove slowly past a procession of captive Republican soldiers. In one burning village, a small child was walking round and round in a circle. Bodies hanging from the branch of a tree. A heap of people shot with harquebuses in an open field. They lay shoved together in the shuddering wagon. A stop on the side of a dirt road. The doors of the ambulance were wrenched open, they jumped out, the driver saluted, hopped into his seat, turned around, the car disappearing in a cloud of dust. He had fulfilled his mission, said Gallego, we had to go on alone. Thirty men, politically persecuted, we discussed what we should do. The entrances to the coastal cities were under surveillance. The harbors were overflowing with people looking for freight ships, fishing boats, that could take them across the sea to Africa. Off the coast the Italian fleet was waiting. I set off toward Mazarrón, he said, to rustle up a boat. The others waited behind a mound of earth next to an olive grove. Looking for a way out, but with no idea where I might find it, I ran into a pilot, in the middle of the road, who I recognized as a member of our air force. He drove us to a nearby military airport. Holding out his revolver, he explained to the soldiers, who were under Casado's command, that he had been issued the task of escorting us out of the country.

The pilots, confused by the general chaos, powered up the engines of eleven planes, those little Natachas, the light bombers, and soon enough they were ready to go. Gallego returned once more to what seemed arbitrary, coincidental. There is no such thing as a coincidence, he said, and neither is anything impossible, for they had always seemed to overcome the impossible. If I hadn't sought out what was then unknown, he said, I wouldn't have encountered the pilot, and if his demeanor had not been so assertive, then we wouldn't have coaxed the crew out of their doubts. There was also no such thing as foolhardiness. Everything during the last few years had been a risk, we were well acquainted with this situation, and when something had to be altered, we knew no hesitation. Later we found out that our helper had been Carrasco, a hero of the Republic. The planes that were sent after us to shoot us down were manned by Communists who feigned a few maneuvers before turning back, since they didn't have enough fuel for the flight to Africa. The pilots who brought us to Oran decided to stay with us. And now, immediately upon our arrival, the next phase of the civil war began: the battle without weapons, in exile. Our adversaries were now the French. We were penned up in the fortress of the harbor city. The things we had heard about the reception of Spanish refugees in France were repeated in Algeria. Colonial troops picked up the people on the ships that had managed to get through the sea blockade to Oran and stuck them in camps. We protested against the treatment that was meted out to us. We were not at war with France and so we also didn't want to demand the fulfillment of conventions that applied to prisoners of war. But we weren't even considered prisoners of war, much less captive officers. In the eyes of French institutions, the Republican army didn't exist. They only entertained diplomatic relations with the army of the fascists. Incessantly, taking shifts, we demanded to be released; yelled, whistled, hammered on the bars of the cells. Gallego saw Oran in front of him, that white, glowing city. Around the citadel, the steep alleys and stairwells of the old Spanish quarter climbed up toward Djebel Murdjadjo. Below, to the west of the bay lay the main commercial harbor; opposite, behind the throngs of Arabic houses, the modern French district and its wide avenues opened out like an amphitheater. We directed all of our energy, he said, toward forcing our release. When we were picked up from the fortress to be taken to an internment camp, it seemed like a victory. Our pressuring had achieved something; we believed that from the interior of the country it would be easier to flee. The first commandment was to never accept what one was given. Initially, the transfer to the Bogari garrison, three hundred kilometers away, at the foot of the Hauts Plateaux bordering the Saharan Atlas, was evidence of the strength we still had. However it soon became evident that life in the desert was more difficult to bear than imprisonment in the fort. From the south, the Simoom whipped up dust and clouds of sand over the camp. By day, we often had temperatures of up to fifty degrees; the nights were ice cold. Yet here we were, a mere sixty to seventy kilometers from Algiers, having already escaped from Madrid; it had to be possible to also overcome the walls around these barracks. There was a French regiment stationed there and a regiment of Foreign Legionnaires. The majority of the troops were off monitoring Bedouin tribes or hunting apes in the mountains. The soldiers who stayed behind mostly sat around dozing during the day, or hung around at the nearby oasis, where there were a few date palms and they had planted some tobacco plants. Because it is the duty of every prisoner to flee, said Gallego, we constantly thought about the escape that could begin at any moment, but whose execution remained unclear. Almost three months had passed since the flight from Spain when we decided to make a run for it. In our impatience, we chose the wrong option, the option which, had we taken it, would have led to our certain death in the desert. At the same time though, we continued to pursue the other possibility, the one we had ceased to believe in, of forcing the colonial authorities to move us through our tireless expression of outrage about our unlawful imprisonment; and thus, before we were able to seize the ill-advised chance to climb over the walls from the washing station on the edge of the barracks, salvation arrived in the form of a convoy of trucks that took us through the desert to Algiers. This in turn was a result of the negotiations regarding the deportation of Spanish refugees to the Soviet Union, which had taken place in May and June in

Paris. In a contingent of three hundred members of the Republican Army, we were first shipped out to Marseille. Since the cabins were overflowing with priests traveling to an ecumenical congress, we had been housed in the hold with sheep and mules. Here, in the depths, in the stench, many of us became seasick; we had heard there was supposed to be a point in the hull somewhere where the lurching was minimal. We spent the night searching for that point, which we didn't find, and then returned to the livestock, which to me at least was familiar from my youth. We were transported through France in a livestock wagon as well, behind sealed doors; through a vent in the wall I saw the country that had so often been praised to us and had inflicted so much suffering upon us. A one-hour stop in Paris. At the thought of that, a warmth overcame him. The international solidarity that he had never ceased to believe in was confirmed in the embraces of the French metalworkers who greeted them, giving them food, wine, cigarettes. An hour on the platform of the Gare de l'Est in Paris, the city in which they were not allowed to set foot, before continuing on to Le Havre. And then, together with Stahlmann—who after traversing the Pyrenees had arrived in Paris illegally, had been taken in by comrades and hidden for months—the walk across the gangway to the Soviet ship. For Gallego and many other Spaniards traveling with him, making it to Soviet soil was the fulfillment of a long-standing dream. Now, in the breeze, in the green wind, it seemed to him as if he had to recount everything once more, as if what he had just recounted had already drawn away from him; he searched for words to conjure up the face of the anarchist in the Pardo, the face of the pilot on the country road, all the faces of the friends and helpers, and the detested faces of the enemy.

BLINDINGLY empty, the path along the waterfront stretched out ahead of her, the water of Lake Mälaren lay still as glass, with the skiffs, barges, and small steamers huddling around the docks. The sun, having just risen above Kastellholmen, shone onto the tower of the townhouse, the cupola of the town hall, and the façades of the buildings on the northern side of the bay, which were broken up by black channels. Behind the railway embankment, the old town was shrouded in misty shade. Bischoff had headed off early, had taken the tram to the Västerbron, then gone down to Pålsundet, through the park, past the dockyard, the sheds, and the warehouses toward the sluice. On the hillside to the right extended the brick buildings of the Münchenbryggeriet, with stepped gables, balconies, and merlons, with the cathedral of the boiler house and its enormous chimney. On the left, between white piles of sand, the cranes stood on tracks, legs splayed, their necks stretched skyward. Hawsers were pulled taut between the iron bolts on the edge of the wall and the bows and sterns of the ships. As on every Thursday morning, today, the twenty-fourth of August, she would be going over to the construction sites on Kungsklippan during the breakfast break to collect for the Red Aid. She didn't yet know how she should answer the questions that would be directed at her—she herself was searching for explanations—but she didn't want to avoid an encounter with the workers. It is important, she thought, that I face up to them, especially today. Rising up steeply on her right was the cliff face—moist here and there from the groundwater—into which was cut the Maria Elevator building, which was also adorned with ogive windows, arcades, bay windows, and turrets. Up above, the castle-like building that crowned the old town on the southern slope protruded from the green of the hilltop. Bischoff read the inscriptions on the façades. The words *Machine Workshop*, on the gable wall from the top of which the beam of a hoist protruded, was difficult to decipher, for traces of letters indicated that there had previously been a blacksmith and wagon factory here, and an even earlier, almost invisible layer of lettering adverted to Stockholm's Electric Boiler Cleaning Company. The building of the construction materials firm Ernström and Company adjoined a narrow wooden stairwell leading to a series of forecourts; farther back, among hard shadows and snatches of glinting walls on the sides, behind the parapet of a balcony, she could see the dog-legged firewall of the laundry and shower block. She felt as if the interpretation of all these inscriptions allowed her to attain something like stability. She lingered in front of the wooden shed with the large letters ZEMENT on it. The blocks of freight goods on the dock, under the sharply sun-chiseled tarpaulin, resembled sarcophagi. Ramparts made from the rubble of torn-down walls climbed up toward Hornsgatan, from which the first groups of dockworkers were approaching along sloping paths. Just now, a train emerged from the tunnel, emitting its high-pitched signal, and rolled down from the hill and across the bridge. The traffic on the winding roads around the sluice grew heavier, the arms of the clock on the tower of the Maria Magdalena Church edged toward six o'clock. Everything was inexorable. Soon, Bischoff would approach the path along the sluice, reach the marketplace where the fishmongers and the greengrocers were setting up their stands, and enter the office on Mälartorget, where she would be briefed about the situation that had emerged. Three hours later she found herself in front of the carpenters and bricklayers. The old foreman, who had always welcomed her warmly, stood there in silence, his arms crossed. A few of the young workers were already picking up stones. Nazi-Communist, one of them yelled at her. She stepped closer to them. The earlier discussion in the Red Aid offices had led to conflicting opinions. Someone had invoked Lenin's principle that Communist politics should always be carried out in a way that everybody could understand. But the situation was now so complicated, so menacing, that all available chances for protection had to be seized, even if they could not be immediately explained. Yesterday, the Party newspaper had designated the signing of the nonaggression pact between the Soviet Union and Germany as a victory of Soviet diplomacy. For more than a year, all suggestions of entering into an alliance against fascism had been rejected by England and France. What's more, Chamberlain and Daladier had pursued the tactic of pushing Germany into a war with the Soviet state; and now, the moment of self-preservation had arrived. The accord meant the dissolution of the Anti-Comintern Pact. Yet it remained unclear what would happen with Poland. Why, people asked, did the agreement not contain the otherwise normal proviso that the mutual assurances would be nullified in the event of an attack on a third country. Though it was still possible to read the pact as a final means of compelling an alliance with the Western powers, there was no justification for the declarations of friendship toward the German Reich. You've allied yourselves with the fascists, yelled one of them at Bischoff, and pointed to a newspaper picture showing the delegates making a toast at the gala dinner in Moscow. Walrus moustache, trimmed moustache, pince-nez, monocle, smiles frozen in the corners of their mouths. A non-aggression pact, she said, was no alliance. The fact that they had managed to force Germany to cooperate could be part of the struggle against fascism. The pact had driven a wedge into the conspiracy for the capitalist **153** redistribution of the world. Don't try to lie your way out of it, cried the worker holding the newspaper, it says in here something about an unbreakable agreement between the partners. The pact served to maintain the peace, said Bischoff; to divide up Poland, answered another, coiling his arm back to hurl the stone at her. You'd better go, said the foreman, I can no longer guarantee your safety. The Soviet Union, said Bischoff, had to choose between the risks of being exposed to German aggression or of being misunderstood in the process of preventing war; it chose the lesser evil. Just look, she said, at how England and France had allowed the German war machine to grow, how they had consented to the conquest of Austria, Czechoslovakia, and the Memel Territory, to the crushing of the Spanish Republic, how all their actions were calculated to ensure they remained unscathed. The stone hit her in the head, and blood ran across her brow; the bloody lump was still clearly visible when she took part in the afternoon meeting that Tombrock had organized at Brecht's house. Once again we sat among the tables in the smoke, but this time the attentiveness of the group was shot through with an uneasy suspense. Brecht asked what effect the pact would have on the Communists in France and on the German opposition. Mewis was present, as was Warnke. They talked to each other in whispers. In order to avoid jeopardizing the pact, said Warnke, our Party organizations had to exercise restraint. We have to assume that the Germans want peace. Though fascism never provides guarantees for the cessation of its advances, the Soviet Union must have received assurances that its spheres of interest would remain untouched. Hodann, who was in attendance this time, asked how the division into spheres of interest was reconcilable with the internationalism propounded by the Soviet Union. Whether, in taking a step that seemed right at this point in time, they might not be abandoning the workers of all countries in the longer term, robbing them of their most basic tenets and leaving them bereft of new guiding principles. Mewis reacted angrily. The new guiding principles were given by the pact, he said. They could be found in the attempt to achieve a rapprochement between the Soviet people and the German working class. This was a great gain for socialism. Let's suppose, said Brecht, that Germany were to attack Poland and the Baltic states: that would necessarily provoke an invasion by the Red Army. How, he asked, could such a step be justified to the global proletariat. If it came to that, said Mewis, then the decision would be justified because it would be purely in the service of containing the war. Why, it was asked, had the Soviet Union not resisted the previous German land grabs. How

could they have done that, cried Mewis, when the Western powers were just waiting for them to expose themselves. No, he said, when it comes to combating the injustice of Versailles, we have to side with Germany. Cries of outrage could be heard. The Soviet Union is on its own, said Mewis. The threats against it have not been neutralized. To consolidate its security, borders might have to be shifted. But we mustn't see our main foe in Germany but in the governments of England and France, for it is they who are seeking to provoke war. It was clear that Brecht harbored skepticism toward these explanations. The Social Democrats, he said, can now offer a combative position. Look, they'll cry, how the Communists have cast aside the Popular Front. If the Social Democrats are getting indignant about Soviet policies, said Warnke, then it's because things have not conformed to their expectations. They had never uttered a word of approval regarding the Soviet efforts to enter into an alliance with the Western powers. On the contrary, they bought the British fabrication that it was impossible to fulfill Moscow's wishes. Having contributed to the rejection of a joint security program, they now paint themselves as upstanding socialists, and under the guise of their liberal democracy the bourgeoisie is standing right there beside them. An atmosphere of distrust, of mutual surveillance, had developed. The studio, with the figures sitting crouched over, the blurring shelving, resembled a kind of interrogation room. Brecht pressed again for information about the situation of the French Communists and the antifascists in the German underground. As far as France goes, said Mewis, in a slightly reprimanding tone, there was no talk of an agreement between the Party and the reactionary forces. There, the nonaggression pact was being seen as a matter of military policy and not as an ideological provision. In Germany as well, not a single Communist had reconciled themselves with fascism. Yet we had to follow the directive, he said, of assuming a posture toward the regime that mirrored that of the Chinese Communists under the dictatorship of Chiang Kai-shek, and work toward winning back our legality. It is too early, he responded to another of Brecht's questions, to expect an immediate release of prisoners, but the growing embitterment in the country, the decay of morale in the army and the mass organizations have certainly benefited us. Since Ribbentrop's visit to Moscow, the impression of Germany's invincibility had faded. Intelligence suggested that the food shortages and the fear of war could provoke revolts. In the group by the door to the hallway, a heated discussion had broken out. The pact, yelled a woman, will only deepen fascism's corruption of the German workers. Then Lindner's voice could be heard. She spoke of the weakening, the disempowerment, of the French Party. It won't be of much help to the French Communists, she said, if the agreement is framed as a sign of the German desire for peace. Their forced neutrality toward fascism is robbing them of their last remnants of strength. Not only are they made to look despicable in light of the steadfastness and patriotism of France and England; their Party, beholden to the Soviet Union, is also threatened with being banned. The dark-haired woman in the background, Weigel, yelled that the working class, confused by the Soviet directives, are laying down their weapons. Assuaging her, Mewis countered that a rebirth of proletarian cooperation was imminent, but in an altered form. In the shadow cast by the back of his chair, Brecht's narrow face displayed a mask-like astonishment. We couldn't get past the clash of opinions. Only the spokespeople of the Party were convinced that the Soviet Union's decision, in this cutthroat climate, was the only valid one. Even if others were willing to consent to this perspective, there was still a lack of clarity evoked by the conflict between the wishful thinking that the logic of the decision might reveal itself and the attempt to fall into line with these contradictions out of discipline. We felt ourselves to be at the mercy of a politics that could not be influenced and that crushed all individual considerations. The nightmarishness of it resided in the fact that a seemingly unreal entity was claiming to be the sole representative of reality. What was really engulfing us at that moment was the renewed realization of how divorced we were from everything that made up the affairs of the state. We had become accustomed to accepting the deformities that were nothing but a reflection of our own insignificance and mental weakness. The Party functionaries were prepared to view the combination of irreconcilable elements as a necessity;

they accepted the skewed, fragile constructions as a makeshift means of finding any kind of stability at all in an environment which threatened to erode all understanding. The destructive forces were so strong that they could only be circumvented via secret paths, with cunning; anybody who wanted to withstand them had to become tough, callous. A system that we wanted to call ludicrous had to be considered normal. Toasts were made with revolvers pressed against one another's chests. Contemplation could only be a sign of deviousness. This left its mark on the faces of the delegates. Their features had drawn narrow, their gazes suspicious, their mouths clenched. Once there had been faces like those of Bebel, Liebknecht, Luxemburg, Lenin, Trotsky, Antonov-Ovseyenko, Bukharin, Schlyapnikov, and Tretyakov—but how, we asked ourselves, could such faces show themselves today, among this scratching and burrowing.

Crawling through the morass, we were happy if we managed to arrive at even a hint of a path. None of what was accessible to us could be compared to the plans of the masters. We were invertebrate animals, washed onto the sand by the breaking waves, floundering among alien formations: even the smallest forward motion between logs and jagged edges was a triumph. Brecht sat in his deep armchair, his hand cupped behind his ear. The brown Venetian leather of his jacket, full of black, horizontal creases, melted into the contours of the dark red leather of the recliner. His face glowed ivory from the cavity, shielded by a flat cap. His shoulders fell away steeply. Head held by a thin neck. Off to the side, his colleague Steffin leaned against the wall, askew and stiff like a chess piece. Guests next to one another on stools, elbows propped on their knees. Others, a clump with nubs against the glowing depths of the adjoining room. Brecht abstained from taking a position. Just posed questions. I tried to divine something about what he was thinking. During my earlier encounter with Grieg I had gained a mere intimation of the clash between politics and literature. Now I was being subjected to a shock, and becoming aware of this collision led me to long to exit my anonymity as well. But I had nothing to show that might arouse the interest of others. Behind me the tabletops were floating and laden with papers, columns and pedestals shooting up between them. The mechanism of the production that was taking place here was still unfamiliar to me. The fact that Brecht withdrew into a sheath of coldness was irrelevant; the only thing that mattered were the works, which right down to the smallest poem spoke of an involvement with the events that were related to my own existence. Calling together experts, lurking as if inside a giant listening device, rushing to absorb information, recasting impulses—all seemed to constitute elements of his working method. The collective knowledge that he absorbed like a sponge lent everything that he put on paper a universal, political significance. Yet the political was to be understood here as something that drew its impact from the field of human coexistence. He absorbed the oscillations in perspective with seeming arrogance, and it was as if I could hear the hammering with which he manufactured a chain of congruousness out of the contradictory. But how, I asked myself, was it possible to transfer this political capacity to the medium of literature so completely that it seemed to be embedded entirely in the present while simultaneously asserting a sense of total autonomy. We tended to agree that politics, which determined the fates of nations, had to force everything that belonged to artistic language into the background. Considering forms of expression other than those that directly referred to current problems would almost have been tantamount to turning our backs on the enormous struggle to maintain peace. And yet, after all this preparation, I was edging closer to that which I saw as my vocation. Professional writer: that sounded like professional revolutionary. And just as the many who carried out the revolution stood behind the latter, so too they stood behind the writer, examining what he had dreamt up in isolation; and it was only through their mental concentration that his words finally received their true life. We were all planners, inventors. We had to seek out the tool that we were best able to wield. Had I been alone with Brecht, I would have told him that the clash of two instruments that had previously seemed to me of equal value had suddenly forced me to choose one of them, the artistic one. In making this choice, I was not distancing myself from my political path, the bonds I had formed, my fundamental convictions; all of that continued to exist. Nevertheless, I recognized that I had been seized by the desire to become a student of my own experiences, to stop repressing them and to attempt to articulate them as precisely as possible. I stood up; eyes turned toward me, and a moment later, because I said nothing, away from me again. I found myself in a large workshop; or, since the effort of acquainting myself with the instruments and machines here nearly caused me to pass out, in a torture chamber. Brecht was at home among these menacing structures and workbenches. He sat there slyly in his leather trench, his bony hands clasped together. He was able to find his way through the web of language that glimmered out against the decay we were unable to halt. Unable to say anything that would confront the tortures, I could offer little more than deranged screams. Prognoses for the next stages of development swept over the manuscripts, notes, stage models. In the same way as the possible became a gushing wave of vowels and consonants that surged toward me and hammered into me, everything I had carried within me through the endless days in the factories and workshops was washed together and pounded into each other. The answers that I wanted to give had to free themselves from pressure that had been building over my entire life. The machinery thrummed in the room. Mewis, Warnke, and a few others whose names I didn't know were building a structure to place in front of the decay, the catastrophe. Time and again they were able to contrive new forms of defense. Brecht too, in a different way, was grappling with permanence. Light reflecting on the lenses of his glasses gave the impression of two glowing pupils. His nose tapered to a point. The corners of his mouth were tinted brown from the sap of his chewed-up cigar. A girl, about eight years old, Brecht's daughter, walked among the people sitting in the room, stepping on their feet. Brecht scolded her. Everything on the ground, said the child in Danish, is there to be stepped on. The conversation suddenly dissipated. Final phrases evaporated. Only here and there a whispered, mumbled word. A figure rose up from the shadows, presenting himself as a poet-prince, strapping, with a long mane, dramatically set yet deliquescent facial features, and bent over Brecht, cooing to him. Brecht turned away from him, dodging the spraying saliva. Greid, like the two Swedish writers Matthis and Ljungdal, was a member of his staff of aids and advisers. Not only had Greid secured himself an overblown position among the emigrants through his marriage to the sister of the banker Aschberg; his training as an actor also enabled him to lend his every word a significance and solemnity. Some of his remarks implied that he had inspired Brecht to produce a collection of aphorisms. His Swedish friends too had approached him; he sat slumped, listened tiredly to reports related to literary plans. I saw Rosalinde's face, yellowish in the doorway to the hall. Weigel, in a washed-out, blue apron, waited impatiently for the guests to depart. Bischoff and Lindner headed off. Other groups stood up slowly, weaving between the tables and chests, their legs lost in dark trenches. Outside, the reflection of the setting sun lay red on the trunks of the pine trees. I tried to remember what had swept through me earlier, like a presentiment of new possibilities, but found only emptiness. It was no longer possible to approach Brecht. Nobody said goodbye. One by one, at long intervals, the visitors stole out of the garden. Mewis waved me over to him and his companions. Before we went our separate ways I had received an assignment from him. As I walked through the door Steffin came over to me. She placed her hand gently on my arm. One day later this week, she said, I could come by in the afternoon.

When I spoke to Rosalinde about these hours, the work that had been assigned to me was already sitting inside of me like a block encased in silence. Participation in conspiratorial activity had something simple, self-evident, to it and didn't seem to involve risks. I carried out the job with confidence, according to Bischoff's rule, like a pedestrian who refuses to be blindsided by any unforeseen incidents, staunchly insisting on their legality in the face of any questions that might arise. My assignment immediately slotted into an everyday routine. Perhaps during my conversation with Rosalinde it still possessed a trace of novelty, but this manifested itself at most in the thought that I would never say anything about it. If the undertaking originally placed me in a state of tension, it was only because it reinserted me into a larger context. We were walking through the city in the heat of the final days of August. Alongside me I was pushing my bicycle, which I had bought for ten kronor at the lost and found office at the police station down on Drottninggatan. Rosalinde resisted my assertion that the tangled confusion of our days could be surmounted with sober judgment; that the horror, the faulty circuits and shocks could be picked apart like normal events. She refused to see anything desirable in the ability to adapt to this twisted situation. To treat this like something valid—that would be giving in, capitulating in the face of this campaign of terror against thought. If a war comes, she said, it won't come because we have failed to sufficiently adjust to the distortions but because we have made far too many compromises with them. I brought up her father's struggle. His pacifism, I said, his decades-long attacks against the militarists and chauvinists, were a component of the greater effort to overcome the drive for annihilation. Tens of thousands stood beside him, and they were still not strong enough. The phantasmagoria could only be torn down once it had been pierced by reason. I conceded that, through continual interaction with sick regimes, disfigurements were also bound to develop within us as well, but this was the price we had to pay if any resistance at all were to take place. It wasn't simply about fighting fascism. Even if the violence of fascism displayed itself most clearly, it remained only a single element in a worldwide plan of destruction behind which were the switchgears of cartels and trusts. All continents were rife with thievery, enslavement, and exploitation, and the powers that sought to terrify and paralyze us were no phantoms but could each be called out by name. The tiniest sign of surrender on our part helped to promote their growth, and our knowledge was too limited to confront their ever-increasing depredation. If war were to eventuate, the most terrible thing would be the fact that it would not yet be a war

for the creation of justice but a war between business giants, not a revolutionary war to topple the exploiters but a war for raw materials for the
capitalist market. And now, said Rosalinde, millions of working people
have to let themselves be dragged into this mayhem because the politicians who call themselves progressive were unable to explain their situation to them clearly, because for twenty years, instead of making use of
their supposed knowledge, they had been bickering with one another and
wasting their time tearing each other to pieces. They had never wanted
the unity about which they had expended so many words; they were only
ever interested in advancing their position. The people leading the parties are monopolists, like the leaders of commerce. As ideologues, they
cannot be distinguished from the speculators on the stock markets.
Nothing new can come from their world, for they refuse to relinquish

their washed-out criteria, they cling to their privileges, their sense of superiority, their envy, their thirst for validation. What sort of analyses was
I on about, she asked. And I heard within me the doubts that I myself
was trying to fend off. Was it not mere verbiage, I asked myself, when the
Communist Party ascribed the blame for the threat of war to the British
barons of finance, the French banker families; were not Communists
and fascists equal to one another in that they both locked up in prisons
and camps anyone who didn't toe the line; was not their final word always the liquidation order, had they not, because they wanted the same
paternalistic system, again ended up at war, the most enduring argument
in their common language. But everything on our side was aimed at preventing war, I said, countless people were still fighting in the underground to change the situation. I mentioned Spain, but in Spain of all
places, she said, the remaining will to revolt had been crushed by the
machinations of the powerful. I tried to explain that the shift in perspective, the apparent inconsistency of our politics was necessary, but she
stuck to her position that nothing could be achieved any longer with rhetoric and pretense. She parried my objection. How is politics supposed to
help us, she said, when it is politics that has got us into this hopeless situation in the first place. Again she interrupted as I went to answer. You
believe in reason as if it were a miracle, she said. As if it were still possible
for reason to suddenly sprout from an epoch of idiocy. Yes, she said, her
understanding of the situation was limited, but she couldn't help but see
what I called the politics of reason as a mere red herring that kept us
shackled in self-deception. Everything that had value for us, she said, lay
buried beneath an avalanche of commonplaces. Our personal reactions
cannot achieve anything at the moment, she said. The only thing we can

do in this fragmentary landscape is pick out the pieces that can best be brought into alignment with our intentions. She didn't understand, she said, how I could freely submit to that kind of reduction of my self, that it contradicts everything I had previously told her about my work plans. Accepting limitations in the political arena, I said, did not preclude the demand for integrity in artistic work. Such a desire for freedom, she countered, could only be laughable to those who determine our fates from above. I too sensed the inadequacy of my statements, for I knew that my relationship with art and with politics could not be separated from one another, and that the ongoing uncertainties in the field of politics also impeded the clarification of my artistic intentions. My background hung from me again like a weight; as with my every attempt to find my way to myself, I continually ran up against this basic condition of disenfranchisement, voicelessness. When Rosalinde now spoke of Toller, it was in all likelihood to stress to me that she didn't expect to get the help she needed from me. She clung to the idealized figure of this dead man; her imagination was filled by his warmth, benevolence, and spontaneity, his understanding for the hardship of others. She portrayed him to me like a lover, dressed up as the father she wished she'd had; but he didn't even know how to help himself, I said, he killed himself because he could no longer see any way out politically. Is that supposed to be the solution then, I asked, to be sunk by the mourning of our powerlessness, the incomprehensibility of events. Angrily she said he had lived for the revolution, had spent five of his best years in prison, had fought against the narrow-mindedness of party politics. All of his work, she said, was a condemnation of the disempowerment of the individual; sick, psychologically shattered, he had stood up for the weak, he didn't spare himself for a single day, he never attempted to make peace with makeshift solutions or half-measures; yes, she said, he had to allow himself to be crushed, and yet in his vulnerability he was still more honest than the others who hid themselves behind their composure. I have no doubt, she said, that someday, when we have made it through this time, we will recognize him and his like as the most insightful. Now, and once again came this *yes*, which was like a loud groan, now you all see them as lost souls, because they hang themselves, because they drink poison, put a bullet in their heads; perhaps later on you lot will recognize in this a dignified response to an all-encompassing extortion. What use is their despair, their flight, I said. But the sallowness of her face terrified me. We stopped still, on the corner of Kungsgatan, in front of Stureplan, the blue trams rattling past. Had there been more of them, she said, and had people listened to them and not only to the others, with their regurgitated slogans, the world would look different today. My demurral sounded hollow; I paused. I thought about the other person whom I had left a few hours ago, the gray-haired gnome in the narrow room on Upplandsgatan. He sat with the curtains drawn shut, muttering as he filled folio pages with his scrawling, sitting up every now and then, whistling and humming in his Viennese intonations as he read through what he had written. A member of the secretariat of the Comintern, smuggled into Sweden covertly, commissioned by Dimitrov to prepare the weekly paper, the first edition of which was to appear in September. Lager, editor of the Party paper *Ny Dag* [New Day], member of the Politburo, had briefed me on my duties. I went to visit Rosner with German and Swedish newspapers bought at the train station, announced my arrival with a special knock, translated the

Swedish news for him, provided him with the supplementary information that he needed, took the old newspapers with me, cut-up sheets divided into small amounts, in order to toss them into the next wastepaper basket, the next trash can. His dwarf-like body with its large head disappeared behind the reams of paper on the table that stood perpendicular to the window. The modest room in which he resided was no more than three and a half meters long and two meters wide. It was located beside the kitchen, with panes of glass set into the doors. In the front corner, next to the door to the hallway stood a white tiled stove; crumpled maps of Europe hung against the greenish wallpaper. Newspapers and books lay stacked on the floor, the chairs, the sofa. The comrades who were harboring Rosner were not there during the day; the man was a taxi driver, the woman a waitress at Café Tranan, just down on Odenplan. Peering through the slit into the courtyard, I asked if the closed curtains didn't arouse attention in the neighborhood. At most during the first week, he answered, then people grew accustomed to it. The apartment was on the ground floor; directly to the left, the tower-like stairwell rose up, jutting out from the body of the building; off in the distance, behind the walls that broke up the row of courtyards, tall façades limited the field of vision, and sparrows chirped in the ivy on the walls of the building opposite. The courtyards also extended to the right, with tool sheds, metal frames for beating rugs, bicycle racks, and wash houses. A cast-iron fence with lance-shaped bars divided the junkyard of the neighboring plumber's workshop from the adjacent yard. Everything was gray, dreary; the windows, lined up above one another in endless rows over four, five stories, looked opaque. Nobody could suspect that, way down here, these floral curtains could conceal the editor of a periodical that sought to disseminate the directives of the Communist International. No place corresponded less to the title of the publication, *Die Welt* [The World], than this room in this unseemly building on Upplandsgatan. Yet he brimmed with pride as he uttered the name. The whole world lay out there, and he was connected to it through the lines he penned. The newspaper, comprising thirty-two pages, would be produced on the Party's printing press in a run of a thousand copies. The printed word, he said, beaming at me from behind the thick lenses of his glasses, has a power that no walls can withstand; there is always a crack somewhere that it can penetrate. He asked me to look for Jewish names in the telephone book so as to add them to the register of people who were to be sent sample copies of the paper. He refused to believe that the Jacobssons, Danielssons, and Rosengrens had deep Swedish roots. Jakobsohn, Danielsohn, and Rosenzweig, he said, shaking his head of tousled hair, and the Lewins and the Blumenbergs—you're telling me they're Christians in this country. From my very first visit he had afforded me unmitigated trust. He never doubted that the people sent to him by the Party to deliver materials and pick up the finished manuscript pages were absolutely reliable. This interdependence also produced a feeling of security in me. I accepted my work as the continuation of a test, the beginnings of which could be traced back to my time together with Coppi and Heilmann. Thus, as I walked with Rosalinde to Humlegården, past the strategic corner between the Royal Library, where I copied out excerpts from the international press, and Sandberg's bookstore, where I could leaf through the international new releases in the reading room, I saw Rosner's laughing face, his short-sighted gaze, heard him sing through the gap in his teeth of the city of his dreams. Rosalinde was on her way to the suburban train that would take her to Viggbyholm, where in the afternoon she had to work in the laundry of the boarding school. I couldn't help her, didn't know what to say to console her. I could have told her about Rosner. The fact that I was prohibited from saying anything about it made the gulf between us even wider. Rosner had asked me to track down a dentist who could fit him for a set of dentures. I was also supposed to get a radio for him; he wanted to listen to music in his hermitage. An appointment was arranged with Doctor Wolff; Rosner felt safe in his projection of a shared confession with the Jewish doctor. Pettersson, the comrade who was putting him up, would pick him up one evening after the surgery had closed. I saw myself on my bike, on my way from Rosner's, gliding down the long, straight Upplandsgatan, that virtually empty street on the northern edge of the city, the street which people called Siberia and on which the houses possessed that uniformity and anonymity that illegals look for in a hideout. I could feel the air stroking past me as I rode along Karlbergsvägen, past Odenplan, Tegnérlunden, where Strindberg sat on the hill, naked and muscular, his arms jammed into the ground behind him, and approached the copper-green roofs and cupolas overlooking Norra Bantorget. I calculated how many hours I had left in which to visit Brecht. It was four o'clock. Twelve hours had passed since the beginning of the morning shift. The eight-hour working day, my time with Rosner, and the hour with Rosalinde formed sealed entities. Before me, a half-hour trip to Lidingö. Two to three hours in Brecht's studio. A half-hour journey back. I had to be home by eight at the latest. A hasty meal in the kitchen. Potatoes, tinned meat, a glass of milk. I needed at least seven hours of sleep to get through the coming day. I had my right hand wrapped around the handlebar of my bike and my left hand holding Rosalinde's. We had arrived at the stop at Engelbrektsgatan. Everything we were lacking was palpable as Rosalinde leaned out of the train window and, full of exhaustion, said that, soon, she too would be left with no alternative but to follow Toller's example.

For today, let's leave it at what the experts are telling us, Brecht said, chanting hollowly: there will be no war. That sounded as if it came from the prologue of a play, but it was part of the introduction to a series of work conversations that initially stretched over some two weeks. If the studies, which generated a mass of detailed plans, did not lead to the production of the work about Engelbrekt, it was not so much because in mid-September Brecht began to develop and write *Mother Courage*, and in October was preoccupied with the composition of the radio play *The Interrogation of Lucullus*, commissioned by the Swedish Broadcasting Service, but because the material we examined in connection with Engelbrekt's epoch was so broad that it was not yet possible to find a dramatic form for it. It was certainly not that there had not been enough time to conceive and produce a piece: he had needed a month for *Mother Courage*, fourteen days for *Lucullus*. He approached a work as if it already lay finished within him, needing only to be coaxed out into the light of day. But the story of Engelbrekt could not be made into the fable which he—to my bemusement—desired. Now and then he would grow tired, dismiss the topic, and then he seemed to set to work drafting a dramatic epic that could do justice to the continual bifurcations and ruptures, the contradictions and ambiguities of the events. The snatches of conversation that I caught as I entered implied that, despite the looming threat of war, indeed, even if war were to break out, the work was to be continued. Under all circumstances, the craft of writing was on a par with political events. On the afternoon of the thirty-first of August and on the first of September, during the hourly radio transmissions, after a short discussion of the state of the world, Brecht steered the conversation back to the day's workload. Especially now that external forces were gaining ascendency, he urged us to cling to that which we had created under our own steam. He would circle his way into the material that Matthis and Ljungdal had put together for him, turning back to revisit, reinterpret, and delve deeper into specific images. This time, Brecht's constant need for impulses that could be elaborated upon was focused upon an event about which Matthis had provided information. With short strides, hunched over, Brecht paced back and forth through the room along the paths created by the tables. He had interrupted Ljungdal, who had come from the public library after his shift and was reading out loud from the books he had brought, and ordered Matthis to go back over the course of events which had produced the original impetus to develop the piece. Who is she anyway, he yelled. Doesn't she know who she's dealing with. Treating my work like that. We should storm the building. Seize possession of the stage. He wanted to hear how she had sat up there on her high horse, in her stronghold. Matthis had given Brunius, the director of the Royal Dramatic Theater, the manuscript for *Galileo*, and her response had been that they don't do religious plays. Him: it is not about the Galileans but about an Italian scientist from the Renaissance. That could hardly be of interest either, she said, and placed the booklet among other texts on the shelf, where it would probably lie unread for twenty years. Embittered and outraged after this initial report, Brecht had asked Matthis which forces there had been against the rulers, which freedom fighters, popular leaders, there had been in Sweden. The mention of Engelbrekt—or Engelbrecht, as Brecht called him at first, after his original German name—had immediately made an impression on him; he placed his ferocity, his wrath, in this figure, was already sketching him out before he even learned the details of his character and deeds. By taking on Engelbrekt, he could also take a stance on the history of this country in which he had ended up. A prevailing sense of horror seemed to preside here in the face of the foreign, the different; he was distressed by the apparent tendency to capitulate to the flattening of thought that had driven him out of Germany. And yet he wanted to stay in Sweden. He had been provided with a house here as well as in Skovsbostrand, on the island of Fyn, where he could work; he was also interested in observing how the tussles between democratic and reactionary forces would pan out. When he said he would be willing to interrupt his work at any time and continue on to somewhere else, however, he was merely describing his method of adapting to the condition of life in exile. In Sweden, as in his six years previous in Denmark, he remained close to Germany: he wanted to be able to return as quickly as possible should the opportunity arise. But the chance of that was now growing increasingly remote, and, by way of precaution, he had asked friends to resume their efforts to obtain the American visa that he had previously rejected and then reapplied for. Ljungdal went to make a gesture as if he wanted to encompass the panorama of the fourteenth century, but Brecht was not done with the Royal Theater yet, and Matthis had to recommence with the description of the setting. The director's office was not pompous but of restrained appearance, the walls a matte gray, divided by strips of wood. Squat bookshelves, green plush

curtains on the two windows looking out onto Nybrogatan, a green sofa in front of the empire desk in the corner, a conference table made of russet mahogany, about two and a half meters long, the seats upholstered with burgundy fabric. Which floor was it on, how do you get there, asked Brecht. From the front office up two wide flights of stairs, then up a spiral staircase to the antechamber. After checking in at reception and a long wait, in through the paneled door. Inside, the windows were open. The tower of the insurance company Fylgia was visible on the corner of Birger Jarlsgatan, its flag flapping. Red company name on a white background. The wind was blowing over from Berzelii Park and carried the scent of the acacias. The traffic hummed around the roundabout at Nybro harbor, one of the skerry steamers let out its huffing departure signal. Behind the brass lamp with the green shade sat the mistress of the house. Matthis handed her the copy of the piece. The large format alone, the brownish paper of the manuscript, was unusual for her, displeased her. She weighed it in her hand. She was familiar with Brecht as the author of the text of *The Threepenny Opera*. She thought of him primarily as someone who adapted old plays. Rustling on the wall beside her were theater bills, announcing *Gustav Vasa* at the top, directed by Sjöberg. What was her face like, asked Brecht. Expansive, cool, said Matthis. It couldn't be called beautiful, as it lacked personal features. More like a mask. As if she were playing the role of a queen. A high brow. Hair brushed back slick. White pearls in her ears. White pearls around her neck. In order to understand Engelbrekt and the revolution of fourteen thirty-four, said Ljungdal, we first of all need to address the era of Margaret and the Kalmar Union. As if he hadn't heard the remark, picturing the director's office with its open windows, Brecht said: that's so we know which way the wind blows. He asked if anything else had stuck out to Matthis. There was a glass door on the left, half covered by a curtain, he said. Through a pane decorated with Jugendstil vines, a section of the colonnade in front of the theater's upper circle could be glimpsed. The closed nature of the room in which his play had been dismissed was pierced by the glass door. The direct access to the auditorium, to the stage, this seemed to preoccupy Brecht, who never went to the theater. We should try to win over Sjöberg, said Matthis. Brecht waved that away in an instant. Just as he had met with a lack of understanding from the director of the theater, he now showed disdain toward the other representatives of the establishment. The piece could only be realized under our own direction, said Brecht. The directors here are unfamiliar with our theories. And when he spoke of *us*, he meant his willingness to engage in collective work on the text, his openness to a range of suggestions, while the task of deciding on a selection remained his—although particular images, confrontations, and plot developments were then put back up for discussion. His digressions from the topic, which could have the appearance of inattentiveness, interruptions—something he didn't tolerate in others—quickly revealed their relevance to the discussion. Right from the start, the form of the work was lit up before us. It was to comprise two distinct parts, each full of contradictions, but in the first the powers from above would prevail, and in the second, the forces from below. Developing commerce, building cities, the early bourgeoisie rose up against the society of the knights and prelates in their fortified castles and churches. For a century, a new class had been forging ahead, its contours still hazy, here dependent upon the local nobility, there linking up with foreign enterprises, gaining advantages over static, landed property with mobile capital. The clash of two worlds: one losing its old means of compulsion yet still capable of retaining its privileges through diplomacy and military supremacy; the other progressive, in that it removed feudal forms of exploitation, while simultaneously grasping for a new, economic form of despoliation. The great majority of them, the peasantry, descending from the primal society of the freeholders who had kept workforces under their yoke. This is where the broad, enduring strength was to be found; in the village communities the vestiges of independence had been maintained. Individual landowners reached the rank of lords and squires, and, driven by the upheavals, they turned to the lucrative business of mining; the smallholders, by contrast, found themselves on a downward trajectory, weighed down ever more by the burden of taxes. Lacking rights, scarcely able to break free of their abasement, in their exodus into the mining districts, during the initial phases of industrialization as day laborers and wage laborers, the peasants formed the foundation for the emergence of an insurrectionary class. Initially as a result of the encroachment of the aristocracy and later of the expansion of the middle classes, the king had been forced to forfeit his despotism; to maintain his power he now needed both the favor of the nobles and the support of the artisans and tradespeople. Margaret, daughter of the Danish King Valdemar IV Atterdag, betrothed to the king of Norway at the age of ten, raised by Märta, the daughter of the seer Bridget, of Swedish royalty, was elected to elevate the status of the royal line once again, and, following the establishment of the union between Denmark and Norway, to take Sweden as well and unite the three Nordic realms, creating a single great power under Denmark's leadership. First scene, fitting of the child as a model for the queen, as she is later to appear. Anointed and combed by the maids, in a gown of golden, shimmering brocade, her face tiny in the headscarf falling over her shoulders, enveloped by the bell-shaped robe held together by an enormous gemstone brooch, the child stood like a doll before the stamping royal household. The child was then passed to the sickly, gauche king, who, in his tight-fitting jacket, covered in embroidered axe-wielding lions, with a low-sitting belt, his dagger hanging from the middle, in two-tone stockings, his feet in pearl-embroidered poulaines, his shoulders broadened by his ermine-lined robe, straining to hold his head up under the heavy crown, holding his slack hand toward her. Surrounding them, the knights, in basinets with nose guards, pointed helmets with visors raised, tall chain-mail collars, polished breastplates, leather vests, arm guards, and greaves, clasping hefty swords. To litanies, accompanied by trumpets, cymbals, and drumming, on the Sunday after Easter, the ninth of April, thirteen sixty-three, Margaret was wed to Haakon by an archbishop and two bishops. In the fall of the same year, Albert of Mecklenburg rode into Stockholm to have himself named king of Sweden. Brecht was considering a simultaneous scene in the style of medieval drama, in which Margaret's antagonist would be introduced. Then, in working with the historical documents, the necessity of creating a contrast arose. The mention of the long-running feud between the Swedish noble families, of the battle for the crown, between son and father, brother and brother, the reference to the struggle for castles and fiefs, the continual shifting of the borders of the three monarchies in the north, the pillaging and plundering, the selling off and pawning of provinces and shipping channels, the devastation of the soil, the blind robbery of the people through exploitative tributes, the starvation, the treacherous murders and unsuccessful military campaigns of the Folkung dynasty, and finally the reports about the era reigned over by angels of death, by death dances and Black Masses—all of this gave form to the backdrop to Albert's appearance for Brecht. The aftereffects of the Great Plague—which had taken more than a third of the population and rendered idle large sectors of agriculture and mining—hung over the arrival of the man from Mecklenburg, who did not master the language of the land, who represented the business interests of the Hanseatic League, and who drew his legionnaires from the armed forces of the Teutonic Order. His appointment by the ruling classes, who needed a dictator from outside of their competing clans—their enmity fueled by the intrigues to secure the throne—and who would resolve the grievances with terror while remaining their instrument; the calculations of the risks and the gains associated with his installation; the hope of the ruling classes that Albert, supported by his powerful coastal cities, could stave off the Danish advance and allow them to retain their position of power; the expectations harbored by the territorial lords, mine owners, and merchants of generating an increase in their capital, an economic boom, a boost in production through the consolidation of their connections with the Hanseatic League; all the efforts to curry favor with foreign princes, with all manner of self-interest lurking in the backs of their minds; and then also the peasants' fears of raised interest rates and tax payments, the unrest of the cottagers, who saw no escape from their plight; all this had to find expression in the presentation of the new monarch. The ten-year-old girl was still standing in wait, only hinting at what was to come. The German, on the other hand, was immediately able to unfurl the full breadth of his thirst for power, boasting about his connections, which stretched from Novgorod to Bruges, his people also having long ago infiltrated Stockholm. Thanks to their diligence and skill, they'd got hold of the transshipment centers, the commerce, and guilds; the harbors held the freight ships from Lübeck, Wismar, Rostock, Stralsund; for the most part, the most eminent families of the capital were of German extraction. He entailed something of the epoch of upheaval, a cunning representative of the nobility, hungry for the lucrative evolution of his office; at the same time, however, he was open to the social changes in Europe, where feudal domination was being shattered by peasant insurrections and the bourgeoisie were asserting themselves against the courts, where emperor and pope were losing authority, government administration was moving toward centralization, and handiwork, commodities trading, and finance were finding increasingly stronger forms of organization. In addition to the war specialists, his staff included representatives of the merchant class, the shipping companies, and banks, as well as experts in mining, who were supposed to get to work driving forward the extraction of iron in Dalarna. From ancient times, the Germans—who had acquired stakes in the mines and ironworks—had been entitled to privileges in the form of exemptions from taxes and duties. The production of copper and valuable iron was the foundation for the increase in exports. Apart from wax—always in demand with the continental church administrations—and furs, Sweden scarcely had goods to offer. The far-sighted, enterprising landowners, in alliance with the wholesalers, were the ones who had organized Albert's recruitment. During the period of decline, of the shortage of labor power, they had secured themselves the majority of the ownership of the pits; the discovery sites were rich with ore, inexhaustible even, and anybody who rose to prominence here could be sure not only of a leading role in the realm, but also of gaining a foothold in international commerce. The most powerful local lord, Jonsson Grip, who had taken the farms of one peasant after another and had acquired most of the mines in Dalarna, now stood as one of the preeminent members of the high council that was preparing to receive the duke. With both the accoutrements of the royal child and the inauguration of the prince from Mecklenburg, the aim was to present a symbol of sovereignty to represent the two respective quests to establish a great power. The forces standing behind each would have to measure themselves against each other, dragging the lower classes along with them and gradually driving them to revolt. The institutions were the same on both sides, shot through with conflict, their internal divisions already containing the seeds of their rupture. With the well-equipped fleet from Warnemünde and heavily armed mercenaries behind him, the emissary of the Hanseatic cities addressed the Swedish nobility with condescension. They were unable to read and write, nor could they express themselves in a global language, and were at a loss among the modern rules of business. Regardless of whether they possessed enormous swaths of arable land, forests, and mines, in his eyes they were nothing but filthy farmers, dressed in stinking rags and animal skins; they stepped before him as supplicants, relying on interpreters, which allowed him to keep his remarks ambiguous. Grip, having never been knighted because he was too stingy to turn up with armor and charger at the annual weapons show and place himself at the services of the royal armed forces, was nevertheless from the upper nobility, that of the financiers, and held the title of steward, his coat of arms bearing the griffin's head with a drop of blood on its beak. Well-versed in all manner of intrigue, he thought himself a match for the man from Mecklenburg, capable of getting anything he wanted out of him. Picturing the offices, homesteads, and castles that he would receive, the mountains of grain, the herds of livestock, the iron ingots, he led the welcoming party for the new arrival. In a violent shift from the rigid hierarchies of the wedding— with its blank, metallic procession and the rustling carmine and violet of the church elders—creaking carts smeared with feces and packed with corpses drove in, followed by grave diggers, wailing women and monks. At the foot of a beam structure swarmed the lowly and the impoverished, the beggars, some crawling crippled, hobbling on crutches, petty sinners and outlaws sat locked in the stocks, other prisoners, ropes around their necks, were shoved past by henchman with kicks and blows of the lance; conjurors and acrobats attracted small groups of onlookers around them; another mob, in provincial dress, knives and axes in their belts, stood off to the side waiting. We discussed how we could convey something of the character of the Stockholm of the day, that stilt city. Thick stakes, posts, ringed the islet, and double rows of planks, connected by roughly hewn trunks, had been rammed into the water in front of the city wall to pro-tect against waves and attacks from seamen. We gathered impressions from looking at old images. Before sketching out the play's plot, Brecht decided on the appearance of the stage. Only once a material space had been produced could the figures also become concrete in their arrange-ment and distribution, their relations to one another. The notion of a below and an above formed part of the fundamental conception. Yet con-tained within these were the internal divisions, the contradictions that were constantly emerging. The wooden platform was at once bulwark, walkway, and castle floor, uniting inside and outside. Brecht was consid-ering a mystery play which, accompanied by shawms, pipes, and fiddles, could be performed by jugglers who, swinging scythes and dressed as skeletons, evoked the calamity that primarily affected the poorest, while the rich were not only able to remain unscathed but, in the midst of the terror and desolation, to indulge in the pleasures of life. The mention of the rhymed chronicle, in which the events from the end of the fourteenth century up to and beyond the struggles for independence had been deliv-ered in song form, sparked the idea of writing the play—or at least inter-spersed sections of it—in these simple, stilted verses. Street theater could provide the natural prelude. The actors would be swept from the stage by the noblemen as they arrived, to show who was in charge. Down below: convulsing, scuffling, lying in the muck; up above: a broad, regimented parade, rising up level by level. In front of the flag-bearing mast of the cogs out in the harbor, standards, tufts of feathers, and shields jostling about.

171

Down below: earthy gray, black, umber; above: red, white, silver, gold. The festively dressed citizenry stepped forward from the wings to the blaring of horns and drums, partially concealing the clayey hues with their broad robes and wide-brimmed hats. Once Albert had positioned himself in the middle of the hosts with his retinue, everything below fell to its knees. Only the spokesperson of the hoard of peasants climbed up onto a barrel, tilted his face upward and raised his hand, as if he wanted to break into a desperate cry. But above him soldiers in chain mail beat their spears and crossbows on the ground. Meekly, the compatriot backed off. Albert wore a sleeveless cloak, peppered with uncut rubies and emeralds, which a number of Swedish courtiers admired to such an extent that, when it was removed by a page, they grabbed it and fondled it. Even the bottle of perfume with which he was sprayed aroused such curiosity that, with a dis-

missive flick of the wrist, he bequeathed it to the noblemen, who couldn't get enough of splashing it around and then sniffing at one another. In a short, custom-tailored jacket with peacock feathers sewn into it and silken hose, he sat on the throne, behind which the Mecklenburg coat of arms, the black, silver-horned bull's head against a golden background, was being held aloft. Up above, the confrontation between the free territorial lords—the small group who, thanks to ancient traditions, could afford to brutally maltreat their subordinates and who had become the filchers of the people's labor—and those exponents of an urban culture that had already revealed that the rates of profit could be increased if the living conditions of the producers were to undergo certain improvements. Up above, peers invested with unlimited powers yet acting according to different principles; on the one side the men of practical speculation, au fait with the global market, and on the other side the barbaric robber barons, with their shortsighted racketeering and frugal planning; the primitive barter economy up against the knowledge of manufacturing processes and large-scale workshops. Up above, the overlords of the worldly and ecclesiastical realms, who under the pressure of crisis were compelled to open their sparsely populated, expansive domain to new members from without, and the experienced travelers, coming from densely populated, exploited regions. Below, the burgeoning bourgeoisie, the representatives of the guilds, and the magistrate officials, who would soon assume the podium up above. On this level too, both solidarity and conflict. United in their rejection of absolute rule from above, the self-assurance of the masters clashed with the hubris of the patricians, who, due to the possessions they had amassed, thought themselves better than the others. Above, the haggling for ranks and titles, for land rights, fiefdoms, and benefices, for tax exemptions and access to trade routes; below, the friction around differences in status, the already emerging division into haute and petite bourgeoisie, the brewing of deeper unrest through a new division between tradespeople and the protoproletarian masses. Standing on the tribune, the councillor of the realm announced that the appointment of Albert as king was contingent upon his pledge to unfailingly govern in accordance with the will of the Swedish nobility. Only in name was he to be at the helm; they intended to manage the affairs of the state themselves. Above, people talked at cross-purposes, false clashes were rehearsed over issues that had already been agreed upon. What was accomplished by the antics of the pickpockets down below was enacted by the conspirators above on a larger scale, accompanied by solemn verbiage. Up there, the future captains, vice regents, bailiffs, and judges practiced their craft; here, a slashed bag was all that could be had. A speech **173** was delivered in the tongue of the Mecklenburger. Albert provided the assurance that had been demanded of him. Was full of gratitude that he could now settle in the country that he and his ilk had considered their home now for some time. He would be sure, he said, turning to face those below, to work for the good of all in this city, whose castle, house of God, monastery, trading posts, and harbor had been constructed by Germans, and whose borders he intended to expand to include the surrounding islets. The adulation that he received from below, the silence from above, revealed the contradictions between town and country. By raising the emblem of Mecklenburg, the two-headed eagle of Lübeck, and the vivid insignia of the guilds of German origin, the bourgeoisie and the tradespeople declared where they considered their loyalties to lie, and the councillors launched into a surprising announcement, pledging their allegiance to the esteemed prince of the cities of the Hanseatic League. That they did this before the knightly and ecclesiastical council had even completed the coronation was a grave violation of custom; it was as if the representatives of the bourgeois classes wanted to get in the first word, ahead of the autocrats, who had never sought their opinion. The peasant used the confusion to mount the barrel again, high-borns, he cried, removing his cap with its flaps that fell down over his ears, most humbly we wish to beseech you, but was instantly knocked down by a man-at-arms. We must, said Brecht, give an impression of the ongoing skirmishes. The attempts by the aristocrats to oblige and pin down the duke were met with his well-honed evasive maneuvers. If, for example, they spoke of the necessity of domestic dominance over the ore mines, then he would have his interpreter convey that, in order to improve output, he had brought with him a shipload of experienced miners from the pits in the Harz Mountains. Bo Jonsson Grip, sensing that the foreigner was trying to cheat him out of what was his, enjoined him to replace the military flag he bore with a different coat of arms that conveyed Sweden's supremacy; whatever you want, answered Albert, give me a banner with three crowns, and I will bear it for you. Perhaps, said Brecht, the event could be concluded with the voice of the church, with a severe sermon delivered by Bishop de Vadaterra, the emissary of Bridget in Rome. Previously, the worldly powers had featured; now it was time to hear the voice of the power whose weakening had been declared but which would nevertheless continue to assert itself for centuries to come, castigating, casting darkness, provoking confusion and wars. Amassing riches for itself, it preached the virtue of poverty. Smothering revolts, it called for patience,

174 promising rewards in the afterlife for suffering endured in this one. With the delivery of the message, the haggling for arable land and forests, for mines and smelting furnaces, for palaces and castles, taxes and customs was replaced by feigned gestures of piety and contrition. The confidant of the holy woman, in soutane and lace apron, vividly portrayed Bridget's vision of the death of Christ to the gathering. If she calls herself the bride of Christ, said Brecht during Ljungdal's discussion of the revelation, then the fate of her fiancé ought to be lamented even more. What an unloading of hatred onto that man, what lust in the description of his humiliation and torture. She saw him before her, her beloved, completely naked, the whip having shredded his flesh down to the ribs. Brecht imagined Bridget composing her *Revelationes*. How she kneeled on the stone floor, running her fingers over her skin at the sight of the blue-bleached skin of the crucified man, who couldn't lay a hand on her. His face wet from gobs of spit, his tongue bloody in his open mouth, his stomach pressed flat against his spine because all the liquid had drained from his viscera, his hands and feet wrenched by the nails to the point of tearing apart, at the moment of death the holes still dilated by the weight of his body, his shoulder blades pressed hard against the wood in their final twitching. With the invasion of the German troops into Poland, with the dizzying speed of their advance, we thought of that dreadful and prophetic address, which spoke of the mutilation of the human being and of the pain of taking part in it. I myself, the possessed woman screamed at us, closed his mouth with my fingers and closed his eyes, but no matter how I pressed, as he was taken down from the wooden beams, I couldn't bend his stiffened arms, and his knee could not be straightened. Now that the knights and the dignitaries of the city had been admonished in this way to look inside themselves

and to commemorate the one who had suffered for them, Brecht claimed, the Christian education of the young Margaret could now be portrayed, tying it back in with the opening scene. As a sixteen-year-old, in the burlap robe of a nun, a thick rope tied around her waist, head shaved bare, pale, slender, she would pray on her knees before her foster mother. Before she was to be draped in the king's bed for copulation, to inculcate in her that she was to face her coming obligations with severe self-discipline, she was given a caning in an elaborate ritual, to which she submitted, lying prone over a wooden railing, her dress hitched up, her hands folded in devotion, her eyes wide open and face unmoved. Kissing the punishing hand. Enter the maids again. They remove her hemp cloth, put on her wig, her brocade dress, its curved neckline tightly clasping the bust, sweeping out widely at the base, with its gold-embroidered pomegranate design over a purple background. The sudden transformation of the gray nun into the triumphant regent, said Brecht, had to be retained as an impression on the retina, so that her form would shine through into the following scenes, as it were, until she reenters the action in Kalmar, to reinstate the Nordic independence and reunite the three realms.

As the reports came in of the German victories, of England's and France's entry into the war, we were reviving the era of Margaret's arrival on the stage of history. In order to assure his military ascendency, directly after his accession to power Albert organized the expansion of the mines in Jarnberaland, the old iron-producing region. Letters of privilege were handed out to the owners of the mines and smelters, who were all presided over by the treasurer Jonsson Grip. In order to spur production in the industry, which comprised more than fifty pits and their attendant smelting facilities, labor power first had to be enticed through the promise of incentives. Thus, starving and rudderless, peasants and maidservants, freed prisoners, adventurers, and vagrants moved into the region around Kopparberg and Norberg, and they were promised not only rations of grains, butter, meat, herring, and salt, but also goods to the value of three marks, which they were allowed to pick out once a year from the local merchant's stock. Outlaws received the right of asylum, even those who had been accused of theft and murder could find employment, the recruiters weren't overly conscientious, the bounties being offered were smaller than the premiums they received for complete workforces. But soon enough the incentives alone were not sufficient to guarantee willing workers; wherever extra hands were needed, peasants were dug up: bailiffs decided on the profitability of a farm, and if it wasn't producing enough they would drive man, woman, and children from their land and force them to take up quarters at a pit for six months to a year. German miners were employed to dig and build adits; as experts in surveying, draining, and ventilating the pits; in the processing and smelting of the ore. Their rations were twice those of the unskilled workers and carriers, and, on top of that, they received their wages in cash. With their capital, German merchants also had stakes in the extraction, the local traders supervised the mining shares, and, with the stiff competition between the groups, those who had acquired specialist knowledge were able to increase the productivity of their lots. Through the competition among these early corporations, concerns began to form, new class strata began to emerge, of industrialists, financiers, tradespeople, and the masses who had just been freed from enslavement. The potential for large profits re-

quired increases in security personnel, the wage slaves had to be held down by mercenaries, subjected to continual threats and exemplary pun-ishments. In the medieval mines, the masters and miners had worked together cooperatively in mutual agreement; the new division of labor provoked violent antagonisms between the original bosses of the mines, who issued from the landowning class, and the encroaching aristocrats, the royal inspectors and shareholders, the foremen and the carters, load carriers and charcoal burners; and beneath, the rebelliousness of the scat-tered masses was fermenting, stored in miserable huts around the pits and smelting furnaces. Only those who were skilled in mine surveying were allowed to possess weapons, only the directors got about in armor and helmets, and any servants caught carrying a knife or a dagger were flogged. Nevertheless, certain rules of peasant society were maintained in Dalarna: the townships had their own governing assemblies, the ownership of the forests was untouchable, and the landowners preserved their independence from the royal household. And yet because privileges only ever applied to the upper classes, indignation began to grow among the oppressed, who, having made it a rung higher than their former, beastly existence, were now edging toward self-consciousness. Why, we asked ourselves while listening to the radio reports, were we not hearing about any Soviet response to the German invasion; and why were the Western powers doing nothing to come to the aid of Poland. The Soviet Union might have been caught unawares, or might have consented to the Ger-man offensive; perhaps England and France only wanted to give the ap-pearance of a willingness to intervene while they waited for the clash between the German troops and the Red Army. Meanwhile, the Party revealed itself to be just as clueless as we were, being unable to report anything in its press except declarations about the imperialist character of the war, in which Sweden's main priority ought to be maintaining neutrality, national freedom. Albert had sent out his fleet squadron and laid waste to the Danish coastline, troops from Mecklenburg and Sweden had invaded Norway, Haakon was unable to cobble together any kind of defense, Atterdag was forced to capitulate, in thirteen seventy a peace was negotiated in Stralsund which forced both conquered countries to hand over key harbors and forts and to recognize Hanseatic control over maritime routes. Just as today's Germany projected an image of invincibility, the Hanseatic League, comprising seventy-seven cities, then stood at the height of its power. It had possession of Visby, on the island of Gotland, and of a number of trade centers in southern Sweden that had previously been ruled by the Danish. Even Stockholm had become part of the Hanseatic League. In the depiction of the events of the years before **177** Margaret fully assumed her role, Brecht began his search for a form that corresponded to the rhymed chronicle, in which—drastically, boldly—a new event was described with every line. He had in mind a procession that progressed quickly through its stations—ballad singers, choruses, pantomimes, and dances—to the music of hurdy-gurdies and bagpipes. Details from the wealth of historical events were picked up and sketched out: the battle of Albert and the Swedish knights against the Danish monarch; the Danish preparations to recapture their lost holdings; the burgeoning rebellion among the Swedish nobility against the Hanseatic hegemony and the high-handedness of the king; the disappointed expectations in the country; instead of a stabilization of trade after the initial military success, a continued anxiety due to the expanded armament and new campaigns; instead of the shoring up of capital investments, tax decrees from which even the wholesale merchants were not exempt; instead of the alleviation of penury, new starvation diets for the people; instead of a restoration of agriculture, plundering and pillaging by gallivanting mobs of soldiers; instead of a strengthening of national unity, an intensification of disputes among all segments of society. Accompanied by the images of the devastated fields and ruined cities in Poland, of the imported masses of prisoners, the dismembered corpses, the continual keening, faced with the terrifying thought of what would happen if the German troops reached the sphere of Soviet influence, we turned to the Sweden that had become a colony of Mecklenburg, where foreign lieges and bailiffs fleeced the autochthonous landowners unless they were among the privileged few allowed to line their own pockets, like Grip, who had now amassed two thousand estates. Brecht was fascinated by the thieving steward and chief judge, who, deformed by rickets, was able to stab rivals to death unpunished, even before the altar of the monastery church in Stockholm, who possessed a monopoly on the trade in grains, in sable-fur goods, and in candle manufacture, who was in charge of the mint, and who eventually, having grown too strong, fell out of favor with his royal ruler. Now that Albert—having been driven to war by Grip and used as cover for his raids—wanted to take a portion of Grip's ill-gotten goods away from him, Grip found himself haunted by the fear of being murdered by the regent, who was deeply indebted to him through loans, and he set about assembling co-conspirators in the Council of the Realm, this time to rid himself of the foreigner. Yet he died before the time was ripe for the uprising against the Mecklenburger, a victim of his own insatiability. Following Grip's death, Albert seized his country estates and ore

178   mines, which, now that the great magnate had fallen, led to a rebellion among the Swedish nobles. Brecht made a number of attempts at depicting this phase, which stretched over two decades, and he demanded a concentrated dramatic form that could nevertheless make the power relations transparent. But no simplifying structure could be laid over the chaos: again and again, that which was arising produced new foundations, exhibited new lines of development. The expansion of the northern Germans, the disunity of the Swedish nobility and the big merchants, on the one hand interwoven with the interests of Hanseatic high finance, on the other animated by the desire to found their own Scandinavian cartels; the battles among the knightly families for influence in producing a convincing claimant to the throne; the growing influence of the patricians over the affairs of the government, the hunger for progress among the bourgeoisie and tradespeople, the impatience of the urban and rural workforce— all of these were harbingers of an erosion of the old form of the state, the rise of a revolutionary movement. Grip had replaced the traditional patriarchal rule with the rule of the supremacy of money, he had made use of all forms of economic compulsion to maintain the privileges of his class, had militarized the government bodies; then, once the patron of the rich he had deployed had grown too big for him to control, he called together the oligarchies he had always denigrated and turned toward Denmark, with whom he had only moments earlier been feuding, to win them over for an alliance against the dictatorial king. After this flickering, hectic, still fragmentary moment, in which grafters and underhanded assassins skulked around one another, in thirteen eighty-six, on the thirteenth of July, Margaret, who had been Norway's regent since Haakon's death, met with Albert in Lübeck for the diet of the Hanseatic League. Margaret

brought her sixteen-year-old son and heir to the crown, Olaf. All motives for the meeting had to be considered. Albert, weakened by the opposition in the country, was turning to the German princes to fill his coffers, to bolster his army, his fleets. Margaret was concerned with establishing business relations, securing peace on the seas, and guarantees for the possessions that had previously been pledged to the Hanseatic League and since bought back. Albert, aware of the Swedish plans to topple him, attempted to win over the woman who dazzled the assembly of senators, though the assertions that he was vying for her hand in marriage were questionable. Yet there was theatrical potential in his attempt to woo her, his efforts to outbid the Swedish nobles and to convince Margaret of the benefit of a union between Mecklenburg and Denmark. Margaret's cool rejection. An antagonism which was an expression not only of a financial contest but also of a battle of the sexes. A royal drama in the Shakespearean sense. While Albert passionately enumerated the advantages of a union, Margaret was calculating what she could extract from an alliance with the Swedish nobility. The funds for a military campaign had to be raised, but in terms of populace and agricultural production, Denmark was still the richest land in the North. A year of doubled taxes would cover the military costs. In exchange for her military assistance, the Swedish emissaries had promised her not just the throne but also a large number of estates, palaces, and castles. Secretly she was negotiating for the mines in Dalarna to be signed over to her. The Swedish entrepreneurs had to weigh Margaret's stipulations against Albert's ambitions of being restored. In either case, the greater portion of the industrial capital would remain in the hands of Hanseatic bankers. They preferred Margaret's rule because she, governing from Denmark, would be further away and would consequently be able interfere less in their affairs than a king residing in Stockholm. Securing a partnership in the mining enterprises was also a topic of discussion between Margaret and the North German councillors. Though she may have been buying their favor, they too had an interest in forming a bloc with Denmark at a time when, in the west, the competition from Burgundy was growing, and in the east the Polish-Lithuanian Union was on the rise, and both Russia and England too were making moves to increase their trade rights. The financiers therefore made concessions to Margaret, while still hoping to profit from Albert's rule for as long as possible. Until it had been decided who would be the victor in Sweden, they supported both. Knowing she had secured Hanseatic backing, Margaret returned to Denmark, and Albert traveled back to Stockholm with a fleet full of soldiers provided to him by the Margrave of

Brandenburg. The city, he announced, was to be transformed into an impregnable fortress. After his creditor died and he was able to tear up his borrower's notes, he sent his henchmen out to plunder the country ruthlessly and to sow chaos in anticipation of the Danish invasion, with the intention of making organized local attacks against him impossible. One last time, before Margaret gave her troops their marching orders, a classically condensed vision of royalist power emerged, shot through with obstinacy toward the members of one's own clan, with the resolve to stop at nothing. Educated by the rod, castigating herself yet filled with ambitions to trump her late father and achieve everything that her sickly spouse had left unfulfilled, she showed her son, the young heir to the throne, a severity which ultimately broke him. Olaf died at seventeen years of age. The material provided by this incident allowed Brecht to

sketch out a scene that revealed the perversion of the autocrat. Embodying a principle in which the worldly and spiritual powers pervaded one another, she alternated between giving her power a veneer first of religious fervor, then of national utility. Thus, she began to present herself in heraldic mourning, her face made up white as chalk, no eyebrows, her mouth a stroke of black. Having grown up in the cult surrounding Bridget, she knew how to imitate the saints; she stood there like a ghost, holding her dead son in her arms, stretched out on his back, and, but a moment after she had handed him over to the priests to be laid out, she summoned her commanders with a wave of her hand, had them unfurl their field maps, and set out the directions of the attacks. A battle on the stage could no longer be portrayed through yelling, swishing sabers, and dying men falling to the ground. Even abstractions in the form of hauling onto the stage panels outlining allegiances, the kind and number of troop units, would seem too playful in light of the military actions now being shown in the newsreels. Any attempt to act out a massacre would have been an affront, and the incorporation of the audience into some overpowering event was to be rejected out of hand. During the war, it is only possible to talk about war, said Brecht, if the aim is to investigate its causes. Wars had always, as people said, descended upon the people. Today too, the people had allowed themselves to be driven blindly into calamity by higher powers, hoping right up until the last minute for mystical salvation. Even the Party itself had considered the outbreak of war impossible on its very eve. Lacking Soviet communiqués, their press indulged in speculations about the aggressiveness of the Western powers, which had declared war on Germany, and about the openness to peace of the German army, which on the third of September stood at the Vistula, on the ninth in Warsaw, crossing the San on the eleventh on their way toward the Curzon Line. Then came the first murmurs within their commentary that Poland's right to exist was questionable, because it had stolen its western border from the German Reich and its eastern one from Russia. They're trying to prepare us for an agreement to divide the country, said Brecht. In thirteen eighty-nine, on the twenty-fifth of February, on the plains of Falan in Västergötland, the main bodies of the armored knights approached one another in rectangular formations, the infantry trudging through the snow behind them. Yet nothing could be seen or heard of the clash of the warriors. A horrible silence and gloom prevailed. In the foreground, sitting backward on the shoulders of knights, Margaret. Brecht wanted to show that on both sides it was individuals who hurled the countless, nameless masses to their annihilation. In this first part of the play, he was concerned with making evident the enormous rift **181** between those who were swallowed up by history and the crowned heads that rose up as historical markers. The image of history as a history of the rulers was intended to cause the audience members to think about the necessary inversion intended for the play's second part. There were still four decades before Engelbrekt would appear, before the popular uprising. But in looking at our situation today, having once again been duped, fallen into the trap, we could already sense how dark and divisive this phase would be as well. Individuals still determined our fates. Before Brecht set about depicting the effects of the war on the lowly and their behavior, he demonstrated what kind of people it was who were leading and deceiving them. He highlighted the selfishness of the two figures, the ridicule they heaped on each other. Instead of the turmoil, the reddening snow, he sketched out two instants, one at the beginning and one at the conclusion of their struggle. While Margaret was biding her time, sending out scouts, she was brought a whetstone on a cushion, a gift from Albert, addressed to King No-Pants, with a message that the recipient should give up governing and go back to sharpening her sewing needles and scissors. Later, after her troops had been victorious and her captive enemy had been hauled in, she had him dressed in a fifteen-cubit-long jester's cloak, placed a cap with brightly colored trains on his head, and had him brought to her curtained canopy bed, his hands and feet in chains. The humiliation of the man who had offered himself to her as a spouse surpassed the joys of a wedding. A new emblem of power, the standard of the Swedish realm, was handed over to Margaret. The coat of arms, originally produced for Albert, bore three golden crowns over a blue background. Three crowns: the first for the country's grandeur, the second for its honor, the third for its riches. The toppling of the foreign regent was followed by the execution of transactions that had been previously set out in contracts. The Swedish nobles named Margaret their rightful ruler and pledged to faithfully serve her and her appointed heir. A series of castles and fortified harbors on the west coast were bequeathed to her to consolidate her dominance over the Kattegat and the Öresund. She received the majority of Jonsson Grip's estate, which extended from Kalmar and Öresten across half of Sweden up to the ore mines around Falun, Kopparberg, Norberg, and over to Vyborg in the Finnish east. Meanwhile, Stockholm sealed itself off from her; even with the incarceration of Albert and his sons in the fort at Falköping, the war did not end; it would continue for the better part of ten years before the capital's garrison would fall and Sweden was liberated from the Mecklenburgers. Key moments from the material that

we had collected from the libraries and inspected: countermeasures by the Hanseatic League to force the extradition of the imprisoned nobles from Ruppin, Stargard, and Schwerin; arrival of an expedition corps from Rostock; total maritime blockade, to make clear that it was still the Hanseatic League that controlled trade; the country ruined by rampant theft and war; the security of the coasts compromised by Mecklenburg privateers; murder or exile of everyone in Stockholm who did not remain loyal to Albert; Margaret's negotiations for a ceasefire and for the conditions of release for Albert and his son; stipulation of a sum of sixty thousand marks in silver; until the sum was provided, Stockholm as collateral; efforts of the Mecklenburgers to persuade the grand master of the Teutonic Order to advance them the ransom money; Stockholm this time used as bait by Albert's adherents; Albert's release; installation of the Hanseatic League as the neutral protecting power of Stockholm; arrival of the occupying troops from Lübeck, Stralsund, and Greifswald, from Danzig, Elbing, and Thorn; a forest of flags, solemn speeches, citizen demonstrations; Albert and the princes of the Order plot their revenge; preparation of military activities; conflict with the Hanseatic merchants who demand the resumption of trade; finally, on Trinity Sunday, the seventeenth of June thirteen ninety-seven, the act of union in Kalmar, in concert with the coronation of the young Eric of Pomerania, nephew of Margaret, whom she had made her pupil and selected as her successor. Just as Brecht had dealt in detail with the postures, the gestures, of the protagonists when delivering the whetstone and during the humiliation of the defeated king, he meticulously set out the sequence of the movements in this scene. The behavior and the gestures of the figures, their distribution on the stage, the relationships between the different individuals and groups were to be so emphatic that words would scarcely be necessary. The economy of the dialogue also corresponded with the turn toward the cantor or chorus, which commented upon or summarized the plot. We discussed how Margaret could be viewed by the people as a liberator. She had alms distributed among the poor. The fact that those who had always had every last thing taken from them were given a coin, a little bag of flour, or a loaf of bread must have made the donor seem like a savior. She presented herself as pious and penitent, had her servants carry around an image of Bridget. A chorale about her pilgrimage to Vadstena, to the Abbey of Our Lady and of Saint Bridget. The nuns and monks made it known that in that very place she had kissed their feet. The prelates stuck the bribes she had given them in their pouches and sang a mass in her honor. The lowly looked up to her as to a sovereign. Finally, hope for peace and calm. The elite also expected peace from Margaret's regency, and it was peace that they needed to consolidate their positions. The praise she received from the upper echelons was not a response to her but to the chance to lay the foundations for expanding their estates. The poor's expressions of deference were like a hurried prayer born of enduring need. Only the country folk now stood mute once more, evincing a hint of their threatening force yet incapable of voicing their demands in the face of this growing power. The council of the spiritual and worldly rulers had always chosen the sovereign according to their own interests. They would not let themselves be outfoxed again, as they had with Albert. Their collective goal was now to overpower the Mecklenburg soldiers that were still marauding through the land, to neutralize the pirates on the seas, and to achieve independence from the Hanseatic League. The advantages of a union of the three Nordic realms caused the conflicts among the noble houses and dynastic interests to subside. Scandinavian unity could counter the North German efforts at expansion. Within the alliance, each of the three states harbored the desire for ascendancy; the Swedish aristocrats were forced to bend to the will of the Dane, not so much because of their agreement with Margaret but because of the supremacy of her fighting forces on land and at sea. As the victor and founder of the union, she could afford to speak of equality, yet she and her courtiers knew that she would give her own country priority. Above all, the participants at the meeting could revel in presenting the immutability of their status as a superior class once again. Only the nobles took part in the meeting. The advance of the bourgeoisie had been halted, and they had been relegated to their position in the urban economy. The necessity of the Nordic alliance was underlined further by the fact that

Gotland was then occupied by an army of the Teutonic Order. The news that forty-two warships had landed in Visby intruded upon the ritual of the coronation. Present at Kalmar Castle were the archbishop of Uppsala, ten bishops, four other high-level church dignitaries, and over fifty representatives from the most distinguished families, with Eric knighting one hundred thirty-three lords. But Eric, though he was king, had to reckon with being able to exercise his reign only after Margaret's death. She had secured her power over him contractually. The goods and industries that had come into her personal possession were likewise untouchable. As before, when her son was still alive, she reigned in the stead of the actual king. Thanks to her diplomatic skill, as the creator of the Scandinavian trinity, she was rewarded with being allowed to rise above the installed king. Brecht rejected the suggestion of further elaborating the conflict between the strong mother and the weak son. He was afraid that to do so would cause the play to plunge too deeply into tragedy, which would cause it to depart from its balladic character. He was more interested in showing how Margaret's almost modern-seeming intentions were deformed and disabled by old-fashioned self-interest. It made an impression upon him when Ljungdal read out the charter that was drafted in Kalmar. It could have led to an enduring union if the people who laid down this text under Margaret's leadership had already belonged more to the modern age, rather than still being largely rooted in the Middle Ages. The document, with its nine key points, in which the ideals of equality and justice resounded, was based on the decision-making power of the elite and ignored the demands of the people. Though it also dealt with the powers and responsibilities of the states in a far-sighted fashion, it excluded the fates of the great majority of their inhabitants. It provided a clear image of how an intellect could be directed at the future and yet be unable to transcend the conditions of its society. The notion of centralization was expressed in the dictate that the three realms were to be joined together for eternity under one king. Alongside this bond, which served to maintain peace and harmony, the integrity of each individual realm was guaranteed through the retention of their own laws and jurisprudence. The military and political side of the alliance was revealed in the stipulation that, in the case of an attack on one of the realms from abroad, all were obliged to provide assistance with all of their might. But in other provisions—that those banished from one realm were also banished from the others; that everyone must collectively support the king against all those who rose up against the accord—it became clear just who was claiming the right to protection here. The binding of the realms and the assurance of their supranational defense was a deed well ahead of its time. But the realization that the rapid development of world trade demanded a concentration of power in states was still a far cry from the acknowledgment that it is the working populace who carry the small class of leaders. After establishing unity as an abstract ideal, Margaret immediately went on to vitiate it in practice. She entrusted her local lackeys with vacant posts and employed them as administrators in the castles and forts. Though she did leave a number of the posts to the Swedish councillors, in order to stem their dissatisfaction, taxes were collected for her by Danish lords and bailiffs. From the moment the Kalmar letter was sealed, it was clear that Sweden would once again find itself under foreign rule, that the domestic peace would be pregnant with revolt. The solemnly celebrated meeting of the worldly and spiritual aristocracies, said Brecht, was to be concluded by a procession of peasants, **185** returning to their daily hardship, still blinded by all the dazzling pomp. During those days, around the fifteenth of September, such pressure descended upon us that we were scarcely able to follow Brecht's exhortations to continue with the conception of the play. All of our fears were now being confirmed. Molotov declared that two weeks of war had demonstrated Poland's untenability. The Red Army had been issued with the order to move into the country to protect the populations of Belarus and western Ukraine. A collective communiqué announced that it was the duty of the Soviet and German military forces to provide peace and order in the fallen Poland. The Soviet decision was welcomed in the Party press and by Rosner in the Comintern's paper as an active intervention in the interests of peace, and they spoke of the liberation of the peasants and workers who had been held down by the feudalist Polish regime. But Brecht was disturbed by the similarity between the Soviet and German programs; he found a treacherous echo in the nationalist talk of provinces having been occupied which had once belonged to the Russian Empire. Once again, he said, it was the government that had decided for the people, and not the people for themselves. In anticipation of the confrontation between the fascist and socialist armies, Steffin noted down what we managed to summarize, and I too filled my notebook with suggestions that I worked up in the evenings from memory. The central theme of the play as the first part drew to a close would be the truce reached after a century plagued by war. Margaret had absorbed Stockholm into the realm, chased the buccaneers from the seas, and sold off Gotland to the Teutonic Order for eighty thousand marks. The restoration of agriculture and trade, the recommencement of production in the mining regions, the formation of a collective army and fleet, the glorious appearance of the regent; all of this added to the security of the lands of the Nordic union and lent them a new impetus. Though hardship might not yet have been resolved, a wide-ranging national development was nevertheless taking shape in Sweden. It was not just the large landowners and industrialists who could expect profits; merchants, tradespeople, and business owners were also able to reassert themselves. The aristocracy and the bourgeoisie alike learned to recognize the rule of the Dane. As long as she presided over the three-state realm, the disagreements among the noble houses receded into the background. During the last ten years of her life she was the guarantor of peace, and this reputation clung to her, despite the amount of conflict concealed within the peace she created. Thus, her death, which befell her aboard her ship in Flensburg Harbor, was be-

moaned not only by the upper classes, who had managed to turn their loyalty to their own advantage, but also by the people, for whom the freedom from war must have been a relief; while King Eric and his counselors were now poised to fully unfurl their power. Margaret had made sure to resolve the conflicts arising from the foundation of the Nordic alliance through negotiations. The times of war had taught her that diplomacy could often achieve more than military enterprises in which she would lose many of her best knights. She maintained her strong army to lend force to her claims. Her realm of unity stood out from the rest of Europe, which was riven by unrest. Union feuds were taking place on the Iberian peninsula; England was at war with France and simultaneously facing insurrections among the rural population; revolts had begun in Bohemia, and in Lübeck the tradespeople were rising up against the patricians. She saw that the antagonistic forces in her countries could only be held in check by a precisely balanced alternation between threats and concessions, attacks and evasion. She made gifts to the aristocrats of goods that she had originally taken from them, she flattered the bishops, sent them stolen treasures, used customs perks to win over the large merchants, she renewed the letters of privilege for her partners in the ore mines, sowed gratitude among the peasants by reducing the amount of goods owed as tribute, and she awarded small plots of arable land to discharged men-at-arms. The lowest she didn't consider. Only in her final hour would she recall the shadowy, nameless masses. She had traveled to Flensburg in order to resolve the conflicts with the Holstein nobility, who were making a claim to Schleswig, and had already sent cavalry into the Danish countryside. She was willing to cede a part of South Jutland in order to put an end to the armed clashes, but during the negotiations she fell ill with the plague which had broken out in the city. Before putting our work on hold for an extended period of time, Brecht sketched out the concluding image for us. Friday the twenty-eighth of October, fourteen hundred twelve. Margaret feverish in the cabin of the royal cog. Without a wig, her head shaved bare, she once again resembled a novice. Brecht wanted to see her divested of all external defenses. Her precious robe, her jewelry and insignia hung over a stand; in her nightshirt, wet with sweat, her face bluish and blotchy, she sat in bed, just a few confidants by her side. Now that it was too late, she was to be confronted once more with the dream of unity that her statecraft had been unable to bring about. Powerless and face-to-face with death, she was to be compelled to recognize her failures. The contradiction between her visionary vows and her betrayal of herself and her subjects was to be cruelly revealed. The fact that she had been more advanced than many later regents was no longer **187** of any use to her; her absolutist rule could not be freed of the faults that kept it mired in its age. Even in her decay, shivering, her teeth clattering, she still attempted to pull herself together to gain a perspective of the extent of her power. The abbots of Sorø and Esrom, the bishop and the prioress of the Abbey of Our Lady in Roskilde, who belonged to her entourage, murmured over their rosaries. In order to confront the disputes in a world whose dimensions could no longer be made out, she had her adviser and treasurer, Kröpelin, a born Prussian, read out the amounts that she had at her disposal, a total of twenty-six thousand three hundred thirty-seven Lübeck marks. Every now and then overcome by wheezing and retching, she calculated the contributions that were to be given to the churches and cloisters, to fund pilgrimages to Jerusalem, Bethlehem, Rome, and Assisi, and for Masses to ensure her salvation on Judgment Day. The clerics received her instructions with an *amen* and a *hallelujah*. Then the forces set upon her; through the windows they came, crawling out of the trapdoors, brachiating along the beams under the ceiling; they cropped up behind the pylons; pallid, grimy apparitions, some maimed, with bloodied bandages; among them peasants, laborers from the mines, women in tattered clothes carrying emaciated children; beggars, madmen, prisoners in chains. Handmaids toweled off her face, held a golden bowl to catch the sputum. While she listed the names of the courtiers to whom she wanted to leave her forts and fiefdoms, the figures crowded around her bed. Turning to Kröpelin, she said he should be the bailiff of Bohus from this day forth, in recognition of his service; and Stockholm, Kröpelin replied, he wanted to be named governor of the castle in Stockholm. Then corpses were laid on the bedding before her, hands grabbed her throat from behind, no, she cried, the domains and cities should belong to their residents. The clerics prayed more loudly, she wrested herself free, the duties, she cried, the duties from Öresund, from Kalmarsund, from the Kattegat should go to Denmark, and once again hands tightened around her throat, she vomited, wrong, she screamed, it was wrong to hold onto our privileges, it had been wrong to fill the highest positions with our counts, it had been wrong not to allow freely elected councils and judges to administer justice, it had been wrong to never listen to the farmers, the tradespeople, this whole belief in the indissoluble nature of the rule we had created had been wrong. The church dignitaries stepped up to perform an exorcism, waved the crucifix above her, sprayed her with holy water, attempted to drown out her screaming with litanies. The dying woman was now completely surrounded by the encroaching masses. Look at me, she cried, and the scribe at the lectern scratched out her rapid-fire words with his quill; I belong to the poorest, I am the very lowest of them, and thus I wish to perish. That which I called my property is to be distributed among those whom I aggrieved and humiliated in all the lands. My houses should go to those who have no roof above their heads, my clothes should be worn by those who are getting about in rags. I want, I want, I wanted, she cried into the choir of the prelates, I wanted to found the realm of peace on Earth, but there was nobody listening to her anymore, there was only the heaving singing, and so she turned, straining upward, to face the one who was least able to help her, pleaded with him for forgiveness, for deliverance, sank back down, nothing but a heap of festering flesh.

Then came the crows. With the arrival of the evening frost they gathered together in flocks in Humlegården, flew screeching to Berzelii Park, hung in packs in the trees there, rose up out of the flurry of the yellowing foliage, hurled themselves, flapping black clouds, over to the palace, where they settled on the eaves in long, menacing rows. Every evening, for an hour after sundown, the birds stormed from spot to spot with shrill and bitter shrieks, returned from the façade of the palace on Strömmen, back into the thinning branches of the chestnut trees to spend the night. A package had been delivered to Rosalinde; inside, wrapped up in newspaper, with no accompanying note, lay the golden medallion of the Nobel Prize that had been awarded to her father. She had arranged the small table in her room with the coin resplendent on the brown, crumpled envelope, between the stamps of eagles with outspread wings. She ran out of the hot steam of the laundry and into the field, flung off her apron, shirt, and wooden shoes, lay down in the cold furrows in the earth. Every evening, after she had toiled at the tubs and the wringer to the praise of the mistress, she hurried into the darkness, and it amazed her that it took so long before she began to cough, to break into a fever. Talking to herself in the field, she noticed with a laugh that her father had bequeathed her a strong constitution, that she, just like him, wouldn't be done in easily. She took on the task of wearing herself down on her own. Finally, nearly unconscious, lying outstretched, her teeth bared in a grin, she was able to stare up hopefully into a starry sky that provided her with a familiar sense of icy infinity. As she broke down at her workstation, spewing blood, the housekeeper initially accused her of faking; but then, after the school physician was summoned, she was taken to the hospital in Mörby, where I visited her at the end of October. I had not seen her for more than a month. Looking into her shrunken, yellow face, which now resembled that of her father in a terrifying way, it seemed pointless to tell her about the writing work that was occupying my time. It wasn't estrangement that had developed between us; I could have easily found a way to relate to her reality, I understood the expression of pride etched in her features, but my political exile had eaten away at something in me—it was as if I had to extend the secretive silence that accompanied my illegal activities to all my personal relationships as well. I also had not met with Hodann for a long time, to avoid having to hide things from him. Confronted with Rosalinde's haggard face, I could sense the renunciation into which I had entered but saw no way of breaking out of the structure that had been applied to my days. And even still, the task I had set myself was near impossible to realize. Rosalinde's mouth remained closed, but in her eyes I read the question of whether the path I was taking might not lead me astray instead of giving me satisfaction. I too sometimes perceived the strictly regimented activities of my afternoons as a chore. Only my meetings with Rogeby and Bischoff afforded me brief spells of relief. With them, the absence of questions, our isolation from each other, was also a form of understanding. But accepting sole responsibility was the prerequisite for my work. I could not expect any support whatsoever, had to deny all connections to the Party. Continually feigning neutrality, I shifted between destinations that seemed to lie in a no-man's-land. Now that parts of the separator plant had been incorporated into the arms industry, as a foreigner I had to expect to be let go. It was only the lack of labor power—with many reservists having been called up for military service—and perhaps also the low wage that explained the fact that I was still able to creep into a cavity on the lowest level of the production site, whose capital amounted to eighty-two million kronor and whose net profits that year came in at eight million. Thus, a faceless foreigner, despite being destined to be discarded, I was still of use as cheap unskilled labor down below in the tin workshop and was contributing to the economic growth of Sweden. Nevertheless, I preferred the dubiousness of my situation to the insecure life of the emigrants. If I was a collaborator, they were ejecta. Though my independence might have been illusory, they were condemned to passivity. Their days consisted of nothing but waiting, waiting to be issued subsidies, food stamps, and shabby items of clothing, waiting for a visa so they could continue on to some other place. They would sit in the International Foyer on Västerlånggatan, consuming the bread rolls that were handed out to them there, reading the newspapers that were placed on the tables, or they could be found in Café Ogo on Kungsgatan, or in

the cellar of Brända Tomten on Stureplan, where they could kill a few hours chatting in small groups, over a cup of tea, a glass of water. On the streets, you could tell them from the inhabitants of the city by their sluggish gait, their aimless gaze, the way they would come to a sudden halt with extinguished faces. Perhaps I owed Brecht's acceptance of me to Steffin, who may have recognized in me something of her own past as a child of working-class parents in Berlin. But this had not sparked personal questions, neither from her nor from Brecht; I was permitted to enter his studio, permitted to sit in a corner and listen, and the indifference that was shown to me intensified my timidity, I couldn't understand why they had invited me in the first place. Stepping into his office always made me freeze at first. Despite Brecht's restlessness, a peculiar despondency and paralysis could be sensed in the atmosphere. This might have been related to Weigel's presence, who, cut off from her profession, scuffed and banged about upstairs, and whose facial features— which longed to express something other than sullenness and self-sacrifice—were sometimes, when she cropped up in the doorway to the hall, pierced by a bitter wrath. Brecht turned toward her with indignation, before flinching. Steffin, on the other hand, he wanted to have right next to him while he worked, with a sharpened pencil hovering over the paper; and he was most content when he could see Berlau, his elegant girlfriend, speeding off on her motorcycle, clad in leather. It wasn't until Brecht suddenly demanded my opinion on a few dramaturgical questions that had arisen, and I, already resigned to the notion that I wouldn't be tolerated here much longer, emphasized my lack of interest in the fable and suggested constructing the plot purely out of the clashes of historical forces, making the figures jump erratically into diametrically opposed positions, that I—with a slight sneer from Brecht, as this was precisely what he was thinking about doing—was incorporated into the planning process. I was instantly tasked with plowing through some source material, which would correspond to one working day for someone in Brecht's situation but which I could only manage by working late into the night. I read between my stints operating the tin crucible, while riding my bike; I learned to pick out a usable sentence with a single glance at a page, learned to quickly connect a found image with a series of other fragments; and, even if Brecht assumed that everything that we uncovered belonged to him, this inventing, intertwining, and refining became my education. The things I wrote down I did for him, for the work that would have him as its author; but at the same time, I did it in order to be able to retain and pass on a few tiny pieces of documentation in the event of the arrival of the catastrophe that would violently disrupt our efforts. The fact that our work was broken off after the intensive process of sketching out the first section strengthened my resolve to bring as much as possible of what had been outlined to fruition, and while I was making my notes I often forgot that I had someone else's work in front of me. And yet this too formed part of the conditions under which I lived—as a messenger, a medium, a servant—and I often indulged in the idea that these almost completely unrecognized efforts might yet one day lead me to tasks that I could call my own. I had been let go by Brecht for the moment, with a fleeting reference to resuming the work later; I was now no longer needed as a contributor on a project with which he had moodily, hectically, and violently experimented; he locked himself away again, moved on to other material, with only Steffin helping him, occasionally also Matthis and Ljungdal. I did not belong to his circle of friends. I was never a guest at his house like the Social Democratic politicians Branting and Ström, to whom he was indebted because they had procured his Swedish entry visa; like the doctors Hodann and Goldschmidt, the writers Blomberg and Edfelt, the actors Greid and Wifstrand, the academics Steinitz, Scholz, and Ziedorn, the politicians Enderle and Plenikovski. I suspected that Brecht didn't even know that I worked in a factory; I never had the opportunity to tell him about it. Regardless of what he might have made of my contributions to the discussion, I was one of the young refugees, who, due to their participation in the fight for the Spanish Republic, could presumably be viewed as reliable but who otherwise possessed none of the qualities which for him would have justified their participation in the gatherings of an intellectual elite whose tasks included the planning and founding of an antifascist alliance. Though I had heard Brecht speak disparagingly about intellectuals—we could place no faith in them, he would say—the acquaintances that he sought consisted primarily of academically educated or politically influential personalities. Once, when I met up with Matthis, he gave me a sense of the formation of this intellectual front, this Voltaire Club. Through the participation of Swedish professors, journalists, and liberally minded patrons, a committee was forming that was not only going to produce an encyclopedia of National Socialism, but was also going to confront the issue of exile, an undertaking that Brecht had been thinking about for many years and that aroused mistrust among the Party functionaries because it was closely related to a project of Münzenberg's, which meant it could be assumed that Brecht and Münzenberg had exchanged ideas about it. The breadth of the project also impeded its organization and public presentation. Talking to Matthis about *Mother Courage* and *Lucullus*, I realized that he had worked elements from our conversations into these pieces. The depiction of the sutler seemed to be marked by the same odd ambivalence that he had shown toward the queen of the Union. Just as with Margaret, who, having been ferociously caricatured, was then able to assume a certain grandeur, he was also ultimately seized by Mother Courage, whom he had wanted to depict as a terrifying figure. The last judgment of the lowly and suffering, presaged in the facial expressions of the dying queen, found a simpler variation in the radio play in the appearance of the plaintiff against the commander. It was a relief for me that I now only had my trips to Rosner. Now, when I came from Rosalinde's place, I would be able to devote myself more amply to the Saint Jerome of the Comintern. The fact that she was asleep when I left seemed for a moment to be the sign of a complete separation. I wanted to be able to wait, but I was driven out by restlessness. The trip on my bike through the cold October air to the train station, up Upplandsgatan—which lay barren as usual—past the house in which Rosner lived to Vanadisvägen, where I left my bike, the leisurely stroll back, hammers beating on tin, the hissing of the welding guns in the basement of the workshop, the arched entranceway with the number seventy-seven, meager stucco work above it, a few steps, a folding door with glass panels, a hallway, at the end of which the stairs coiled around the central pylon, the bell on the right, the prearranged signal, inside, the hobbling steps accompanied by the thudding of the cane, waiting, the noise from the workshop, the signal again, as agreed, Rosner appearing, with glistening eyes, whistling cheerfully, on the left, the door to the kitchen open, at the front, beside an inbuilt cupboard and facing the street, the closed doors to the family's rooms, and then into the kitchen, where his host had prepared him a meal and a thermos of coffee. Sitting down at the table on the wall that curved around the stairwell, he showed me his new dentures, described to me how he had been transported to the dentist in the trunk of a car, how the dentist, in a single nighttime sitting, had pulled his rotting teeth and fitted the prosthetics. His feigned distress—quickly replaced by a grin—at the fee demanded of him by his dentist and fellow believer, whom he had taken for a philanthropist, amounting to the exorbitant sum of one thousand five hundred kronor, which the Communist International had to front. At the kitchen table, which he had loaded up with newspapers, he explained to me how things stood now that Poland had been divided. His hideout seemed to contradict the health and reach of the global movement of which he was a representative, but, he said, for anybody who has spent years in prison and is used to carrying out their work in hiding, this kitchen with a sink, oven, and firewood box, this room, even if it is scarcely larger than a wardrobe, is the epitome of freedom of movement. Also, he said, the dialectics of history are proven here, in that a concealed action at the right moment can counterbalance or even outweigh a public strategy. The expansion of the agreement with Germany from a nonaggression pact to a pact of friendship should be interpreted as facilitating a renewal of revolutionary possibilities of the kind that arose toward the end of the previous war. An accord between the Soviet Union and the German people would lay the foundations for a future cooperation. The declaration of friendship, he said, was meant to convey that there is no land in which the working population wants war, that the offer of friendship was intended for the workers. This didn't mean that a fraternity was immanent, for fascism always carries war in its core. The crucial thing now was the degree to which the German working class was capable of appreciating the new relationship. Great demands had also been placed on the international proletariat to trust Soviet policy, to refuse to be influenced by the bourgeois propaganda that portrayed the agreement as a betrayal. Through the advance of the Red Army, he said, pouring coffee from the thermos into our cups, and in coordination with the negotiations of recent weeks, the border between the Soviet Union and Germany had been established. The Western powers had opposed the Soviets' freedom of movement because they were expecting the Germans to conquer all of Poland. Rejected by England and France, the Soviet Union had taken the necessary step to protect their own territory, neutralizing a German military objective and establishing a ceasefire. Only the West was pushing for a continuation of the war, in the hope that the German attack would be directed against the

Soviet state. This is what we have to make clear now, he said, pushing the crockery aside, that having been driven into isolation by the Western powers, it is the Soviet Union that is attempting to calm tensions by way of an alliance between the peoples. Provocatively, in pursuit of their own interests, the bourgeois governments had turned their backs on them, had accused the Soviets—who were fighting for nothing but the maintenance of peace—of a policy of aggression; and the Social Democratic movement, by expelling the Soviet trade unions from the International Federation of Trade Unions, had eradicated every last hope of cooperation. That's what it's all about, he said, sitting down to write his weekly report, asserting our perspective, despite the defamation to which the Communist Party is being subjected. Rosner, with his big, curved nose, his blinking mole's eyes, Rosner, smacking his lips, wheezing, Rosner, holed up in a foreign land and at home in his beliefs, Rosner, denied the possibility of moving about freely on the streets, rummaged through the heap of newspapers, handed me the sheets of paper covered in scribbles to be made into fair copies. Often, while he worked he would have the radio that the Party had provided him switched on, the volume turned down low. Stop, he would call out suddenly, when a piece of music spoke to him, throwing his head back, rocking to and fro, this time to the voice of Edvard Persson from Skåne, whose folk songs he particularly loved. The schmaltzy, dialect-inflected singing formed the background to my report on the conditions in the separator plant, where, as in all other industries, the Communists were being put under pressure by the union leadership. The metalworkers' association recommended removing members of the Communist Party from positions of import. It claimed that because of its allegiance to the Comintern, the Party could no longer continue to exist within a democratic context. They were striving to have the Party banned, as had happened in France. While Persson conveyed an unconcerned unity in peacefulness, in a sense of belonging, I brought up how comrades in many industries were now being subjected to daily denunciations, attacks. Acts of sabotage were being carried out at their workbenches, they themselves were then being held responsible for the destruction, for the loss of productivity. Humming along to the blaring melody, Rosner replied that we were only facing preliminary bouts of a harmless nature at the moment, but that soon we would be facing very different clashes. He spoke of the dangers brewing next door in Finland. We must assume, he said, regardless of what we might say about a Soviet-German friendship, that this peace is nothing but a mere postponement of armed confrontation. The anti-Communist slander in Sweden is being spread by groups—plenty of them from among the top rungs of the military—who have an interest in provoking the outbreak of war between Finland and the Soviet Union. They are promising the profascist Finnish government military support and encouraging their rejection of Soviet suggestions on regularizing their borders. The proposals—of pushing back the northeastern Finnish border due to the precariousness of Leningrad and of leasing Hanko, at the mouth of the Gulf of Finland, offering Soviet regions in Karelia in return—are already being construed in the bourgeois press as a sign of Soviet plans of aggression. Desperate to be cut loose, the generals declared that Finland's struggle was Sweden's business. We sorted and numbered the pages that, subject to strict precautionary measures, were to be picked up in the evenings and taken to the printers. The gated entrance to number eighty-four Kungsgatan, which led to the courtyard buildings of the Party headquarters, was monitored by police informants. Despite the fact that the Communist Party enjoyed complete legality and was represented in the national parliament, members were subject to sudden arrests, house searches, the confiscation of materials. The singer with the soothing, slick voice had not prevented Rosner from unfurling the map of Scandinavia on the table in front of him. Have you ever been to Lapland, he asked, and traced his knobbly index finger along the rivers running down from the mountains to the Gulf of Bothnia. He pointed to the gnarled walking stick standing by the kitchen door and said we have to be prepared to hike, across the highlands to Lake Inari and on to Petsamo, with nothing but emergency rations in our packs. Here at the kitchen table, he seemed to view the enormous trek, equal to walking down to Italy, as nothing more than a light stroll. And yet, the first guard on the edge of the city would arrest him, for who, I thought, could look more suspicious than this disheveled Wandering Jew schlepping the International around on his hunchback. He wanted to hear more about my day in the factory. How could the workers, he asked, be freed from mechanistic thought and reoriented toward an offensive position. The international unity of action of the working class is ongoing, he wrote on his corrections sheet. I need local color, he said, I want to touch and smell what's going on in the workshops, in the cafeteria, in the union meetings. It was as if he were straining against a tiny sliver of light that I had opened up, as if he wanted to haul the whole factory into his kitchen nook, with its smoke and din. We heat a lot with peat now, I said, it leaves an earthy effluvium hanging over the courtyards. There's a lack of tin; trucks bustle in loaded to the top with scrap iron to be melted down to recover raw materials. Tin bars are being stolen; a stockpile was found in a shed on the canal intended for sale on the black market. Separators are now being created only for large dairy farms, not for use by individual farmers. The lathes in the bigger machinery halls have been converted to produce artillery shells. The parts are delivered from the steelworks in the north, the shells produced are seven and ten-and-a-half centimeters in caliber. People from the Landstormen monitor the packaging departments. I watch without being noticed. I listen and keep quiet. I take part in the union meetings. I invoke my Social Democratic background. My father's name is familiar to the union functionaries. As a member of the union I am also affiliated with the Social Democratic Party. And though joining the Party is no longer compulsory—as had initially been decided at the founding congress of the national organization in eighteen eighty-nine—anybody who makes use of their right to abstain makes themselves identifiable as a Communist or arouses suspicions of at least being sympathetic to the Communist Party. In this way, Communists can simultaneously belong to their own Party and to that of the Social Democrats. The struggle of the Swedish workers' movement is identical with the struggle of the trade unions. To push through the objectives of their struggle, the trade unions need a governing Social Democratic Party. In an interplay of interests, the Party draws its strength from the unions while the unions draw their strength from the Party. What is necessary is for the Party to reach an absolute majority. If, in the continual balancing act, the scales tip toward the bourgeois parties, the demands of the unions cannot be realized. Scorned as an ideological enemy, the small Communist Party nevertheless helps the Social Democratic Party to reach a narrow socialist majority. Despite the disputes, there are still Communist shop stewards within the trade unions. They can be supported in the union elections. My membership in the trade union and the Party makes me eligible to take part in the elections. I pay five kronor a month to my division, the metal division. Of that, four kronor a year are handed over to the Social Democratic Party. Even though most of the union initiatives in our workplace are issued by Selin and other Communists in positions of power, and though solidarity still reigns on the workplace floor, the slander spread by the leadership of the metalworkers' union has still borne fruit. They tie the antifascist struggle to the struggle against the bolshefascists. The trade unions make gains among militants by emphasizing what is suppressed by the Communist press. The German victories, justified by the Communists, are pilloried. The trust lost by the Communist Party through its cover-ups is gained by the Social Democratic Party through its apparent honesty. The workforce is being fractured by the ongoing scheming. Because everyone is worried about keeping their jobs, caution and passivity are intensifying. Even in addressing union issues, an awkwardness, a hush sometimes descends. It's not only the threats and blackmailing that are driving many to leave the Communist Party but also the inconsistency of its political positions. Fundamental solidarity at the workbenches, but when you look further, exhaustion and demoralization. As always, in the interests of national unity, a depoliticization of the workers. A focus on the most immediate interests. Our problem: there's no soap in the washrooms. The rations of crystalline soft soap are unusable. Our problem: no hot water in the showers. The food is getting worse: nothing but cabbage and potatoes hollowed out by worms. We demand better food in the cafeteria, and at cost price, one krona fifty. Numerous accidents, which the factory doctor hardly ever treats anymore. The nurse wraps an emergency dressing around a black fist with a severed finger, around a gaping foot, a brow pelted by a drive belt. Grievances of that nature are discussed. Letters are written to Fossberg, the technical director, who skirts the questions and speaks about the difficulty of keeping production and sales going at all, who yells *sacrifices must be made* when wage increases are requested. It isn't raises we should expect but reductions, further cutbacks, remember, it's wartime. A brief consensus in the assessments of the employers and the union fat cats. Then back to exhaustion. You've got to keep your mouth shut, for tactical reasons. Look how they pit us against each other, you'd like to say, just like they always have. You only dare to agitate among the barking of the tin cauldron. And on top of all that, I said, I'm trying to help out with the draft of a play about Engelbrekt; Engelbrekt, leader of the Swedish struggle for freedom, in the thirties of the fifteenth century; Rosner interrupted: now that would be something, that could mobilize the workers, he yelled, something has to be written about that in the magazine; but it's too early, I said, it's Brecht's play, I'm collating the material for him, he wants to put it on the stage in the winter; and I was overcome by a sudden feeling of dizziness.

We began in late November, as the Finnish-Soviet conflict was threatening to escalate into all-out acts of war. As each day passed, the pressure on our project intensified; it was as if every thought, every image, every word had to battle for its right to exist. Everything we wrote down was opposed by crushing dismissal. And though it was anxiety that drove Brecht to work, this time the difficulty of finding focus was compounded by the unwieldy nature of the subject matter. According to the history books, Engelbrekt had suddenly emerged from the darkness when the hour was ripe; and then, having shaped an entire epoch, vanished without a trace. The lack of a past; the brief duration of his activity, one year and ten months, from mid-summer of thirty-four to the twenty-seventh of April thirty-six; the impossibility of ascertaining the location where he was slain by axe and hastily buried; the various motivations for letting him vanish into obscurity—either to rob his actions of significance, to divest him of his exemplary quality, to make him seem like a failure rather than a figure to be emulated, or, by amping up his mystique, to idealize him, to declare him a saint—these were the negations we had to contest with. Such a man does not come out of nowhere, said Brecht. We had to investigate historical facts from which this ambivalent figure could be carved out, had to analyze mechanisms that set this still faceless man in

198   motion, caused him to act, and brought about his downfall. A number of early sketches—which Brecht had produced as Matthis had told him about Engelbrekt for the first time and read to him from Grimberg's work—had already been cast aside during the meetings in September as misinterpretations. Engelbrekt could not, as Brecht had assumed back then, be viewed as a popular leader of peasant origins. In the poem by Thomas Simonsson, the bishop of Strängnäs, he was described as *then litzla man*. This could be taken as a characterization of his short stature, as the Swedish historians of the fifteenth century Ericus Olai and Olaus Petri had read it, but could also, as is suggested in the rhymed *Karlskrönikan*, refer to a lowly heritage. Because in this text, however, the aim was to praise the truly great man, Karl Knutsson, Engelbrekt's rival and successor from the Bonde dynasty, who had to share the title of commander of the realm with Engelbrekt before having himself elected king; and because Thomas, the owner of mines and smelting works in the region around Norberg, was familiar with Engelbrekt's rank, we stuck with the idea of the diminutive, stocky miner. Brecht associated the expression *then litzla man* with the image of a kobold, a Rumpelstiltskin, a forest spirit; he liked the idea of connecting him with this gnome-like quality, which was at odds with Engelbrekt's fabled strength and booming voice. Our work in September had provided us with a broad foundation. Looking back, the song about Margaret and her Union appeared easy enough to sing; the courts and kings had been clearly outlined. Now, however, it became almost impossible to knead the shadowy, earthy, loamy mass into this small figure who was said to have inspired the country to rise up against foreign domination. And yet here it was that we had to look for our sense of belonging and understanding. We were so disfigured by the

events of our age, had been made so alien to ourselves by the disempow-
ering developments, that every glimmer of revolt seemed to become shot
through with doubt, that with every upswing we immediately saw those
who had been betrayed. The unrest began in the iron mines among
those who had nothing left to lose, the miners and farmworkers rose up
against the plunder, and a popular militia began to form, but soon enough
traders, merchants, large landowners, knights, and clerics joined them,
the revolutionary struggle transformed into a national war—and after
this collective effort, the nobles and the bourgeoisie made off with the
victory. Realizing that it could never have turned out differently, once
again defeated and outgunned right around the world, we turned to this
period of history to analyze the interplay between past and present experience, in the hope of discovering something about the roots of the developments that continued to repeat themselves. But our goal was not so
much to compare the betrayed movement of unity from back then with
the fallen front of our own times, but to uncover their particularities and
specificities. We needed to find another way to draw lessons from our
current failures, which were still so hazy and unclear. Never before had
dealing with an artistic problem presented itself to me under such relentless antagonism as during that winter; it had never been more clear to me
how artistic activity was played out right where the forces of society
clashed most violently. Standing in the center of the contradictions, it
faced the threat of being pulverized, but its driving force was the desire to
assert itself in the face of these forces. For that reason, with everything
seeking to annihilate us, we clung to our task, which was interrupted
multiple times until, with us still waiting to resume the work despite its
fragmentary state, it came to a halt. The jerking, uneven nature of our
progression matched the kind of activity we had become familiar with in
the autumn, and which reflected not just the shifting winds of external
events but also the differences between us and Brecht. It was not possible
for me to dabble in more than one project at the same time; Ljungdal was
able, with all the literary sources at his disposal, to work on multiple
things at once, was preparing a book about the Marxist worldview and
writing reviews; Matthis was also writing articles on the side and planning a film; but Brecht was constantly exposed to a glut of ideas and yet
remained capable of organizing the diverse themes, setting them on their
tracks, treating them according to a set system. He rushed to and fro in
his bustling factory, overseeing all departments, issuing brief instructions here and there, following the paths of the different products, inspecting the outcomes and always coming up with further applications.

With the Engelbrekt piece, as I later came to understand, he was mainly interested in exercises of style, investigations of dramatic forms. Occasionally, hastily stroking her platinum blonde hair, he would have Steffin read him prose pieces, meditations that he had dictated during the night, or notes from conversations with refugees, theses for a wide-ranging essay on literary realism; sometimes he also spent time working on a novel about Caesar—for relaxation, as he used to say. He was using ideas brought to him by Greid for a composition that he called the *Book of Changes*, even though as soon as the actor left he would make snide remarks about his dilettantism. Goldschmidt, on the other hand, he was happy to listen to. The famous surgeon from Vienna—who, as usual, was not allowed to practice his profession in Sweden, allowed at most to help a resident at the Karolinska hospital analyze X-rays for a paltry sum—would tell him

anecdotes about this work, which Brecht often inserted word-for-word into the dialogue of his figures Ziffel and Kalle. What attracted him about these reports was their tone. Though Goldschmidt had every reason to complain, they had nothing of the usual litanies delivered by other emigrants. Most of all, Brecht wanted to hear Goldschmidt's recollections of his time in prison in Russia during the First World War. The reports were burlesque, of a half-Hasidic, half-Slavic flavor. He was talking about his aide, a Romanian gypsy named Juan, who had made Goldschmidt's stay in the camp as a field medic more bearable through his farcical wit, his good-natured mischief. A kind of Švejk figure, said Brecht, already planning a new piece, which he wanted to work on with Goldschmidt. The search for a pseudonym for this character was like a scene from the play. Considering the practical difficulties of staging a play, the name couldn't sound Jewish. Erzhauer was suggested, Steinklopfer, Schmied, Maurer, and finally Koch. Despite my apparent autonomy, Brecht's air of authority—which never left a doubt that it was he who would reap the profits from everything that was produced in his workshop—made it clear that I remained a kind of employee, though without him ever asking how I actually made my living. My efforts to overcome this unsatisfactory situation were bolstered by the idea that I was participating in the construction of a work that was also my own. For myself, for my development, for my path to becoming a writer, I carried out studies that had to be carefully slotted into my timetable—though I couldn't help but notice the levity with which Brecht attended to the material he received, in contrast to the harried way that I went about my research. What he found entertaining were the things we translated for him from magazines and books. Pushing his cap—made not of leather but of cloth, though it looked like leather due to its filthy, oily sheen—down even further, imitating the expression of a detective, he pulled the evidentiary exhibits out of our notes and set out to solve a case from the history of Sweden. He wasn't worried at all by the press campaign against the Soviet Union, which, so they said, was merely looking to secure its remaining spheres of influence, which was also why it wanted to attack Finland. He didn't believe that the Western powers would establish a front in northern Scandinavia to come to Finland's aid or to cut off the shipments of Swedish ore to Germany. The only thing he feared was the creation of a Soviet-German military alliance, to which he felt Molotov was alluding in his statement about a friendship cemented in blood between the two peoples. He was in favor of regularizing the borders to protect the Soviet Union but condemned the statements about the need to liberate the Finnish proletariat. And yet, said Ljungdal, soon everything would revolve around the iron ore that Germany needed for its armament. If the English didn't come to Sweden via Narvik and Tromsø, the German armies would come to secure the raw materials they needed. Ore was also a key issue when unrest first broke out in Dalarna in the fall of fourteen thirty-two. The second part of the play had to begin in the mining districts, for it was here that Engelbrekt's ancestors had resided since the thirteenth century. In twelve ninety-six, under Birger Magnusson's regency, the name of a citizen of German extraction, Ingilbertus, had been recorded in the registry list of the city of Uppsala. In thirteen twenty-one, records allude to an Engilbertus, who bore a triangle of halved fleurs-de-lis on his coat of arms. Originally tradespeople, soon residing in the fiefdoms around Västerås, and then in Dalarna, the family became landowners involved in ore mining. In the title registers at the beginning of the fourteenth century, the names Englika, Englike, and Engliko could be found. One Engliko settled not far from Norberg, the site of the largest iron discovery, founded the Englikohof estate, bought into a mine lot, and set up a smelting works. The registers of thirteen sixty-seven revealed that the son of Engliko, in addition to being awarded tax-exempt status by Albert, had been made a nobleman. The coat of arms of this Engelbrekt Englikosson bore a downward-facing wing on the left side and a halved fleur-de-lis on the right. He died in thirteen ninety-nine and left behind two sons, of which the elder, Engelbrekt Engelbrektsson, was mentioned for the first time in the year fourteen thirty-two when he stamped an official document with his seal, consisting of a triangle formed of halved fleurs-de-lis. Referred to as a mountain man, *montanus*, he must have been well over forty years old even then. He owned shares in mines and smelting works in Norberg and, together with his brother, was heir to four estates: in addition to Englikohof, ones in Tjurbo, Snäfringe, and Siende. His noble rank was a lowly one; perhaps he stood in the service of a nobleman as a squire. It was already quite something, said Brecht, to have this family tree, for this succession of names not only produced a biblical, incantatory tone but also allowed the figures to be woven into the sequence of historical facts we had explored earlier. Though we knew nothing about his childhood or the background of the mature Engelbrekt, it was possible to draw conclusions about his personal characteristics and behavior from the information recorded about his ancestors and from the accounts of the manner of his appearance on the stage of history. The fact that they were awarded a noble rank confirmed that the Engelbrekt family had grown wealthy and gained influence. Spelling their name according to Swedish pronunciation rather than the German announced where the bearers felt their loyalties lay. Given that they worked in one of the most important sectors of production and were dependent upon international commerce, however, they would have maintained close ties with the major traders of the Hanseatic League, probably also sharing with them the capital invested in the pits. Since Englikosson was among those who had received his privileges from King Albert, it could be assumed that, for his part, he had been an advocate of the Mecklenburgers. He must have been able to maintain Albert's patronage through loyalty, or through lending him money, for he was also able to maintain control of his estates, mines, and smelting works while Jonsson Grip was expanding his power across Dalarna. His business acumen was apparent in the fact that he was harmed neither by the expulsion of Albert nor by the arrival of the Danish governors. It wasn't until thirteen ninety-six, shortly before his death, as Margaret began to bring large swaths of the mining regions under her personal control, that his previous privileges were curtailed. He no longer had unfettered access to trade with the Hanseatic League, having instead to defer to the agents who had been sent out by the regent to take over the export business. If they wanted to retain possession of their transport posts and smelting works, the mine owners now had to put down— depending on their production volume—up to twenty-six ship-pounds of iron for a share in a mining company. In fourteen hundred two, at war with Holstein, the Dane was already circumventing these agreements in many locations and she ordered some of the most productive mines to be occupied. The young Engelbrekt was one of the miners whose rights were threatened, who had to pay bribes and make continual concessions in order to be allowed to retain a portion of their lots. Gradually a sense of indignation began to build up within him that would later lead to revolt. Yet with his coat of arms, he still belonged to the privileged. He could attain an education. His friendships with aristocrats suggested he had been educated on noble estates, perhaps at Rossvik, the estate of the knight Nils Gustafsson Båt, whose son Puke, the same age as Engelbrekt, would become his most intimate confidant during the battles for freedom. As the owner of a mine, he had to oversee the transportation of the iron downriver to Västerås, and from there to Stockholm via Lake Mälaren. In Stockholm, at the transshipment point just on the other side of the sluice, at the Iron Canal, the cargo destined for the Hanseatic cities was weighed and loaded onto the big cogs. He might have traveled on these vessels to visit his trading partners in Lübeck, Wismar, or Rostock, where he could have learned about the sprawling social struggles in central Europe, particularly the revolts of the Bohemian peasants, the effects   **203** of which were spreading all the way to the coastal cities. Engelbrekt had supported the Union so long as it served to maintain the free exchange of commodities and provided protection from foreign attack, but it would seem that, when Eric assumed office, he entered a period of doubt, of restlessness, which continued until the outbreak of the revolts. At the outset he had perhaps hoped that he could attain a favorable position in the realm united under Margaret's successor. There were indications that he, as a member of the cavalry, had taken part in Eric's campaigns against the Holsteiners and the Hanseatic League, at a time when the Teutonic Order was weakened by its war against the Polish-Lithuanian Union. But this must have placed him in an ambivalent position, for the advantages that were secured in terms of Denmark's position as a naval power were offset by his losses in valuable trading partners. As a man whose later life would be shaped by his sense of justice, he was thrust into a moral dilemma by breaching the trust of the Hanseatic traders; at the same time, though, it was here that he gained the military experience that would serve him in organizing and leading his people's army. It was only when Eric broke his promise to guarantee Swedish independence, filling all crucial posts with his own vassals, sending his governors, bailiffs, and bands of mercenaries into Dalarna, doubling taxes, driving down the price of iron, sowing terror among the populace with his slashing and burning, that Engelbrekt began to resist the Danish regent. Slowly, a transformation took place, from the stance of a businessman and financier rooted in a particular class, from his outrage over personal injuries, to a broad, altruistic vision. Based on the high-level functions assigned to him with apparent popular support and on the assertiveness and confidence with which he immediately and without opposition assumed his duties, we could conclude that he had long ago demonstrated his abilities and won the respect of the miners. The suddenness of his appearance was simply due to the fact that the close circle in which he had previously been active had broken open, expanding its reach. It wasn't that he had suddenly transformed from an insignificant individual into a key historical figure, but that from one moment to the next, history threw light on the field in which he had long served as an elected leader. It was impossible to determine the extent to which his first steps into the public sphere were motivated more by personal interests than by those of the greater good; likewise, the question of whether he had progressed to armed resistance through his own convictions or due to pressure on the part of the people would also have to remain unanswered. Even though he might have initially been concerned only with getting his business up and running again, with normalizing trade, he nevertheless became known as the spokesperson for the peasants and miners, who had designated him to present their complaints to the king regarding the injustices in the country. The time was not yet ripe for a military campaign. But the tactician recognized the prerevolutionary situation. He needed the people to achieve his own goals, but he might have also been swept up in the force issuing from the people. Previously, in a covert ritual, the supreme councillors had been responsible for all decisions; now, a public power was emerging from the populace. The revolutionary force could be glimpsed in the altered posture of the workers, the way they began to grasp their tools as if they were weapons. In the first part of the play, the lords had dominated. Now the action would issue from the lowly. Yet as we planned the scenes, the rulers imposed themselves upon us once more, for they occupied the bulk of all the chronicles; their intrigues overshadowed everything that occurred below, down among the earth and the rocks, events that were seldom deemed worth mentioning. We discussed how we could express the shift in power as an epoch dawned in which, once again, peace was being replaced by wars and Sweden was succumbing to a regime of violence that exceeded everything from which they had secured their liberation through effort and sacrifice. And since events were dictated from above, and mistreatment was always foisted upon the people from above, these heights also exuded an awful attraction, which also seduced the historians into turning their dazzled gazes toward the heavens. The decrees could not be evaded, just as decrees determined our daily lives, today, in nineteen thirty-nine. We have to try, said Brecht, to transfer our current anxiety to our treatment of the circumstances from back then, such that the depiction incorporates our defeat, our limited perspective, our continual guessing. Fateful decisions are being made above our heads, sometimes from quite a distance, with their effects then revealing themselves right before our faces. We refuse to allow ourselves to be assaulted, we are drawn into decisions that arouse utter confusion and force us to sketch out our own image of the situation as best we can. The explanations we come up with may well be mistaken—and as such they correspond to much of what was thought up, resolved, and revoked in Engelbrekt's time. The most important thing was to place the workers, the exploited, in the foreground, to overlay our own plane, and to search for allies there, while the enemies were sent to the back disdainfully and faced off against only from a distance. It was significant that we were dealing with rebelliousness, that the beginning of this part would not be shrouded in a powerlessness in which the rage would dwindle miserably. **205** The elites had to be portrayed in the piece in the same way that the newsreels and the photos in our newspapers conveyed gray impressions of the meetings of the famous leaders, of their supercilious smiles or grim facial features, in the same way that we read their declarations, so abstract and yet so dangerous, aimed as they were at our extinction. Before anything was conveyed about Eric, who eroded Margaret's Union and destroyed everything she had striven for during the final years of her life, the context of Norberg was to be put on the stage. Brecht's desire for exact details had Ljungdal, Matthis, and me in the libraries, collecting excerpts from obscure works, sketching devices, constructions, machines. On the tall table Brecht erected a model made of cardboard, bits of wood, and modeling clay that gave an impression of what had been documented in writing and drawings. Pieces of wood were piled up before the stones and set alight, the heated strips of ore were doused in water and made to split, the clumps were hewn out of the mountain and broken down with picks and sledgehammers, the fully laden baskets then hauled up by the winches of the huge treadmill. Buckets full of groundwater were hoisted up, wooden beams lowered down on ropes and fixed together to form supports: each motion of those involved in the operation, the surveyors, the diggers, the carriers and helpers—the latter including women and children—the barrow-pushers and wagoners who carted the raw pieces to the smelting ovens, was intertwined in a deliberate and stable order. The activities around the conical, charcoal-heated smelting hut proceeded in a similar fashion, where the water wheel powered the bellows, the smelted metal ran its course to be cleaned and refined and ultimately worked by the blacksmiths. In contrast to the simple verses that Brecht wanted to use as linguistic material, in his discussion and visualization of the mine structure he seemed to have a universal theater in mind. Perhaps this was in defiance of the fact that even the smallest stage was beyond his reach. He answered our questions in a range of ways. To begin with, he said that we needed to be familiar with the entire, complicated mechanism before we could proceed to restrictions. Then that he felt it was not impossible that such scenes from working life could be set on the stage in the future; that is, in a future dominated by productive forces. The centrality and physicality of the people involved in the production, the power and conviction in their actions, their cooperation, the impression that it was they who bore the burden of building the world, this was all to be decisive for the continued progression of the plot. The crackling of the fire, the beating of the hammers, the rattling of the cogs and the creaking

of the wooden frameworks, the climbing and dragging, the blackened faces, sooty caps, filthy boots, and leather aprons, these were component parts of an entirety that was impinged upon by foreign, disruptive elements. If earlier it had been mercenaries from Mecklenburg who had descended upon the peasants, a black bull's head on their standard, to wrest from them grain and livestock, now heavily armed soldiers stepped forward whose banner of arms bore the Pomeranian red griffin against a silver background or the blue, elongated Danish leopard. They had a few bound women with them, one of the men had a dead child on his leg, which he swung back and forth, and skulking behind them was the country bailiff's emissary. The men in armor moved cautiously, so as not to sully their polished leg pieces. Even the officer popping his head out was careful not to step in a puddle with his spurred shoes. Hay for the horses was requested; a farmhand brought the bundles over from the stalls. The activity in the mines had not yet drawn to a close. A number of peasants were brought over from the side. The lord had come to collect the taxes, and his bookkeeper read out the names of those who had not made their payments. One of them, stepping forward with his fists pressed on his hips, explained that he had needed to buy back his ox from the bailiff—who had taken it from him during the previous tax collection, valuing it at twelve öre, and then sold it back to him at the going rate of four marks—which had left him broke, and that he was therefore requesting an extension. Hand over the ox, said the collector. The peasant countered that, without the ox, he would be unable to cultivate his land, but two soldiers immediately seized hold of him and led him away. He was tasked, said the officer, with collecting the legally stipulated sums and, in the event of refusal, was authorized to confiscate farms and livestock as security. It was no longer possible, he was told, to provide him with minted money to the value of everything that had previously been handed over in grain, crops, poultry, and skins, as they also had to bear the costs of the board and lodging of the troops and make annual contributions to the costs of fort building. Now all the surrounding ears pricked up. The baskets ceased to stir, the wheelbarrows were set down. The emissary called for the owner of the mine, announcing that the bailiff, Jösse Eriksson, was awaiting the delivery of the iron ingots. In the ensuing silence, one of the peasants dared to say that for a year he had been asking for payment of his wages for services rendered to the bailiff, and that now he was going to be made to do forced labor simply because he had demanded what he was owed. With a wave of the officer's hand, he was beaten and hauled off. Now the miners emerged from the pits. Marksmen sprang to the front and loaded their crossbows with their feet. The workers stood across from the menacing gang, holding their tools. A stocky figure climbed up over the rampart in a thick doublet and soft, pointed cap. What's going on, he asked. I demand to see the owner of the mine, said the bailiff. You're looking at him, replied the figure exiting the mine as he patted the dust from his clothes. The officer was unsure how to behave; the man who had just appeared more closely resembled a day laborer than the proprietor of a mine and a landowner, but he considered it appropriate to bow, for the king of the Union, the so-called Eric of Farther Pomerania, progeny of Duke Wartislaw and of a granddaughter of the great Valdemar, this foster son of the distinguished Margaret, governing the three realms from her seat in Denmark, was, it was said, well disposed toward Engelbrekt, so the tax collector of the Danish bailiff installed by Eric ought to show him respect as well. He ordered the soldiers to lower their weapons. Twenty ship-pounds of forging-grade iron, said Engelbrekt, so all together four hundred Livonian pounds, a tenth of our yield, have been loaded as stipulated by the court. It could be more, if we were allowed to work in peace and all this harassment wasn't driving off our workforce. And why, asked the bailiff, has the iron not yet arrived in Västerås. The loads are on their way, said Engelbrekt, but the roads are in such a sorry state that they are not making any progress. And why don't you repair them, asked the officer. Because the people we would need to do that, said Engelbrekt, were slain in the military campaigns. Though Lord Eriksson might not have personally felt the pangs of hunger plaguing the people, said Engelbrekt, he might have been miffed by the under-salted meat on his table; that could be remedied if an end were finally put to this war and the cargo in Lübeck harbor were allowed to enter. But the peasants, cried the emissary, have not met their obligations. Yes, the peasants, said Engelbrekt, I would also like to lure them out of the forests into which they fled from the thieves; my own fields are going to ruin because I have no cottagers left. I will report everything to my lord, said the messenger, and then I shall return.

Hours spent at Rosner's kitchen table were squeezed between my other commitments. We asked ourselves how all these things that imposed themselves upon us could be systematized, categorized. Digressions were countered with lists, tables; visions were substituted for registers and protocols. We could no longer retreat into a history with which we could do as we pleased; the reports, telegrams, and decrees, the small, gray newspaper images in halftone forced us to engage with what was irrevo-

cably predetermined. The mining landscape of Norberg had become more familiar to us than the arena of today's events; while the era of half a millennium ago could be interpreted and took on a reality in which we were able to live, we watched our speculations about the immediate present become untenable and collapse time and again. For Rosner, the search for historical comparisons had lost importance, for him, what was happening around us was palpable, he stuck the things that were constantly slipping away from us into boxes, crates, he drew lines connecting the various complexes, plotted relations of magnitude in the muted light of the kitchen, and used figures and concentrations of power to calculate the impending shifts. The sheets he produced contained a reality in which individual names stood for forces in society, in which numbers of shares and economic speculation influenced the movement of troop divisions, fleets, and air force squadrons, in which even an apparently isolated silhouette could be related to remote contexts. Everything on his table was rational. Once deciphered, the rows of figures stated objective facts. Before progressing to larger groupings, he pried open a tiny window onto the internal structure that was held together by the command posts. He described two cells in the remand center on Bergsgatan. Warnke and Verner on mattresses. Each with two police officers holding their arms and legs, while one held their heads down and another poured milk through a glass tube stuck in their nostrils. The two German Communists, members of the exiled Party leadership, had begun a hunger strike because the authorities had rejected their demand to be treated as political refugees. They were suspected of having planned acts of sabotage against ships taking ore to Germany. In their files they were described as ringleaders and terrorists. Half of the nutrient-enriched liquid dribbled out, mixed with the blood from the lacerations in their mucous membranes. The head supervisor of the police station, Paulsson, a specialist in enhanced interrogation with a close relationship with the German secret police, pressured them to provide a confession. Two small torture chambers in the building representing the Swedish state. Two political prisoners, among hundreds of others who, after weeks of fruitless questioning, would be transferred to the camp in Långmora, the prison in Falun, the Kalmar penitentiary. A neutral, democratic state. In the neighboring state to the east, war. Finland had rejected the Soviet offers to regularize their borders. The value the Soviet Union placed on the pact with Germany was demonstrated by their efforts to secure their northeastern border. The Finnish army was under the command of the same individual who twenty years earlier had led the White Guards against the revolutionaries in their own land and against Russia. Mannerheim was backed up by the top brass of the Swedish military, who had joined forces with his men back in the day and were now once again offering their support, disguised as patriotic empathy. At their insistence, and in response to their anticipation that war in the North would be the signal for a German advance into Poland, Finland had bolstered its defensive capabilities. The small state had every right to defend itself in the face of a threat from a major power. Considering that Finland was facing the possibility of becoming a deployment zone for enemy forces, the Soviet Union's request to lease Hanko and exchange a few parcels of land had been a paltry demand. For the Swedish generals, Finland was an outpost in the battle against the Communist menace. With their actions in early December of thirty-nine, they were the ones who conveyed an appraisal of the German-Soviet agreement that ought to have provoked a response in public opinion that departed from the widespread national intoxication. In their willingness to relieve the burden on Germany, to make a large portion of their military firepower available to Finland, they showed that they were convinced of the untenability of the nonaggression pact. But the intentions of the Swedish and Finnish generals did not assist the Germans in the way they had intended; instead, the war provided the German military leadership with a theater in which the offensive power of the Red Army could be examined without incurring losses themselves. In the first clashes it seemed that the Finnish troops had the advantage over the Soviet soldiers, who were thrown into combat underequipped for winter fighting and with no consideration of losses. The bourgeois, liberal, and Social Democratic press couldn't get enough of expressing their joy about the instantly recognizable defeat of the invaders. Showering scorn on the proclaimed intention of protecting the Finnish working class. Disdain for the thesis that, following the formation of Kuusinen's government in exile in Moscow, a situation of civil war had developed in Finland. Because he had published Kuusinen's program, Lager, the editor in chief of *Ny Dag*, had been arrested. The advocates of Finnish Lappo-fascism on the other hand were not subject to any censorship, and the leadership of the Swedish army came out in favor of participation in the war without facing any opposition. Here, the squares, with thick outlines, referring to the centers of financial capital. Underneath, the pyramid of the intervention bloc. At the apex, the commander in chief, General Thörnell. Moving down the levels, Admiral Tamm, General Major Rappe, right-hand man of the commander in chief, General Douglas, chief of the Second Army Corps in Norrbotten, General Ehrensvärd, chief of the Defense Staff, Colonel Adlercreutz, chief of the Secret Service, and General Törngren—all former members of the Finnish White Guards. An inserted report from April of this year, when Thörnell and Tamm visited the German dictator for his fiftieth birthday, presenting him with a statuette of Charles XII of Sweden, the great enemy of Russia, as a symbol of their common bond. Lists of numerous officers who had been charged with disseminating propaganda, recruiting volunteers for the Expeditionary Corps, and sourcing and sending out munitions. The line of attack for this activism being issued by the banks and financial monopolies. Connected with the big banks were the corporations, predominantly in the hands of fifteen families. An empire, subject to the stiffest internal competition, held together by a common interest in the maintenance of free enterprise. A reference to the entanglements of the Wallenberg family companies: Jacob Wallenberg on the board of the commission for transactions with Germany; Marcus Wallenberg a member of the Swedish-British chamber of commerce. The two of them controlling the country's economy. From their private bank, strands running to the major industrial concerns, LM Ericsson, Atlas Copco, Asea, Separator. A thin thread to the boiler room, outlined in red, in which I cart tin about. Hundreds of other affiliated firms. A trembling of powerful names in all branches, from ironworks, chemical combines, matchstick factories, transport companies, through to the West Indian and East Asian Company. Gray boxes swelling with the throngs of hundreds of thousands working for the magnates. Direct channels to the generals. One lot planning, money-grubbing, the others setting up armed defenses. Consultations with General Major Jung, chief of the armed forces, about the relative strength of the militaries, in this instance regarding the relationship with Great Britain. The summoning of Count Douglas in relation to the transport of ball bearings and ore shipments to Germany. Wenner-Gren, a confidant of Krupp, partner in the Bochum steel foundry, in his head office out on the islands of the Bahamas, issuing instructions to Malm, the chair of the board of directors of Handelsbanken. The conspiring of military and industry to found the Finland Committee, to launch a crusade against Communism. Imperceptible voices from the depositories of capital, a little clearer around the employers' association, gaining resonance among the generals and in the leadership offices of the bourgeois parties, resounding in the conservative education system, the national associations, and hitting full volume in the Party presses. The government was partly bound to the major employers, partly battling for their integrity. An ongoing seesawing of the scales; one moment, out of longstanding tradition, the balance tipping in favor of amity toward the Germans; and then, out of liberal ambitions, toward the Western European powers. Foreign Minister Sandler, Minister of Trade Möller, Defense Minister Sköld, head of the right wing of the Social Democrats for a quarter century, gave their support to the endeavors of the military leadership. Aligned with them, Attorney General Westman, from the Farmers' League, and the leaders of the Right Party, Bagge and Domö. In the Social Democratic parliamentary caucus as well, the majority in favor of military support for Finland. Rosner's finger slid from name to name. Dissenting positions were expressed in parliament by Branting and the member of the People's Party, Andersson i Rasjön, the Social Democratic Finance Minister Wigforss, the Minister of Agriculture Bramstorp, from the Farmers' League, and the Secretary of State Eriksson, a Social Democrat, and Quensel, an independent. For and against, right across all political formations. From both right and left, the demands to intervene and to maintain neutrality. Per Albin Hansson, leader of the patriarchal assembly, had to maintain the equilibrium. What united the war-minded, regardless of whether they sympathized with National Socialism or were swaddling themselves in the security blanket of Anglophilia, was the hope of crushing the Soviet Union. On the one side, the people who saw Germany as responsible for this; on the other those who wanted to consent to England's request to march into Finland via northern Sweden. All that was to be decided was which alliance promised the best prospects for the future. In the end though, it was the desire to remain independent that prevailed, to stand by Finland as they saw fit. Thirteenth of December, government reshuffle, wrote Rosner. Hansson remained prime minister. Sandler, who had urged for Swedish troops to be sent to Åland, was replaced by Günther, who, of German extraction, was amenable to Berlin, and was also au fait with the necessary diplomacy of evasion. Möller was named minister of social affairs and minister of police, charged with monitoring the political opposition; Bagge became minister of culture, Domö minister of trade, in order to keep financial affairs under the control of the ultraconservatives. Andersson assumed the office of communications minister, Eriksson the ministry of the economy, while Sköld, Wigforss, Westman, Bramstorp, and Quensel retained their posts. No intervention, but comprehensive military assistance and the smuggling of volunteers. Disappointed that they weren't allowed to participate in Field Marshal Baron Mannerheim's war, the Swedish generals emptied their arsenals so they could at least contribute to the victory over the Red Army on a material level. In the absence of personal triumphs on the battlefield, the old commanders fanned

the hatred of the Bolsheviks in their own country. Outstanding in this domain was Count Douglas, whose father, as marshal of the realm, had advocated an alliance with Germany during the World War. At Rosner's, we saw the violence that was gathering together like a clenching fist, ready to rain down upon us; but also the signs of resilience, of the effort to maintain the foundations of democracy. At Brecht's, we saw the signs of the approaching apocalyptical storm; overlaying the images of the frozen corpses in the Karelian snow, we saw the peasants of the Dalarna, strung up in the chimneys of their smelting huts, bound to the stake, chained by the neck and flogged, we heard the wailing of the women yoked to the plough, the whimpering of abandoned children.

The owner of the mine, a member of the merchants' guild, Engelbrekt Engelbrektsson, had been summoned to appear before the bailiff Jösse Eriksson. Why had he not come earlier, why had they had to bring him in, asked the Dane, sitting on an elevated chair dressed in a velvet robe adorned with ribbons covered in bells. The smallest motion provoked a jingling. Engelbrekt had also gotten dressed up for the visit, wearing a floor-length, wide-sleeved cloak, hemmed with fur and with slits on the sides, and a broad-brimmed hat. Almost in admiration, he grasped one of the dangling strips of fabric, shaking it. The latest fashion, he said with a laugh. The man from Jutland informed him in a nasal voice that they were supposed to call to mind the peals of the church bells after the burning of the heretic Joan of Arc. Then began to hold forth about this vixen, this goatherd from a village in Lorraine, who had run away from her parents and sown turmoil. That slip of a woman, who could only seem large when sitting on a horse, he said, looking down upon on the thickset, cloaked figure before him; and she was almost always sitting on a horse, until she was seized in the forest of Compiègne; a monster she was, and she was justly punished in Rouen for her hubris. Of course, the people in France say she acted heroically against the British, said Engelbrekt. Possessed, a witch she was, answered Eriksson, those who condemned her ought to have known, around a hundred of them sat above her in judgment, the most eminent clerics, theologians, and doctors of philosophy; then, accompanied by vigorous jingling, that he knows full well the reasons why the invited guest did not want to show up, that Engelbrekt was trying to withhold his foreign coins in silver and gold from the king, in violation of the stipulations of the law. Engelbrekt looked at him in bewilderment. You yourself exchanged my money, he said, for worthless currency, and even if I did still possess any of it, it could hardly contribute to a victory in our wars against the Hanseatic League, which will soon have endured for twenty years. Why doesn't he give up his beloved Schleswig. Who are you talking about, asked the bailiff. His Royal Highness, said Engelbrekt. Have we perhaps become disloyal, asked Lord Eriksson. I have always served him faithfully, said Engelbrekt. Yet one notes a reluctant tone in your voice. Question: Do you wish to join the rebel camp. I was for the Union, said Engelbrekt, but under the conditions that currently prevail it can no longer be maintained, harmony must be established, work and trade must be promoted. Then, peasants and miners in tattered clothing descended upon the chamber in the castle of Västerås. The treadwheels of the mine stood still, the adits had collapsed, the fires in the smelting ovens and at the blacksmiths had gone out. Engelbrekt, his robe undone, a breastplate and sword underneath, was surrounded. No more complaints about torments, just explosive rage, the demand that the message, that the people's patience has been exhausted, be delivered to the king in Denmark. Question to Engelbrekt of whether he, with his skills in conversation and negotiation, would be willing to travel to Copenhagen on behalf of the countryfolk to present their cause. Fall of fourteen thirty-two. The meeting of Engelbrekt, leader of the iron-producing regions, with his ruler. This scene, said Brecht, should have something of a canto from the circles of hell to it, but distorted by elements from Gothic novels and the colorful language of the sensationalist press. Eric, a decrepit-looking youth, his white-blonde hair in a pageboy cut, his lace shirt unbuttoned, one foot bare, the other in a satin slipper, surrounded by scantily clad concubines, a few courtiers scoffing food and guzzling booze, and a bishop in tattered vestments. The court jester juggling crown and scepter, the clergyman ranting and raving, drowned out by the screeching of parrots in cages. What will become of me now that they no longer want me in office in Iceland either and are threatening to drown me, Bishop Gerekesson, me, Johannes Gerechini. Be off with you, cried Eric. In response: you allowed them to dismiss me from my office as archbishop in Uppsala, you should have come to my aid, after all I've done for you, you'd have been lost without the riches that I brought in for you with our privateers. Go back to Skálholt, cried Eric, they should boil you in the spring waters. The king threw himself onto the cushions, sobbing, while the women caressed him and stroked his face with peacock feathers. My Philippa, he cried, why were you taken from me. Then Engelbrekt stepped in with his entourage. Travel clothes, spurs on his clay-smeared boots. Said he came as the emissary of the people of Dalarna to most humbly beg him to see to an investigation into the ills in the country entrusted to his care. The king: but do you not see that I am suffering; and, once more: Philippa, how could I ever have hit you. It pains him, the jester whispered to Engelbrekt, that he beat his wife to death, and the king again: oh the pain, the pain. Countless are feeling pain where I've come from, said Engelbrekt. They want relief, action. You could never compete with my suffering, countered the king, yet I wish to display my grace with an order to the Council of the Realm to kindly investigate the matter. He wrote a few words on a sheet of parchment, had it sealed, handed it to Engelbrekt, waved him away with a trembling hand, and lay straight back down whimpering on the soft bed of skin. And now, said Brecht, we had to depict the period leading up to the summer of thirty-four, perhaps in a call and response arrangement, or in scraps of conversation, incorporating the discussions deep down below concerning conditions at the top. The councillors had probably arrived on their horses, accompanied by the bailiff Jösse Eriksson, infuriated that their horses couldn't carry them all the way up through the rugged terrain, strutting about among the starving, holding their noses at the stench from the smelters, bowing and shaking their heads and then scampering off again. Just as we, said Brecht, are following the moves in the games of chess to secure accords, treaties, alliances, nonaggression pacts, border defenses, border crossings, defensive measures and defensive wars, the peasants and miners in the muck, the prisoners in the straw, the poachers in the forests, also had to address the question of what would happen to them now. Wasn't a peace supposed to have been agreed to, in Horsens; where's Horsens; in Jutland, there, the peasants don't have to front up for military service anymore, yet Danish squadrons were setting off once again to face the Wendish cities of the Hanseatic League; why, because Eric would sooner let Nordland fall than give up control over the Baltic Sea; but then there was a cease-fire after all, where they had gathered together in Svenborg, on Fyn, and come to an agreement; peace at last; no, Eric couldn't take the fact that the Holsteiners wanted to keep South Jutland; new concentrations of masses of cavalry, new massacres, renewed tax gouging; but now, in Vordingborg, at the strait of Falster, a big conference, lofty speeches and solemn promises; so who was there, there were the emissaries from Lübeck, Wismar, Hamburg, Lüneburg, and Flensburg, there were the Danish and Swedish noblemen, the bishops Sigge of Skara and Thomas of Strängnäs; but why was Eric's contingent so small; because most of his knights were still out in the countryside trying to scrounge better conditions for a peace treaty through their plundering. The chant, the round, entered an elevated tempo, Engelbrekt had traveled to Copenhagen once again, you can go to hell with your endless complaints, the king had cried, I never want to see you again; and the leader responded, I shall return once more. Because it was now a struggle for liberation, a civil war, said Brecht, the events had to be depicted palpably. No longer a view from a dispassionate height, no blind and august gaze, but setting to work, bundling lengths of timber together which were coated in pitch and wedged against the forts. Behind the protection of the palisades, carrying axes, hammers, pitchforks, iron bars, clubs, seized swords and lances, the army of peasants and workers approached the fortresses of the enemy. If earlier only the rulers had been visible, now, it was only the people who could be seen, no trace of the men of God, they had made tracks at the sight of the masses traversing the fields. They headed for Borganäs. Fire, the crumbling of the walls under the axes. It was Midsummer of fourteen thirty-four. Now, the bells were ringing in the people's first victory. In the villages, the fiddlers were playing, the shawms were blaring for their side. On it went, into Västmanland, toward Köping and Västerås. They'd been able to take Borganäs in a surprise strike, but the castle of Köping was more strongly fortified. But when the lord of the castle, Johan Vale, an Italian whose real name was Giovanni Franco—they might be able to get some material out of him, said Brecht—jumped onto his horse and fled to Stäkeborg without even having had time to put on his armor, Köpingshus was burned to the ground as well. The army marched at quick time to the harbor city of Västerås. At the gates, Engelbrekt was lifted onto the shoulders of the masses, and the short, bearded leader, cupping his hands around his mouth, demonstrated what people meant when they spoke about his booming voice. He called upon the locals to follow him, then ordered the representatives of the nobility to show themselves and submit to the power of the people; otherwise, he threatened, they would be relieved of their property and their lives. A series of increasingly tall walls. The gates within were slowly opened from behind. Frightened, bowing deeply—while Jösse Eriksson stole off through a hatch in the distance—the deputy bailiff Melchior Görtz stepped forward and handed Engelbrekt the keys to the city, whereupon Engelbrekt, apparently acting upon a prior agreement, named the knight Gustafsson Båt lord of the castle in Västerås. Thus, barely a week after departing Dalarna, the appearance of the revolution had already begun to transform, with the aristocrats rushing across to join the militant rural masses. We mustn't seem to be conveying a history lesson, said Brecht, we only had to highlight a number of key moments that enabled a reading of the violent historical transformations. There was a whole host of evidence of the upheaval, which was consummated within a month and which brought Dalarna, Västmanland, and Uppland, the center of the realm, into the hands of the people's army, which had now swollen to fifty thousand men. Even though many of their privileges had been taken away by Eric, the nobles had opposed a confrontation with the Danish supremacy for as long as possible. The signs of an independent movement among the populace unsettled them more than the acts of violence of the regent of the Union. Despite all the warnings, they had done nothing to assuage the hardship of the people and had instead carried out internal negotiations with the Danish court aimed at striking a deal to regain the rights they had conceded in Kalmar. Since Engelbrekt's second visit to Eric in thirteen thirty-three had also been fruitless—the ignominy heaped upon the people having increased, if anything—he had marched to Västerås, a horde of fighters already at his back, in order to oust the bailiff. The knights and prelates had barred his way, had vowed to bring about improvements in the country immediately, and, to avoid a scuffle, Engelbrekt had withdrawn. This did not mean that he stood with the elite; rather, his caution seemed to prove that he had already come up with a revolutionary plan and did not want to jeopardize it, was still waiting for the moment to strike. He didn't want to risk a clash that could lead to a break with the aristocrats but wanted instead to draw them to the side of the people. He knew that it would be impossible to secure victory without them; from the first moment to the last, he was focused on establishing unity, was willing to make any compromise for the sake of preventing their struggle for freedom from turning into a civil war. He had to win over the knights with cunning, with persuasion, and the most convincing factor now was the size of the army standing behind him. The rallying cries to band together, to take up arms and form regiments, had been passed along from village to village. The excitement building among the people was unstoppable. The day of the harvest festival was chosen to launch the campaign. As the throngs of farmworkers and miners streamed together, the first nobles began to see the advantages of joining forces with this army. Perhaps, with the protection of the masses, they would be able to regain the estates and castles of theirs that had been occupied by foreign counts. While the workers were fighting for their survival, the focus of the nobles was on filling their coffers. Though generations had suffered the abuse of foreign rulers, it had never made much difference to the lowly whether it was Germans or Danes at the top; the lowly knew only oppressors. They had always been without a fatherland, even when local princes had reigned. The idea of a nation, a national ethos, was only implanted in them later, from above. That **217** Engelbrekt was of German extraction didn't concern them, for them he was autochthonous to their landscape. Given the hatred toward the Germans from Albert's time, his origins actually managed to reinforce his reputation as a man of integrity. While Engelbrekt made use of the people, extracting their violent intervention from the revolutionary conditions, this well-traveled and experienced mine owner was likewise of use to the people, who were the source of the initiative to rebel. What was undeniable, though, was that the workers cast aside their submissiveness and rose up, and that Engelbrekt grew with his mission. It was also possible that he saw himself as a man of the people. The gulf between him as a mine owner and the pitmen may have still been fluid: he participated personally in the work in the pits, worked side by side with tradespeople and smiths, intervened with the bailiffs on behalf of his wage laborers. Yet the closest members of his entourage came from the nobility. There were various reasons for this. The knights possessed armor and warhorses, were skillful in handling weapons. He needed the cavalry to be able to advance quickly and seize the enemy's estates by surprise. Denmark was still strong, as was now being revealed on the approach to Stockholm, with the main fortresses still housing heavily armed garrisons. The rural folk, who had risen up spontaneously, had to be shaped into disciplined battle formations. So he brought in professional soldiers, even if they came from different social ranks than those of the groups that had constituted the initial incarnation of the revolution. And behind this, time and again, his vision of all social levels and classes working together, his hope for the reestablishment of the judiciary, the foundation of a council representing all classes of society. In this transitional phase in which consensus was essential, he courted the nobles, offered them high-level positions, appealed to their ambition, but also threatened them when they showed reluctance, always anticipating that the successes in their advance would compel them to loyalty. And yet this would also be his undoing. For while he presumed that the dignitaries were interested in liberating their country, they were merely feigning their support in order to prepare themselves to resist popular rule. Aligning himself with the people, he still failed to consult them for the most important decisions; availing himself of the nobility, he also allowed them to retain their influence; promoting the bourgeoisie, he secured them an elevated position. Though there was always talk of rural folk from all provinces joining his agitation, stepping in to defend him when the nobles attacked him and attempted to rob him of his status, with the expansion of the struggle, the commoners began to take a back seat, and the elite scored one win after the other. In many aspects, the strategy that Engelbrekt developed resembled a campaign of guerrilla warfare, with brutal, unexpected attacks, hasty retreats, and flanking maneuvers, but the victories could never be consolidated among the populace. Though he did convoke assemblies in the villages, he had always already set his sights on the next castle still occupied by the enemy, and the minute it fell, it had a highborn Swedish administrator sitting in it. The people just wanted to burn down the castles, those symbols of power strewn across the entire country. Engelbrekt's assertion—that with the arrival of knights loyal to him, they had won bases from which to continue the struggle—was deceptive. He too was still unable to countenance the idea that the castles and fortified estates could be handed over to the workers. He might have been audacious enough to prepare the aristocrats for the prospect of expropriation, but in his eyes the only suitable successors were those of noble standing. The structure of feudalism had impressed itself so deeply in the consciousness that even the first signs of its collapse were not yet able to provoke the will to discard it entirely. The rebellion was of an elementary nature, had initially been aimed at casting off a mass of unbearable pressure. The lashing out and the forward rush engendered relief. Those revolting had never intended to take the estates or even government affairs into their own hands; the fighters demanded no more than a small piece of arable land, the abolition of forced labor, and the lowering of taxes. When their captain promised them that their wishes were to be fulfilled, they instantly saw in him a new Saint Eric, under whose regency in the early times of legend a realm of freedom and fraternity was said to have existed. Perhaps Engelbrekt wanted to become such a king. But for all his aptitude as a commander, his visions of a new form of politics, for all the energy he exuded, as attested to by his contemporaries, he was not equal to the plotting against him by the elites. In the face of these conspirators, for whom no betrayal was too great, no murder too treacherous, his honesty was deformed into a weakness. Today, in the course of our research, the things that he realized too late moved into the foreground for us. By the time he reached the outskirts of Stockholm in July, his enemies' plots were already flourishing widely. Messengers had rushed news of the insurrection to the members of the Council of the Realm, who were in Vordingborg to participate in the peace negotiations with the representatives of the Hanseatic League. The threat of a plebeian seizure of power accelerated the agreement among the elites: the Swedish lords deferred their demands for sovereignty. Needing help from Denmark, they pledged their loyalty to Eric, who for his part needed an alliance with the Hanseatic League to strengthen his rule over Sweden; and the Hanseatic League was provided with the assurance that Stockholm would remain under its flags. While Engelbrekt was camped in Normmalm, looking across onto Stockholm's fortified Helgeandsholmen, the Swedish and Danish aristocrats agreed to support one another in the battle against the rebels in accordance with the theses of the Union document. The defeat of Spain was still on our minds as we contemplated the courage and enthusiasm of the peasant soldiers in medieval Sweden. From Engelbrekt's camp north of the city, we turned to his final hour, on the small island in Lake Hjälmaren, asked ourselves where the people had been. We can only inquire, said Brecht, into how it happened that they went from this show of strength to their loss of power and ultimate defeat, and in doing so, provide a contribution to the understanding of the irregularities, fluctuations, ruptures, and jumps involved in the process of world revolution. Engelbrekt had been let in through the northern gate of the Islet of the Holy Spirit. Stood with his entourage, in the forecourt of the church, in anticipation of negotiations with the leader of the city's armed forces. The walls of the fort rose up behind the narrow arm of the stream. The bridge leading into town ran between two square defense towers. Though the powerful might have been sitting up above, out front, directly before the castle, it was now the commoners who were standing armed and ready. From above, laughter, scornful jeers. The demand to hand over the city to the people's army sounded foolhardy. Kröpelin, German-born, former courtier to Margaret and now the lord of the castle of Stockholm, showed himself through an arrow slit. He rejected Engelbrekt's demand, invoking the oath that he had sworn to King Eric and his duties to the inhabitants of the capital as mayor. This sounded honorable, but it was dripping with contempt. Discussions between Engelbrekt and his people. The fort impossible to take, given they had no fleet. A siege pointless, as the city has plenty of provisions. Losing time grave, given the expectation of a Danish invasion in the west. Essential not to interrupt the advance and to immediately continue on to take other forts. Suggestion to leave the city to its own devices until the beginning of winter. It would fall once the country had been liberated, or they'd take it on their way across the ice. Agreement of a ceasefire. Until the eleventh of November, cried Engelbrekt, Saint Martin's Day. Then, they said below, we'll eat our roast goose in the castle. This rapid decision altered the relationship between the horde of country folk and the guard details of the patricians. Those standing out front, who had just a moment ago seemed small, insignificant, would gain the upper hand, the armored figures on the walls would be made to yield. Not the sensation of failure, but the intimation of the possible. Puke led an army to Norrland and Finland; on the Bothnian coast, Vaxholm was razed, and Kastelholm on Åland capitulated without a fight; in early August, Puke rejoined Engelbrekt again, to whom Uppsala and Gripsholm had now fallen. Nyköping, too strongly fortified, was bypassed, but as Ringstadaholm came within reach, Engelbrekt learned that the councillors of the realm and the church dignitaries had come from Denmark and were gathered in Vadstena on Lake Vättern. The scene of Engelbrekt's entrance into the meeting of the noblemen, on which Brecht had focused in the very first sketches for the piece, was now reconceived. The ancestors could happily be depicted in all their exaggerated grandeur to begin with, standing at the podium and sitting around the enormous table; but soon enough, those from below would come marching in to meet them and leave them speechless. The bishops of Strängnäs and Skara could still hold forth in a duet about the evil—just now butchered in the figure of the Hussite leader Prokop, near Lipany, east of Prague—that now sought to rear its head in their own land; they could still gleefully praise the victory of the Bohemian emperor, accompanied by the choir of the knights, but a second later they were set upon by the peasant throng, armed with clubs and flails. What did these peasants think they were doing, yammered the bishop of Linköping, raising his hand to cross himself, admonishing those who had previously been nothing but humble to return to their senses. Engelbrekt stood above him on the chair, lifted him up by the collar of his cassock and yelled that he would throw him to the peasants like all the others who failed to immediately declare their willingness to join the side of the people; then pulled out a piece of paper and ordered a letter to be written to the king relieving him of all his offices. Then the clerics, Thomas of Strängnäs, Sigge of Skara, Knut of Linköping, the knights Bo Stensson and Bengt Stensson of the House of Natt och Dag, Magnus Birgersson and Guse Nilsson of the House of Båt, Erengisle Nilsson and Nils Erengislesson Hammersta, Karl Magnusson and Greger Magnusson from the House of Eka, Gustav Algotsson from the Sture Dynasty, and all the rest of them bent over the table, scribbling, muttering away, interrupted by cries of *Your Grace, Venerable King*; no grace, no veneration; we have gathered together; were beaten up, shoved together; would gladly like to resolve in your favor; get rid of the favor; would like of our own free will; forced, seized by weapon-wielding hands; as administrators of the highest offices of the land; in loyalty to Engelbrekt and the peasants, to absolve ourselves herewith of our oath; the Dane broke **221** his oath long ago; but we will not undertake anything against you; will remove you from the Swedish throne; are sending up a prayer from our pit of despair; are polishing our suits of armor, saddling our horses; request compensation; will sweep the land clean of your riff-raff. Wax dripped onto the paper, the seal pressed on top, and thumbs from all sides. Engelbrekt's behavior after the conference at Vadstena could only be explained by his desire to build a nation; his undertaking seemed to occur as if in a state of blindness but was an expression of an absolute longing for legality. For him, even though they had reached their posts through personal violence, the prelates and knights remained the absolute authorities of the realm; he wanted to establish his state for the good of all, not against them but with them. In Vadstena, a triumphant gesture sufficed the powerful Engelbrekt. In order to demonstrate his trust in the high lords and to make his alliance with them unbreakable, he placed them at the head of his armies. And what followed initially gave the impression that the nobles had been convinced by the supremacy of this minor squire. Engelbrekt had one corps, led by Bo Stensson and Erengisle Nilsson, take on Stäkeholm; a second, under Junker Herman Berman, headed to Småland to conquer Rumlaborg, Trolleborg, and Piksborg. He himself returned with Nils Erengislesson to Castle Ringstadaholm, which he bequeathed to his companion following a rapid victory. Then continued straight on with his troops to Stäkeborg, chasing off Giovanni Franco once again, where he installed Bishop Knut, also born a Natt och Dag, as lord of the castle. Knut also snared himself Rönö, placing it under the supervision of another family member, Erik Stensson. Once the rumor had spread that the nobility could get their hands on castles for cheap, knights rushed over from all counties, among them Magnus Gren, Bo Knutsson Grip, descendants of the powerful treasurer Bo Jonsson Grip, and the young Karl Knutsson Bonde, who would soon become Engelbrekt's strongest adversary. While Engelbrekt took control of the castle of Örebro, one of the strongest in the land, for a sum of one thousand marks and named his brother the commander there, the nobles had no luck at Stäkeholm; after repeated assaults they continued on toward Kalmar, which also refused to be taken. Berman conquered the forts in Småland, and Engelbrekt set off for Värmland and Västergötland together with Puke, received help from the country folk everywhere he went, smoked out the castles around Lake Vänern, Agneholm, Edsholm, and Dalaborg, ordered Puke to besiege Axvall, conquered Opensten, Öresten, arrived in Halland, won over the citizens of Varberg with promises of trade privileges, left the Danish bailiff in the city's castle, pushed on to Falkenberg, Halmstad, where his troops united with Berman's army, secured a separate peace with the capitulating Laholm, wanted to add Skåne to the realm as well and have himself ferried over to Denmark to keep his promise of a final visit, but since there was word that Eric was on the way to Stockholm with his fleet and Saint Martin's Day was drawing close, he rushed off toward the capital, having liberated the entire country, but for a few castles still holding out, in four months. When he arrived the bay was filled with Danish warships, and the Swedish councillors and the king and his army were meeting in the House of the Holy Spirit, chaired by the mayor Hans Kröpelin. Engelbrekt was not allowed in: crossbows peered out from the loopholes in the walls, the bridges were drawn, the gates barricaded. For a second time the military leader stood before the bulwarks of the island city. There could no longer be any doubt that the nobles had betrayed him and the people. There was no longer any discernible reason for Engelbrekt's continued hesitation to declare war on the nobility. He could have begun the siege and stormed the city in the winter once the ships had sailed off, providing they didn't get frozen in place. He had gathered together an army before the southern gate, another before the fortifications in the north; he himself was camped on the island of Långholmen, where today the Västerbron begins its powerful, upward arc over Lake Mälaren. The peasant ranks heavily outnumbered the few thousand soldiers in the castle. Why, we asked ourselves, did Engelbrekt not respond to the announcement of the agreement between the aristocrats and the regent that all discord was to be brought to an end and that in the autumn of the following year, the treaty would be ratified in a court session. We worked until after Christmas on this scene, which had to convey the end of the first phase of the revolution. What's with the roast goose, cried one of the soldiers. And it was brought from an abandoned estate in the surrounding area, where the outer baileys had been burned down by the defenders of the city. It was roasted over the fire. Eating now, among the steaming pots of the sutlers, the conversation covered the topics that we ultimately considered were most likely. First, rage, demands for the revocation of the ceasefire. It wasn't the knights who bore the burdens of the war, it was us. We seized this victory, and we want our reward. We won't let ourselves be ordered around by those lords in there any longer. Messengers delivered details of the accord sealed on Helgeandsholmen. Eric has surrendered all his previous authority, vowed to withdraw his bailiffs and governors and henceforth hand over the administration of the entire realm to the local noblemen. Sweden's autonomy has been confirmed. Eric now only wears the crown as the Union's head of state, in a symbolic role, practically divested of all power. The councillors had declared the agreement a great success, also bestowing praise and thanks upon the leader Engelbrekt, who, with the great sacrifices of the people, had ushered in an epoch of peace. Thus Engelbrekt was supposed to surrender, return to the pits with his miners, send the country folk back to their villages and leave the knights and merchants to manage their hard-earned share. We had to concede that Engelbrekt's decision was a reflection of his circumstances. He was as revolutionary as he could be for his time, indeed, he was ahead of his time, but was held down, pushed back by the viscous progression of the evolution of society. He had made it infinitely further than Margaret, but it would be almost four hundred years before the kind of progress was made that we would have wished to see, from our contemporary perspective. Had Engelbrekt been an adventurer rather than a revolutionary, he'd have allowed himself to be seized by the hatred that erupted toward the aristocracy, he'd have led the exhausted troops to storm the city, and probably would have taken it too, before unleashing civil war, taking on the Danish cavalry, the Swedish knights, the Hanseatic League, and the Teutonic Order. Nothing could be done any more about the fact that he had been deceived. Of course the upper classes preferred the fickle king of the Union to the unbending leader of the people, for they knew well that they could only retain their privileges under Eric. But there were also a few, like Nils Gustafsson Båt and Thomas of Strängnäs, who had some sympathy for Engelbrekt's far-sighted aspirations. Puke, Berman, Bengt Gotskalksson and Gotskalk Bengtsson, Johan Karlsson Färla, Claus Plata, and other knights and lords stuck by him; as a progressive movement,

223

the insurgency had also taken root among the elite, and Engelbrekt remained committed to bringing this thirst for renewal to a wide-reaching
realization. Engelbrekt resisted the temptation to jeopardize the goal of
national unity—as difficult as it would have been to achieve—in the interests of securing a brief, spectacular victory, even though many of his
fighters were urging him to do so. Though some might have called it
weakness, a lack of daring, we decided that during the brief period of his
appearance on the stage of history, he had shown more prudence and
determination than any other statesman before him in these parts ever
had. He retained a standing army, sent all others in ordered groups back
to their homelands for them to resume their work, elect their representatives, form their councils, stay in constant contact with him, ready, if
necessary, to mobilize once more. In January, after Twelfth Night, on the
Feast of the Three Kings, he would call a conference at which the representatives of all classes would decide upon the fate of the realm.

In January Brecht was unwell, lay mostly on the sofa in a frayed bathrobe,
a woolen scarf around his neck. A draft came from the floor, from the
windows; despite the fire in the iron stove, the room was cold. Our work
began to stall, all our senses froze. A new law had been issued giving the
police the power to open letters, listen in to phone conversations, carry
out home searches, body searches, arrest any random suspect and keep
them in custody for up to sixty days without the possibility of representation. We had gathered together material on the meeting in Arboga and
on Engelbrekt's demise, material whose drama was as icy as the air outside. We attempted to overcome our torpor and begin to draft the final
scenes, but Brecht seemed to have given up on the piece. Though he still
had us read aloud from the history books and prepare sketches of some of
the confrontations, he hardly listened any more. One time Greid entered
the room, his arms flung wide, his coat and his mane of hair full of snow,
crying that God had appeared to him, that he'd seen the face of the moral
and ethical agendas that had to shape Marxist ideology if it was to avoid
wallowing in materialism. The city's entire atmosphere was as spectral
as the vision of this actor and amateur philosopher. The circular *Eleven
Forty-Four* had been sent out to the workplaces by the union leadership,
with the instruction to remove Communists from union posts. The divisions of the federation had to join the National Coalition for Finland. Specific days were introduced on which the workers had to give up their wage
for the struggle of the Finnish people. On the tenth of February, more than
three thousand police officers took part in raids on the headquarters and

editorial offices of the Communist Party. Sacks and crates full of documents were taken from the occupied Party headquarters on Kungsgatan to the headquarters of the security service. The sale and postage of Party papers was forbidden, as was putting up flyers. The so-called Transport Ban circumvented the law on freedom of the press, which had been enshrined in the constitution for more than a hundred years. The texts were permitted to be produced, they just couldn't be distributed. The involvement of the Social Democrats—who had previously been affected by the efforts of the bourgeoisie to limit press freedoms—was tantamount to total censorship. Even ministers like Branting had voted in favor of the parliamentary resolution. Thus, the Swedish Communists who had begun delivering the papers themselves were now thrust into the illegal struggle as well. Many members whose addresses were identified in the confiscated lists were subsequently arrested and interrogated as enemies of the state. The comrades harboring Rosner remained undetected. Either they hadn't been identified as suspects, or the building was already under special surveillance. From now on, when I went to see the representative of the Comintern, I would leave from Västmannagatan, which ran parallel to Upplandsgatan, passing through the courtyards and a building out the back. Until this point, he had signed his lead articles as Franz Lang. From December, he called himself Hauser, perhaps in memory of the foundling in the tower. His pseudonym was surrounded by a host of well-known names, including Dimitrov, Marty, Pieck, Florin, Ulbricht, Thorez, Cachin, Šmeral, Andersen Nexø, La Pasionaria, and Mao Zedong. The Swedish Party leaders Linderot, Sillén, and Hagberg also wrote for the paper, which was produced legally on the Party printing press in Västermalm. The cover was total. The paper had existed as a Swedish publication for two years. Now it appeared only as a German-language edition. The Communist Party was responsible for the content. No editor in chief was named. Earlier the material had also been primarily provided by the Comintern. There was no evidence to suggest that the Comintern was now located in Stockholm. The police could try to identify the pseudonyms, they could search for potential employees living in the underground, but they could not raise any objections against the paper itself, which was aimed at German émigrés and addressed questions of international politics and economics. But after the Transport Ban, many of the copies that were sent out were left lying in the basement of the central post office. Being shut off from the public was like a confirmation of the isolation the Party had retreated into in September. The directives issued by the paper must have been confusing for many of the members. By abstaining from directly criticizing fascism, by continuing to portray the Western powers as the primary enemy and the cause of the continuation of the war, they suppressed the proactive energy that had earlier made them into a party of struggle. During these months, they lost seven thousand of their nineteen thousand members. But indirectly, with their justification of the actions of the Red Army, they identified the actual motive of the conflict with Finland. No pact could hide the fact that the Soviet invasion, as earlier in Poland, served solely to avert or delay a clash with Germany. England and France were hoping for the outbreak of war between the two powers; the lack of action behind the Maginot Line provided the proof of that. But when the Party emphasized the peaceful intentions of the Soviet Union, when they advocated for the maintenance of neutrality out of their commitment to the Comintern and de-

nounced the Swedish desire for intervention, this was dismissed with scorn by the press. Antifascism was now the business of Social Democracy, the progressive bourgeoisie, even the liberal aristocrats. Princes, counts, bank directors, professors, lawyers, and journalists were showing generosity and offering to help Jewish and non-Communist refugees, while it was left to the Communist Party to declare a state of emergency on itself. The committees, platforms, and organizations, with their charitableness, their emphasis on common cultural bonds, their soirées and bazaars, their training courses, their attempts to find jobs and apartments, operated under the banner of an unimpeachable humanism. Up until September thirty-nine, isolated instances of cooperation with the Red Aid had been possible. Now, the activities of this institution had been cut back dramatically, and aid efforts were confined to the underground. Hodann seemed to have joined the side on which the concept of freedom and justice was concomitant with a condemnation of Communism. I visited him together with Brecht's girlfriend, Berlau, who for a long time had put up Hodann's daughter from his first marriage, Sonja, at her place in Denmark. Since the masses of snow on the streets made cycling impossible, she had picked me up on her motorbike, as she often did to take me to Lidingö. Hodann lived with his wife and his one-month-old son on Lidnersplan in Kristineberg, in one of the new buildings on Lake Ulvsunda, overlooking the Traneberg bridge. He was haggard, seemed exhausted, the smell of diapers was accompanied by the smell of the expectorated mucus that I knew all too well. His strength was sapped by the tram trip along the endless Drottningholmsvägen and Hantverkargatan, change at Tegelbacken, then Vasagatan, Kungsgatan, on to his workplace and then back again. He had to pay one hundred fifteen kronor for the small apartment, almost half of his wage as a consultant. I tried to imagine him in the uniform of the Spanish Republican Army, tried to reinitiate our earlier conversations, but that time in Cueva la Potita and Denia slipped away from me. Something had happened to him during the past year, something that had left him shattered, and yet he still managed to muster a friendly demeanor. On the verge of a breakdown, he immediately offered to look into ways that I could be fostered in my professional development. He wanted to speak to Professor Tegen, the chair of the refugee committee, to Gillis Hammar, the director of the adult education center in Birkagården, he wanted to recommend me to Miss Hellner, in the aid office on Vanadisvägen, and I could have accepted all of this if not for the fact that I had enough responsibilities already—and that his own deterioration demonstrated the futility of all such activities. While Berlau and the woman from Prague sat in the living room, which was cluttered with furniture, we sat in the bathroom, Hodann on the toilet seat, me on a stool; I thought that we might now be able to speak with one another. I brought up the distinction between the nonpolitical and political refugees, the neutralization of the Red Aid. Compared to the economically feeble leftist organizations, he said, the bourgeois and Social Democratic initiatives offered the exiles their only chance of safety. With their official approval of the aggression of the fascists, it was no longer possible to place trust in the Communist Party. And anybody who looks at the German workers—who were so willing to carry the burden of building up arms and going off to war—and sees future combatants for socialism, has lost their faculty of judgment. The explanation that the Soviet Union had scored a diplomatic victory over the German government had to be rejected. He could see no sign of strength in the Soviet state acquiescing, after the extinction of an entire generation of pioneers, to the sacrificing of the global Communist movement as well. Now, as earlier, fascist Germany—which enjoys the support of the overwhelming majority of the population—represents the main foe. By continuing to portray the Western powers as their sole opposition, and with their attack on Finland, the Soviet Union had created the impression that their aim was to divide Europe between them and Germany. This could lead to devastating consequences if England were to enter the conflict from northern Scandinavia to relieve Finland. It was an illusion, he said, to expect, as the Communist Party did, the Finnish working class and the Red Army to come together and form a revolutionary Finnish government. We were once again forced to face the question of how we should behave in this escalated situation, whether we ought to turn our backs on anybody who opposed the Party line, or, in our uncertainty, open ourselves up to any and every perspective so as to gain our own picture of the complexity of the competing forces. Yet I knew I wouldn't be able to break with a friend with whom, though he had taken a conflicting stance, I nevertheless shared a belief in criticism and the free exchange of opinions. I had always presupposed that party loyalties could never be associated with dogma, that self-examination could never be abandoned, that nothing could be taken to be definitive, final. When the bourgeoisie made a show of its progressive attitudes and in the process carried out their class justice, we had to stand up even more vehemently for the reestablishment of the concept of human rights. As long as the Party existed in its current form, Hodann viewed this as an impossible endeavor. Then I rode with Berlau back through the city, my arms wrapped around her creaking leather jacket,

riding through the spray of shards of ice. We pushed the motorbike up the slick, steep slope to the red wooden house among the pines. Arboga, the thirteenth of January, fourteen thirty-five. A brick façade, with windows and a round gate, the countryfolk out front with their carts, carrying their tools, some with a sword or crossbow as well, all bundled up in quilted jackets, fur caps pulled down over their ears, pacing back and forth in the dense snowdrift, stamping their feet, slapping their arms together. Since the people were not allowed to participate in the conference, Brecht had said, distracted, blowing his nose, we'd have to move the conference onto the street, show not the speakers inside but the commentators outside. That's where the revolutionary force was first articulated. Listen, it's not just knights and clerics gathered together over there, there are others too. Who then, people asked. The gatekeeper passed along the messages, he had found out what was going on up above from a guard in the stairwell, who had received whispered reports from the bailiffs. Yes, it was not just the usual aristocratic councillors sitting there, there were also representatives from the lower echelons of the nobility, from commerce, from the peasantry. And it isn't just twelve of them, as it was before, but a whole thirty-six. Now—and this was directed against the nobles in Stockholm—a government and a head of state was to be elected. So the events taking place inside were no longer unfolding with the consent of the lords in Stockholm but against them. The elite, loyal to the king, had become isolated; the broader community, the *allmoge*, had to formulate their own decisions. Did they do that, we asked ourselves. Even those standing outside must have wondered what kind of decisions those would be. Not in the way that we asked today, but from within their time. Had they been capable of asking why no peasants, no wage laborers from the pits, were sitting in the hall, they would have resumed the revolution of their own accord. But since even today, regardless of the fact that they constituted the overwhelming majority of the people, they had not taken the reins from below, instead placing their trust in representatives who only rarely came from their own ranks and who told them what to do—back then they could likewise only stand by in anticipation. Though their questions were forceful, demanding to know where they stood, they felt fairly secure once the report was relayed that Engelbrekt was sitting alongside his comrades in arms Puke, Berman, Gotskalksson, Bengtsson, Färla, and Plata. When they heard that the bishops Thomas, Sigge, and Knut were present, the knights Magnus Birgersson and Nils Gustafsson Båt, Nils Erengislesson Hammarstad, Gustav Algotsson Sture, Greger Magnusson Eka, Bo Knutsson Grip, Knut Karlsson Örnfot, Bo Stensson and Nils Stensson Natt och Dag—all of whom, in addition to holding public offices, were also major landowners, mine owners—they interpreted this in their favor. If these people were now openly pledging their allegiance to Engelbrekt, they said, they must also be willing to undertake land redistribution, tax relief, the abolition of the punitive measures of the bailiffs. However their petty concerns were not the topic of discussion; there were more important things to be dealt with up there. It was probably also the case that insufficient attention was being paid to the decisions being made inside, since everything was overshadowed by the news that Engelbrekt had been elevated to the rank of commander in chief. That was a new title. Does that mean king, people asked. Not a king, a marshal. Predictions of how the situation in the country would now be different were cut through by the cries coming from the gate declaring who would assume control over the various provinces. Engelbrekt himself took over Uppland, Nils Erengislesson Östergötland, Bishop Sigge Västergötland, Nils Stensson Småland, Bo Knutsson Tjust, Knut Karlsson Södermanland. After all, somebody had to preside over the territories. And at least it was those who were now proving that they wanted nothing more to do with Eric. What they couldn't understand, though, was that down below everybody was supposed to give up their weapons. The order had come from the guards. Shouts of: don't hand over your weapons, that's what our fathers did, and our fathers' fathers, they shouldn't have done it. But that's the order, because it is peacetime. Peace isn't reigning yet. We want to hear it from Engelbrekt himself. He showed himself at the window. Shouts of: we want to keep our weapons. We have decided, he said, that all weapons are to be handed in and stored in the arsenals. We're keeping the weapons, came the answer. The realm will see to it that the weapons are looked after, he said. The response: we want to guard the arsenal. Guards will be elected, said Engelbrekt, the weapons will remain within reach. What we have to do now, he said, is win over the knights who still refuse to recognize us, and show them that our intentions are peaceful. The attempts undertaken by Engelbrekt during the year of thirty-five to reach an agreement with the nobles didn't arouse any interest in Brecht. Representatives of the lower classes were excluded from the meetings in Sigtuna, Vadstena, Halmstad; all matters relating to government affairs seemed to have once again been handed to the elites. Whenever Engelbrekt was able to chalk up a success, it was paid for with concessions to groups of nobles who were also still scheming to reinstate Eric. If sometimes the impression emerged that the country was in the hands of Engelbrekt and his followers, it was nevertheless impossible to

230   conceal a growing catastrophe. The Danish-occupied castles of Kalmar, Nyköping, Stäkeholm, and Axvall were still standing, threatening the realm, and Stockholm also remained with the king of the Union, refusing to open its gates to Engelbrekt's people. It wasn't until we mentioned Engelbrekt's canal construction, quoting a few lines from the rhymed chronicle, that Brecht tuned in. While the commander was stuck in terse diplomatic negotiations with an adversary who wanted nothing but his ousting, he initiated a project with which he demonstrated his capacity for a forward-looking politics aimed at securing lasting peace. Through the hostility of the knights and the haute bourgeoisie in Stockholm, the passage out to sea via Lake Mälaren had been blocked. The trade in ore lay idle, and the importing of goods into the interior of the country was likewise hampered. After the preceding year of war, hunger reigned, and the clan of the Union aristocrats intended to demoralize the commoners, who had once again been driven to a state of misery. Evading confrontation with the nobility, preparing for a prolonged siege, a drawn out social tug-of-war, driven by the necessity of reestablishing the food supply and securing capital through the sale of iron, he began his project, which represented a transition from the war effort to economic development. He may well have received encouragement from some of the cities of the Hanseatic League with which he still had a relationship, and which had a stake in the resumption of commercial relations. Barely two months after the conference in Arboga, he sent an army to Tälje, this time armed with picks and shovels. The barges coming from Västerås were fully laden with carts, buckets, baskets, and pointed pickets. Here, at the tip of Lake Mälaren, southwest of the blockaded Stockholm, from the point where in prehistoric times an inlet had led to the sea and now a swale with patches of swamp extended to the open waters, the shipping lane was to be dug. At the narrowest point in the lake, just outside the city—whose gray log houses were clustered around the Saint Ragnhild Church—stood the palisade-ringed castle held by Lord Bengt Stensson Natt och Dag, one of the leaders of the opposition camp. While Puke kept watch on the fortified island with a small group of soldiers, the workers set about digging up the sand and mud in the southern valley, so as to make use of Lake Mälaren's higher springtime water levels, steering the southward current into the canal. The construction of the canal, said Brecht, would almost merit a play of its own. Here, the principle of collective labor could be set against the force of self-interest and the rabid pursuit of profit. Thought it might have seemed as if the war of liberation had aroused in the people an awareness of their own power, soon enough the persistence of the forces of oppression showed itself again. The strug- **231** gle to dominate nature could have been won through the efforts of the masses. The miners who had been brought in, with their experience in excavation, and the thousands of farm workers burrowed into the loose earth, transported the stones, beat posts into the ground to form rows, wove them together with twigs, dug day and night in ground that was continually seeping back together, installed the walls for a sluice up at the tip of the lake, stood up to their necks in water when the tides burst through; they couldn't expect to open the access route this spring or even summer, but perhaps the next year. A number of the Hanseatic cogs from Lübeck were already sitting in the outer harbor, and the cargo was loaded onto flat-bottomed boats, which were rolled on tree trunks over land to Lake Mälaren; in the opposite direction, the first barrels of raw ore were transported to the cargo vessels. Pulling and hauling, toiling like slaves— but doing so freely, with purpose, as after a victorious revolution. But although here they were able to overcome all difficulties through technical skill, the same could not be said of their efforts to drive out the enemy, which reared its many heads again, spreading out across the land, scheming to destroy what was emerging. In late July word arrived suddenly that the king of the Union, invited by the nobility of Stockholm, was preparing his voyage to receive solemn confirmation in the capital of that which the councillors of the realm had promised him in the Halmstad negotiations in May, namely, his right to the throne and the restoration of all the castles, forts, cities, and provinces that had been taken from him. The revolution was to be declared illegitimate. Engelbrekt now had to face off with the self-appointed countergovernment and force a decision. The populace stood behind him, ready to head to war again. Thus, the large-scale endeavor had to be interrupted, the horde of workers turned back into a horde of soldiers. Puke stayed behind in Tälje to protect the canal, where he soon found himself in a conflict with Bengt Stensson. Stensson had his men plunder one of the cogs from Lübeck, whereupon Puke stormed the castle with his troops and chased the knight off. At the beginning of August, Engelbrekt set up camp for the third time just outside Stockholm, again on the island of Långholmen, while the knights and clerics gathered together in the Church of the Holy Spirit. The city preened itself to receive the king. The aristocrats continued their duplicity, traveling from Stockholm and their castles in the countryside to visit the rightfully elected commander in chief and attempting to assuage him, explaining that, in truth, the meeting of reconciliation represented Eric's ousting. Though he would get some of his old possessions back, he would not be allowed to assume any government office in Sweden, and the Union would continue to guarantee the invulnerability of the Nordic countries. That Bengt Stensson also came with his entourage and joined up with Karl Knutsson Bonde, Krister Nilsson Vasa, and the newly named member of the Council of the Realm, Magnus Gren, demonstrated clearly enough whose interests were going to be presented to the Danish king; but Engelbrekt trusted Bishop Thomas and Nils Gustafsson Båt, who would be among the negotiators. He handed them a written statement in the name of the people. It read that Eric had proven himself incapable of implementing law and order in the land. The people had stood up as one to rid themselves of him. But despite their victory over the tyrant, calm had not yet graced the realm. Efforts were underway to reintroduce the old conditions. The people cannot tolerate such a thing. Never again the violence of the bailiffs. Never again the thievery of rogue tax collectors. Never again the torture and shackling of the peasants. Away with this dishonorable alliance. Away with the false king. The flaky Eric arrived in Stockholm late, in early September. Then the haggling began, behind the walls of the castle, initially overseen by Kröpelin. But it became evident that the mayor had drifted too close to the Swedish side and was removed from his office, replaced by one of the regent's lackeys. Once again, the potentates off on their own and, waiting outside, the people. Inside, away from prying eyes, they decided upon what was ultimately advantageous for each of them. Well-versed in extortion and deception, regardless of how they had fleeced and tormented one another, they now had to declare a triumph any outcome that would leave their murderous regime in place. Eric was allowed to regain control over Halland, Stockholm, Kalmar, and Nyköping. The remaining provinces and castles, however, were to be managed by local lords. These lords swore their loyalty to him and the king vowed to buy the freedom of the Swedish warriors who were still wallowing in Hanseatic dungeons. From now on, justice was to be upheld in accordance with the laws of the land. The people's taxes, on the other hand, were to be determined by Eric and to flow to Eric's court. Retaining their exemptions from tax payments, the spiritual and earthly nobility were afforded the right to occupy the posts in the Council of the Realm; however, the right to name the treasurer and the marshal was reserved for the king. His choice would take effect once approved by the high council. Consensus was achieved, with Eric's confidant Krister Nilsson Vasa being given the office of treasurer, a choice that would be offset by Karl Knutsson Bonde—the speaker of the nobility—being made marshal. As sworn enemies of Engelbrekt, both were congenial to the rulers, though it was also immediately clear that, being rivals, they would antagonize each other. The reconciliation festival of Stockholm, then, at which Eric bought himself the crown and the aristocrats won back their old privileges, was at the same time a manifestation of discord. To the peals of the bells in the cloisters and churches, Krister Nilsson received a silver staff from the hand of the king and Karl Knutsson a sword. Nils Gustafsson Båt was the only one present who did not give his seal of approval to the agreement. Engelbrekt was never mentioned by name. After the departure of the sixty ships of the Danish fleet, he gathered his army. In November, he called for a second revolution.

233

We found ourselves caught in a war on two fronts, followed Engelbrekt through the snowdrift, and entrenched ourselves in our besieged city. Every morning, in the factory, I anticipated my dismissal. Every afternoon, upon entering the building in which Rosner lived, I expected to be stopped by police officers. Every evening, before going to sleep, the thought that something had to arrive that would change my life was overlaid by powerlessness. The union leaders were waging their campaign of terror against the Communist workplace representatives, attempting to force their exclusion with one circular after the other. But many trade union federations rebelled against the directives. While the reactionary forces seemed to be gaining the upper hand, the representatives of the democratic tradition gathered together to mount a defense. Engelbrekt had headed off to Stockholm for the fourth time, with peasant armies from Dalarna, Hälsingland, and Ångermanland. He was joined by the inhabitants of the skerries, who had been robbed by Eric's sailors as they approached from the southeast. They took up their positions on the hills overlooking the southern city gate. And now that the power of the people was again revealing itself, their outrage spreading throughout the entire land, a whole host of nobles came across as well to offer their support to the commander in chief. There was no parchment on which their signatures would be have been worth anything; they would exchange one vow for another, one alliance for another, at the drop of a hat if it promised more at that particular moment in time. Stockholm would not be able to withstand the tens of thousands camped on the hills in the snow flurry. Might as well march into the city alongside them rather than having to receive them behind the walls. And if the nobles then joined their continued advances, shifting the responsibility for it onto the people, they would also be able to take possession of the remaining fortified cities without the need to break with the king of the Union. We asked ourselves how Engelbrekt could have let them come back to him, the brothers Nils, Bengt, and Bo Stensson Natt och Dag, Bo Knutsson Grip, Magnus Gren, and look, even Karl Knutsson, the king's field marshal, and we felt that we had to accept that, in the end, he remained a man of the ruling classes, that he fought for their interests, and ultimately turned his back on the people. Even when we turned our attention to his demise, to attempt an interpretation from that perspective, we couldn't get past the impression that the aristocrats had availed themselves of him for as long as he could be of use to them, only to then cast him aside once they had achieved their goal. Though this was true, it didn't resolve our inquiry. The forces that had been set in motion by the rebellion were too complex and full of contradictions to be interpreted from a single standpoint. The historians had viewed him as a representative of the nobility, of the bourgeoisie, of the Hanseatic League, of the countryfolk; as a saint, as the founder of a nation. We could only base our conclusions on what he had achieved in a material sense. He had grown up in the age of the robber barons. He was dependent upon trade with the cities of the Hanseatic League. The deeds of the local and Danish lords had a negative effect on his production. He wanted peace for economic reasons. The high nobility was riven with conflict, and its members sought the support of lower classes to consolidate their individual positions of power; they were against the foreign king one moment and for him the next, if an alliance with him could be used to thwart their rivals back home. That's the way it had been since Albert's reign. An enduring conflict had descended upon the people, had devastated their work, their lives. Engelbrekt the miner wanted to protect his pits from ruin. Engelbrekt the businessman wanted to reestablish the disrupted business relationships with the Hanseatic League. Engelbrekt the nobleman wanted to seek unity in his circles, to win over influential groups to defend against the campaigns of despoliation. Engelbrekt the bourgeois wanted to strengthen the merchants against the parasitic nobles. Engelbrekt the countryman wanted to stand by the people, for he recognized that only through their strength could a revolution be brought to fruition. The dawning of a revolution carried out by large peasant armies showed that the epoch of petty thievery was over: it wasn't knights with pillaging mobs heading out but the masses, fed up with misery and squalor. Regardless of the ends that Engelbrekt might have been pursuing at the outset, the power that he attained and was then able to direct was aimed at eradicating oppression, establishing just conditions. The unity that he sought was not national in nature, and perhaps also not yet democratic, but practical. As many as possible had to stand together in order to lift the weight of hardship; the stronger the will of the majority, the less the regressive forces would be able to have their way. It wasn't naïveté or even agreement that led him to welcome the knights into the fold but rather the expectation that the supremacy of his army would command their respect. His miscalculations became apparent with his murder. At that moment, his lack of ruthlessness was revealed, his unwillingness to engage in the ultimate, revolutionary violence. He didn't push those who had continually stabbed him in the back into the abyss in which they belonged because he had comrades in arms beside him—like Erik Nilsson Puke, Herman Berman, Gotskalk Bengtsson Ulv, Nils Jönsson Oxenstierna, Johan Karlsson Färla, and Claus Plata—who would protect him against any attack, of that he was certain. So he went to the edge of the mountain with his vanguard, to begin the descent to the bridge. In Norrbotten Count Archibald Douglas and his generals Nordqvist, Högberg, and Nygren were preparing to crush the Communist stronghold in the province. The major general had ordered the construction of the first concentration camps in Storsien, east of Morjärv, not far from the Arctic Circle. The roundup of everyone at the Party offices and of the printers of the newspaper *Norrskenflamman* [The Flame of the Northern Lights] was planned by the count's adjutant, Captain Svanbom. Consultations took place with Danielsson, the bailiff of the province, Hallberg, the police prosecutor in Luleå, and Meyerhöffer, the mayor of Boden. The pogrom-like mood was whipped up in the right-wing newspaper *Norrbottens-Kuriren* [North Bothnia Courier] by the journalists Hedenström, Lindberg, and Moberg, and by Holmberg and Ericsson in the Social Democratic paper *Norrländskan*. Four members of the pioneer troop of the second army corps, the ensigns Borgström, Norström, and Krendel, along with the conscript Palmqvist, had been charged with carrying out the attack. In the enormous apparatus in which the murder was unfolding, there were direct lines of connection running from the military and police apparatus to the chair of the Finland Committee, Professor Linblom, the director of the Nordic Museum and the Skansen National Parks, the leader of the People's Party in Stockholm, the engineer Wretlind, and Attorney General Westman, a champion of Germany, who back in nineteen fourteen had been a member of the ultrareactionary government and was now responsible for combating Communism in the country. Once again names, names in cold and deadly succession, emerging from the dense network of relationships. The traces were covered over from above by powerful allies, always from above and in a downward motion. Up above was the king, the generals, up above were civil servants, party functionaries, politicians, industrialists, up above was the cultural establishment; down below, a few young men were picked out, with blank faces and idealistic, patriotic beliefs. The fifteenth of January fourteen thirty-six. The city hid itself from the armed figures on the hilltops, the storm winds whipped up clouds of snow, only the two bridge towers and the occasional glimpse of sections of the wall emerged behind the stilts in the ice like shadows. But Brecht couldn't shake the image that we had stumbled upon in drafting the scene, that medieval cityscape with the astronomical depiction of the reflection of the sun. In the panel, Stockholm was a jewel, glassy, painted in exquisite detail, surrounded by gracefully breaking waves, verdant islands, and high up in the clear sky above, sun rings and sun dogs, circles of their orbits, comet trails and arcs resembling the aurora borealis. Brecht wanted to incorporate cosmic phenomena, which contrasted with the revolutionary moment by indexing great stretches of time, while also placing it in a continuity. Perhaps, he said, there could be a prospect of the city with the firmament, the northern lights, above the gloom. As they reached every town, the outer baileys, the bulwarks, the bridges and walls had to be overcome before the rebels could take possession of the elegant buildings within. Reflecting the convergence of distant connections, said Brecht, the perspective of the stage also needed to be foreshortened, like looking through a telescope, making the fortifications and flickering walls of the buildings behind them seem to occupy the same focal plane, and the massive tower in front two-dimensional, shoved up against the foremost fortification tower as if there were no path between them, and directly in front of this loomed the cliff top from which Engelbrekt and his companions were descending. Heading toward the curved gate, the troop first disappeared as they plunged into the depths, before cropping up again in front of the planks of wood. Then came the soldiers, in chain mail, gray doublets, with leather helmets and a motley selection of weapons. Up in the loopholes, archers and the Danish castle commander Erik Nilsson. Their demand that the gates be opened was met with the response that this could only take place on the king's instruction. The Council of the Realm, cried Karl Knutsson, demands the surrender of the city. They recognized the marshal. You yourselves have decided that Stockholm belongs to Eric, came the cry. Answer: the decree is invalid. Nilsson said he would have to confer with lord Kröpelin, who happened to be in the city at the time. But they were already hacking at the gate with axes. Erik Nilsson warned that he had five thousand armed men in the castle; it's barely five hundred, came a cry from the rear tower, and they're too scared to come out anyway. Then the city gate was pushed open from the other side; out front as well, the noise of bolts being pulled **237** back, beams being lifted, a rumbling of footsteps on the bridge, and the workers of the city welcomed the peasant soldiers. The ignition charges in the Party building in Luleå were detonated. Five people lost their lives: the district head, Hellberg, his wife, the treasurer of the youth organization, Granberg, and her two children. They had to be carried to their graves via remote side streets with a police escort. No death notices were accepted by the papers, no venue was made available in which the mourners could gather. At the same time, crowds of people paraded through the main streets of Stockholm with the coffins of a handful of Finland volunteers. Brecht had us read out everything that we could find out about the attack. The court proceedings were slated for the end of April. Lenient sentences were expected for the culprits, who claimed they had only wanted to give the enemy a warning, a fright, to secure the printers for the major general so that he could use them to produce a newspaper for the soldiers on the front. Brecht wanted to hear about the recruitment activities within the army associations, about the selection of the agents, the procurement of the explosives and fuses from the depots, about the declarations from the detained men that they had acted on orders, about the prevarications of those who gave the orders and their intermediaries, about the rapid diversion of attention from the murder to the illegal activities of the Communists, the national exculpation, which received important support from the voices of Archbishop Hultgren, Bishop Cullberg, and other church dignitaries, from the old socialists Ström, Höglund, Kilbom, Nerman, and Lindhagen, the distinguished working-class writers Vilhelm Moberg, Eyvind Johnson, and Harry Martinson. We attempted to return to Engelbrekt, but Brecht was already planning a new documentary play structured as a trial, *Die Drahtzieher*. An impossible play, a play that the state was sure to attack. The play's new title: *The Deportation of Brecht*. Douglas stepped out from the darkness above, the hero who had vowed to cleanse the country of dangerous elements. He gave a big, patriotic speech. Lindberg, the boss of the union organization, agreed with him, ringed by red flags. In the Stockholm that Engelbrekt had liberated for them, the knights and prelates immediately began meeting in secret. In consultation with Kröpelin and the major merchants, they divvied up the posts for a government that would be independent from Denmark. Engelbrekt had the ports and warehouses prepared for the spring trade and ordered the expansion of the access roads, and then set off for Nyköping with his troops. No sooner had he instigated the siege of the fort than he received word that the high council was meeting in the capital. Karl Knutsson, whom he had en-

trusted with managing Stockholm and taking the castle, was to be named commander in chief, they said. Leaving the siege of Nyköping to Puke, Berman, Färla, and Plata, he hurried back and found the conspirators gathered together in the monastery of the Black Friars. The archbishop of Uppsala, Olof, and the bishops Knut of Linköping and Sigge of Skara, as well as the other attendees, thirty lords in all, had just robbed him of his title and bequeathed it to the knight Bonde. Only three votes had been cast for Engelbrekt. The city was in turmoil; working people, tradespeople, and peasants besieged the house on the steep alley overlooking Järntorget, only Engelbrekt, they cried, was entitled to the rank of commander in chief. But the aristocrats had read the situation astutely: regardless of whether the people were ready to tear them to shreds, they knew that right now, having just entered the final phase of his military campaign, Engelbrekt wouldn't let it come to open hostilities with them, which would ignite a civil war. They were also familiar with his indifference toward titles, had most likely already considered the possibility that the title of commander in chief could be shared between him and Karl Knutsson Bonde. They moved on to praising his military abilities, wanted to make him believe that he was destined to receive other honors than those he could secure through affairs of the state. That his place was at the head of the army, that the knights wanted nothing more than to walk behind him on a victory march. And things went as they had expected; Engelbrekt said he was willing to share the highest position of power with Karl Knutsson Bonde until the conclusion of the struggle. The nobles assumed he would never again be able to claim the title for himself alone, for, if he were to complete his task, his life would also be complete, and the people would exhaust themselves in liberating the country. And so, having assuaged the workers in the city, Engelbrekt returned to Nyköping, left Färla and Plata to continue the siege, headed off with his other comrades in arms to Östergötland, tasked Erengisle Nilsson with the encirclement of Stäkeborg and Bo Knutsson Grip with storming Stäkeholm in Tjust. He headed to Kalmar, which was to be conquered by Nils Stensson Natt och Dag, and forged ahead toward Blekinge, took Ronneby, where he installed Claus Lange as lord of the castle, reached the west coast, placed the fallen Laholm in the custody of Arvid Svan, put Halmstad under the control of Bo Stensson and Varberg Herman Berman, secured a peace accord with Älvsborg, before finally reaching the heavily fortified Axvall with Puke. Engelbrekt's path down the east coast, turning off to the west before Skåne, heading up through the Danish province of Halland; this journey lit by torches, with musters in every village; this journey that traced a ring around the country and confirmed the rule of the people, was **239** for him also a journey to exhaustion, to ruin. Riding through the winter and the frigid spring without so much as a break, camping out in the open air, had wrecked his health; feverish, plagued by aching muscles, barely able to stand upright anymore, he left Axvall under Puke's guard to seek a moment of respite in his castle in Örebro before continuing on to Stockholm. At the end of February, having turned our attention to the ailing, aging Engelbrekt, to follow him in his final hours, we had to pause because the flu Brecht had been lugging around flared up again. Not far from Örebro, on the southern banks of Lake Hjälmaren, Bengt Stensson Natt och Dag had been living in Castle Göksholm since being chased out of Tälje, and he visited Engelbrekt in the castle to attempt a reconciliation. Also present was his son Måns Bengtsson, who had won Engelbrekt's trust on the field of battle and whom Engelbrekt had made his squire. The commander, crippled by gout, hobbling about on crutches, fed the visitors after coming to an agreement with the knight to make peace. The presence of young Måns erased all distrust. But their only intention was to determine the condition of the people's leader. They saw that he wouldn't be able to raise his sword in defense, that it would be simple enough, as the councillors in Stockholm had decided, to kill him at any opportune moment. It wasn't long before the opportunity arose. He informed them that he planned to set off for Stockholm the following day, by boat, in order to spare his health. He sought the advice of these compassionate men about the most favorable route, and they suggested he row through Hemfjärden and Ässundet, then through Mellanfjärden to Björksundet and Sundholmen, where he would be able to rest. But the nights are still cold, said Bengt Stensson, and, as the islands were not far from Göksholm, he offered to put Engelbrekt up at his place. Engelbrekt thanked him, said he couldn't waste any more time, had to set off early if he wanted to reach Rossvik on the eastern tip of Lake Hjälmaren by the coming evening, where Nils Gustafsson Båt was expecting him. In that case, said Måns, he could choose one of the larger islets to make camp, since there would be plenty of wood there for a fire. Our further analysis inspired only antipathy in Brecht. It was not just his illness in which he shrouded himself, as it were, but also a sudden desire to shield himself from Engelbrekt's unbearable end that made it impossible to continue working on the piece. Interrupted by a barking cough, he had still shown an interest in the paradoxical historical condition according to which Engelbrekt, though he had led the people to victory, never entrusted them with the top positions, and according to which the people—who were actually already standing out in front—

left the leadership to others, as if they too were unaware of their capacity to make decisions. Brecht's final remark on the project, which I jotted down in my notebook, was that the members of the House of Natt och Dag were to be called Night and Day in our version. That was shortly before the twelfth of March, the end of the Winter War between the Soviet Union and Finland.

At Brecht's house an intellectual freedom had established itself that allowed us to overcome the current plight and made historical perspectives possible. When I left the factory or met up with Rogeby I was governed by the everyday, and the gate to the world of sweeping interpretations and connections sought to slam shut in my face; what was directly before us and holding us down demanded to be investigated. While we had been working on the Engelbrekt piece, something like a feeling of belonging in this country had grown within me; I saw myself putting down roots in Sweden. Germany no longer had anything to do with my heritage; I only had a few friends left there, in the underground. Czechoslovakia, whose citizenship I had once possessed, was foreign, Paris was miles away, Spain laid to waste. The whereabouts of my parents was unknown. Now, if I acquired a picture of the political reality that surrounded me, of the conditions to which I was attempting to adapt, this happened between two poles, as it were, in a continual shifting of perspectives. In Brecht's field there was luminance, unbound imagination, while the things Rogeby conveyed to me were afflicted by severity, the fog of working life. The contradictions permeated one another, bled into one another, and a fabric emerged that could serve as a backdrop to my current existence. From this point on, a point which would become like the date of my birth, I developed a desire to get to know the history of this country. By looking into the Middle Ages, or, as earlier, into antiquity, I had developed a feel for universal connections. Now, after my hours at the laundry boiler and the smelting furnace, in the drafty cellars and corridors, the machinery rooms which with their rods, pipes, and belts sprawled like vined forests, a wish surged up within me, to not just be an observer in a stopgap solution, but to enter into a present that was replete with the experiences of these last few decades. I wasn't seeking a national identity—the concept of having a homeland had no validity for me—the point rather was to consolidate my own function by intensifying my relationship to a totality. For more than a year I had been positioned at a particular workplace, as one wage laborer among others, and had participated in practical and union matters, but my activities after my day's work in the factory shut me off from my coworkers. Having been made a member of the Social Democratic Party en masse, I was camouflaged by the governing party itself; as a foreigner, I was not allowed to belong to the Communist Party. The risk of my conspiratorial meetings with German Communists being discovered meant I had to remain alert and reserved at all times, even in the presence of like-minded individuals. Even though I was a messenger in the service of the Comintern, I was not beholden to any organization. Though I was involved in the procurement of material that would be used in the antifascist struggle and was aware of the efforts within the Party to expand its illegal German support points, I had no intention of returning to Germany. I had to piece together this existence— sometimes seemingly spent in a vacuum, sometimes surrounded by many-sided and palpable realities—to form a single entity. Stateless, in possession of an alien's passport that was only ever valid for three months, I had begun to prepare myself for a future in a country to which I had hardly given a thought only a year and a half earlier. Only the language that I had brought with me into exile, this language that took on form through reading and writing together with Brecht, Hodann, Bischoff, made me somehow incongruous with this new environment, and perhaps this isolating effect would endure even if I were able to express myself like a native. The existence of another language inside of me had to be accepted. This interior language was my only possession; preserving it formed part of my self-preservation, although this prerequisite was entirely different from the unquestioning manner in which Brecht—the accomplished one, at peace with himself—interacted with his idiom abroad. Making use of insights I had picked up while passing through areas in which national borders had been annulled and only the movements of collectivity had force, I began to make my language into a tool that I could wield. With Brecht I experienced the first impulse to attempt to give the current moment a historical charge. Ström, the chairman of the city council, one-time cofounder of the Left Party, the Communist Party, who had subsequently returned to the Social Democrats, had come over for a visit. A remark by the deputy had steered the conversation to Brecht's book about Caesar. The right-wing press had compared him with Catiline, said Ström, when he had been appointed to the First Chamber of parliament in the fall of nineteen fifteen. The agitator, they said, secures his entry to the senate. The Catiline conspiracy, used by Brecht as material to depict in parable form the period leading up to the emergence of fascist domination, was transferred by Ström to the period of the previous war, and it was as if Brecht suddenly had doubts as to whether Caesar, or even

Engelbrekt, could be used as figures whose actions could illustrate something about the conflicts of our times. In the difficulty of finding explanations for the catastrophe that afflicted us, he had sought events that appeared to contain recognizable patterns. That Brecht gave up his work on both the Caesar novel and on the piece about Engelbrekt in mid-March might have had to do with the realization that those models were subjected to their own historical laws and couldn't help us out of our crisis situations. In his youth, Ström had read the book by the Danish historian Bang, with which Brecht was also familiar, in which Catiline—unlike in bourgeois historiography, which portrayed him as a violent criminal and demagogue—was portrayed as a social reformer. The clash between the Roman owners of capital and the impoverished populace was the main theme of this work. As in Brecht's novel, the emphasis was placed on the efforts of the ambitious, heavily indebted Caesar to latch onto the revolting forces in order to then rise to power himself once they had been crushed. Being called Catiline, said Ström, was not inaccurate, for he too—then the secretary of the Social Democratic Party and the leader of its left faction—had belonged to a wealthy family, as had the leader of the slave hordes and initiator of the street clubs. And ultimately, after all the political intrigues, the fact that he was able to fulfill the economic requirements to be eligible to run for a seat in the upper house once he had turned thirty-five had been crucial. That meant he possessed property valued in excess of fifty thousand kronor and had paid tax on an annual income of at least three thousand kronor, which, with the value of the currency at the time, was only possible for a small, moneyed minority. It was not due to general elections but to internal dealings among city councillors that he joined the forum of the elite. For their part, the high-ranking electors had been entrusted with the municipal administration by a vote, the outcome of which was determined by the propertied classes: participation was limited to people aged twenty-eight and older who had reached the minimum income threshold of four hundred fifty kronor, had never received support, had paid off all debts, and maintained a fixed address. On top of this, the results of municipal elections were scaled according to a forty-degree curve, which meant that the votes of people of means were worth up to forty times more than the votes of those who only just managed to reach the first rung. And yet, the fortyfold system set down in nineteen hundred nine, which took into account not just capital, real estate ownership, and the number and size of production sites possessed but also livestock numbers and the number of workers employed, was a step forward from the prior five-thousand-degree model, which had guaranteed the domination of a number of potentates over the disenfranchised populace. In the election of the Second Chamber, the principle of one man, one vote applied, but only those who paid tax on an income of at least eight hundred kronor and could show property to the value of at least six thousand kronor were eligible to vote. This meant that, here too, most of the workers—especially the younger ones, lacking permanent employment, regularly changing their place of residence— were excluded. As a result of the mass campaigns, the large-scale strikes of nineteen hundred two and nineteen hundred nine, and the growing influence of the Social Democratic Party, lawmakers were forced to revoke the financial census, and only a minimum age and the requirement to have paid taxes in the preceding three years was retained. In nineteen hundred eleven, the new laws entered into force. Women remained without the right to vote for another decade. Though the workers had now managed to get their party into the Second Chamber as well, and in the same numbers as the right-wing coalition, the bourgeoisie—to whom the main faction of the Liberal Party belonged—still outnumbered them almost three to one, and from their position in the upper house, which they dominated completely, they could dismiss all motions that were passed up to them. In the history of suffrage, Brecht saw the class struggle progressing in its most dour form. In this realm, legally founded bastions could to be seized, backwardness was propped up by legislative periods, and strategies could be continually developed to combat the slightest hint of radical ideas. Brecht wanted Ström to tell us more about Swedish parliamentary democracy, the progression of which had determined the position of the bourgeoisie and the essence of the workers' movement, first in the lead-up to nineteen hundred eleven—considered the year of democracy's breakthrough—and then up until the time that the Social Democrats first formed part of the government, in March of nineteen twenty; and on into the thirties. In order to understand the impact of Social Democracy within Swedish society, we had to place it in the context of the of the liberalization of the bourgeoisie. From the first socialist cells through to the formation of the unions and the Party, liberalism had also been developing; skillfully adapting to the desire for renewal, often charging ahead, picking up the latent strands, redirecting them and weaving them into their own causes. With its progressive wing engaging in collaborations with the Social Democratic leadership groups, the bourgeoisie—in possession of the means of production and bolstered on the right by the police and the military—was able to maintain its predominance. Guided by the principle that changes had to take place through peaceful, parliamentary channels, with each endeavor, Social Democracy remained in a dependent relationship with its ideological opponent, and everything it gained from this opponent had to be paid for by sacrificing their original objectives. It was not that socialism, borne by the majority of the voters, slowly infiltrated the flesh of capitalism; instead, capitalism simply absorbed this social movement into itself. Almost imperceptibly, revolutionary ideas evolved into their reformist, pragmatic form, the combative organizations of the populace, surging forward, often manifesting a revolutionary strength, were made into tools of revisionism. It wasn't just the bourgeoisie's peacekeeping forces—mobilized the moment a flashpoint emerged—who fought off the proletarian demands; the leaders of their own party also played their part, silencing them with appeals to the need for reasoned patience. During the conversation, which continued over a few afternoons that month, Ström presented this process of back and forth as the sole possibility of attaining a just, liberal, and democratic regime, and it was precisely the years of deviation, of the search for a quicker alternative, he said, which had confirmed his viewpoint. He saw the defensive character of his party politics not as a renunciation of socialist ideals but a compliance with historical conditions. Basing his position upon the value of the individual human life, he adhered to a transformation secured through consensus, even if time and time again it was made evident that this collective entity, this state of free solidarity, was unable to emerge due to the unshakeable violence of the bourgeoisie. At the same time as the first reading groups were founded, around eighteen forty-five, by journeymen arriving from Paris, where they had become acquainted with the doctrines of Cabet, Proudhon, and Blanc, the Friends of Reform societies appeared, organized by bourgeois groups. In the former, initial steps were taken in the struggle for a people's parliament, for universal suffrage, and the shortening of the working day, which could last up to sixteen hours; in the latter, the young journeymen, having been freed from the yoke of the masters after the dissolution of the guilds, were to be won over for new forms of paternal guidance in educational associations. The impulses issuing from France brought a League of the Just to Stockholm as well, but Cabet's Icaria—the realm of peaceful Communism, in which everything belonged to everyone and total equality ruled, in which the people themselves reigned, anyone could be elected to any position, in which the fraternity of true Christianity was brought to life, as Götrek the bookseller had claimed—was all too utopian to endanger the suggested foundations of the liberals. To the extent that it was possible in the still half-feudal, agrarian countryside, Götrek kept himself informed regarding the upheavals that had shaken Europe in eighteen forty-eight. He was the one who translated and published *The Communist Manifesto* that same year, who spurred the typographers to form the first trade union, and he was also the first person to be subjected to the blows of the police and thrown in a prison cell for standing up for the rights of the working class. The preparations for the conversion of the old house of the estates into the house of representatives, with two chambers, were controlled by the bourgeoisie, with the workers, lacking comprehensive organizations, still unable to push through their initiatives. Steering the country economically, setting the development of industry in motion, the bourgeoisie was able to present itself as a progressive force, distracting from the fermenting social conflicts through advances in constitutional reform. The final phase of the bourgeois revolution had taken place, if somewhat late, toward the middle of the nineteenth century. The transition from the feudalist to the capitalist system of domination had been accompanied by compromises and extortionate deals within the upper classes. Behind this economic revolution, this transfer of power from the patronage of the landed gentry to the top posts of the financial world, a revolutionary transformation of consciousness took place, set in motion by the demands of the workers; the bourgeoisie, up above, armed with the weapon of money and with their sights set on raising profits, drifted toward increased opportunities for exploitation, while below, the forces that bore this new era within itself were shifting. While revolutionizing production methods and finding effective applications for their wealth, the owners of capital were afraid of the strength of the working masses and were forced to show them a certain amount of goodwill, a readiness to make concessions, and yet time and again they managed to impressively thwart these forces through sophisticated chicanery. The duplicity of liberalist thought extended all the way to the king, the patriarchal figure of Oscar. His hand forced by the unrest in France and Germany, the regent donated five hundred riksdaler every year to support the expansion of the worker's education associations, while he had courtiers and respectable citizens ensure that, rather than discussions of political and social problems, the associations hosted lectures of an exclusively ethical and moral nature. And yet, from Almqvist and Blanche right through to Strindberg fifty years later, all the best minds had been on the left side of the democratic movement, just as, with their intertwining strands of socialist and liberal thought, the workers' party had also possessed a critical, left wing from the outset. The later battle of the right against the rebels, which led to the victory of conservatism within the Social Democratic Party, reproduced the early predominance of the tendencies aimed at striking a reconciliation between the classes. When the bourgeoisie reformed the parliament in eighteen sixty-six, given the nepotism that had hitherto prevailed, it seemed to be a decisive step toward democracy. Lacking centralized leadership, and disguising their political gatherings with cover associations in response to the increased surveillance in the wake of the formation of the First International, the workers were forced to bend to the will of the bourgeoisie—particularly since the bourgeoisie had promised them a second chamber of democratic representation. Previously, the representatives of the four estates had convened separately. The first estate, comprising ten thousand people, had its seat in the house of nobility. Fourteen thousand belonged to the second estate, the clergy, sixty-six thousand to the third estate, the bourgeoisie, and two million to the fourth estate, the peasantry. Nowhere was the fifth estate, the proletariat, represented. Yet the power possessed by the four governing estates to pass resolutions was not proportionate to their size; rather each received a quarter of the whole. That which was discussed separately was then brought to collective negotiations and ultimately enacted by political coalitions and alliances, to the benefit of the nobility and the prelates. The elimination of the disproportionate distribution of votes in the rule of the estates, along with the rapid rise of reform-minded liberal organizations, gave the impression that the hegemony of the upper classes had now been broken, but in truth, the bourgeoisie, in alliance with the estate owners and in cooperation with the aristocrats, had managed to crush the first charges toward the organization of a proletarian class, and for a few years, with their revolution from above, they took the wind out of the sails of the still heterogeneous masses of workers streaming from the countryside to the cities, from artisanal trades to the factories. Legally tying suffrage to property relations, they also protected the privileges of the nobility, which, with the approach of the socialist menace, had recognized that an alliance with the bourgeoisie was necessary to ensure their own survival. The social reforms that, up to the present day, formed the basis of Social Democratic politics had come about under Prime Minister De Geer, who—a banker, industrialist, and landowner of noble lineage—personified the alliance between the ruling classes. Sometimes appearing as a harbinger of democracy, sometimes reveling shamelessly in their status as a chosen few, a cultural elite had infiltrated the educational organizations and workers' associations; the Liberal Party, which had been founded in eighteen sixty-eight, more than two decades earlier than the Social Democratic Party, was already determining the makeup of many of the workers' clubs through the introduction of idealistically tinged topics. Setting up savings accounts and taking out insurance policies, the establishment of consumer cooperatives and questions of temperance and morals were to replace the demands for universal and equal suffrage and the shortening of the working day. Following the defeat of the Paris Commune, a consortium of the richest citizens gifted the workers an organization to support their associations. Here, under this supposed patronage, they were able to erect an apparatus for investigating revolutionary tendencies, often working hand in glove with right-wing labor leaders. In eighteen eighty-one, as Master Palm, the Swedish Bebel, held the first socialist gatherings, the Liberal Party controlled the milieu surrounding the workers' organizations, and the Party combated the Socialist Club—which would go on to join the International—with an umbrella workers' association headed up by antisocialists. Barred from participating in elections, workers began expressing their opinions, turning to strikes and mass demonstrations, causing an immediate split in the movement that would lead to the formation of the Social Democratic Party, with one side demanding a unicameral parliament, the abolition of the standing army, the arming of the people, and the revolutionary transition to a socialist society, and the other arguing for the parliamentary conquest of the state. Reformism and revolution clashed, and the contradictions in the Party worked out to the benefit of the bourgeois bloc. Branting came from the liberal camp. Quickly sidelining Palm and maintaining close connections with the liberals, he also had the ability to draw in the proletariat with radical slogans. Under the red flag of internationalism he spoke of the liberation of all the oppressed and exploited, of the party they aspired to create as a revolutionary party. He could also be viewed as a revolutionary, having been sentenced to prison time for publishing offensive articles, but the progressively minded bourgeoisie allowed him to lead; they knew they could rely on him, for he personally ensured that the left-wing leaders Palm, Wermelin, and Danielsson were neutralized and sent into exile. Before going on to tell us about his Communist interregnum, Ström argued that the path that Branting had taken was the right one; Branting, the pragmatic proponent of realpolitik, did not praise refusal in the face of the bourgeois state but an engagement with the state, which they could turn into their own means of power. He condemned the outbreaks of anarchy and actions that lacked the support of the majority of the people, and he focused on the most immediate tasks, on pushing through the right to vote, the eight-hour day; he championed

what was achievable within the context of the capitalist system— portrayed not as riven by crises at all but actually rather robust—and in doing so he attempted to win over the majority, through alliances with groups from outside the working class who wanted to contribute to an expansion of the rights of the people. Alongside the emergence of the mass party, that instrument for achieving the workers' increasingly combative demands, the bourgeois union for parliamentary reform had also grown, and the universal suffrage alliance competed with the Social Democratic Workers' Party to appeal for parliamentary improvements. The bourgeois government, backed up by the First Chamber—which was dominated by the Liberal Party and the right-wing groups—could rest assured that no changes that might endanger society would get through. In order to increase its number of seats in the Second Chamber, Social Democracy had to conceal its inner antagonism and project an image of unity. Torn between revisionist hope and revolutionary illusion, the workers supported their party in the elections, but, in the intervening period, they drifted increasingly into extraparliamentary action. Just as the bourgeoisie had immediately opposed the committee of the confederation of trade unions with a worker's association that ran job placement programs and negotiated individual wage agreements, so too in response to the union organizations' joining the Party did they form their own workers' federation, which, in the escalating conflicts, provided them with strikebreakers with a legally protected right to work. The bourgeoisie still called the product they were proposing to the workers a people's parliament, but, after crippling the feudal state, the workers now began to call for a general strike. This first major campaign, in April of nineteen hundred two, was at once an announcement of proletarian solidarity and of secession from the right-wing party leadership. The contradiction between the positions was now brought into focus, and the antagonism—between those who rejected collaboration with the bourgeoisie, whose police troops had beaten down the strikers; and Branting's supporters, who remained willing to cooperate—became irreconcilable. During those days the populace had seized control of the Party, had exercised social democratic power from the streets and squares of the cities, and in so doing had given teeth to the negotiations for voting rights taking place in the parliament. Another seven years would pass before a provisional, deficient electoral reform would be added to the constitution; but while the Party was being driven in an increasingly revolutionary direction by its leftist ideologues, by its radical youth arm and the impatient workforce, the owners of capital were also strengthening their own organizations. Immediately after the strike they came together to form an employers' association and took measures more forceful and severe than any of the actions that the workers had ever considered employing against them. The strike leaders were dismissed, their names put on blacklists; many of the workers who had participated in the strike lost their apartments in the factory housing and then, now homeless, were prosecuted by the courts for vagrancy, thereby losing their right to vote; and henceforth, the columns of strikebreakers were supplied with clubs and revolvers. Organizing the economy, the business owners stipulated the fundamental principles which, some three and a half decades later, set down in the Saltsjöbaden Agreement and sealed under a Social Democratic government, the union spokespeople were still unable to overcome. In paragraph twenty-three of the statutes of the agreement, today inverted to paragraph thirty-two, they appropriated for themselves the right to discretionary power over the management and distribution of work, to freely hire and fire their workforces. And, just as they did in in December of thirty-eight, as a concession, they approved the right of the workers to expand their union organizations without hindrance; at the elections, however, it became evident that the bourgeoisie had managed to drive a wedge into the working class, to deepen the chasm that had opened up around the turn of the century between a favored stratum and the masses of wage slaves. Those who defended the reformist path could be pitted against those who, remaining below the income threshold, wanted to take up violent methods. Thus, the aristocracy of the working class, who wanted to retain what had already been achieved and who sought to secure what further improvements could be afforded by capitalism, became the most avid watchdog in the quest to prevent a leftward drift. Following

Bernstein's thesis that the capitalist state, with its capacity for rapid industrialization and increases in production, created the material security necessary for the development of a democracy, Branting—angling for an electoral alliance—consolidated his relations with the Liberal Party and, with calls for calm, peacefulness, and frugality, attempted to fend off the storm that was once again threatening to gather into a general strike. It was understandable, said Ström, that at that time Branting's main focus was on increasing the Social Democrats' seats in the parliament; his party still only had thirty-four representatives in the lower house, compared to a hundred representatives from the Liberal Party and roughly sixty members of the bourgeois right. There was no point in saying that the majority of the people couldn't bring their vote to bear; justice had to be introduced legally, and that could be achieved if everybody fulfilled

250 the conditions of suffrage through industriousness, having a fixed residence, committing to sustained work and the punctual payment of their taxes. Action on the streets could only rob the Party of its good reputation. But in August of nineteen hundred nine, after Branting had given in to the bourgeois demands—approving a minimum age of twenty-four for the right to participate in the elections for the Second Chamber (instead of twenty-three, as had been suggested) and continuing to exclude women altogether—a second major strike ensued. Once again, the masses stood alone with their discipline and endurance. By distancing themselves from the strike, the Party and union leadership subjected the workers' movement to universal condemnation and the demonstrations to horrible reactionary ignorance. The king traveled to his tennis match in Särö; Lindman, prime minister, leader of the Right, was settling into his summer house in Hälsingland; Staaff, leader of the Liberal Party, headed off to the spa town of Furusund; and Branting traveled to Germany for his vacations. They were all banking on the police troops, together with the civil guards called together by Sydow, the boss of the employers' association, to keep the hundreds of thousands in check. Only one politician from the Liberal Party followed the events with extreme attention, in a mixture of sympathy and terror. He firmly believed that the working class had been spiritually deformed by poverty and hunger and that, through the provision of nutrition, structured living conditions, and stable schooling, they would be able to be imbued with a patriotic mindset. Belonging to a noble house that had become Pietist, he grew up in the presence of officers, courtiers, and diplomats, was raised with strict rules, reluctantly became a naval cadet as a twelve-year-old, went from the school ship to the Naval Academy; artistically minded, conscience-driven, a bible-reader and

scholastic, having taken leave after coming of age and reaching the rank of reserve captain, Palmstierna had turned to charity and become, despite his family's opposition, secretary of the Central Association for Social Work, chairman of the first Congress for Poor Relief, and a city councillor with the Liberals. He saw the powerlessness, the hardship of the people in this late-summer month. The businesspeople had taken out long-term credit from the banks just in time; after four weeks of lost wages, the workers were demoralized. He was familiar with the cramped, meager quarters of the working families, he had often caught glimpses of them, their sour stench had repulsed him, he had never been able to overcome the nausea, just like the seasickness of his youth; and yet time and again, accompanying the soup wagon of the poor relief, he wanted to enter the homes of these strangers, who would often throw him out. He felt drawn to them in some strange way, he knew he would become their redeemer, **251** would protect them from the perils of godlessness, of feral revolutionary thought. Now he could see his big chance, the strikers had been defeated, the union leaders had negotiated with the employers behind their backs, they were left with no choice but to return to work, to head back to the factories, he could empathize with their humiliation, he had also had to suffer abuse on the frigate, and now he wanted to work for them, in their party, which would inherit the future if it could only be cleansed of falsehood and fanaticism. He had long ago noticed Branting's isolation, and he wanted to stand by this great pioneer, would say to him, you and I, we are kindred spirits; we both want to put an end to torment and misery, establish mutual trust, human dignity, but you are afflicted by the mediocrity and ignorance that surround you, I want to help you to lift the intellectual level of the Party, to make the Party into a truly democratic party. And Branting welcomed him into the fold. With Palmstierna joining the Party, the alliance between Social Democracy and liberalism was sealed. Now, a liberal government in which Social Democrats would occupy ministerial posts was within reach. The fact that this coalition, characterized by an ideal of ministerial socialism, had still not materialized two years later, as Lindman had to make way for Staaff, could be put down to the fact that the heretical left had rejected every agreement with the liberal bourgeoisie. Now that the Social Democrats had doubled their seats in the Second Chamber and had reached parity with the right-wing bloc (made up of the protectionists and free trade enthusiasts of the moderate group, the Agrarian Party, and the National Progress Party) it had become necessary to take measures to expel the opposition. Palmstierna was well-suited to tackling this task. Quickly making his way into the

Party leadership, the parliamentary caucus, he could fully realize his dream of making himself useful. Fearing that, next time, the workers would not make their demands when economic conditions were poor, which would prevent their success, but during a boom, he placed all emphasis on alleviating the conditions of their struggle for survival, on reducing the cost of living, increasing wages; it made him dizzy to see them coming out of the factories, pale and hunched over. He wanted to impart his idealism to them. He hated the agitators who wanted to drive them to crude and riotous protest, but he also demanded from them the composure and discipline that he had been forced to learn, punctuated by the terrifying nocturnal experience of hanging high above in the crow's nest, of plummeting into the depths. He who had been subjected to constant pressure in order to prove himself strong enough to manage the inheritance of his class, was now using this toughness to cleanse the great movement of the people, to make it respectable, presentable. The image of the masses on the streets and squares of the city would not leave him alone; he had to seek relaxation every so often on his estate in Dalarna, enjoying the beauty of the forests and Lake Siljan. Rejuvenated after his hikes, he took up the fight against the leftists, who had founded their own alliance within the Party. No longer from outside the worker's party but from within, a position that promised greater impact, he went on the attack against the antimilitarists, advocating the expansion of the defense budget, declaring the extirpation of Bolshevism his first concern, revealing what had motivated his move into the field of power politics. His willingness to make sacrifices corresponded to his inner nature; he had to accept being spat upon by the nobility, on whom he had turned his back, had to put up with vilification from the right-wing press, with threats to his family from the haute bourgeoisie, but he knew that he had dedicated himself to a just cause. And even if the masses of workers didn't want to pay him any mind, he kept struggling for their benefit, he could see his mission clearly, standing alongside the mustachioed Branting, gazing out over Europe with his dark eyes, the great mission of his time: the constitutional establishment of solidarity between labor and capital.

The decision of the union leadership to call off the strike led to the workers' first major crisis of confidence in their organizations. Within three years the number of union members dropped from one hundred eighty-six thousand to eighty thousand. The condemnation of the strike actions coming from the Party and the reprisals meted out by the employers forced the emigration of many of the activists who could no longer expect to find employment. Toward the end of the previous century it was primarily the impoverished rural proletariat who had left Sweden; now, many of the best industrial workers were migrating, the people who would have been central to powering a revolutionary movement. This loss, along with a spiraling mood of demoralization, characterized the years leading up to the outbreak of war. In August of nineteen fourteen, the Social Democrats' wartime truce with the newly established right-wing government of the royalist Hammarskjöld—which included a banker, Wallenberg, as minister of foreign affairs, the shipping entrepreneur Broström as naval minister, the industrial magnate Vennersten as finance minister, the estate owner Beck Friis as minister of agriculture, the head of the employers' association, Sydow, as minister of the interior, and Westman, the propagandist for joining the war on Germany's side, as minister of education—also meant the demise of the Second International in Sweden. Nevertheless, the left didn't want a split to occur; they insisted on their right to fight for socialist principles within the Party, but, while they were attempting to build up the Party for an all-out assault against the bourgeoisie, the right-wing Social Democrats were seeking to use the Party to protect the country from unrest and economic crisis. The party was able to grow because it represented the interests of all groupings within the workers' movement. The leaders of the left wing were still able to assert themselves without resistance; Ström, who in nineteen twelve had been involved in the formation of the left alliance, took on the post of Party secretary; and rightists in the leadership such as Palmstierna and Per Albin Hansson were now joined by new forces, such as Wigforss, Möller, Schlyter, and Undén, who, though they supported Branting, advanced progressive positions. With their wealth of ideas, the spokespeople of the left—which at the time also included Sandler—had it over the gang surrounding Branting. But while they were still searching for forms of action, the right were developing a tactic with which they would win over the masses. Holding the nation together, guaranteeing neutrality and simultaneously fighting for social reforms, Branting managed to make the workers' party the largest party in the parliament in the fall of nineteen seventeen. It wasn't until the following year, after a delegation from the left had taken part in the meeting in Zimmerwald, that the attacks against the opposing side were amped up in an effort to bring about a split. According to all estimations, said Ström, the majority of the workers stood behind the leader of the Party. In response to the increasingly radical antimilitarism in the Party and accusations from the left of having thrown in his lot with the reactionaries, Branting was now characterizing the war as a clash between the capitalist powers and heaping scorn on the senselessness of the arms race. He responded to the appeals of his critics with answers that made no commitments but that had an air of radicalism about them. He described the call for a Third International as a betrayal of the working class and began readying himself, in the event of a split in the Party, to shift the blame to the left, which had allowed itself to become seduced by Bolshevism. The Young Socialists and the Left Alliance were still struggling to maintain their legitimacy, but when they adopted the slogan of making the imperialist war into a war of the oppressed against their oppressors, the right began to publicly denounce them with venom. Hansson spoke of a monstrous erosion infecting the thought of the youth, and Branting dubbed the Zimmerwald line the revolutionary romanticism of rootless emigrants. The rants of rabid, small-minded bourgeois thought didn't worry the workers; they were more convinced by Branting's efforts to confront the looming chaos with resolve and reason than they were by revolutionary pamphlets. If the left did not wish to return to a healthy functioning of the Party and to prove their loyalty before the next attack was launched, they said, then they could expect to be kicked out. It was at this time that Ström was appointed to the First Chamber. Branting had promoted him with the consent of the Liberals, aiming to pacify him and to alienate his allies. Circles within the Right Party, who had just as much riding on a splintering of the Social Democratic opposition as he did, had accommodated the move. Ström, the representative of the Zimmerwald group, joined up with the other member of the left alliance in the upper house, Lindhagen, who like Palmstierna had come across from the Liberal Party. An extreme individualist and a leading force in the struggle for suffrage for men and women alike, he assumed the office of mayor of Stockholm. The filling of such positions with radical socialists, said Ström, indicated that the Party had already begun to take control of the state via parliamentary channels. The Left also saw the basis for social transformation in parliamentary rule. Unlike Branting's group, which assumed an agreement would be reached with the bourgeoisie, they anticipated that the bourgeoisie would strike back, yet they failed to develop any strategy for such an eventuality, instead maintaining a fatalistic belief in a democratic transition to socialism. Their images of a socialist order also remained unclear and variegated. Even Höglund, who had a Marxist education and who, together with Nerman, the modernist poet, had pledged himself to Lenin's International in Zimmerwald, combined half-anarchist tendencies with his concept of freedom, while Ström, the most pugnacious advocate of a new party, placed more emphasis on the significance of mental forces than material ones. The journalists Vennerström and Carleson held to generally humanist ideas, while Fabian Månsson followed a populist, spontaneitist, antibureaucratic line. A popular agitator like Månsson, Kata Dalström, the friend of Kollontai and Balabanoff, preached her doctrine of salvation, inflected by a primeval Christianity. She openly called herself a Communist but was already getting caught up in theosophical musings which a few years later would push her into mysticism. Though the goals of these leftist personalities might still have been primarily of an idealistic, utopian, philosophical, poetic, visionary nature, Branting was nevertheless determined to take the wind out of their sails, for the revolutionarily minded youth league—whose leaders included Kilbom and Linderot, both experienced in practical union work—was increasingly driving them to make the mass party a tool of a politics of confrontation. Branting, who wanted to form a government with the Liberals, now rejected all initiatives from the left to preserve the unity of the Party. It was no longer possible to realize his reformist vision while maintaining their critical platform. Warning against what was occurring in Germany, where the first Spartacus Letters had been published, Branting led a press campaign against the antagonists in the Party. Before presenting his ultimatum to the Party, he strengthened his promises to the workers until he believed he had convinced them that the youth association and left alliance were impeding the struggle for equal voting rights, for the eight-hour day, and for social welfare. After he had allowed the congress of the Young Socialists for Disarmament and World Peace to be broken up by the police and authorized the arrest of Höglund, the congress chairman, as a traitor and enemy of the people, in February of nineteen seventeen he provoked the break. Right up to the end, said Ström, we had attempted to facilitate an amicable division into various directions within the Party, but the resolution of the leadership, with the demand that all submit to the directives of the right, could only lead to our leaving the Party. With the heightening tensions on the international scene, he said, Branting was taking a risk that could have annihilated his party. He lost the entire youth league, the radical cadres, the best-known theorists; nevertheless, said Ström, he had no other option, for otherwise he'd have run the risk of allowing us to pull the Party to the left. Inspired by the February Revolution in Russia, said Ström, we appealed for the constitution of a popular socialist party. It was the mention of the names— of the right-wing Social Democrats who were still leading the Party today and assuming government positions, and of the leftists who with few exceptions had rejoined the Social Democrats—which made the political continuity evident to me, as well as the contradiction between the widespread will for renewal, which, half a year before the October Revolution, brought about an internationalist party seeking a transition to Communism, and the Party founders' gradual renunciation of their work. But the investigation of their behavior had to be excavated from material that consisted of many layers. Tracing the symptoms and tendencies that seemed to point to the reasons for their deviation, we ran into contradictions that threatened to compromise our whole project. The conversation between Ström and Brecht also initially provided insights into the mechanisms of writing. In picking up on conflicting themes, in the abrupt shifts in perspectives, the following of contradictory impulses, the continual openness to new suggestions, I recognized something of Brecht's

working technique. He listed a mass of authors whose books he had used as material for the novel. After producing excerpts, he said, the writing followed almost automatically, in a kind of montage. With the same apparent condescension toward his own text, he said of the Engelbrekt piece that he was only continuing and transposing to the stage that which he had received from historians such as Grimberg, Schück, Lönnroth, Kumlien, Carlsson, or Nyström. He compared himself to a scientist in a laboratory who, always relying on the earlier work of others, produced new products through the chemical combination of elements. He glossed over how fundamentally the texts he produced differed from the material he used. Only with the care that he brought to each page of his manuscript did he indicate that he viewed this vastly improved, pasted over, neatly formatted object as something unique and autonomous. Otherwise he was more interested in experimentation than the effort to create a finished work. The concept of failure didn't seem to exist for him. Every fragment, every partial result had its own value. He told Ström that in depicting Caesar's Rome, with its market speculation and its corrupt senate, its party imbroglios and rigged elections, its terrorist upper class and its plebs, who were so easily won over for wars of conquest, he had sought too much of the present in the past, had gotten too deep into a historicism in which he had lost track of part of what was actually historical, from which he might have been able to learn more. As if history repeated itself, he had compared Caesar's time with Nazified bourgeois society. The insurrectionary movement was annihilated, Catiline had been driven out and fell in battle, henchmen had caught his co-conspirators and strangled them in the dungeon late at night on the sixth of November in the year sixty-three before the common era. Caesar, supported by the owners of capital, had become a dictator and was now fanning the flames of the war that was to resolve all the contradictions in the state with a single blow. His army's march toward Spain, as preparation for the subjugation of Gaul and Britain, could still be fit into a contemporary frame. But then the analogies were lost. The current war took up where the earlier imperialist war had left off, but whereas back then the revolution had erupted from the colossal destruction, today, from the outset, it was the counterrevolution which stood behind the clashes, with the intention of misleading the masses being hurled into battle so drastically that initiatives to revolt would be impossible. Ström returned to his role as Catiline. It would also have been possible to transport the Roman businesspeople and military, the corrupt government functionaries and demagogues, the hordes of slaves and burial societies into the impoverished Stockholm of nineteen seventeen. In the senate, Ström, Catiline, was now attacked fiercely by Cicero, Branting. It was no longer mere denunciations that the consul poured on the apostate but rather veiled accusations that the insurgent was plotting to kill him. With his meekness and conscientiousness, his philosophical bent and his republican candor, Lindhagen would have been able to play a Cato, while Nerman, as Cinna, could be placed in the milieu around the Neoteric poet Catullus. A Sulla could have been found in Kilbom as well; and thus, on the morning of the thirteenth of April nineteen seventeen, the four conspirators went to the Stockholm train station to pick up Lenin, who was traveling from Zurich. They escorted him and his entourage via Vasagatan to Drottninggatan, where Ström had rented rooms for the guests at Hotel Regina. Of the roughly twenty people, said the minister, he had recognized Krupskaya, Inessa Armand, Zinoviev, Sokolnikov, and Radek. Lenin was surprisingly short. He was wearing a shabby, almost floor-length coat and a tattered felt hat, carrying an umbrella, and wearing clunky hiking boots. Lenin was hurrying everyone along, wanted to continue on that night; the group didn't arouse any attention, people were used to seeing flocks of ragged people on the streets, on their way somewhere, to get bread from the distribution stations, milk for the children, on a hunger march; it was only the porter who grew suspicious at the sight of the travelers with their bundles over their shoulders and their old-fashioned suitcases, and he demanded the money in advance. Lenin had none on him, Ström paid, alerted the local Party office, had them collect a few hundred kronor for the purchase of the tickets to the Finnish border, bought them breakfast, then sat in a dialogue with the leader of the Bolsheviks in a small room. At first Ström claimed not to remember what had been said, digressed, told them about their visit to the Bergström warehouse at Hötorget, as clothes were needed; he described Lenin's threadbare trousers, the holes in his laced boots. Brecht pressured him, gradually got him to tell us something about the conversation. Brecht wanted to know Lenin's opinion of the Swedish left, who were in the process of forming their own party. A few days earlier, the Independent Social Democratic Party of Germany had been founded in Gotha, and the Spartacus Group had joined them. Lenin must have wanted to be informed about the formation of the Left Party, said Brecht. Lenin's theory that the events in Russia were just a warm-up for the transformations in the countries of Western Europe seemed to have been confirmed, but he also recognized that the counterrevolution would confront the insurrections here even more strongly than in Russia. The German Independent Party already carried the antagonism within itself. Its raison d'être was not so much to distance itself from the Social Democratic Party as it was to neutralize leftist forces and keep them from converting to Bolshevism. The Spartacus League, which was attempting to push the Party's evolution in a revolutionary direction, would sooner or later be expelled. If Lenin was in conversation with one of the leaders of the new party, said Brecht, then he would probably have addressed the question of how the dangers that were becoming evident in Germany could be avoided in Sweden. Lenin warned us, said Ström, that the actions of the workers could be headed off by the bourgeoisie. In Russia, Lenin had said, the right-wing forces in the worker's movement, the Social Patriots, the Kadets, had placed themselves on the side of the landowners and the bourgeoisie to prevent a proletarian revolution. A convergence of workers, soldiers, and peasants had to be created. Ström asked whether the fragmentation of the populace might not bring about the fall of the revolution. The revolution will collapse, Lenin had replied, if we do not act and seize the leadership. Petit-bourgeois revolutions will become tools of capitalism, of imperialism. Our fellow party members on the right of the Social Democrats don't seem to understand this; they are walking blindly through time and history. We deliberated, said Ström, on the character of the Party, whereupon the contradictions in our perspectives became apparent. Lenin demanded a strictly disciplined elite party, while for us a party could only be functional if it stood in close contact with all sections of the working people. Lenin also spoke of the Party as an instrument of the masses, of the seizure of power by a class-conscious proletariat, and yet, said Ström, at the mention of democratic centralism, I couldn't help but hear something of the demand to fall in line, of the position that the working class could only be brought to class consciousness by the leadership. Lenin must have understood, said Brecht, that the Swedish left would end up in the same conflict with the Bolsheviks as the Spartacists, and Ström confirmed that in their discussion of the concept of democracy, the conflict between Luxemburg and Lenin had been reactivated. He had, he said, rejected the notion that the Party constituted the vanguard of the revolution, had expressed his mistrust toward all leaders. I might have claimed, said Ström, that we were supporters of peace, of the individual freedom of movement, for I can still hear Lenin's voice ringing in my ears as he retorted: you're pacifists, even you lot, on the extreme left, are petit bourgeois pacifists. You love peace, but you are not willing to fight for peace. A Tsarist Russia remains a menace for the Scandinavian peoples as well. The army of the Tsar will not be defeated with prayers. The Russian Revolution will be armed. It is with arms that it will remove the continual threat of war and give Finland back its independence as well. **259** Ström asked whether the revolution could turn into a military dictatorship. Yes, Lenin replied, if the soldiers and workers didn't take over the army, if it continued to be led by the generals and trust bosses, then the bourgeois military dictatorship will prevail, in one country after the other. To Lenin's question about our party's program, said Ström, he had countered that there was still no such thing, that it had to be drawn up by the people themselves, in response to the conditions in the country. Lenin was indignant about our lack of decisiveness and insight, said Ström. Our job was to look forward, to capitalize on the lessons from the first stage of the Russian Revolution, to educate the masses and provide them with instruction. We were still massively outnumbered, Ström answered. In that case, said Lenin, what we needed to do was to identify what was keeping the Party in the minority and to draw in the workers through convincingly identifying the country's problems and making suggestions for their improvement. We grew up with a democratic mindset, said Ström, and that he understands the democratic foundations of the Party to mean that the leadership can only reside at the bottom, with the members, and that decisions cannot be foisted upon them from above. Lenin agreed with him that, of all European countries, democracy was the most advanced in Sweden. But then he immediately asked how things were with Höglund, wasn't he in prison, just like Liebknecht in Germany, and MacDonald in England. So where was the democracy in that, the freedom of the word, personal security. Do all workers in Sweden have the right to vote, he asked, is there protection from exploitation in Sweden. No. You have broken with Branting, but you have not yet realized that true freedom and democracy can only be reached via revolution. What guarantee was there, Ström had asked. The guarantee lies in the working class seizing control of the means of production, Lenin replied. For us, said Ström, the principle of the dictatorship of the proletariat could have no validity, we had no reason to ascribe the revolutionary mission exclusively to the proletariat, from the very beginning, the democratic movement had been backed by people of diverse backgrounds. The dictatorship of the proletariat, said Lenin, means that the fundamental producing class is afforded all authority during a brief transition period to protect the revolution. The dictatorship of the proletariat produces an extreme centralization of forces. It was precisely because of his centralism, his undemocratic actions, said Ström, that we turned away from Branting. Branting is smarter than you are, retorted Lenin. But his

politics are wrong. He is a Menshevik, he is banking on the Entente Powers instead of the working class. You think you possess the spirit of the revolution. Spirit, great. The only thing you need now is method. Perhaps history will teach you the right method. Even back then, said Ström, it was clear to me how far away we were from Lenin's revolutionary goals, how irreconcilable the conception of the Bolsheviks was with the guidelines we needed to draw up for our party. In our country, in which the foundations for democratic institutions had been laid, and in which there was a hundred-year tradition of peace, different steps had to be taken than in backward, isolated Russia, in which only now the bourgeois revolution against feudalism and absolutism was taking place. We knew that, with an industrial proletariat that had been educated in democracy and trade unionism, with an expansive, still largely unpoliticized class of peasants, a broad, partially progressive middle class, and many intellectuals of radical yet humanist convictions, we would not be able to go on the attack as a conspiratorial vanguard of professional revolutionaries, but that we needed a party of the masses in which numerous groupings, all united by the fight against all forms of oppression, would be pieced together into a bloc. If we have learned something from history, said Ström, then it was this, that we must never allow ourselves to be diverted from our independence, from the specific constitution of our class situation. In my conversation with Lenin, and in the ensuing, documented discussion in a larger group, said Ström, we touched upon the problems which, just as they provoked disagreement in Lenin back then, would later force us to clash with the theses of the Soviet Party and the Comintern. We envisioned a party that reflected the concerns of the workers in our country, we didn't yet want to commit to particulars, we had our own way of addressing the populace, we didn't reject the proclivities of the numerous Good Templars and utilitarians, we didn't deny the influence of Dalström, of Fabian Månsson, who combined the Sermon on the Mount with the *Communist Manifesto*, we were familiar with the people's aversion to authoritarian ambitions, we ourselves preferred romantic declarations of fraternity to forming a rigidly disciplined party. We would have found our path, our own path, the need for a new party was profound, a strike movement was in the making. In addition to demands for equal suffrage, the eight-hour day, there was agitation for increased food rations for the workers, for reductions in the price of bread and milk, for rent gouging to be outlawed and amnesty to be granted to political prisoners. Here, our party would be able to take the lead and show the voters that addressing immediate problems was no longer the sole remit of the right-wing Social Democratic propagandists. In April of seventeen, said Ström, we were full of hope; then, perhaps due to the power exuded by Lenin's personality, due to our admiration for the young Soviet state, we allowed ourselves to be made to renounce our right to self-determination, a decision that drove the Party from one phase of failure to the next. Radek, who had stayed behind in Stockholm to attend the founding congress of the Social Democratic Left Party on the twelfth of May with Münzenberg, produced a caricature of the meeting in Lenin's honor, some ten years later, which suggested that the Bolsheviks' trust in Ström and his comrades must have been minimal. With a feel for nuances, for all signs of doubt and hesitation, the satirist, who had now been eliminated by his own people just like Zinoviev and Sokolnikov, depicted where Lenin's hosts would end up. Not Lenin nor one of his Russian companions, not even the memorable Armand—Who, Brecht mused, would one day write the book about her, about whom so little is known—were present at the food-laden table. For, as Radek was trying to say, the radical leftist intellectuals were not seeking an alliance with them; they were already looking for other participants for their circle. They didn't drink to the revolution but to Lindman, Trygger, and Hederstierna, the leaders of the bourgeois Right Party. This drawing, said Ström, as he held up the sheet to us, expressed the Bolsheviks' lack of understanding of the political situation in Western Europe. Radek wanted to show that the founders of the Swedish Party would never have been able to become Communists. When we left the Party, he said, as far as Radek was concerned, this could only be traced back to long-standing reactionary motivations. This made it possible to justify the measures taken against us. It was not us who had walked out; the Comintern-backed sect had forced us out of the Party with their continual scheming. We had been made into the guilty parties because we had wanted to create a party in accordance with what was possible for us instead of clinging to the heroic epoch of the workers' state and bowing to the demand for unconditional and irrational observance of Soviet directives. I am, said Ström, stroking his white moustache, an enemy of fanaticism and totalitarianism. The only things that had proved tenable in the disappointing, disillusioning, embittering, destructive struggle for a new party, he said, were humanistic values. Brecht looked at him with derision. He knew that the politician would turn around and go straight back to attacking the Soviet Union in articles and speeches. It was true that Ström had been willing to stand by political refugees; together with Höglund and the younger Branting he had opposed the restrictions on the right to asylum, but he

was wary of falling under suspicion as a protector of antifascists who were working illegally. He looked past Brecht's Communism; for him, Brecht was somebody who stood above the Party. And Brecht happily let him believe that, for Brecht needed him. Ström, Höglund, and Branting could assist him in renewing his residency permit and, should it become necessary, in procuring papers to travel farther afield. Ström had handed Lenin the tickets. Finnish comrades would receive him in Haparanda and accompany him to Petrograd. But while Lenin and his companions were traveling north, feverish activities were taking place among the leadership of the Social Democratic Party. On the fourteenth of April, Branting had returned from Petrograd, where he had informed Kerensky of Lenin's impending arrival. They were cut off from all news about the international situation there and believed that a bourgeois revolution was also imminent in Germany. A peace accord could not yet be anticipated, Branting had said, urging Kerensky to keep Russia in the war to lessen the strain on the Entente Powers. He had also been successful, he reported, in mediating between the provisional government and the workers' councils to this end. And what had become of his actual mission, asked Palmstierna, who had sent him to exert all of his influence upon Kerensky to convince him to seize the opportunity to have Lenin killed on his way to the Russian capital. The problem was that Kerensky didn't seem to have ascribed any particular significance to the arrival of the revolutionary leader. Rather he wanted to show—and Branting supported him in this—that democracy reigned in Russia. If somebody feared Lenin's arrival, he maintained, then it was the people, who had just attained their freedom. The workers' councils, which only represented a tiny portion of the populace, he pointed out, were only interested in maintaining their organizations, they were not interested in taking over the government. And these groups, which were suited to toppling but incapable of building up something new would also have allowed the bourgeoisie to take control without objections. Still buzzing from the memory of his evening in the Tsar's box at the opera, where he had been cheered by the audience as he congratulated them on their victorious revolution, Branting recommended following the Russian example of confronting the actions of the left with the weapon of democratization. Just as the wandering rabble in Russia would not be able to achieve anything, the Party of the Swedish insurrectionists would also remain powerless. For two more days, Palmstierna sent flash telegrams to Kerensky. Kerensky, consider what is approaching you. Kerensky, do not underestimate the danger. Kerensky, respond to our urgent request. Years later, as an envoy in London, Palmstierna spoke about that fateful failure. Everything would have turned out differently, he exclaimed, had they followed his suggestion back then. But on the morning of April seventeenth, in the Tauride Palace, Lenin read out his ten theses.

Actually, said Rogeby, Palmstierna had more integrity than the rebels who had returned, disappointed and remorseful, to the bosom of the mother party, for he had never disavowed his intention to smother all revolutionary unrest, had never seen the Party as anything but a bastion against Bolshevism. The lesson in the schoolbooks during the war—that, after the voting reforms, the great mass of the people could not automatically exploit their majority position but could only assume possession of their civil rights after considered education—had come from him, said Rogeby. As a child born into poverty, as a young unskilled laborer in the raft builders' quarters, Rogeby had heard the blind wrath expressed by the elders who had been witnesses to the process of transformation in the Party. Many of them would tell stories about the expectations that had arisen around the turn of the century with the consolidation of the organizations. Those who had been most devastated by the decline were the ones who were old enough to have known Palm, Danielsson, and Wermelin. August Palm, who trained as a tailor in Germany before being expelled because he had also gotten an education in socialist agitation, had been broken by the discord in the Party. He, the limping master tailor, known to all proletarians, ended up blustering on in his mélange of German, Danish, and Swedish about nothing but moral decay and alcoholism in an Old Testament tone. Danielsson and Wermelin, on the other hand, cast out by Branting, had held onto their revolutionary convictions. Wermelin and Danielsson, mentioned only in passing by Ström, stood at the forefront of the workers' movement, as far as Rogeby was concerned. They were too idiosyncratic, incorruptible, to be able to assert themselves among the careerists. Danielsson had shaped the ideological foundations of the Party, and Branting had taken from him that which could be used in his diplomatic balancing acts with the Liberals. While Branting never showed his weaknesses, Danielsson had exposed himself to all attacks, scorned all protective measures. Through him, the workers had gained an education about the system of the capitalist concentration of power. Having been kicked off the editorial team of the Party paper by Branting, in his own paper, *Arbetet* [Labor], signing his articles as Marat, he had not just conveyed the goals of socialism but through his depictions of the conditions under which working people were living, he had also initiated Swedish workers' literature. As a twenty-five-year-old, in eighteen eighty-eight, he'd ended up in prison for a year and a half for slandering the government, to the benefit of Branting, who was about to found the Party. The health of the strong, tall man was eroded by his time behind bars, and after his release he only lasted another decade. He died two days before the dawn of the new century, worn down by his time in the hospitals, the continual attacks on his newspaper, the denunciations coming from the Party leadership. His rejection of the state as an instrument of domination necessarily collided with Branting's aspirations to take the state by parliamentary means, to establish a form of state socialism. The existing institutions of the state, he expounded, could never be taken over by the working class; they had to be smashed before a socialist society could be constructed, to prevent the old from eating away at the new. But, he went on to say, a revolution could only be successful if it were borne by the majority of the people and took place on an international scale. Studying the Paris Commune, he made the question of proletarian violence dependent upon the violence that the bourgeoisie would use against the workers. His closest comrade in arms, Wermelin, who had introduced him to Marxist writings in his youth, had been ejected from the country; one last time, the poet with the round, wan moon face traveled from America to visit Danielsson in the site of his exile, Malmö, oh Malmö, that city where the petit bourgeois try to choke the reason out of you, where you're condemned to perish among the half-hearted and the lethargic. Rogeby pictured them, the two exiles, the one gigantic, the other a short and stocky figure, two of the original thinkers in that dark and stodgy time of an intellectual desertification that drove other artists of the era—like Fröding, Josephson, Hill, and Strindberg—mad as well; he wondered what they might have talked about as they strolled along the shoreline in the moist wind blowing across from Öresund. Not about illness, ridicule, expulsion, but about what they called the struggle of the intelligence against barbarism, the struggle of the imagination against sterility; perhaps, he said, they broached the question that was now becoming relevant again in our time, the thesis of the reconception of the notion of class, the removal of the borders between intellectual and physical workers, the acquisition of cultural values by those who, without being aware of it, had made their creation possible; about alliances which in turn could be traced back to connections from the past, to Götrek, to Cabet—and at the mention of Cabet I suddenly remembered Meryon's depiction of Marat's house, in the inscription on the turret, *Cabat*, I now felt I had recognized the connection between the names Marat and Cabet. Much of what Rogeby disclosed was encrypted, just like that old etching. **265** Just as he pointed up to a couple of low, narrow windows while walking across Järntorget, in the old town, saying, that's where the Icarian crew lived, at Strömmen his finger slid in a semicircle around the islands, the inns under the bridge in front of the palace, the boulevard leading into the royal gardens, that's where in June of seventeen the officers had to gather their men who refused to fire on the workers during the mass demonstrations. From intimations, supplemented or contradicted by Ström's statements, my image of the course of the political developments gradually crystallized. Even though there was often a groaning about the dishonor and wounds they had to bear, though people said that the pressure had become impossible to withstand, though torpor and exhaustion had set in again, the workers, said Rogeby, had never lost their instincts. People always said that they had allowed themselves to be led astray, but they were doing what they could. It was easy to say they should take what they needed, but what, he asked, could they do against a single strategically positioned machine gun. For those who had money and military might behind them, everything was possible, the doors of the enormous edifice of civilization were open to the owners, as soon as they took their first steps it was decided who would stay below and who would make it to the top; in the schools and barracks, the divisions had long ago been drawn, one lot get the secure jobs, the others head to the workbenches. What the propertyless wanted to achieve was something entirely different, an inversion of everything we had known, of all forms of life; in that context, it was craven to say they had given up, had submitted, when their efforts and the sacrifices they had made were infinitely greater than the energy the other side needed to invest to achieve their self-affirmation.

Ström spoke of the advocates of realpolitik who, with endurance and calculation, concentrated on what could be achieved; sure, they had been able to tally tiny gains, and that was better than having to cop the trouncings that came after overly ambitious lunges at lofty endeavors. Rogeby spoke of the voices that rise up from the humiliation, the wasting, the accumulated and restless brooding, from the outsiders who were familiar with the sucking spiral into numbness. Ström followed those who would soon occupy government posts which, in their continual contest with the bourgeoisie, they would lose, win back, hold onto, and be forced to surrender again. Rogeby saw the overcoming of anonymity, the effort to gain access to their own voices, he saw the accumulation of the documents bearing witness to an arduously acquired literacy. Among the poets and orators who captured the forces surrounding them like mediums and brought them to voice, speakers from proletarian backgrounds were now appearing: a cork-cutter called Menander, a day-laborer, Gabrielsson, a printing plate maker by the name of Hellborg, a seamstress, Maria Sandel, a sawyer, Östman, a raft-maker and tracklayer, Hedenvind-Eriksson, a mechanic, Larsson, a farm worker, Moa Martinson. The concept of education was shifting, the school of reality could be found everywhere, and everywhere, visions could emerge, all experiences began to resound in a commonality, individual experience and collective knowledge, the national language and the language of the world pervaded one another, slowly laying the foundations for the imagination of a classless society. Time and again, up until the strike movement of the thirties, said Rogeby, genuine spokespeople were found among the workers; even today, with the density of the repression, there were many people in every workplace who knew the issues in detail; but who, we asked ourselves, bore the blame for the uninterrupted domination of finance, why had the working people not been able to bring about the overthrow. Rogeby rejected the notion that the compromises of Social Democracy alone were responsible for the fact that there had not been a decisive change in the circumstances of wage laborers or in the dynamic between the classes since Branting's first government, pointing as well to the incapacity of the Communist Party to convey a convincing political alternative. In June of nineteen seventeen, he said, the objective preconditions for the development of a revolutionary situation were there. The Left Socialists had called for a general strike, the workers had headed in to the parliament from the outskirts of the city, the workers and the soldiers had begun to band together, the opportunity to pull away from Social Democratic politics was there—but even before its first test of strength, the new party failed. The masses were willing to act, but there was a lack of leadership capable of coordinating the impulses, of consolidating the spontaneous alliance between the striking workers and the young conscripts who had left their units, and of getting the weapons—indispensable for the insurrection—into the hands of the people. Tens of thousands stood on Helgeandsholmen and in the surrounding streets and squares chanting their demands to abolish the First Chamber and the monarchy, to begin forming workers' councils. Branting, however, in order to give an appearance of decisiveness, had already put together a workers' committee straight after the constitution of the Left Party—but one tasked with averting calls for strikes and diverting their energies into election preparations. Units of cadets broke up the crowd and blocked off the Riksbron from Gustav Adolf Square with their bayonets raised; up in the castle courtyard waited Count Douglas, who in nineteen hundred nine, as a company commander, had kept reserves at the ready, the troops armed as if for war; and now the mounted police joined the party, charging into the crowds. Those seconds on the fifth of June, the blurred slashing of the saber blades, the prancing horses, with tails trimmed short, the masses of people fleeing every which way, the windows in the façade of the foreign ministry packed with onlookers, the fallen figure, legs pulled up to his torso, arms wrapped around his head to protect it, the surrounding area cleared, the gendarmes off in the distance having lost interest in him, the throng of bodies on the bridge, a boy climbing a lamppost, instantly caught by the lash of a whip, and the arrested worker between the two men in uniform, his hands held together behind his back, right and left the greatcoats, the rows of glistening buttons, the glinting sables, tassels on the handles, the grim, gray faces under spiked helmets, straps under the chin, and in the middle the face stretching upward into the light, neck straining out from an open shirt, the pride in the features winning out over the breathless surprise. Instead of Höglund, who had declared the streets to be the parliament from the balcony of the Riksdag, it was Branting who, rushing out to call the hordes to order and leading them to the workers' club on Barnhusgatan, was able to assume the role of the tribune of the people. The appeal for unity, previously issued by the Left, was now picked up by Branting's party; the union leaders demanded an end to the strike, which had been called illegitimately; the autumn elections promised to be a success for the Social Democratic Party, where they were expecting not just to increase their share of the seats but also to occupy ministerial posts; their nonviolent rise to participation in government was imminent. For a few days, the Swedish workers had been way ahead of the situation in Western Europe with their counterslogan that power could only be won by toppling the reign of capital. For the first time, the confidence of the bourgeoisie had been shaken. Then came the hesitation, the confusion. The threat of expulsion from the confederation of trade unions forced the workers to break off the strike that had been called by the Left. As unified as the workers were on the fifth of June, they still didn't want to risk splitting from their organizations. Without union membership they would have become isolated penitents. The bond between the conservative party leadership and the union bosses proved once again to be stronger than the cumulative will of the masses to achieve radical change. The inexperienced Left Party was not able to assert itself in the face of the established Social Democrats. If the frustration among the workers lingered for a few weeks,

268 soon enough the restraint and caution urged by Branting was smothering the insurrectionary energy. As after the major strike in nineteen hundred nine, in June of seventeen the union functionaries once again strengthened their right to determine the political action of the working class. The reprimanded had to bow to the fact that a general strike demanded centralized initiative and leadership. Industrial peace also had to be reached, without which, as contractually stipulated, the planned negotiations with the employers association could not take place. After the retreat into the factories, Branting's workers' committee was dissolved. It was no longer needed. In the German Social Democratic Party, the events in Sweden had been followed with consternation and anxiety; a year later, the lessons that had been learned were put into practice. It had been shown that the power of the people could achieve nothing without a strong party and far-sighted leaders, which is why the murder of the key figures of the German Revolution became the first concern of the bourgeois-socialist alliance. When Ström said there had been no revolutionary situation in Sweden, although this conclusion was correct in hindsight, it also attested to the indecisiveness of the Left Socialists when faced with the opportunity to contribute to the emergence of such a situation. Even if we had been in agreement, said the lawmaker, we would still have been no match for Branting's personality, around which a cult had been built up after the model of the German Social Democrats. In October of seventeen, four Social Democrats were appointed to the newly formed national unity government, headed up by the Liberal Edén, with Branting as finance minister, Palmstierna as naval minister, Rydén as minister of education, and Undén as a minister without portfolio. The next government was to belong to the workers—and to the members of the Left Party, who had formed an electoral coalition with the Social Democratic Party—and it would be led by Branting. Despite their organizational weakness, the Left Party comprised twenty thousand members and had won eleven seats in the Second Chamber. Not up to the task of street fighting, their leadership group turned toward parliamentary confrontations, which promised more success. The radicalization of the working populace seemed unstoppable. They would no longer be pushing for universal suffrage, the eight-hour day, but for the construction of the socialist republic, the appropriation of the country's goods and means of production by the working class. And yet it was not the upsurge of the Left but the measuredness of the right wing of Social Democracy that came to be seen as a sign of strength. No longer confined to the opposition, the Social Democratic Party could offer the workers a program that addressed their most immediate objectives. Despite the fact that the Left **269** Party's diversity of perspectives better reflected the situation, their theoretical approach meant that they were unable to appeal to the masses. For the voters, the arguments in the Left Socialists' program about the dangers of the Social Democratic Party's philosophy of power and its belief in authority and its bureaucratization were less decisive than the fact that the two parties agreed about the centrality of parliamentary democracy; and in this domain they preferred the Social Democratic Party, which with over eighty seats was by far the largest party in the Second Chamber, making it better positioned to represent their interests. If we could just achieve universal suffrage, went the prevailing belief, we would also be able to make social justice a reality. By entering into an electoral coalition despite the fact that they were competing with each other for seats, the two workers' parties had built that bloc of mutual condemnation and dependence which had remained necessary for every subsequent attempt to assert themselves against the bourgeois hegemony. The party of the Left Socialists, later the Communist Party, was decisive in the battle against the cobbled-together Right Party, the Liberal Party, and the newly founded Farmers' League, but in the process it ended up in the very position its founders had wanted to avoid, that of an avant-garde which, as a result of internal divisions, did more to provide wind for the sails of reformism than to push the working class toward revolutionary consciousness. Rogeby, with his broad face and flat nose, hands clasped under his chin, stared into the darkness that contained his childhood and this political turning point. He saw himself in his father's drab kitchenette. Before him lay the years of arduous forward motion through the sediment of the failed insurrection. Late at night on the sixth of November,

Lenin had proved that the moment to roll the dice of revolution had to be chosen carefully, and in Sweden this historical moment had been missed. The resolve required to face off against such an overpowering adversary had only existed in Russia, he said. The magnitude of the achievement of Russia's steadfastness could be measured against the crushing of the German Revolution, the failure of the European proletariat, the rapid expansion of capital, the conspiring of the Western powers against Russia. Here, he said, working together with the bourgeoisie and the army, the Social Democratic Party was advocating for intervention in Finland, where, after the declaration of national independence, Mannerheim's White Guards and German battalions were staring down the workers who had proclaimed a popular government. In defense of freedom, the freedom of bourgeois domination, Palmstierna had weapons delivered to Mannerheim, his declared sympathy for the people of Finland excusing this breech of the laws of neutrality; and Douglas, after secret negotiations with German Foreign Minister Kühlmann, put together an expeditionary corps. The slaughter of the Finnish socialists allowed a generation of Swedish generals to cut their teeth, providing them with experience that was able to be put into practice again on the same stage today. Condemning the Swedish intervention in Finland, declaring their solidarity with the Russian and Finnish revolutionaries, calling for an immediate ceasefire, the Left Party demonstrated its internationalist stance. Though many workers had been cowed by the victory of the counterrevolution in Finland and were given to entertaining the slander of the Social Democratic Party against the splintered Bolshevik revolution, which they accused of sowing nothing but calamity; for others, those November days in Germany had aroused a sympathy for the slogans of the Left. Once more fear spread through the bourgeoisie that the workers would band together to demand the formation of workers' councils, the ousting of the king, the dissolution of the army, the arming of the people, and control of production, and people sat in their barricaded houses, money was sent overseas, suitcases were packed. And like in August of fourteen, at the end of the war, Social Democracy once again worked to ensure the maintenance of the status quo. Palmstierna had sent out armored cars, and their guns would be aimed at the workers. Once more the hesitation, the bated breath. The outcome of the German Revolution was uncertain; there too, the proletariat seemed to be overpowered by reactionary forces, and anything the powerful working class of Germany couldn't achieve would never be able to be won in Sweden. After the bloody German January, the bourgeoisie could open their shutters once more. The financial oligarchy quickly recovered from its fright, and rising up behind this group that had long been involved in world finance were the Entente Powers, who would not allow menaces of the kind that had just been weathered to emerge in Sweden. When the Communist International was formed in March of nineteen nineteen, the Second International too—strengthened through agreements with the owners of capital, the generals—was ready to enter this new epoch. And all those who had still hoped for a collective front of all workers had to witness their betrayal, and every attempt during the following two decades to salvage the notion of unity was doomed to be smashed by this underlying betrayal. The Social Democratic Party, providing assurances that the monarchy and the First Chamber would be maintained, ascended to assume the government, while the Left Party, after having joined the Third International in June, became a cadre party which never again reached the membership numbers of its early years. In nineteen twenty, said Rogeby, with the introduction of universal and equal suffrage, the eight-hour day—even if there were still restrictions—and the formal establishment of democracy, access to the actual power of the people was cut off. Ever since the workers had gotten their mass party into government, they had achieved nothing through class struggle; everything was now given to them from above, by the Party, by the state, and their defeats too were no longer brought about through large actions of solidarity but through failed negotiations up above, in the parliament, or between the union leadership and the employers' association. Most of us, said Rogeby, saw the twenties, in which exploitation was supposed to be abolished with the ballot, as lost years.

But the Social Democrats were governing as a minority, said Ström. In the Second Chamber, one hundred thirty-three representatives of the bourgeois parties sat across from eighty-six Social Democrats and eleven Left Socialists; in the First Chamber, the bourgeois parties had double the number of seats as the other side. Instead of finally seizing success after almost a hundred years of beating at the gates, the Social Democratic Party had to lead a state that had been declared bankrupt by the business owners. Let's see how you do with this, they cried out to the government, and it was obvious that they would soon have to give up. The postwar boom had brought in maximum profits for the industrialists. The workers had had every last drop sucked out of them, they could be left to their own devices for a while, kept as a reserve that cost the factory owners nothing. Induced market crashes and factory closures were used to suppress wages, often by up to fifty percent. Recalcitrant union sectors were shut out. The crisis could not be tackled with strikes. Soon, the number of unemployed had risen to a hundred thousand. In the metal industry alone over ten thousand workers were laid off. There could be no thought of social reform, all motions were voted down, the focus was now on providing financial aid to the affected families. Later we had to concede, said Ström, that by holding fast to their democratic principles despite attempts to bring them to their knees through extortion, the Social Democratic Party was actually promoting the course of progress. We too, he said, were closer to the Social Democrats' rejection of violence and their condemnation of a coup d'état than to the dictatorship of the proletariat that we had now recognized in our program. Our bond with the Soviet state was of a moral kind; we were fighting against ourselves when we claimed to be opponents of Branting, who emphasized the notion of socialist evolution over socialism as a dogma, and who reproached us, former adherents of Luxemburg, with her erstwhile fear that the dictatorship of the proletariat could become a dictatorship of the Party apparatus over the proletariat. In the conflict, said Ström, between the task of placing all our energy in the defense of Soviet Russia and the realization that we needed to create a national basis for the guiding principles of our party, we ended up in a state of paralysis, unable to act. The revolutionary catchwords that had been conveyed to us by the Soviet Party corresponded less than ever before to the power relations in the country, and yet we couldn't abandon them, as that would have led to our exclusion from the Comintern. The notion that we could exist purely as part of the global organization led by the Soviet Party clashed with the opinion that we would only be viable once we had established our autonomy; and both were correct, a destruction of the Soviet order would also have meant our own destruction, just as the lack of practical suggestions on everyday issues robbed us of credibility in the eyes of the populace, who didn't want myths but bread and work. We attempted to combine these two extreme needs; Lindhagen, Höglund, Kilbom, and Aschberg, the banker, traveled multiple times to Moscow—against the wishes of the government, which had broken off diplomatic relations with Soviet Russia—to put aid operations in place and to open up trade routes; and at the same time, we set about once more sketching out our conception of a socialist party based on humanist foundations and incorporating all democratic rights. Had we been able to deliver on our prevailing intentions, he said, we would have formed a party with a future, but by nineteen twenty, when the Comintern issued its theses distancing itself from the Second International, the Central Committee already considered us sectarians, opportunists, petit-bourgeois elements, unworthy of belonging to a section of the Communist International. What we wanted was distorted and decried, as the doctrines of the early socialists had once been. With the rise of a strictly disciplined, hierarchically structured party, the scientific rigor of thinkers such as Babeuf, Buonarotti, Owen, Blanc, and Cabet had been dismissed; they were at best recognized as sources of inspiration and otherwise declared dreamers and fantasists. For us, their utopias were still something worth striving for; supplemented with new economic findings, they could be forged into an image of society that fit with our views and with the traditions in the country better than the authoritarian model with which we were supposed to be falling in line. But at this time of civil war, of the Entente Powers' blockade measures and plans of attack, the Soviet Party needed to be able to trust the foreign Parties, said Rogeby, they needed a support structure and had to be certain that the structure was not dominated by Social Democratic interests. That which had been achieved in Russia and was now being put to the test was to be adopted and extended in the West; and there, time and again we saw the failure of the proletariat in the face of military and economic institutions and in the face of Social Democracy, which claimed sole title over the workers' movement. Feigning radicalism, in their new program the Social Democratic leadership returned to the definition of the antagonistic conflict between work and capital, spoke not of concessions and reconciliation but of class struggle as the sole means of removing the system of depredation. At the same time, though, this militancy was annulled with the assertion that capitalism was not capable of exploiting the growing productive forces. Upon reaching the highest level of accumulation, it would void itself of its own productive force and have to make way for industrial democracy. Thus, in its decline, the Social Democratic Party gave the impression that the crisis, which had been conjured up by the owners of capital, was the preliminary stage on the way to a socialized society. As happened so often in the following years, Social Democracy co-opted the challenges issued by the left wing. Wigforss, the Social Democratic finance expert, was adept at instantly adapting the questions posed by the Left Party—about participation in matters related to production and about the economic struggle against the punitive measures of the employers—and adjusting them to fit their reformist program, nullifying the demand for workers' councils. While the Communist practitioners Kilbom and Linderot were working within the unions to activate them at the level of rank and file, the Social Democratic functionaries propounded the formation of works councils, which masqueraded as a platform for securing the right to workplace participation, but which actually served as instruments for controlling events in the workplace. When the Left Party made appeals for extraparliamentary action against the bourgeois attempts at restoration and for the arming of the working class, the Social Democratic Party pointed to the calm, experimental progress of their activities. Above all, said Rogeby, this offensive line clashed with the liberal and pacifist attitude within the Left Party itself. The group around Lindhagen put together a *Humanist Manifesto* as an alternative to the *Communist Manifesto*; Kata Dalström, having converted to Buddhism, agitated for religious freedom; and Höglund, the leader, and Ström, the Party secretary, preferred to speak not of arming the proletariat but merely of disarming the bourgeoisie. We needed time, said Ström. But there was no time, said Rogeby. Lenin's writings hadn't even been published here, said Ström; we sketched out a political strategy, a theory of the state, investigated the possibility of an alliance with the Social Democratic Party, and we received nothing but directives aligned with Russia's war Communism; what's more, Radek and Zinoviev were already driving a wedge between us—who they viewed as revisionists— and those who were determined to fall in line with the Comintern. We could have forged a synthesis from the differences of opinion and pushed the progression to the left with a unified party and a consideration of our specific conditions, but, against our better judgment, we had to choose the path of fragmentation. Now that the Social Democratic Party had proven itself to be incapable of relieving the misery in the country, the call could be made to return the bourgeoisie to the ministries in order to rectify the labor situation, and by October, after the election of the Second Chamber, in which the Social Democrats lost eleven seats, the king asked the Right Party, which had gained fifteen seats, to form a government. When Rogeby thought back to the years of his youth, he sensed the feeling of being roped in that had become part of the inheritance of the working class. It was in the countryside that the backwardness was all-encompassing: there was no eight-hour day out there; out there people worked twelve to fourteen hours, sometimes even longer, for starvation wages. And the thing with the right to vote was that, for the Second Chamber elections, men could only head to the polls once they had turned twenty-five (and women not even then); for the municipal elections it was twenty-eight, and with the gap between the elections that often meant an additional deferral, as well as the exclusion of many of the younger, active workers. In March of nineteen twenty-one, said Ström, we contributed to the further weakening of the socialist bloc by tearing our Party apart in the conflict over the acceptance of the twenty-one theses outlining the conditions of membership to the Comintern. Unintentionally, he said, we had ended up carrying out one of these so-called purges, like those now beginning in the German Party. Not yet having recognized how tightly we were binding ourselves to the Comintern, we pushed out Lindhagen, Vennerström, and Fabian Månsson, who wanted an independent party. Our membership numbers, which by this point had dropped to sixteen thousand, shrank by another six. The Party lost almost half of its members of parliament. The faction that Lindhagen headed up for another two years under its old party name before being absorbed into the Social Democratic Party, received five seats, while the Communist Party, as it was henceforth called, had only two members in the Second Chamber. In the fall of twenty-one, with women also having received the right to vote, Social Democracy managed to climb from seventy-five to ninety-three seats and, in this saga of fluctuating figures, retake the government from the Right Party, which had surrendered ten of its seventy-two seats. The business owners immediately went on the offensive. In January of twenty-two, more than two hundred thousand were calculated as unemployed when the youth were included, almost twenty percent of the entire working-age population. The Social Democratic Party was now presenting itself as a radical opposition party. With Palmstierna's relocation to London as an ambassador and the promotion of the economist Wigforss, the old, patriarchal, liberal position seemed to have been exchanged for a line in keeping with modern, rationalized forms of production. With the revolt in Kronstadt, the failed insurrections in Germany, the rejection of world revolution, the introduction of the New Economic Policy for the Development of Socialism in One Country, the wrangling for succession upon the deterioration of Lenin's health, and with our internal discord, which was once again threatening to explode, said Ström, the Social Democratic Party, with its unerring parliamentary activities, its leadership—which had remained static for years and would do so for many more—conveyed an impression of solidarity. With the Soviet Party now attempting to catch up to capitalist working conditions, handing out concessions and profit incentives to industry and agriculture, it was approximating, he said, the methods that Social Democracy was also pursuing in order to reach state socialism via state capitalism. The Social Democratic ideologues were able to capitalize on this in their election propaganda, pitting their peaceful alternative against the Soviets' dictatorial force. When on the first of May, said Rogeby, tens of thousands of Social Democratic workers streamed down Karlavägen beneath red flags

on their way to the gathering at Ladugårdsgärdet, singing the International as they moved through the quarter of the haute bourgeoisie, accompanied by jeers from the windows, it seemed as if there were no differences between the objectives of the workers' parties; but during the working
day the contradictions emerged. Though they still shared the same battle
hymns, the Communists viewed their efforts as connected with the
events in other countries and attempted to strengthen the front against
capitalism, while the others, the great majority, shaped by the policy of
concessions and compromise, took the path of working day reforms,
which promised access to prosperity for all if they could only ensure the
Party was strong enough. Often growing exhausted and then picking
themselves back up, defeated in April of twenty-three, in the autumn of
twenty-four they reclaimed the government for their party. The foundations of the labor movement, however, were the unions, and there the
parties wrestled for the leadership of the workers. It was as if they wanted
to prove, time and again, the thesis that they would never be able to transcend unionist thinking on their own. The Social Democratic functionaries attempted to hold onto the workers through the obligatory membership to the mass party—the same party that was using the unions for
revisionist ends—while the Communist cadre endeavored to prepare
them for revolutionary action. In the efforts of the two parties to form an
alliance between the industrial workers and the rural proletariat, contradictions became apparent that would lead to an intensification of the
antagonism between the parties, and to the second break in the Communist Party. Höglund and Ström wanted to work together with the Social
Democratic leadership to create a common front, but the Comintern ordered that the parties remain separate. In order to become an effective
front against monopoly capital, the United Front had to be under the
leadership of the Communist Party. The workers were to be won over for
this front. Once again, the Party's top-ranking committees were concerned with questions of principles, hair-splitting, debates on whether
capitalism was in the epoch of its demise, which would make the revolutionary concentration of the proletariat appropriate, or rather in a phase
of stabilization, which would necessitate a tactical retreat. In the lower
ranks of the Party, the reasons for the disputes remained incomprehen-
sible; the rank and file, who now numbered only nine thousand four hundred in total and were willing to enter a coalition with the Social Democratic workers, were surprised by the split. After Lenin's death, said
Ström, the executive committee of the Communist International had become nothing but a body for carrying out interrogations, meting out pun-

ishments and demanding apologies, confessions, penance. Höglund, who had declared his allegiance to Trotsky, had been vilified in Moscow by Zinoviev and Bukharin; I was also accused of having an un-Marxist, un-revolutionary attitude, said Ström, because in one of my books I had mentioned Balabanoff, who had just been expelled from the Soviet Party. And thus, shortly before the elections for which the Social Democratic Party was gathering the populace together, we ended up in a quarrel over the one true faith. The two groups—one demanding a break with the International, the restoration of autonomy, the other arguing that our key task was to protect the Soviet Union, which had been forced into isolation—managed to keep the Party on its feet until the elections were over. The Party lost two of the seven seats they had won the previous year. The Social Democrats, strengthened by the dissolution of the Left Party, picked up eleven new seats in the Second Chamber. At the congress in November, the explosion that led to the formation of two Communist Parties occurred. Höglund, the previous leader, and Ström, the Party secretary, had the majority of the Central Committee and the members behind them. Claiming the legitimate leadership of the Party for themselves, they shut out Kilbom, Linderot, Sillén, and Nerman, who made up the majority of the editorial team of the Party newspaper. They, in turn, having been granted authority over the Party by the Comintern, shut out Höglund's group. In the vicious struggle for the newspaper *Folkets Dagblad* [The People's Daily], the minority snatched victory, and the independents set up a competing newspaper, *Nya Folkets Dagblad* [The New People's Daily]. Since both parties claimed to be the true Communist Party, they spent a year spreading confusion among the workers, but after that, said Rogeby, most of those who had followed Höglund and Ström returned to the Comintern Party. The reformist tendencies in the independent Party had become increasingly manifest; the need for a proletarian party was becoming more evident; and what's more, the Comintern's attacks on Social Democracy had grown more convincing. Basically, said Ström, we had initially accepted the principle of the dictatorship of the proletariat for a transitional period, as had been set out by Lenin. We had also been willing to make our decisions in accordance with democratic centralism, provided that it indeed operated from the ground up. But then, as Soviet centralism began deciding on our decisions, we saw ourselves compelled to return to our original concepts. We offered to maintain close relations with the Comintern. Their doctrine wouldn't allow for that. We were condemned as heretics, which only strengthened our desire to establish a socialist party in our own image. But in nineteen twenty-six, following Branting's death and Sandler's brief assumption of government, we came to the realization that nothing could be achieved from within this small party, that we would never get beyond submitting motions that were either voted down or had to be adopted by the Social Democrats, that we needed the mass party, as it was only there that we would have access to the full spectrum of working people. Initially we perceived our return as a humiliation, but the Social Democratic Party had also suffered a defeat that year, and had to surrender the government once more to the bourgeois camp. With the renewed rise of a reactionary wave, they required all the support they could get. And he turned right around and started currying favor with his old comrades, said Rogeby, and venerating Branting, the patriarch, in his writings. The departure of the reformists proved to be a boon for the Communist Party. During

nineteen twenty-eight, the membership numbers rose from four thousand to eighteen thousand. In the elections that year, they reached their highest tally, snaring eight seats with almost six and a half percent of the vote. For those of us who were then finding our way to Communism, said Rogeby, it was a given that the Party would act in concord with the Soviet state, which was being threatened by the Western powers. We attended less to the brutal regulations in the Soviet Union than to its successes in industrialization and collectivization. The foreign policy of the bourgeois government—once again with Lindman, the leader of the Right Party, as prime minister—conformed with the request from the Western powers to destroy development in the Soviet Union. Domestically, they attacked the union organizations, strengthened the strikebreaker commandos, and had prison sentences handed out to Communist agitators. More and more, the industrial democracy that Wigforss had added to the Party program had revealed itself as a tool for establishing harmony between employers and employees. Precisely because he was considered progressive, Wigforss was best positioned to deceive the workers. He dismissed their power to create revolutionary change in society and pointed to their inability to assume high-level posts in industry and the state. But to avoid completely turning his back on the plans for socialization, he promised schools and other institutions, under union management, where workers could be trained to become future managers. The industrial pseudodemocracy only benefited the business owners, for under the pretense of giving the workers a say, but with no talk of collective decision-making, such platforms could utilize workers' technical experience and insights to increase productivity. The strike in the mining districts, which was maintained for half a year, did not lead to major united struggles against finance capital—which had now, according to the analysis of the Comintern, reached its imperial stage in Sweden—but rather to an agreement that only reemphasized the powerlessness of the workers' organizations. The agreements made between the union bureaucrats and the employers' association after the capitulation of the general strike in nineteen hundred two were set in law, and new paragraphs were drawn up which would be ratified a decade later, in Saltsjöbaden. Collective wage agreements complying with the conditions of the employers were forced on the trade union associations. Industrial peace was manufactured by banning strike actions for the duration of a wage agreement. The owners were afforded the privilege of hiring and firing workers as they saw fit, and of merging or shutting down factories. In conflict situations, strikebreakers had the right to freely exercise their profession. Not just the union organization but every single worker was henceforth responsible for observing these ordinances. Transgressions were punished by a labor court. The law, said Rogeby, was whatever served the owners of the means of production; crime was anything the workers initiated themselves. When Ström spoke about this era it was as if he had always propounded the arguments of Social Democracy. So durable was the fabric of the Social Democratic Party that all deviations disappeared into it like chance occurrences. He saw no betrayal in the collaborationist policy of the union leadership. They were merely responding to the circumstances. The means of production were in the hands of the capitalists, the economy was booming, attacks against the existing society would have jeopardized their own livelihood. In the Second Chamber, ninety Social Democrats and eight Communists faced off against seventy-three representatives of the Right Party, twenty-seven members of the Farmers' League, and thirty-two Liberals; in the First Chamber, fifty-two Social Democrats and one Communist were dominated by ninety-seven members of the bourgeois parties. If we didn't want all our achievements in social reform to be crushed, said Ström, we had to make concessions on economic matters. The slogans of the Comintern, said Rogeby, class against class, which took aim both at the owners of capital and at Social Democracy, were justified. If war was to be declared on imperialism, then Social Democracy, which had become its handmaid, had to be included. The designation of the Social Democrats as Social Fascists, however, poisoned the atmosphere within the unions. Once again, opinions diverged in the Communist Party as to how the union should go about its business. In the estimations of the Comintern, the capitalist system was facing a worldwide crisis as a consequence of overproduction and unrestrained speculation. The moment of revolutionary possibilities had arrived. A United Front of the working class would be able to bring down imperialism in this weakened state. In the attacks on Social Democracy, however, a strict distinction had to be made between the workers and the leadership. Linderot and Sillén convened a unity committee that was supposed to mobilize the union membership. The group around Flyg and Kilbom, however, were anticipating that the boom would continue. They also considered the opposition too weak to withstand the countermeasures of the Social Democrats. Leading Communists had immediately been shut out, the threat of being excluded from the unions hung over anyone who wanted to join the committee or sympathized with them. Kilbom, and with him the majority of the union functionaries, assumed that the United Front could only be realized in cooperation with the Social Democratic Party. The unions

had to remain intact. The Communist cadres must not be isolated from the members of the other workers' party. It was an impossible dilemma. The Social Democratic leadership was not willing to enter into any alliance, and the Comintern likewise rejected the suggestion of establishing a United Front from above in coalition with the Social Democratic Party leadership, describing it as pacifist and opportunistic. The unity committee, said Ström, did not want to create unity but rather to splinter the national confederation of trade unions. In the group faithful to the Comintern, there was an expectation that the workers would join a front that was formed from the ground up. But few were willing to accept being ejected from the union for joining the opposition, which would mean risking their job. The Comintern pressed for escalated confrontations; Kilbom's group demanded that order be maintained in the unions. Here too, said Rogeby, it was unimaginable that the Party would shatter under the weight of these controversies. The members were sure that the Central Committee would not be willing to endanger the Party in its strengthened position purely in the interests of dogmatism. But instead of further expanding the work of the union, said Ström, the Party severed itself from its base. What played out in the days of October nineteen twenty-nine, he said, no longer had anything to do with Marxist rigor, with discipline, proletarian responsibility. Flyg, the leader of the Party, and Kilbom, editor in chief of the Party paper, with the majority of the Central Committee, the members of parliament, and the union workplace representatives behind them, shut out Sillén, Linderot, and their supporters. Meanwhile, these two, who had been conferred the right to lead the Party by a commission of the Comintern led by Manuilsky and Ulbricht, shut out the majority group. The events that had taken place five years earlier at the instruction of the Comintern were being repeated, but this time, said Ström, in the escalating madness, the coming degeneration within the Soviet Party was beginning to reveal itself. The persecution of dissidents began to take on metaphysical dimensions. On the ninth of October, he said, while the Communists were fighting for their Party headquarters, funds, membership registers, for their newspapers and archives, accompanied by brawls and gunshots, I understood why the workers in this country stuck to the Social Democratic Party. The animosity, said Rogeby, was well-founded. Right to the end, the Social Democrats—and with them, the Communists who tended toward the Social Democratic ideology—had held fast to the belief in the stability of the capitalist economy. In doing so, they had given free reign to developments that could only lead to catastrophe. The formation of the proletarian front had been prevented. Because one side wanted to seize the initiative too quickly, by **281** force, said Ström. While the others, said Rogeby, still believed it was possible to negotiate with the bourgeoisie. While the Social Democrats gave in to the vision of the *folkhemmet*, the people's home, which had been decreed by Per Albin Hansson as a veil for all unresolved problems, and while the Communists tore apart their Party—Kilbom's group took the printers of the *Folkets Dagblad* on Luntmakargatan and Sillén's troop the Party headquarters on Torsgatan, while seven thousand members were gathered in the independent Party and only four thousand remained in the Comintern section, with the other seven thousand lost to Party life for some years—capital, according to the prognosis of the Comintern, had reached the limits of its expansion and was moving toward its own violent redistribution. Once again it was time to disempower the working class, to rob them of their capacity to make demands. Though the efforts to annihilate the Soviet Union had fallen short, they could still harm the workers and their organizations through the production of privation and misery. In the process, the anarchic regime of finance did not spare its own camp. It accepted enormous losses in order to maintain its system. On October third, with plummeting stock prices on Wall Street, the maneuvers had been set in motion that were to lead to the annihilation of the weak and the ultimate triumph of the giants. At first it was those without property who were affected. Unemployment would quickly wear them down, soften them up for subservience. Then the smaller and mid-sized traders and savers were devastated; it was business against business, monopoly against monopoly, concern against concern, trust against trust, until only the strongest remained, snapping up the assets of the bankrupt on the cheap. And the leaders of the workers' parties, blinded in their disunity, gave imperialism yet another deadline to allow it to recover and prepare itself for the ultimate arena of thievery: war.

The existence of a second Communist Party didn't worry him, said Rogeby. It made no difference that the Party of Linderot and Sillén, which he had joined in August of nineteen thirty, was small, for it belonged to a movement that encompassed the entire world. For him, the tussle between rich and poor took place on an international scale. Even later, when the German Party had been shattered and the Soviet one left to devour itself, he saw what was emerging in China, in Indochina. Spain had taught him the endurance of proletarian solidarity, and now that Social Democracy was governing together with the bourgeoisie, he was left with his silent activities in the Swedish underground, looking toward the future. In nineteen thirty, he said, the Party was built anew from the ground up. Though many were still clinging to the middle path of the national Communism offered by Flyg and Kilbom, others found their way back to the Comintern Party. Though they managed to win only one percent of the vote at the elections in the fall—in which Kilbom's Party reached three percent—the rise of fascism in Germany, the formation of national socialist brigades in Sweden, the burgeoning effects of the economic crisis, the special divisions of the secret police for persecuting radical workers, the military attacks on strikers, the growing number of unemployed, the wage cuts and lockouts: all called for a Party capable of organizing resistance. But even in the unions, where almost all the Communist functionaries backed Kilbom, the work had to begin from scratch. The union opposition that had been generated was now being combated both by the reformist leadership and the Communist Party that had remained loyal to the unions. Nevertheless, said Rogeby, we often pulled together for joint campaigns. He thought of the bloodbath in Ådalen. The image flared up alongside the execution of the insurgents of Madrid, alongside Guernica. The brutality took form not in the spectral darkness of Goya or Picasso, which created a unity with the event, but was set against the verdant dawning of a Swedish summer. There was no war raging, no foreign hordes had occupied the land; it was simply that work had been stopped in the sawmills and paper factories in Marma, Graninge, Utansjö, and Sandviken, at the mouth of the Ångerman. And Versteegh, the director of the company, had brought in strikebreakers. At midday on Thursday the fourteenth of May, nineteen thirty-one, eight thousand striking workers—Social Democrats, Communists, all of them union members—gathered together out the front of the workers' club in Frånö to set off on a protest march. Under the shining sun, the procession began to move toward Lund, where the ships of the strikebreakers were berthed in the harbor. Many of the older members walking in the procession were reminded of the great demonstrations of two, three decades earlier. In their Sunday best, with the flags and standards of their union confederations, led out by a wind orchestra, the workers walked along the dirt road, between the glittering stream and the hills with the red wooden houses of the villages and the blossoming apple trees. Just short of their destination, the cavalry and reservist units that had been hurriedly mobilized by the company management were awaiting them. Industry and army stood in alliance across from the collectivity of the workers, who were unarmed, as always, trusting only in their numbers, and a few dozen rifles had them infinitely outmatched. Shortly after two o'clock, Captain Mesterton had the demonstration procession in sight, the people were pacing forward calmly, it wasn't revolution they wanted, but their right to work and a living wage; they couldn't see the rifle barrels that were trained on them. The musical instruments drowned out the command to halt, and the captain gave the order to shoot. Those who were hit fell into the dust of the road, their blood blending with the soil, and it wasn't until a fraction of a second later that the cracks were heard, tearing apart that peaceful spring day. Five workers had been killed. On the side of legality was the captain, who was tasked with ensuring the maintenance of order. On the side of legality were the military conscripts, who had orders to follow. On the side of legality, with the right to freely carry out their profession, were the strikebreakers. On the side of legality were the factory owners, upon whom it was incumbent to prevent economic disruptions in the interests of the greater good. Identical with legality were the capitalist conditions of production, which claimed the lives of Eira Söderberg, Erik Bergström, Viktor Eriksson, Evert Nygren, and Sture Larsson. Because they were a danger to the rule of law, lengthy prison terms were handed out to the Communist agitators Nordström, Sjödin, and Forssman, and Linderot, the leader of the Communist Party, received the same for calling a protest meeting. The union leadership backed the class justice and criminalized the unauthorized actions of the workers. The outrage within the workplaces, though, could not be smothered, leading to the second major crisis of trust in the union movement. In Ådalen, a general strike was proclaimed; in Stockholm, one hundred fifty thousand workers demonstrated on the day of the funeral of their murdered comrades. Right across the country, trade union associations joined the strike in defiance of the union leadership. At the same time though, said Rogeby, the workers were faced with the necessity of getting the Social Democratic Party back into government. The Social Democratic electoral campaign in the year of thirty-two was not launched under a slogan of going on the offensive against the bourgeoisie—riven as it was by corruption scandals—but rather of defaming the two Communist Parties, who for their parts had nothing better to do than to feud with each other. While Kilbom continued his efforts to secure a coalition with the Social Democrats, Linderot's Party continued to attack Social Democracy as the number one enemy, which was a waste of energy on both counts; for in the first instance, Hansson's party was never willing to make concessions, and in the second, it simply drew on all its resources to strike back even harder. Still unified on the factory floors, even if this unity was nothing more than the spontaneous unity of class, the ability of the workers to articulate a position was hindered by the predominance of the sectarian clashes between the two Communist groupuscules. The obstinacy of the Party leaderships meant that this unity couldn't be brought to bear. And so the bourgeoisie was able to wield its terror from government over four terms. It wasn't until September of thirty-two, after the fall of the Kreuger empire, when they failed to cobble together their power with new transactions, that they were forced to step down and hand over the formation of the cabinet to the Social Democrats, who had again managed to secure one hundred four seats thanks to the collective effort of the voters. Even with the two seats of the Comintern Party—corresponding to three percent of the vote—and the six seats of Kilbom's Party, which had received five percent, the Social Democratic Party was still three seats behind the bourgeois parties in the Second Chamber. In that year one hundred sixty thousand were without work, and as the year of fascist rule in Germany began, the number of unemployed was one hundred eighty-six thousand; with their family members, they formed an army of almost a million needy souls. We had no option, said Ström, but to attempt to balance and maneuver between the demand of the workers for gainful employment and the demands of the company owners for increased profit margins. We were at the mercy of international finance, were threatened by German fascism and by the chauvinist apparitions in our own country, had to subsidize the industries to reduce unemployment and bring the negotiations between the confederation of trade unions and business owners to a conclusion in order to stabilize the markets. Under these conditions, only cautious reforms were possible. Yet the Social Democratic government, he continued, was embodying the wishes of the workers. Hansson, the prime minister, had already become the national father figure that Branting had represented. Sandler, the foreign minister, was known as the founder of the Workers' Education Association. Vennerström, the minister of defense, Möller, the minister of social services, and Schlyter, the attorney general, were respected as progressive humanists. Sköld, as minister of agriculture, had helped the agricultural workers to improve their living conditions, and Wigforss, minister of finance, represented the rigor of socialist science. Sandler, said Rogeby, immediately sent a circular to all the trade union confederations, calling for Communist representatives to be purged from all unions, and instead of the schools for future factory managers, instead of the socializations that Wigforss had promised, there was only an expansion of the power of the state. Before we could speak about any kind of workers' participation, said Ström, we had to create the economic foundations for it, in the form of state and union funds. Through their eternal willingness to compromise, said Rogeby, the Social Democrats had allowed the bourgeois groups to become so strong again that in June of thirty-six they were able to regain control of the government. But only until September, countered Ström, then we won it back, with an absolute majority for the first time, and we've retained the leadership to this day. He didn't attribute any significance to the recent rise of the Comintern Party; the eighteen thousand members that they now numbered evaporated in the face of the hundreds of thousands in the Social Democratic Party. What were their five seats and the six seats of Kilbom's Party worth, he said, next to the one hundred twelve seats, with which we, all on our own, outnumbered the three bourgeois parties by five seats. The sixteen seats that the conflict-plagued bloc of workers' parties had over the bourgeois factions didn't change the economic situation one bit. The means of production were in the hands of the owners of capital, and there they would stay, even if we did manage to reach parity in the First Chamber. Nevertheless, said Ström, with the reforms we had pushed through—the unemployment insurance, the retirement laws, the regulation of working hours for agricultural workers, the child support, the rent relief for large families, the homes for the elderly, the obligatory two weeks of vacation—we were on the way to becoming the model welfare state. In the early thirties, said Rogeby, Hansson's crisis program had been geared toward tying the working class more tightly to the Social Democratic Party. The complex links between the Social Democratic state apparatus and monopoly capital became evident in December of thirty-eight, when the partnership between the wage laborers and company owners was sealed in Saltsjöbaden. That the state avoided passing legislation did not contradict this bond; rather, the seeming autonomy and equality with which the employers and employees would henceforth sit down together to address any conflicts that might arise emphasized the harmony that was now supposed to prevail. The bourgeois mixed economy of Social Democracy provided a stable backdrop to the quest for industrial peace. Generously, the buyers of labor agreed to give prior notice before layoffs, which had previously taken place without any warning at all, and to refrain from the use of strikebreakers in the event of a strike. In all other matters, as always, they retained sole control over the management and distribution of labor, the expansion or downscaling of production. The ban on strikes for the duration of a collective bargaining agreement—supposedly to protect the rights of a third party, the consumer—benefitted the business owner, since it meant they could rely on a fixed core of workers while restructuring and

improving the efficiency of their factories. The path to prosperity had been paved. The employer gave the worker work; the worker took their wage, which was rising gradually, öre by öre, though never keeping pace with the piece quotas. The Social Democratic Party reached its greatest number of votes and now occupied one hundred thirty-four seats in the Second Chamber and seventy-four in the First Chamber, where, with the help of a single Communist seat, it had become as strong as the bourgeois factions. Kilbom's Party, which had called itself the Socialist Party since thirty-four, had already lost ten thousand of its fifteen thousand members when, in early thirty-seven, a rupture occurred between him—who was hoping to return to the Social Democratic Party—and Flyg, whose national Communism became a national socialism financed by Germany. The share of votes of the Communists faithful to the Comintern remained unchanged at around three percent. Faced with this vanishing minority, Ström could look back on his decision with satisfaction. His face good-natured, well-meaning. When he now looked out beyond the borders of his rich country, it was not to catch a glimpse of the vision of socialism, but to look hopefully for signs of life within the French-English bloc. The thought of the possibility of a clash with the countries which would one day rise up from colonial oppression and demand their share of global goods didn't occur to him. He who had once turned to revolutionary ideas only to then turn back—as the bourgeoisie of nineteen fifteen had correctly guessed—to the forces seeking to protect the structures of society, now stood confidently beside the old guard at the gate of the famous Swedish welfare state. Thus, at Rogeby's place, in his room on Coldinutrappan, looking out onto the leafless Piper garden, I gained a perspective on the Social Democratic syndrome. At its core was that per-

severance at all costs, that terror in the face of fundamental change. Ström would say that this patience had been able to abolish a whole range of social injustices. He would emphasize the democratic freedoms in his land when compared with the Soviet regime. He would credit the humanist traditions of his party with having prevented fascism from further pervading the minds of the people, and he would portray its pacifist stance, which had been subjected to so much pressure, as the guarantee for the endurance of the country's neutrality. If Rogeby countered that no reforms had eliminated the unequal opportunities of education and occupational choices, then Ström would say that the Party was striving to remedy the lingering bourgeois dominance in the universities. He would speak of the adult education centers, as if they were responses to a transitional situation and not institutions for the retention of class society, and he would mention that numerous writers and artists from proletar-   **287**
ian backgrounds had long ago made cultural values into a common good. To the question of the fulfillment of the specific goals of the workers, Ström would respond that the Party had contributed to an expansion of the concept of class. They had managed to draw in a broad spectrum of intellectuals, academics, and functionaries and to convey a new social affiliation to this group which had previously been dependent upon the bourgeoisie. In a certain sense, Rogeby would have agreed with this, for revolutionary changes could no longer be carried out solely by a working class destined to assume a revolutionary role but by all the progressive forces within the populace banding together. But Social Democracy, said Rogeby, had failed to insist upon the right of the workers to participate in decision-making and to play a leadership role in all branches of production. By rooting out radicalism and leaving property relations untouched, they became a conservative force. In the grass roots of the Party, he said, you could find workers with the qualities that had once defined the Social Democratic organizations. But the top was pervaded everywhere by petit-bourgeois aspiration, holding down those who wanted to actively intervene and expand their own research and knowledge. Because such workers could not bring themselves to bear within Social Democracy, which had become a mere employee lobby group, said Rogeby, their place was in the Communist Party. Though here they would also be subjected to a form of constriction that would cut against their personal development. While Social Democracy promoted the depoliticization of their members, the Communist Party held theirs back with outdated dogma. We had replaced the dictatorship of the proletariat with a politics of alliances. Our work in the German underground and in Spain had shown us that the

character of a fighting unit could not be judged by its class affiliation but only according to the convictions to which it attests. When we spoke of class consciousness, we meant joining forces with the most oppressed and collectively revolting against the mechanisms of exploitation. With all the insufficiencies and theoretical quarrels, the lack of critical reflection in light of their misjudgment of German fascism, their subservience to the doctrine of the Comintern, said Rogeby, the essential difference between the two parties lay in the fact that the Communists kept historical consciousness alive, while the Social Democrats, by undoing their ties to the class struggle, robbed the workers of all history. What kept Rogeby and other Communists alive, despite their isolation, were the traditions that lived within them. In contrast to those who found their nourishment in the junk products of bourgeois civilization, they clung tight to their tasks. They resisted becoming alienated from their work, as capitalism wanted them to, in order to get its hands on a steady supply of malleable stooges. The lack of solidarity among the workers and the crippling of their original intentions could be sensed in every factory. The faces of the people standing at the machines were marked by an expression of numbness and emptiness. While the conversations at Brecht's house began from the assumption of a culture that had already been liberated, the place I occupied with Rogeby was miles away from what we understood as culture; we had to traverse a path leading through regions that left one lot with burning legs, bones ground to stubs, lungs heaving, so that the others could position themselves around us as outstanding and responsible planners, protectors, and patrons, as well-to-do windbags and friends of the people. We have already come so far, the foremen cried to us, and the upper levels remained diffuse, where the principle of maximum profit demanded the unending existence of enfeebled masses and a powerful few.

The composition of the notes documenting these conversations was dictated as if by a chorus. It was not just Rogeby's or Ström's voices I heard but the voices of all those who were named, who had appeared and were now taking on form. I began my new occupation as a chronicler who reproduced collective thought. Books, picked up from the library, lay in piles on my table, and I filled in the blanks of the things that I had vaguely intuited. To begin with I found nothing more than scarcely visible signposts appearing in a thicket, but from these points I could make measurements, draw connections, from which I gained a rough notion of expansive, previously unknown realms. From now on, my consciousness was filled with the process of writing, which included registering impulses, statements, recalled images, moments of action; everything that had come before had been a preparatory exercise, all the hesitation, all the fragments and ambiguities, the seething monologues, became the medium in which my thoughts and reflections resonated. I gained a glimpse into a mechanism that sifted and filtered, that brought apparently unconnected elements together into segments, that organized what I had heard and experienced into sentences, that was continually searching for formulations, striving for clarity, ceaselessly forging ahead to new heights of vividness. The moment I woke up first thing in the morning and during my hours in the factory, I was exposed to combinations of words that I jotted down once I was back in my room during those days of melting snow. The monstrous gulf between those of us who were bound to the time clock, where we punched in each day, and those who were able to dedicate themselves independently to literature, to art, was no longer agonizing; it was instead as if the very pressure of real conditions had suggested to me the things that I wanted to express. Because I found something universal in translating the material that was rooted in the language of this country into my own language, the gulf between the languages vanished, and the language that I used became nothing more than an instrument, an element in a global science. While I carted the tin ingots, heated up the ovens, lowered the centrifuges into the acid baths, I fitted together pieces of the recent history of Sweden, turned my mind to Engelbrekt and sketched out the concluding scenes of the epic, even if Brecht had entirely lost interest in it. Engelbrekt had to set off on his journey. From the castle with its four squat, round towers, surrounded by expanses of water, he had to be carried to the stepped slope of the shoreline, to the landing steps, and lifted up into the long, narrow, tarred rowboat that was tethered there. The boat could not stay in Örebro; it had to be pushed away from the stone and steered under the bridge, down the Svartån toward Lake Hjälmaren. It was the morning of the twenty-seventh of April, fourteen thirty-six. Along with a number of faithful followers, the annals recounted that Engelbrekt was accompanied by his wife, whose name was unknown and who was otherwise never mentioned. To the rhythmic beat of the oars, the boat glided past the banks and the freight ships sitting beside their forts. Engelbrekt had not been ill enough to stay in his castle and yet was too weak not to sense an uneasiness, a chill shiver, at the thought of the purpose of his journey, his meeting with the Council of the Realm in Stockholm. The boat could not turn back; it had to set out onto open waters. Spring was beginning, a yellow-green shimmer had been deposited upon the skeletons of the trees. In the evening, the boat landed on an island in the strait, perhaps Västra Sundholm, Valen, or one of the other small skerries. The cliff climbed up on an incline, and the oarsmen appeared from behind, carrying Engelbrekt on a stretcher. They made a place to sleep out of fir branches, Engelbrekt was put to bed, a fire lit. One of the men pointed back into the darkness, said there were lights there, on the southern shore, over there, toward Castle Göksholm, of the House of Night and Day. Shortly afterward, as they were eating their meal, the sentinel called out that a boat was approaching from the other shore. They probably want to invite us over to stay with them, said Engelbrekt, to reciprocate my hospitality; bring them over. The sounds of the boat landing, the clattering of the oars, then footsteps, ominous jangling. Måns Bengtsson appeared, in full armor, a

battle-axe in his hand, followed by archers with crossbows. Engelbrekt got up with a groan, stood hunched forward, leaning on his crutches, ready to greet the squire amicably. When Bengtsson failed to say anything, Engelbrekt thanked him for his visit and explained once more that he could not stop in at his family's house, since he had to set off early the next morning. I have come, said Bengtsson, to put an end to your journey; and Engelbrekt's wife, staring at him, placed her hand over her mouth in horror. For otherwise, cried Bengtsson, we will never have peace, and he raised his axe. Peace, Engelbrekt managed to get out during an infinite moment, but we have secured peace. Then time was split by the slash of the axe. Engelbrekt raised his crutch in defense, the honed iron hit his hand, knocking off three fingers. Engelbrekt turned to his screaming wife, Måns Bengtsson raised his arms once more, and the weapon whistled down onto Engelbrekt's throat. As he tumbled forward he was caught by the third blow, on his bare head. The soldiers shot at the small band; Engelbrekt's body was also perforated by arrows. The dead and the still living, Engelbrekt's wife among them, were dragged up the slope, Engelbrekt by his feet, drenched in blood, one hand clamped around the handle of his crutch, and then pulled down into the depths. And, after this fall, the ascent to the concluding image, one that showed nothing of the people, only the elite, in all their power, once again front and center. On a wide pedestal in the middle, the three bishops, Thomas of Strängnäs, Sigge of Skara, and Knut Bosson Night and Day of Linköping, in glittering regalia, shrouded by the smoke of swinging thuribles. They held up the parchment letter with the list of all the privileges they and the worldly lords had assigned themselves. The cluster of seals dangling from it. To their right stood Lord High Constable Karl Knutsson Bonde, the brothers

Nils, Bo, and Bengt Stensson Night and Day, Måns Bengtsson Night and Day, Nils Erengislesson and Erengisle Nilsson Hammarstad, Bo Knutsson Grip, and Magnus Gren; to the left, Krister Nilsson Vasa, Knut Karlsson Örnfot, Gustav Algotsson Sture, Knut Jönsson Tre Rosor, Karl Magnusson and Greger Magnusson Eka, Magnus Birgersson and Guse Nilsson Båt, along with Nils Jönsson Oxenstierna. And then there were Engelbrekt's comrades in arms Herman Berman, Gotskalk Bengtsson and Bengt Gotskalksson Ulv, Johan Karlsson Färla, Claus Lange, and Arvid Svan. Only Plata and Puke were missing. That which stood up there in iron and silver, in purple robes, presenting itself as the ultimate unity, was riven by jealousy, avarice, and bloodlust, concealed bitter feuds for the greatest estates, the strongest castles, the most important posts, the throne; and behind them, in the windows of the gable-fronted houses, the haute bourgeoisie, dressed in velvet and furs, were awaiting their share of the spoils.   **291**
A prisoner was then hurled at their feet, a peasant, his arms and legs bound with ropes, followed by a second. There they are, the last of them, cried Bengt Stensson Night and Day, they wanted to set fire to Göksholm while we were paying a visit to the knight Nils Erengislesson. They wanted to avenge a certain Engelbrekt. Who was Engelbrekt, cried Karl Knutsson, to bawdy laughter. Never heard of any Engelbrekt. A nobody, like this lot here, he said, pointing at the prisoners. One of them sat up. Hans Mårtensson is my name. One of the soldiers below dealt him a blow with a lance. You are nameless, cried Karl Knutsson. My name is, said the peasant once more, and fell down under the weight of another blow. My name is, said the other prisoner as well, and: your name is nothing, yelled Karl Knutsson, and the lances rained down on the peasant. Each of them is to have a hand and a foot hacked off, ordered the lord high constable. Hans Mårtensson stood up. Engelbrekt's murderers, he cried, had fled to the knight Erengislesson. For him, ordered Karl Knutsson, both hands and both feet. Where are the people, cried Krister Nilsson Vasa, where are they, they were making so much noise just a moment ago. We are they, said Mårtensson, bleeding from his nose and mouth. Uproarious laughter. Away with them, cried the bishops Sigge, Knut, and Thomas. The peasants were dragged away, Engelbrekt's wife was shoved in, her hands bound behind her back. It's the wife of Engelbrekt, cried Färla. She spat at him. A soldier slapped her. Into the tower with her, cried Färla. No, let her walk, cried Bengt Stensson, may she ramble across the countryside, never finding peace, ostracized, with nowhere to take refuge. I have taken Englikohof. And I've got Tjurbo, cried Knutsson Grip. Then I get Snäfringe and Siende, said Karlsson Örnfot. No, cried Grip, they should go to me as

well. No, me, cried Örnfot. Karl Knutsson waved impatiently for the woman to be taken away. Take her into the soldiers' quarters first, cried Berman. Bellowing laughter. Then Claus Plata and Erik Puke were tossed in, in chains. Silence. So you two wanted to band together against us, said Karl Knutsson. You weren't content with Kastelholm and Tälje, Puke, with Rasbo Hundare and Rossvik in Rekarne, what more did you want. Are you listening to me, Puke. Puke kept his head bowed. A soldier wrenched his chin up. You wanted to get rid of us, cried Karl Knutsson. You and your father, you were waiting to take in this cripple, what was his name again, and to continue on with him to Stockholm. You had called upon the peasants in Rekarne to fight. But he didn't come, he yelled. I get Rossvik, yelled Guse Nilsson Båt. And Tälje returns to me, cried Bengt Stensson Night and Day. And I'm taking over Kastelholm, yelled Karl Knutsson Bonde. Your power will be taken from you, said Claus Plata. Shrill laughter. To the rack with him, disembowel him, quarter him, cried Svan, Berman, and Färla. So it shall be, said Karl Knutsson. And this one here, he said, pointing at Puke, shall be treated according to the privileges to which he is entitled. I renounce the privileges of my birth, cried Puke. You who call yourself Bonde, *peasant*, he said, you who are the greatest tormentor of the peasants—let me die like a peasant, on the wheel, at the stake. He'll go to the scaffold, said Knutsson. And we shall invite everybody to the festivities, where they can watch on stage how a head that refuses to think right falls under the swing of the sword. And he waved, and Plata and Puke were dragged out, with a few more blows for good measure. And the aristocrats who had been carried to victory by the people strained skyward, stood there backed by the bourgeoisie of finance, the way rulers always stand there, smiling distortedly with clenched teeth. They stood there with feet spread wide, the earth solid beneath them; it would be a long time before it would fall out from under them. They raised themselves up in splendor, the owners of the soil, the buildings, and the heavens, around them a hissing and slapping of birch rods accompanied by groaning and whimpering, and Karl Knutsson Bonde raised his voice once more, praise be to justice, may the land be cleansed of the revolters. Wherever one of theirs is still to be found, may he be slain like a rabid dog. Peace be to us. Triumphal chorus of the nobles and bourgeoisie, freedom and peace, broken up by the beating of the birches, the cries of agony, peace, and beating and crying, and peace, freedom and peace.

Serfdom, however, was something the Swedish peasants were spared. Though they had been conquered, feudalism was unable to carry out its ultimate violence on them. Never again would they allow themselves to be cast back into the humiliation that held sway before Engelbrekt's great campaign. What fell into oblivion and lay covered over, swamped by new struggles, rose up time and again as confidence, as a strengthening of consciousness, until it became the foundations of the workers' movement. Brecht wasn't listening to me. He was pacing back and forth between the tables. Steffin was arranging manuscripts, diaries, notebooks, newspaper clippings, slips of paper into piles. Inside the house, Weigel, her friend Lazar, Santesson, and the children were making a racket with the furniture, drawers were being pulled out, stuffed rucksacks and suitcases dragged down the stairs. Brecht had been utterly abandoned by sobriety. Hodann, Goldschmidt, Ljungdal, Matthis, and Branting stood helpless in the face of the terror emanating from the forty-two-year-old, who had otherwise always been capable of accepting the necessity of a hasty departure. It was as if only he had been affected by the catastrophe, as if he alone had to bear the burden of persecution. But it was his work that he was worried about. Here lay everything that he had written during his seven years of exile, most of it unpublished. Here lay the value that would confirm his standing in literature. He was almost unknown, ignored; few understood him, even in the Party that he supported. And following the liquidation of his Soviet advocates Tretyakov and Koltsov, he was shown nothing but mistrust and rejection by the first workers' state. He still had to provide the proof that his thinking was crucial for the development of the literary craft. This enormous store of material had to be salvaged. Tuesday, the ninth of April. We heard the news at seven o'clock in the morning. German troops were in Copenhagen. The city had capitulated. Fighting had broken out on the Norwegian coast. Squadrons of bombers were flying over Oslo. A German attack on Sweden was expected. German cruisers were stationed at the maritime borders. There were German freight steamers berthed at the docks on the river that could not be boarded and that might have had weapons hidden on board, under cover of national sovereignty. Sweden still had not mobilized; only an increased readiness had been ordered, but Branting, like other members of parliament and of the government, had made preparations to leave; a plane, it was said, stood ready for those whose safety was under threat. Because the American visa for him and his family had not yet arrived, a few weeks ago Brecht had received an invitation from the writer Wuolijoki to go to Finland. Branting and Ström had secured the necessary papers for him, but the real question was whether a ship would still set sail for Helsinki. Brecht had made the decision to leave

Sweden in March, when the woman who owned the house had run in panting to announce that some officers from the security service were there to see him. They wanted to know if he was hiding a Communist, a woman by the name of Rosenbaum. It was only after ascertaining that this woman was in fact Steffin, who had earlier taken the name Rosenbaum through marriage, and after a guarantee from Swedish friends had been given and doctor's certificates confirming her pulmonary ailment were provided that the warrant for her arrest was revoked. Even during that first visit the police had shown an interest in the books on the shelves, the newspapers and writings lying around, though not before clarifying the question of the position Steffin occupied in his household, and whether Brecht paid her a wage, which because he was a foreigner he was forbidden to do, and by receiving which she, a foreigner herself, would

also have been committing a crime, no, no, they explained, she was like a member of the family, received no wage, lived in a furnished room in the neighborhood, although yes, Brecht did pay for the rent. It seemed likely that they would be back, and so Brecht had a portion of his political literature packed into boxes and taken to the plumber Andersson, who lived on the other side of Lövstigen and was willing to store the dangerous goods in his cellar. There were discussions about what was to be done with the other books. Ljungdal had called the royal library and offered them Brecht's collection, which they had rejected. I was tasked with packing a selection of books and sending them on to Brecht when he reached Finland; the remaining items were to be taken by Santesson and the young doctor Ek who lived nearby. Greid, who Brecht summoned during the night by telephone, wailed that now all was truly lost, hysterical, ruffling his hair, unintentionally caricaturing Brecht in the process. And yet he wanted to accompany Brecht on his trip, along with Ljungdal. If she managed to escape to Sweden, Berlau—who had gone to Denmark shortly beforehand to work in a theater—was to join them in Finland. The plan was to travel on—a prospect that made Brecht tremble—through the Soviet Union to the United States; or, should this prove impossible, to Mexico or Haiti. The thought of what would become of us others and all those interned, those living in illegality, was of no importance. The only consideration now was what Brecht could take with him on his journey. The most important manuscripts, notebooks, and journals were placed in a black seaman's chest along with an extremely pared-down selection of books. In the list I wrote down the *Georgics* by Publius Vergilius Maro, in the translation by Voss; the epic *On the Nature of Things*, by Titus Lucretius Carus, in the version by Knebel, from the year eighteen twenty-one; a collection of poems by Ovid and Catullus, in an edition for use in schools, published in eighteen eighty-two by Teubner, Leipzig; *The Metamorphoses* by Publius Ovidius Naso, printed in Berlin by Mylius, seventeen ninety-one; Plutarch's *Lives*, in a leather-bound volume from the publisher Langen Müller, dated nineteen thirteen; *The Satires of Juvenal*, published by Langenscheidt; Pindar's *Victory Odes*, put out by Diederichs, nineteen twelve; *Panegyric in Praise of Trajan* by Plinius Secundus, published in Leipzig, seventeen ninety-six; *The Letters of Plinius*, in an edition from eighteen twenty-nine; *The Letters of Cicero*, from the publishing house Langen Müller, nineteen twelve; a volume of Aesop, Hesiod, and Quintus, from the Langenscheidt Library; two volumes of Quintus Horatius Flaccus, with satires and odes; the *Annals and Histories* by Tacitus; two rebound, tattered volumes of Homer, published by Cotta; a collection of the writings of Confucius, translated into English by Waley; also by Waley a translation of poems by Li Po and an anthology of Chinese poetry; a popular edition of Hölderlin's poetry by Cotta; the poems of Shelley; *Tristram Shandy* by Sterne; *Ulysses* by Joyce, in two paper-bound volumes by Odyssey Press, Paris, from nineteen thirty-nine; *The Fateful Adventures of the Good Soldier Švejk during the World War* by Hašek, three volumes; Grieg's piece on the Paris Commune, *Nederlaget*, the title underlined, with an exclamation mark added; and then *The Commune*, by Margueritte; *The Paris Commune*, by Jellinek; *Histoire de la commune*, by Lissagaray; and *The Paris Commune: Accounts and Documents from Contemporaries*, published in Berlin in nineteen thirty-one. Some books, which Brecht didn't think he could go without, were to be stashed in other suitcases, to ensure it didn't get too heavy; the only things that could still be packed in the seaman's chest were his little radio, the three painted Japanese face masks, the camera, a silver canteen, a collection of knives and his Chinese parchment picture, fastened to two bamboo poles. The skeptic was curled up, with his bristling beard, sitting and tugging his robe around himself, staring angrily, yet inspired. To a suitcase that Weigel and the children had already half-filled with items of clothing, Brecht added the *Confessions of Saint Augustine*, bound in leather; the *Ulenspiegel* by de Coster, from Borngräber Verlag; *The Social Contract* by Rousseau, in a little Reclam edition; a few cheap editions of Descartes, Kant, and Taine; Herodotus's *Histories of the Oriental Kings*, published by Ullstein; Kleist's *Collected Works*, from Verlag Bong; the short stories of Poe; *Barrack-Room Ballads* by Kipling; *Disraeli* by Maurois, published in nineteen twenty-eight by Fischer; Emil Ludwig's book about Hindenburg, titled *The Sage of the*

German Republic, Querido Verlag, nineteen thirty-five; the *Chess Manual*, by Dufresne; and the *Tobacco Book* by Cudell, expensively bound by Verlag Neuerburg, nineteen twenty-seven, with the chapters "The Introduction of Tobacco to Europe," and "The Culture of Tobacco Consumption." On top, probably because the book had reminded him of the necessity of smoking, he placed two packets of Batavia brand cigars, each packet containing twenty-five cigars and costing seven kronor fifty, a day's wage for me. Wherever there was a sliver of space in the suitcases and cardboard boxes that were to be sent to Helsinki, in which Weigel was stashing copper bowls, teapots, pots, and frying pans, Brecht stuffed books which he pulled from the piles that we had stacked up all over the place. While I was dismantling the library I noticed that the volumes were ordered neither alphabetically nor according to subjects, yet they were clearly not arranged without rules, but rather according to relationships of affinity, a system of mutual sympathies or of relation through argument. Often hefty contrasts resided side by side, which could then lead to unexpected, covert agreements. Brecht appreciated Kafka because Kafka didn't mind if a book received its conclusion or not, because he had left most things unfinished, lending a flawless completion to the fragmentary itself. With *The Trial* and the novel *Amerika* in his hand, sticking the books between the casts of his face in plaster and ore, he said that in actual fact it was only the fragment that bears the imprint of authenticity, because it comes closest to the most intimate function of production, namely a production that reflected breath, bare being, and gave expression to a fleeting period of consciousness that had just been lived through. Kafka lived beside Goldsmith's *The Vicar of Wakefield*, in an Erfurt edition from eighteen thirty-nine; Thackeray's *Book of Snobs*, from Reclam Verlag; *Les Fleurs du mal* by Baudelaire; *My Prisons* and *My Hospitals* by Verlaine; *The Ballad of Reading Gaol* by Wilde in a German translation by Schölermann; the dramatic poem *Manfred*, by Byron, in Seubert's translation; *Malte Laurids Brigge* and *The Book of Hours*, by Rilke; *The Last Days of Mankind*, by Kraus, published by Verlag Die Fackel; the collection of poems *Burning Earth*, by Mühsam; and the *Songs of a Silesian Miner* by Bezruč, from Kurt Wolff Verlag, on the one side, and on the other, *An Essay Concerning Human Understanding* by Locke, two volumes; *The New Organon* by Francis Bacon; *On the Improvement of the Understanding* by Spinoza; *Letters for the Advancement of Humanity* by Herder; *Phädon: or, On the Immortality of the Soul*, by Mendelssohn; *The Expression of the Emotions in Man and Animals* by Darwin, printed in Stuttgart, eighteen seventy-seven; and a volume of Freud, *On the Technique of Psychoanalysis*. All of these works were actually notebooks, full of underlining, annotations, at times Brecht would forget the panic of his exodus, began to read, showed us Goncourt's book about Gavarni, the two tomes of Brueghel's pictures, or the biography of the Viennese actor Alexander Girardi. He couldn't part with this goliard and comedian, who came from the provincial stages and had appeared in lowbrow farces and operettas. His Torelli in *Artist's Blood*, the singspiel, he said, must have been Kafka's inspiration for his characterization of the painter Titorelli in *The Trial*. The thin volume published by Deutsche Verlags-Anstalt in nineteen hundred five also had to go into the seaman's chest, as did *Jewish Theater*, selected by Eliasberg, nineteen nineteen, *The Sagas of Classical Antiquity*, by Schwab, and the small Reclam edition on the *Bänkelgesang* before Goethe. The literature related to the Caesar novel was packed in a special crate. It consisted of the two volumes by Mommsen, *Roman History*, published in eighteen fifty-seven; the book by Meyer, *Caesar's Monarchy and the Principate of Pompey*, in which Brecht had written his name all the way back in nineteen nineteen; the three volumes of Ferrero, *The Greatness and Decline of Rome*, in an edition from nineteen twenty-one; the Danish book by Brandes, *Cajus Julius Caesar*, which bore the stamp of the Svenborg Public Library; as well as the work by Bang that Ström had mentioned, *Catilina: En portraetskitse paa kulturhistorisk baggrund*; Weinstock's version of Sallust, titled *The Century of Revolution*, published in nineteen thirty-nine; *The Twelve Caesars* by Suetonius, translated by Stahr; Appian's *Roman History*, published by Langen Müller Verlag, nineteen eleven; *Roman Agrarian History* by Weber; *Letters from Cicero's Time*, edited by Bardt, Leipzig, nineteen thirty; *Cicero through the Centuries* by Zielinski, eighteen ninety-seven; and the play *Catalina* by Ibsen, from the Copenhagen Library. We had put together a list of the names of the politicians, generals, and industrialists, these enumerations conveyed to us something of the compulsive violence that threatened our thinking; the books on the other hand—every one of them—opened up a path, leading here or there, the books were our allies in the struggle against hostile forces. And yet it was the hour of their burial. They had to be lowered into the boxes. Many had accompanied Brecht since his youth. Time and again he hesitated, held up a work by Grosz, *The Face of the Ruling Classes*, *The System of Nature* by Mirabaud, his volumes of Hegel, his Leibniz, his Lichtenberg, wanted to explain his connection to this book or that one, wanted to read something out, but people yelled out, urging him to hurry. The contraband was over at the plumber's,

Trotsky, *The Real Situation in Russia*, *The History of the Russian Revolution*, *My Life*, *Literature and Revolution*, *Germany: The Key to the International Situation*, *The Soviet Union and the Fourth International*, *Stalinism and Bolshevism*; Zinoviev, *History of the Communist Party of the Soviet Union*; Bukharin, *Imperialism and the Accumulation of Capital*, *The ABC of Communism*; the writings of Rosa Luxemburg, of Spinoza, and *Dialectical Materialism* by Thalheimer; the complete works of Korsch; the trial reports from Moscow; and packed in with them, Marx, Engels, Lassalle, and Bebel, along with Lenin's *Selected Works* and a few volumes of Stalin. Brecht brought over the thick German dictionary by Grimm, which he just couldn't do without, and he wanted to take the *Encyclopædia Britannica* as well, which would take up two boxes all on its own, and I had to promise to at least send the German-English and

English-German dictionaries straight away, with their black-and-red dust covers. And then, in the midst of the chaos, the two secret police officers showed up in the doorway, displaying their order to search the house. They were taken aback when, upon asking to see our papers, they found themselves face-to-face with Branting, who asked them derisively if the right-wing military coup had now been carried out. My personal details, my address, my place of work were taken down, they hinted that in the near future I should expect an interrogation. And once again, this moment in which danger edged closer to me was strangely free of fear; I saw myself, as I had discussed with Rosner, on the trek to Lapland; I would pass myself off as a forester, with sparingly used Swedish no one would suspect me of being a foreigner, everything I wanted to take with me could fit in a small bag or in the pockets of my jacket. The officers asked about political publications. Agitated, Brecht yelled at them that he only stored his artistic property here. He positioned himself in front of the stacks of books as if seeking to protect them with his body; his face was a greenish white, distorted by disgust. He followed every movement of their hands in the pages of a book; careful with that, he cried in his mishmash of Danish and Swedish, don't lick your thumb. Matthis attempted to placate him; he pushed him back and said in German that here too, barbarism was now descending upon literature. Hodann and Goldschmidt had retreated into the corner under the balcony, Goldschmidt sat tiredly, sunken in the leather armchair, which did not belong to Brecht but to Steffin, and which was supposed to go to Hodann, along with the rustic chairs, tables, and chests brought from Denmark in furniture trucks, except for the ones that had been assigned to Santesson. Lazar and Weigel stood clasping one another, the children beside them. Lazar was still expressing her outrage that the officers were not familiar with her pen name, Esther Grenen. I was married to a son of Strindberg and Frida Uhl, she yelled, but one of the officers just waved her off. Only Steffin continued working calmly, placed the bundled papers into numbered folders made of gray cardboard. The police officers could not find anything that seemed suspicious. Finally they paused for a moment, flicking through Sandström's book about the North's first epoch as a great power, depicted for young and old, while we lowered Grimmelshausen and Cervantes, Petronius, Benedetto Croce, and Machiavelli into their common grave; in they went, crammed next to Boccaccio, Savonarola, and Erasmus. What a fidgeting, giggling throng in the darkness; on top of them came Marlowe, Ben Jonson, and Shakespeare, how their blank verses rolled, how the figures they created proliferated, what a world of power and hellish descents enveloped them; Villon and Rabelais and Swift lay down on top of them, no end to the ghostly laughter, the gallows spectacle, the wild dreams; and Goethe came to rest next to the unforgiving Schiller, who shielded him from Novalis, Grabbe, Lenz, and Büchner; Blake was lifted up once more, no burial place could do him justice, but Keats, Burns, and De Quincey consoled him; and Diderot, Voltaire, and Stendhal followed, reminiscing on their melancholic adventures they sprawled beside Hoffmann, Kierkegaard, and Heine; and Hugo, Balzac, and Zola crashed down violently; they had to deal with the fact that Sue too came to join them, and Lesage, and the bedraggled Bretonne, and poor old Nerval, who had hanged himself from a streetlamp; and they also had to accept being outshone by Rimbaud, lying in the desert dust. With Stevenson and Melville, an age surged toward us whose breath was already pervading our present; this age was an ocean which also carried Defoe, Marryat, and Conrad. And Gogol came too, accompanied by Goncharov, Pushkin, Tolstoy, and Gorky; with Jessenin, Blok, and Mandelstam falling beside them, and the howling Mayakovsky, tearing himself apart; and the two-faced Ehrenburg was lowered down, who saw almost everyone fall around him yet was able to protect himself, blessed be he, who would have been worthless as a dead man but who alive would one day be able to bear witness. Now they came from all sides, the chorus leaders Hauptmann, Nexø, Rolland, and Wedekind; the trombone players, Heym, Trakl, and Loerke; the whistlers and drummers, Dehmel, Mombert, and Werfel, Kantorowicz, Kaiser, Pinthus, and Sternheim, announcing the death of an old epoch, the birth of a new one; and Brecht was already with them, he was a survivor, in terrifying proximity to the silence surrounding Toller, Ossietzky, and Tucholsky, and around Mühsam, who they strangled, strung up in the lavatory in Oranienburg. And Lorca came from a sandy pit on the edge of the village of Víznar, near Granada, drenched in blood; along came Horváth, who was so anxious that he preferred climbing all the steps in a hotel to taking the elevator and who, in broad daylight, with a brief gust of wind on the Champs-Élysées, was decapitated by the falling branch of a tree; and Roth, killed by desperation and drink in the expanses of Paris, where Döblin, Feuchtwanger and Arnold Zweig, Heinrich Mann and Benjamin, Polgar, Neumann, Frank, and all the other drifters and homeless, the outcasts and the defamed, waited for a visa to go somewhere; and there was Broch, who scraped by in New York on poor relief and the outlandish Lasker-Schüler, dancing at the Wailing Wall in Jerusalem; and old Marieluise Fleisser, holed up in Ingolstadt; and Jahnn, playing the organ on the island of Bornholm, hoping the Germans would take him for a Dane; and Musil, alone and starving in Zurich; and all the travelers, Kisch, Olden and Graf, Bredel and Renn, Regler, Klaus Mann, Seghers and Uhse, on the way to Haiti, to Mexico. And now and then, lone individuals who didn't fit anywhere tumbled toward us, Cabet with his book about the ideal communist realm of Icaria, published by Dreiländerverlag; Thomas More, with his *Utopia*, published by Rascher in Zurich in nineteen twenty; More, the heretic, had lingered in the Tower, where he was decapitated; Weitling, one of the first German theorists of Communism, member of the League of the Outlaws, then of the League of the Just, founder of the magazine *Republik der Arbeiter* [Republic of the Workers], with a few tattered books, prison poetry, and *Humanity: As It Is and as It Should Be*; or Gregor Gog, present in a small book, *Prelude to a Philosophy of the Road*, with Verlag der Vagabunden, from nineteen twenty-eight. And where, we asked ourselves, should we put the magazines, *Die Neue Zeit* [The New Era], from eighteen eighty-three through to November nineteen seventeen, *Der Jüngste Tag* [Judgment Day], *Die Fackel* [The Torch], *Die Weltbühne* [The World Stage], *Die Linkskurve* [The Left Curve], *Die Sammlung* [The Collection], *Die Zukunft* [The Future], *Das Wort* [The Word], what to do with these inscriptions, these impressions of the history of half a century, this writing on the wall; now, a new decade was dawning, the decade of total deracination, *Deinon* was beginning, Brecht's teeth chattered in fear. Briefly, I had the narrow, green, leather-bound volume of the *Divina Commedia* open, with its bible-paper pages; it was the same edition from Cotta that I read with Heilmann and Coppi in Berlin. Finally I was able to check my recollection of the lines about the noise that arose, about the moaning and the woe and the howling reverberating through the air all around, the various languages, the harrowing babble, the cries of pain and wrath, the screeching and creaking and the slapping of hands; then I heard shrill laughter from Brecht, he had kept the officers from getting at his manuscript folders, Steffin had opened some of the covers, Branting had said he vouched for the fact that the sheets contained exclusively aesthetic texts; yes, screamed Brecht, almost sobbing, beautiful poems, songs, chiseled prose. Indecisively, the police officers strutted around for a while between the tables before heading off. The detective novels, cried Brecht, you've forgotten the detective novels, rushing up the steps to the little mezzanine where he slept, jumped down with stacks of the cheap, dog-eared books that he liked to read in the evening, tore open the window, threw them after the police, and there they lay in the garden, Wallace, Doyle, Christie, Chandler, Carr, Carter, Quentin, Sayers, and all the rest, lying in the puddles and the moldering leaves. And in the studio a fight had broken out between Brecht and Maria Lazar, who, a Social Democrat, was blaming the policies of the Communists for the situation that had arisen. Your Party paper, she yelled, called the British minefields a provocation and has already provided a defense of any German counterstrike. Germany must act to protect Denmark and Norway, you lot say, I don't understand why you are all so worked up, the friends and allies of the Soviet Union are on their way. Brecht leapt up at her, as if he wanted to hit her; Weigel rushed to protect her, who could have been her twin sister; she snapped at Brecht, but they'd already moved on to another topic; she didn't want Berlau to follow them, didn't want to have to put up with the Dane any longer. And then Branting came rushing over from the telephone; just this minute, he cried, he had received word from the foreign ministry that cabin spots had been booked for the next departing ship; when, then; on the seventeenth of April; a whole week, think of everything that can happen in a week. My work with Brecht ended with the same reservation with which it had begun. Only Steffin hugged me, Brecht took my hand briefly, Greid, obsessed by his fear of germs, drew his hand away from me, Weigel urged me to send the boxes and suitcases with all the things she needed for the household as soon as possible, here's the address, Havsgatan seven-A-twelve. One last wave to Hodann, who, standing at the open window, sucking in the mild air, already with a hint of spring to it, turned to me with his dark, indestructible smile, before looking back out the window. At the bridge, which at this hour late in the afternoon was now manned by guards with machine guns, I had to show my papers once more. The reason for my visit to the island. Taking leave from a friend—well, not my friend, my teacher.

They were right next door, the people I grew up among, my generation lined up in rows. We had trodden the same streets, we knew the same cities and times, spoke and dreamed the same language. We had come to the North uninvited, via secret paths, one of us seeking out hiding places, the others traveling to the drumming of boots that we had known since our earliest youth; we had both come under false pretenses. We'd both been cast out by a malignant land, one of us in conspiratorial silence, the others sent to rob and murder. The same threats, orders, and punishments, the same figures in plaster and bronze behind us, behind us the same benches on which we'd worn our trousers thin, behind us a history which had molded our faces and gestures. It would be impossible to distinguish me from them, they would have taken me for one of their own; with the ones from Bremen or Berlin, a horrible familiarity would have emerged. Transport ships had brought them here, many had sunk, hit by aerial bombs, torpedoes, many of them, whose breath had mixed with mine, had been washed up on the shore, lay swollen like sacks, sopping in the sand, in the swell, among shells they couldn't feel, all the others marching, marching down Karl Johans gate in Oslo, across the town hall square in Copenhagen, taking up their posts, occupying, taking possession, arranging themselves beside wind orchestras to serenade the vanquished, enjoying the awe-filled stares of the children, while most of the other gazes turned away from them, their presence felt only as a gray, unspeakably bleak, leaden mass. I could still sense the movement of their arms as they passed, hear their laughter, their whistling, the buzzing of all the words exchanged, they were right next door, I could have stayed; I had left them, they hadn't driven me out, but I had been forced to learn that there was no place for me among them, they want to snuff you out, I had seen in Spain how adroit they were at the business of extinction, but they hadn't been born to do it either, they'd just allowed themselves to be squeezed into this trade, bit by bit, tighter and tighter, with an ever-dwindling measure of mercy. There may have been some among them whose knees quivered, whose heart throbbed in their throat; there might have even been some among them like Heilmann and Coppi. And here, on our side, there was one who had fled from them, he was called Rosner, short, Jewish, they'd have slain him in a second were they ever to get their hands on him, they'd throw him out the window; and of all people, he was the one who, on the ninth of April, with *Das Lied von der Erde* on the radio, scribbled down strange words of praise for them; nodding, whispering, mumbling: now Sweden is no longer under threat, the men from across the way have come to protect the Scandinavian countries, and under the current circumstances, the occupation of Denmark and Norway also means security for the Soviet Union. Rosner, the secret messenger of the Comintern, crouching in his nightshirt behind the newspapers I had brought for him, explained to me how we were supposed to view the situation now. The Germans, I heard him lisp through his dentures, have forestalled the English-French plan of opening a front in the North. Since the winter, when they had the intention of helping Finland, the policy of the Allies has been a policy of false hope, of mistiming. Germany had acted according to the rules of war. The blame for what had eventuated lay with the Western powers. I asked if the minefield off the Norwegian coast had not been aimed at protecting against a pending German invasion, and mentioned the Party paper that had been printed that afternoon, in which—what a shift—the war had been framed as an imperialist war. A confrontation of imperialist powers. With this, the thesis that the Allies wanted to drive Germany into a war against the Soviet Union was revoked. We have to assume that the Soviet Union will consent to Germany's actions. With the establishment of the pact, I heard him mumble, the Soviet Union was attempting to contain the war. England and France's provocation had expanded the war. As long as the pact exists, the Soviet Union was continuing their attempts to bring the war to an end. Rosner sighed heavily, stood up from his seat, which made him shorter, pulled out a bottle from bundles of newspapers, grabbed a couple of glasses, and poured some wine. In this phase of the war, it's about the ore, he said, sitting down: the English want to cut off Germany's supply from Narvik, the Germans want to prevent any Swedish ore from reaching England, and now Sweden is left with no other choice but to give priority to Germany. Mumbling, he raised his glass, reaching across for a toast. Right in front of me, his stubble-covered face, his hair unkempt, his eyes all but blind behind their lenses. Mahler had lived in Vienna as well, his sensibilities and thinking had been shaped there, by the unsteadiness, the roving spirit, the ragged depths and intellect of his adversaries, he had become their cantor, many of those who were on the other side of the border had listened to him, perhaps moved to tears, until, had he still been alive, they'd have shoved him onto the pavement, ground his mouth into the stone. If life is but a dream, Rosner sang along, and jeering could be heard in the background, why then toil and fret. In his hermitage he was constructing his world; now that everything seemed to be collapsing, it was necessary to erect a system that retained its validity. In a moment he would explain to me, he said, why Sweden would be left unscathed. It was thanks to the tactics of the Soviet Union. These tactics had proven their strength. I saw my classmates, their fingers on the hammers of their rifles, they were standing on Scandinavian soil, they would continue on wherever they were ordered to go, and in the East, having murdered the majority of the military leadership of their country in their blindness, stood the trustees of the October Revolution, petrified angular forms overlooking the mausoleum, their spokesperson the dwarf who had been suckled and cradled in the Danube Monarchy. The conflict with Finland was brought to a close. When West Karelia was taken, they had won what was needed to defend Leningrad. No further claims. The Swedish war-mongers had lost. Rummaging through lists, Rosner ran through every-

thing Finland had received. Eighty-four thousand rifles, four hundred fifty machine guns, one thousand two hundred sixteen pistols, eighty-five an-titank cannons, one hundred twelve pieces of heavy artillery, forty-five million rounds, one hundred seven thousand five hundred grenades, fifty radio sets, along with trucks and other equipment for seven artillery divisions. Twenty-three percent of the air force and seventy-two percent of air raid defenses had landed in Finnish hands, as well as hundreds of Swedish-assembled American planes. Then there were another four hundred million kronor in donations. I fill my glass again and drain it to the dregs. In Germany—I listened to his crackling, gritty stutter, set to dark music—the news of the weakening of the Swedish arsenals had been followed with glee. The country could not have withstood an attack. But it was this very fact that also made an attack superfluous. Now all Germany had to do was show a hint of a threat and they would receive whatever they wanted from Sweden. In the event of an invasion, the ore mines could have been blown up. But Germany was interested in maintaining the orderly flow of ore transports. The entire ore production will flow into the German arms industry. Iron, high-grade steel, ball bearings. Though a section of the major industrialists sympathized with the Western Powers, the king and the leadership of the army were on the side of the Germans. This agreement—along with Germany's and the Soviet Union's shared interest in maintaining Sweden's neutrality—prevented an immediate occupation. Now the government, which had been subject to extortion for days, had to show proof that concessions had been made. The fact that in Norrbotten, where the mining districts were located, General Major Douglas was holding an army of a hundred thousand men ready to confront a possible British intervention, that the Cabinet Secretary Boheman was in London to clarify the Swedish position, that there was no mobilization, all bore witness to the fact, said Rosner, that terms had already been agreed upon for a deal, in which Sweden would maintain its appearance of independence but would otherwise have to fulfill the duties of a vassal. Relieved that the war would not also extend into Sweden, as they had feared, the government and Admiral Tamm—the friend of the Greater German Reich who was supposed to be posted to Berlin—had no further objections to the increased demands. For this reason, said Rosner, our work will not be interrupted, and even Brecht can stay, thanks to the ore. He propped himself up on the papers, for what does spring matter to me, he crooned, let me be drunk. A new day came. The tin boiled. Official statements gave off nothing but the stench of carrion. When the rulers yelled that sacrifices had to be made, belts had to be tightened, for the workers this meant wage freezes, more toil, and for the owners, increases in profits. All forces were at odds with each other. Though the Party press emphasized the aggression of England and France to alleviate the precipitous characterization of Germany as an imperialist power, the Communist rank and file condemned the German attack on the neighboring Scandinavian countries. Bourgeois circles meanwhile were urging, on the one hand, the consolidation of the annexation to Germany and the launch of a campaign of vengeance for Finland, and on the other—though likewise in the interests of securing protection from the Soviet Union—calling for an alliance with England. At the same time, the Communist Party was attempting to convince us that the imperialist war could turn into an anticapitalist one, which, through the influence of the Soviet Union, would lead to the triumph of socialism, allowing them to say that that the struggle against capitalism was inextricably linked with antifascism. But, as reports of the first signs of Norwegian resistance filtered through, in order to avoid the impression of an estrangement between the members of the pact, the Comintern issued an order to place faith in Falkenhorst's assurance that the German troops would respect the continued existence of the Norwegian kingdom and would honor the freedom of the Norwegian people. Yet king and government were on the run, and Quisling inspired nothing but disgust. People asked what would await the Communists and socialists in the occupied countries. We couldn't believe that the pact would ensure that their rights would be respected. Thälmann, and tens of thousands of others, were still locked up in Germany. Lindner had heard that arrests had already taken place in Denmark. Members of the opposition were being sacrificed, she said, so as to hold onto the pact. Likewise, the Polish

Communists who wanted to join the Red Army were being turned away and handed over to Germany, much like the antifascists who had sought refuge in the Soviet Union. Rosner would have explained this away by saying that the direction of the Polish Party was not aligned with that of the Comintern, and that right now, with the Soviet Union fighting for its existence, its focus had to be on casting out anyone whose loyalty was questionable. In France too, said Lindner, under the cover of war, the government was disposing of its political opponents. Daladier organized for leaders of the banned Communist Party, former members of parliament, to receive long prison terms, locked up almost every last emigrant in concentration camps, and threatened Republican Spaniards with deportation to el Caudillo's Spain. It was a mere question of arithmetic, said Rosner, popping up from behind stacks of newspapers, of how many

human lives would have to be expended to avoid greater losses. According to Soviet directives, the Norwegian Party had declared itself neutral and willing to cooperate with the occupying forces. They called upon the populace to suspend all forms of insubordination. The fleeing government of Nygaardsvold no longer possessed any legality. Though there were demands for Quisling's coalition government to step down, this seemed to be more a result of the transference of the Soviet-German pact to the national stage, where there was talk of the possibility of an alliance between the Communist Party and the German occupiers. This mistaken belief, provoked by the passivity to which the Communists had been condemned, led to intensified attacks against the Swedish Party. There were renewed calls for it to be banned. While the leading Norwegian Social Democrats headed to England to prepare the fight for the liberation of their country from there, the Communist Party urged against doing anything that could drag Norway into the war. But the declared restraint did not preclude Grieg, the writer and Communist, from transporting the gold reserves of the Norwegian Central Bank to England in a boat with an expeditionary unit, as I found out from Hodann. British units were battling in Narvik to provide cover for the withdrawal of Norwegian regiments. Refugees who made it to Sweden were interned, those suspected of being Communists were subjected to strict surveillance in the camps at Långmora and Smedsbo, and German deserters were sent back across the border, toward their summary execution. But when, on the eleventh, the mobilization was ordered after all, and Per Albin Hansson gave a speech the next day pledging that all German demands for the right to march through the country would be rejected, this might have been intended to strengthen the position of the Swedish emissary negotiating in

Berlin; but Germany didn't need to take any notice of this, for in southern Sweden General Peyron sent over just a single cavalry brigade, and Admiral Tamm fell silent in awe of the gentlemen from the Reich Chancellery, announcing his excitement about the strike-power of the German Wehrmacht and falling into Waidmann's open embrace in Carinhall. The shipments of provisions and medical supplies had been guaranteed by Günther, the foreign minister; regarding the question of the passage of nurses and vacationers, it could only be a matter of settling on numbers, per week or per day; and soon enough they would also give in on the transport of fuel, battlefield provisions, and reinforcements. The mobilization, therefore, was directed primarily at the people, to convince them of the seriousness of the situation, which meant the need to lower living standards, to save, to increase production. Rosner described the policies of the Swedish government as rational, practical, opposed to all forms of suicidal heroism. Selin agreed with him. Pressed by the workforce, he explained the position of the Communist Party in the tin cellar of the factory. Right now, the efforts to maintain peace were more important than the restrictions on freedom they necessitated. To the question of whether we shouldn't support the struggle that was now breaking out in Norway and Denmark, he answered that as long as the army was not controlled by the people, then stoking a defensive spirit, or building up arms, or even joining the war were all useless to us. Military clashes never took place for our benefit, which is also how we ought to understand the directive of the Norwegian Party that no blood should be spilled for imperialist interests. If today we see a policy of peace as a kind of art of the impossible, he said, then we will start to understand the search for escape points, for stopgaps, which makes the position of the Soviet Union suspect in the eyes of many. Any and all measures that seek to stave off a world war are justified. But how are we supposed to confront them, that lot standing over there whose gray impression was staring out at us from the pages of the newspapers; what was to be done with them, how were they supposed to ever change on their own, when they were already starting to stamp their feet, when they received the signal, they wouldn't be able to resist the stamping that was within them. In order to put a stop to this stamping, they had to be struck down. My separation from them had taken place long ago, our experiences were no longer the same; I belonged, like Heilmann, like Coppi, to those who had rebelled against the self-destruction; everything that we shared was now only a mirage, I could hardly imagine anymore how I had managed to resist the compulsion to submit, they were standing next door, those to whom I too could have belonged, but didn't, due to divergent convictions and decisions. I knew that there could be no peace with them, that the final clash with them would soon commence. The sudden calm—as if those troops over there who were now being joined by the ones in black uniforms had already achieved everything, as if only a few more skirmishes had to take place— was a harbinger of a monstrous explosion. Yet it was this pause which, on the seventeenth of April, allowed a ship to depart the Skeppsbron in Stockholm, destined for Helsinki. Matthis, who—along with Santesson, Lazar, and the Goldschmidts—had accompanied Brecht and his entourage to the quay, described the scene to me. On the left, the building of the German embassy on Blasieholmen, and on the right, the German freighters in Stadsgårdhafen, were flying the swastika, the flags flapping in the breeze. Between the two, on his way across the footbridge, Brecht broke down, had to be held up, almost carried on board.

Afterword to the New Berlin Edition

The New Berlin Edition of *The Aesthetics of Resistance* is intended as a definitive version, one which follows the vision of the author as closely as possible. The version of Peter Weiss's "once-in-a-century novel" that was left at the time of his premature death stands as an authentic expression of his intentions and as an enduring testament to his position in history. The problem, however, was that there were two divergent versions. The fact that the Berlin Edition is generally viewed as an *Ausgabe letzter Hand* [a definitive version of a text edited personally by the author—JS] is a product of its publication date. Its first edition was published in 1983 by Henschelverlag, in East Berlin. The author had also heavily revised this publication, and he described the third volume of this edition as a "re-creation" of his original intentions. In the production of the Frankfurt Edition—the volumes of which were released in 1975, 1978, and 1981 by Suhrkamp Verlag—there had been significant conflict between the author and the publisher. The textual interventions of the Suhrkamp editor were a cause of great concern for Peter Weiss. He felt that his relationship with the German language was being questioned. There were perplexed and bitter letters; harsh words were exchanged. Siegfried Unseld was unwilling to retract the editorial revisions to the extent that Weiss desired. Though Weiss stressed that he was very happy to take on many of the editor's suggestions, he felt that his "dynamic, rebellious, sculptural personal style" was being flattened out to an unacceptable extent by the countless corrections. He felt "disempowered" by the publisher.

The New Berlin Edition, which was published in 2016, provides the source text for this translation.

In the GDR, the publication of the novel was approved in the spring of 1981. The publication was preceded by protracted discussions about the novel's depictions of the debates over Communist strategy and tactics and of the catastrophic course of events in the Soviet Union. These discussions involved some of the highest figures in the regime and took place behind closed doors. The possibilities of removing sections or of altering the text were briefly discussed but never seriously considered. Since the agreement with the licensor allowed for the text to be retypeset, Weiss was able to regain full control over his text. Unbeholden to restrictions in terms of corrections or typesetting costs, he was able to arrange the novel to reflect his original intentions. He made particular use of this opportunity in the third volume.

For the New Berlin Edition, the following textual sources were consulted:

— Peter Weiss, *Die Ästhetik des Widerstands*, vols. 1–3, with an afterword by Manfred Haiduk. Licensed for the GDR. East Berlin: Henschelverlag, 1983. The text of the second print run of this edition (dated 1987) is identical with the first.

— Peter Weiss, *Die Ästhetik des Widerstands*, vol. 3. Frankfurt am Main: Suhrkamp Verlag, 1981. Annotated with handwritten and dated corrections by the author: "Final corrections in accordance with original manuscript for new edition PW 22 July 1981." Located in the Akademie der Künste Berlin, Peter Weiss Archive, PWA 1752.

— Peter Weiss, *Die Ästhetik des Widerstands*, vol. 1. Frankfurt am Main: Suhrkamp Verlag, 1976. Annotated with handwritten and typed corrections by the author, dated shortly after December 12, 1975. Originally from the scholarly estate of Günther Schütz. Located in the Akademie der Künste Berlin, Peter Weiss Archive, PWA 5572.

— Peter Weiss, *Die Ästhetik des Widerstands*, vol. 3. Frankfurt am Main: Suhrkamp Verlag: 1981. Annotated with handwritten corrections by the author and Manfred Haiduk, with dedication and date on the endpaper: "9th May 1981." Personal archives of Manfred Haiduk.

— Peter Weiss, *Die Ästhetik des Widerstands*, vol. 3. Frankfurt am Main: Suhrkamp Verlag: 1981. Annotated with handwritten corrections by the author and Manfred Haiduk, with inscription and date on the endpaper: "Corrected copy for re-typesetting P. Weiss 1 sept 81." Personal archives of Manfred Haiduk.

— Further corrections transmitted either in written correspondence or verbally, particularly in Weiss's correspondence with Siegfried Unseld and Manfred Haiduk.

The text of the New Berlin Edition is based on the 2005 paperback edition from Suhrkamp Verlag with continuous pagination. The arrangement of the text follows the visual intentions of the author, so far as these can be ascertained from the aforementioned textual and supplementary sources. To provide a more in-depth exploration, a register of the people and works referenced within the novel—along with a concordance of the various editions and commentary on the artworks mentioned—was published in 2018 (see Jürgen Schutte, in collaboration with Axel Hauff and Stefan Nadolny, *Register zur Ästhetik des Widerstands von Peter Weiss* [Berlin: Verbrecher Verlag, 2018]). Manfred Haiduk has also elaborated upon the divided history of the work in a clear and detailed text (see "Zur Entstehung der Berliner Ausgabe," in *Das Argument* 316 [2016]). I owe special thanks to Haiduk, a longtime colleague and friend of Weiss, for his support during my work on this edition. This edition accommodates Peter Weiss's desire to realize his complete artistic intention in a new edition of *The Aesthetics of Resistance*—a late but wonderful gift for his hundredth birthday.

Jürgen Schutte
Berlin, June 2016

Glossary

Albert of Mecklenburg (c. 1338–1412). From the northern German region of Mecklenburg; invaded Sweden with the support of local nobility and was crowned King of Sweden in 1364; deposed by *Margaret I of Denmark in 1389.

Aschberg (Olof, 1877–1960). Swedish financier and close friend of *Hjalmar Branting and *Willi Münzenberg; founded Nya Banken, the first Swedish bank for trade unions and cooperatives, in 1912; following his departure from the bank in 1919, worked closely with the USSR. In late 1935 he established a kind of politico-cultural salon called the *Cercle des nations* in his residence on Place Casimir-Périer in Paris; at his property La Brévière, located in the forest of Compiègne, his wife, Siri, set up a home for child refugees from Germany and Spain.

Balabanoff (Angelica, 1878–1965). Russian-Jewish-Italian Communist and Social Democratic activist; joined the Bolshevik Party and became secretary of the *Comintern in 1919. Became an open critic of Bolshevism and left Russia in 1922. After World War II, moved to Italy and joined the Socialist Workers' Party, which later became the Italian Democratic Socialist Party.

This glossary is heavily indebted to the work of Robert Cohen in his *Bibliobiografisches Handbuch zu Peter Weiss' "Ästhetik des Widerstands."* The majority of the entries are more or less direct translations from this source, or are taken from the glossary that Cohen prepared for the translation of Volume I. As Cohen pointed out there, many of the names, events, organizations and works of art that figure in *The Aesthetics of Resistance* would be unfamiliar not only to English-language readers, but also to its original German-language readership. Cohen's detailed work aimed to facilitate the process of acquiring the knowledge, the history, that lies under the surface of this work. More recently, Jürgen Schutte has published a *Register zur Ästhetik des Widerstands*, which also includes comprehensive information on the artists and artworks mentioned in the novels, as well as a concordance of the page numbers of the three main editions. I have maintained the structure of Cohen's glossary, in which first names (since they are almost completely absent from the book) are added in parentheses and cross-references to other entries are indicated by asterisks.

Battle of the Ebro. The longest and largest battle of the Spanish Civil War. Lasting from July to November 1938, the Battle of the Ebro caused massive casualties for both Republicans and Nationalists. Ultimately, the conflict was disastrous for the Republicans, essentially destroying their army as an effective fighting force.

Bebel (August, 1840–1913). Cofounder and leader of German Social Democracy; a friend of Marx and Engels; author of *Woman and Socialism*.

Berlau (Ruth, 1906–1974). Danish actor and director; member of the Danish Communist Party; founder of a revolutionary workers' theater; a colleague of *Brecht. A translator and director of Brecht's works, Berlau emigrated with Brecht to Sweden, Finland, and the United States. Following the war she moved to the Soviet Occupation Zone of Berlin, and continued to work in theater in the GDR.

Bridget (Saint Bridget, c. 1303–1373). Swedish author of the *Revelationes coelestes*. Critical of both church and court, Bridget was perhaps the most significant literary and religious figure of the Nordic Middle Ages. She founded the Vadstena Abbey, moved to Rome in 1350, and was canonized posthumously in 1391.

Bischoff (Charlotte, 1901–1994). German Communist and anti-Nazi resistance fighter. In 1941 Bischoff traveled illegally to Germany, disguised as a sailor, on behalf of the German Communist Party in Stockholm; became a member of the Harnack-Schulze-Boysen organization in Berlin; and communicated with Charlotte Eisenblätter and the resistance organization of the KPD (Communist Party of Germany). She worked with Kowalke and Knöchel of the Central Committee and then, following their arrests in 1943, worked as a cleaner. After the arrests of numerous resistance fighters, Bischoff ensured that the illegal newspaper *Die innere Front* [The Internal Front] continued to appear. Following the war, she lived in the GDR.

Branting (Georg, 1897–1965). Son of *Hjalmar; lawyer and Swedish Social Democratic politician; member of the Swedish Commission for Refugees; chair of the Swedish Committee for Spanish Aid.

Branting (Hjalmar, 1860–1925). Father of *Georg; became the first Swedish Social Democratic prime minister in 1920; awarded the Nobel Peace Prize in 1921.

Brecht (Bertolt, 1898–1956). German writer; lived in exile in Denmark from the autumn of 1933, in Sweden from April 1939, and then moved to Finland in April 1940 before heading to the United States in 1941; returned to East Germany after the war.

Bretonne (Restif de la, 1734–1806). French author of often-scandalous and highly erotic literature. A protocommunist, he was later rediscovered by the Surrealists.

Bukharin (Nikolai, 1888–1938). A member of the Bolsheviks, a close collaborator of Lenin, and an important Marxist theorist; elected to the Central Committee of the Russian Communist Party in 1917; became a member of the Politburo in 1924; appointed secretary-general of the *Comintern in 1926; and was relieved of all his Comintern and Politburo duties in 1929. In 1934 many of his Party duties were reinstated; in 1938, during the third of the *Moscow trials, he was sentenced to death and executed.

Cabet (Étienne, 1788–1856). French lawyer and writer, utopian communist, and author of *Voyage en Icarie*.

Comintern. Short for "Communist International" (also sometimes referred to as "the International" or "the Third International"). Founded in Moscow in 1919 as an international association of Communist parties from numerous countries. Under Stalin, it deteriorated into an instrument of Soviet and Stalinist foreign policy and was disbanded in 1943.

Coppi (Hans, 1916–1942). German worker, trained as a turner. At age sixteen, as a member of the Communist Youth Organization, he spent a year in jail for distributing anti-Nazi pamphlets. In 1941, he became a radio operator for the group led by Harro Schulze-Boysen, which was associated with the Red Orchestra resistance organization. On September 12, 1942, he was arrested with other members of the group and was executed in Berlin on December 22.

Daladier (Édouard, 1884–1970). French politician from the center-left Radical-Socialist Party; served as prime minister of France from 1938 to 1940; a signatory to the Munich Agreement.

Deinon. "Used in Swedish philosophy. Not found in German. (The realm of terror, hauntingly amplified) *Deinosis* (from deinos = terrifying, awful, a violent amplification, in rhetoric, exaggeration)." Peter Weiss, *Notizbücher: 1971–1980* (Frankfurt am Main: Suhrkamp Verlag, 1982), 705.

Delacroix (Eugène, 1798–1863). French Romantic painter and creator of the work *Liberty Leading the People*, which hangs in the Louvre.

Douglas (Count Archibald, 1883–1960). Swedish Army lieutenant general and nobleman; served as chief of the Army from 1944 to 1948.

Drögemüller (Alfred, 1913–1988). Hamburg-born, a Communist Party functionary. He went into exile in Denmark in 1934 and returned to Germany in 1945, living initially in the West, where he continued his work for the Party. Arrested and accused of "Trotskyism" in the GDR in 1951, he spent two years in detention without charge before being unofficially rehabilitated. He went on to teach in East German institutions and was officially rehabilitated by the Party of Democratic Socialism in 1990.

Engelbrekt (Englebrekt Engelbrektsson, c. 1390s–1436). Swedish mine owner; elected leader of the miner and peasant rebellion in Dalarna in the spring of 1434. After initial military victories, he formed an alliance with the nobility against *Eric of Pomerania, the king of the *Kalmar Union. Engelbrekt was named *Rikshövitsman* (chief commander) in 1435, and, despite his willingness to negotiate, he was unable to secure a genuine peace and was slain in 1436 in a private feud. During his exile in Sweden, *Brecht began work on a play about the rebel leader but never got further than a dozen or so pages. The manuscript draft ended up in the National Library in Stockholm, where Weiss stumbled across it in 1964. In an interview with the Swedish magazine *Ord och Bild* from 1977, Weiss explained: "in the second part of the novel, the Pergamum motif corresponds with a very large complex dealing with Engelbrekt. It is based on Brecht's plans to develop a play about Engelbrekt. I met him while he was living in Sweden, and at the time he was gathering material on Engelbrekt. Brecht then abandoned the idea. His work on *Mutter Courage* got in the way. I used my memory of that era and studied the literature on Engelbrekt, from Grimberg to Per Nyström. Based on this material, I constructed an imaginary drama developed by Brecht and his circle, which roughly corresponded to the ideas that Brecht had."

Eric of Pomerania (c. 1381–1459). Ruler of the *Kalmar Union from 1396 to 1439, succeeding his adoptive mother, *Margaret. His power was significantly weakened as a consequence of the popular rebellion led by *Engelbrekt.

Folkhemmet (lit., "the people's home"). This concept was central to the ideology of the Swedish Social Democratic Party and to the evolution of the Swedish welfare state.

Gallego (Ignacio, 1914–1990). Spanish Communist leader. After the civil war he was sent to a concentration camp in Algeria but made his way to the Soviet Union, where he lived until 1945. He returned to Spain in secret in 1976, became active as a politician in the PCE (Communist Party of Spain), and later founded the Communist Party of the Peoples of Spain.

Géricault (Théodore, 1791–1824). French painter and one of the founders of Romantic painting; his most famous work, *The Raft of the Medusa*, was created in 1819 and now hangs in the Louvre; died from injuries sustained in a riding accident.

Grieg (Nordahl, 1902–1943). Norwegian writer whose play *The Defeat* (1935) inspired *Brecht's play *The Days of the Commune* (1949). He spent 1933–1935 in Moscow, then became a war correspondent in Spain during the civil war; during World War II, he served in Norway's government-in-exile. He never returned from an Allied bombing mission over Berlin in which he participated as an observer.

Hansson (Per Albin, 1885–1946). Leading Swedish Social Democratic politician; prime minister from 1932 to 1936; introduced the concept of the *Folkhemmet.

Heilmann (Horst, 1923–1942). Anti-Nazi resistance fighter; met Harro Schulze-Boysen, a leading member of the German section of the Red Orchestra resistance group, in 1940 while studying political science in Berlin; volunteered in the German army in August 1941, deciphering Allied documents and secretly passing them on to Schulze-Boysen; arrested with other members of the group on September 9, 1942, and executed in Berlin on December 22.

Hodann (Max, 1894–1946). Physician, psychiatrist, and leading sex reformer of the Weimar Republic; member of the board of directors of the Union of Socialist Doctors; and author of sex education books for the working class. He was incarcerated by the Nazis after the burning of the Reichstag in Berlin in 1933; after his release, he lived in exile in Norway. He served as a physician in the International Brigades during the Spanish Civil War in 1937–38, and in 1940, in exile in Sweden, he became a friend and mentor for the struggling young refugee painter and writer Peter Weiss. He would eventually commit suicide.

Kalmar Union. A personal union lasting from 1397 to 1523 which joined the three kingdoms of Denmark, Sweden, and Norway under a single monarch.

Katz (Otto, also known as André Simone, 1893–1952). Czech journalist and a collaborator of *Münzenberg. He was exiled to Paris, where he continued to work as an editor for Münzenberg's publishing houses; during the Spanish Civil War, he worked for the press office of the Republican government. He returned to Czechoslovakia after World War II; in 1952 he was indicted in the Slansky trials and executed.

Kilbom (Karl, 1885–1961). Swedish metalworker; a founder of the Communist Party of Sweden in 1921; member of the ECCI (Executive Committee of the Communist International); and editor of the Party paper. In 1929 he was expelled from the Communist International, which would lead to his growing estrangement from the Swedish Party.

Krupskaya (Nadezhda, 1869–1939). Bolshevik revolutionary and deputy minister of education in the Soviet Union from 1929; married to Vladimir Lenin from 1898 until his death in 1924.

La Pasionaria (Dolores Ibárruri Gómez, 1895–1989). Daughter of a Basque miner and Spanish mother; Communist functionary, organizer, and propagandist. A member of the Central Committee of the Spanish Communist Party from 1930, she became vice president of the congress of the Second Republic in 1936. She is responsible for the famous antifascist slogan *¡No pasarán!*, which she used in a speech during the battle for Madrid in 1936. She moved to the USSR after the civil war, only returning to Madrid in 1977 and living there until her death.

Marat (Jean-Paul, 1743–1793). French political theorist during the French Revolution; murdered by Charlotte Corday; the subject of Weiss's best-known play, *Marat/Sade*.

Margaret (Margaret I of Denmark, 1387–1412). Queen consort of Norway and later ruler in her own right of Denmark, Norway, and Sweden; founder of the *Kalmar Union.

Meryon (Charles, 1821–1868). French painter and engraver.

Mewis (Karl, also known as Karl Arndt, 1907–1987). Communist politician and member of the anti-Nazi resistance. He initially trained as a locksmith and in 1924 joined the Communist Party of Germany. He would become a leading figure in the Party in exile after 1933; during the civil war, he represented the German Communist Party in Spain; and was later exiled in Sweden. After World War II, he went on to hold high offices in the German Democratic Republic.

Moscow trials. Public trials held in Moscow in the 1930s, at the height of the Stalinist terror, and covered extensively in the international press; refers specifically to the three trials of old Bolsheviks held in August 1936 (among the accused: *Zinoviev and Kamenev), January 1937 (Pyatakov, *Radek, and others), and March 1938 (*Bukharin, Rykov, and others). Most defendants were sentenced to death and executed.

Münzenberg (Willi, 1889–1940). Proletarian youth, and member of the *Spartacus League and the Communist Party of Germany; befriended Lenin in 1916 and would go on to run a Communist publishing empire in Weimar Germany which included newspapers, journals, books, and films. After 1933, he continued his publishing activities in exile in Paris; during the Stalinist terror of the late 1930s he distanced himself from the Soviet Union. Ultimately expelled from the Party, he was found dead in eastern France under unexplained circumstances.

Nerval (Gérard de, pseudonym of Gérard Labrunie, 1808–1855). French Romantic poet. Nerval hanged himself from the bars on a window in Rue de la Vieille-Lanterne in Paris, a street that was destroyed shortly afterwards. In this volume, Weiss writes that Nerval "hanged himself from a streetlamp." This is a common misconception—

possibly derived from the name of the street—and appears in Baudelaire's poem "Le guignon." In Weiss's case, it can be traced back to a note in one of his notebooks.

October. Refers to the Russian Revolution of October 1917, which brought the Bolsheviks, under Lenin's leadership, to power.

Ossietzky-Palm (Rosalinde von, 1919–2000). Daughter of German antiwar activist Carl von Ossietzky; attended the Odenwaldschule before moving to England in 1933 and attending Dartington Hall and receiving support from *Ernst Toller and Bertrand Russell. In late 1935 she relocated to Sweden, where she was active in the efforts to save her father. She was denied permits to study or to work and was forced to labor as a helper in a school laundry. She remained in Sweden after the war.

Palmstierna (Erik, 1877–1959). Swedish Social Democratic politician and diplomat; grandfather of the artist and writer Gunilla Palmstierna-Weiss, who was married to Weiss from 1964 until his death.

Radek (Karl, 1885–1939). Polish revolutionary and intellectual, member of the Bolsheviks, and a collaborator of Lenin; a founding member of the Communist Party of Germany after World War I; held high positions in the *Comintern in the Soviet Union after 1921. He at times took Trotskyite, anti-Stalinist positions and spoke out in support of the *Moscow trials in 1936, before being sentenced to ten years in prison during the second trial in 1937; he died while incarcerated.

Rogeby (Sixten, 1910–1976). Swedish Communist and writer; fought in the Spanish Civil War in the International Brigades before returning to Sweden.

Rosner (Jakob, 1890–1970). Austrian journalist who joined the Communist Party of Austria in 1919; a collaborator of Dimitrov, first in Vienna and then in Berlin. After a stay in Moscow, he traveled to Sweden illegally in 1943 as the editor of the newspaper of the Communist International *Die Welt* [The World]. He returned to Austria in 1945, where he worked for the paper *Volksstimme* [The Voice of the People].

Sandler (Rickard, 1884–1964). Swedish Social Democratic politician; served as prime minister from 1925 to 1926 following the death of *Hjalmar Branting.

Second International. Formed in Paris in 1889, a federation of socialist parties and trade unions. Unlike the centralized organization of the First International, the Second International was a loose federation of national groups. In 1896 it expelled the anarchists from its ranks. As a consequence of the conflicting positions of the various national groups, the Second International ceased to function during World War I. Attempts to revive it after the war failed but eventually led to the formation of the Labor and Socialist International, which opposed the Communist-led Third International (*Comintern).

Spartacus League. Revolutionary left-wing group that split off from the Social Democratic Party of Germany over its support for World War I. Founded by Karl Liebknecht, Rosa Luxemburg, Klara Zetkin, and others, it transformed itself into the Communist Party of Germany on January 1, 1919.

Stahlmann (Richard, 1891–1974). Trained as a carpenter and was a prisoner of war in Britain during World War I. He joined the Communist Party of Germany in 1919, went to the Soviet Union in 1923, and attended military school in Moscow. He was sent by the *Comintern to China, participated in the Spanish Civil War, and was sent to Stockholm by the leadership of the Communist Party of Germany to organize the illegal entry of resistance fighters into Germany. After the arrest of his colleagues *Wehner and *Mewis, Stahlmann went into hiding and returned to the Soviet Union. After the war he worked for the Stasi in the GDR.

Steffin (Margarete, 1908–1941). Writer and translator; a member of the Communist Party of Germany and the Young Communist League; a key collaborator of *Brecht, with whom she went into exile in Denmark, Sweden, and Finland; died of tuberculosis in Moscow while awaiting a visa for the United States.

Strindberg (August, 1849–1912). Swedish author and painter. Tegnérlunden, a park in Stockholm, features a sculpture of Strindberg by Carl Eldh. The protagonist mentions this artwork in this volume although the sculpture was not erected until 1942.

Ström (Fredrik, 1880–1948). Party secretary of the Swedish Social Democrats from 1911 to 1916; greeted Lenin in Stockholm during his return journey to Russia in 1917; party secretary of the Communist Party of Sweden from 1921 to 1924. Following Höglund's split with the Communist International, Ström also returned to the Social Democratic Party and served as a member of parliament from 1930 to 1948.

Sue (Eugène, 1804–1857), French writer, author of *The Mysteries of Paris* (1842).

Toller (Ernst, 1893–1939). Writer and member of the Independent Social Democratic Party of Germany; one of the leaders of the Bavarian Soviet Republic; imprisoned from 1919 to 1924. Toller engaged in various forms of antifascist activity and was involved in the efforts to support Spain during the civil war; he went into exile in Switzerland in 1933, then continued on to France and to the United States. He committed suicide in 1939.

Tombrock (Hans, 1895–1966). Sailor and vagrant, one of the initiators of the International Fraternity of Vagrants; painter and graphic artist; went into exile in 1933 and moved to Sweden in 1936, where he met *Brecht in 1939. In 1946 he moved to East Germany, where he taught art. He moved to the West in 1953, where he died in 1966.

Ulbricht (Walter, 1893–1973). Trained as a carpenter; joined the *Spartacus League; founding member of the Communist Party of Germany and in 1927 became a permanent member of its Central Committee; in 1928, a member of the Reichstag; after 1933, a leading member of the Party in exile in France; in Spain during the civil war; after 1938, in exile in Moscow; returned to Germany after World War II; founding member of the East German Communist Party (SED); 1960–73, president of the German Democratic Republic.

van Gogh (Vincent, 1853–1890). Dutch painter; lived with his brother Theo in Montmartre, Paris, from 1886 to 1889; died in extreme poverty in the village of Auvers-sur-Oise after shooting himself with a revolver.

Warnke (Herbert, 1902–1975). Trained as a metalworker; joined the Communist Party in 1923; a member of the Reichstag from 1932 to 1933; moved to Sweden in 1938 and was interned from 1939 to 1943.

Wehner (Herbert, also known as Kurt Funk, Svensson, 1906–1990). Son of a shoemaker, joined the Communist Party of Germany in 1927; after 1933, engaged in antifascist activities in Germany; after 1935, in exile in the Soviet Union; member of the Central Committee of the exiled Party; after 1940, in exile in Sweden; expelled from the party as a "traitor"; after the war, joined the Social Democratic Party of Germany; in 1949, became a member of the Bundestag (West German Parliament); 1966–69, cabinet minister.

Weigel (Helene, 1900–1971). Austrian actress; married to *Brecht; after World War II artistic director of the Berliner Ensemble Theater in East Berlin.

Wigforss (Ernst, 1881–1977). Swedish Social Democrat and minister of finance.

Zimmerwald. Small central Swiss town that was the site of a conference held by Lenin and his fellow Bolsheviks, as well as other left-wing revolutionaries, in September 1915.

Zinoviev (Grigory, 1883–1936). Met Lenin in 1903 in Switzerland; a member of the Bolsheviks. Zinoviev moved to Switzerland in 1914, was involved in the *Zimmerwald and Kienthal conferences, and returned to Russia in a sealed train with Lenin

in 1917. During the Revolution he expounded positions that clashed with Lenin's. In 1919 he was involved in the founding congress of the Communist International and was elected to lead the organization. He broke with Stalin in 1925, was expelled from the Party in 1927 and then readmitted in 1928 after capitulating to Stalin. He was expelled again in 1932, and after being readmitted in 1934, was expelled for the third time in 1935 and condemned to ten years in prison. In 1936, Zinoviev was sentenced to death along with Kamenev at the first of the *Moscow trials and executed. He was rehabilitated in 1988.